Titles by Meljean Brook

DEMON ANGEL
DEMON MOON
DEMON NIGHT

Anthologies

HOT SPELL
(with Emma Holly, Lora Leigh, and Shiloh Walker)

WILD THING
(with Maggie Shayne, Marjorie Liu, and Alyssa Day)

DEMON NIGHT

meljean brook

BERKLEY SENSATION, NEW YORK

THE BERKLEY PUBLISHING GROUP
Published by the Penguin Group
Penguin Group (USA) Inc.
375 Hudson Street, New York, New York 10014, USA
Penguin Group (Canada), 90 Eglinton Avenue East, Suite 700, Toronto, Ontario M4P 2Y3, Canada
(a division of Pearson Penguin Canada Inc.)
Penguin Books Ltd., 80 Strand, London WC2R 0RL, England
Penguin Group Ireland, 25 St. Stephen's Green, Dublin 2, Ireland (a division of Penguin Books Ltd.)
Penguin Group (Australia), 250 Camberwell Road, Camberwell, Victoria 3124, Australia
(a division of Pearson Australia Group Pty. Ltd.)
Penguin Books India Pvt. Ltd., 11 Community Centre, Panchsheel Park, New Delhi—110 017, India
Penguin Group (NZ), 67 Apollo Drive, Rosedale, North Shore 0632, New Zealand
(a division of Pearson New Zealand Ltd.)
Penguin Books (South Africa) (Pty.) Ltd., 24 Sturdee Avenue, Rosebank, Johannesburg 2196,
South Africa

Penguin Books Ltd., Registered Offices: 80 Strand, London WC2R 0RL, England

This is a work of fiction. Names, characters, places, and incidents either are the product of the author's imagination or are used fictitiously, and any resemblance to actual persons, living or dead, business establishments, events, or locales is entirely coincidental. The publisher does not have any control over and does not assume any responsibility for author or third-party websites or their content.

DEMON NIGHT

A Berkley Sensation Book / published by arrangement with the author

PRINTING HISTORY
Berkley Sensation mass-market edition / February 2008

Copyright © 2008 by Melissa Khan.
Cover design by George Long.
Interior text design by Laura K. Corless.

ISBN: 978-0-425-21977-5

BERKLEY® SENSATION
Berkley Sensation Books are published by The Berkley Publishing Group,
a division of Penguin Group (USA) Inc.,
375 Hudson Street, New York, New York 10014.
BERKLEY SENSATION and the "B" design are trademarks belonging to Penguin Group (USA) Inc.

PRINTED IN THE UNITED STATES OF AMERICA

10 9 8 7 6 5 4 3 2 1

❧

To Bobby, because you're it for me.

And to the Renob Dogs (of the American Society of Barbe-cued Cats for Breakfast): my sisters, Jen, Kate, and Echo. Sorry, Megan, you were born too late to join—but, because you live with me and I'm afraid of waking up with shaved, green, and/or super-glued hair, I guess this is also for you.

Special thanks to my editor, Cindy Hwang, because the first time might have been a fluke, but you went for a second, and that's more than I ever expected. To my agent, Roberta Brown, for making the second time as smooth as possible. And to Leis Pederson, for making sure that every-thing gets to me (and that I get everything back to you).

PROLOGUE

εden, Arizona Territory

1886

"The McCabe boys are coming in, Sheriff. From the west."

A dusty deputy was an unlikely harbinger of doom. Lightning forking across the sky, tremors that fractured earth and ocean—*those* were portents of ruin. Two safecrackers were hardly cause for concern, no matter how many lawmen had died in pursuit of them or how many jail cells they'd escaped, and so it was several hours before Sheriff Samuel Danvers recognized the announcement for what it was.

Danvers eased up from behind his rosewood desk, tipping his hat back and surveying the young deputy. He'd seen rolls of barbed wire less tightly wound.

"Randolph found their campfire up on Webb Ridge, Deputy Erwin, and the latest report over the telegraph was a robbery in Tucson. How is it that they are coming in from the *west*?" A wasteland of scrub and desert stretched for fifty miles in that direction. Nothing to tempt men, whether sinners or saints or all of those in between.

"They're circling around, Sheriff. Like buzzards." On each word, the deputy's Adam's apple bobbed with the force of his excitement.

Vultures. Danvers liked that description; the McCabe boys likely wouldn't. If they stepped foot in his town with the intention of bringing trouble, the only carrion to scavenge would be their own.

Danvers's smile was slow and long, and Erwin visibly brightened beneath it, straightening his shoulders. "Well now, Deputy. We'd best show our visitors the depth of Eden's hospitality."

Erwin nodded, muttering, "Circling around, sneaky as coyotes. Throwing us off the scent."

As the deputy undoubtedly hoped, Danvers was pleased by that comparison as well. "It won't be difficult to sniff them out."

Danvers adjusted the fit of his vest and collected his pistols from a wooden peg, buckling them around his hips. The holsters were a negligible weight, and the threat of their appearance commanded more respect than the gleaming weapons within—so much respect that Danvers hadn't yet fired them.

But then, most outlaws were cowards at heart, and his deputies were eager to please him.

After donning his neatly pressed jacket, he continued, "If not directly to the bank, where do you imagine a pair of iron workers dry from the trail would go first, Erwin?"

"Madam LaFleur's, Sheriff."

Danvers paused on the threshold. "Deputy."

A blush ruddied the young man's tanned skin, and his lanky form wilted under Danvers's disapproving stare. "The saloon, sir. They'd have an almighty powerful thirst."

"Yes." Men were all too often driven by their weaknesses—thirst, hunger, lust—and surely men such as the McCabes were more susceptible than most. "Round up Singleton and Randolph, Erwin. I'll expect you in the saloon by nightfall."

Cowards and coyotes waited to slink in under the cover of darkness; the McCabes wouldn't be any different.

Danvers stepped out onto the stoop. The main street curved snake-like through Eden, east to west, and the sheriff's office was at the head of it. The sun hung low over the flat roofs and peaked façades lining the street, washing the graying buildings with pale gold, casting deep shadows in between. The jagged ridge of mountains on the western horizon appeared lavender—and was quickly deepening to purple.

"You'd best hurry, Deputy," Danvers said softly.

Erwin darted past him, and dust flew from his gelding's hooves as he sent it galloping down the street. Gathered in small groups in front of the general store, several of Eden's citizens turned to watch his winding progress, their concern etched in tight lines near their mouths.

They needn't have worried. Danvers had single-handedly delivered Eden from corruption; he wouldn't allow the little piece of Heaven he'd created for himself to be desecrated by the likes of the McCabes.

He walked loudly down the board sidewalk, alerting the watchers to his approach. He answered their nervous greetings with an easy smile designed to assuage their fears.

These were good people, worth saving: the women in their clean, bright calicos and fresh skin and modest glances; the men with their work-roughened hands and solemn mustaches that always gave the appearance of a frown. Even the whores lounging in Madam LaFleur's parlor across the street had the decency to cover their wares with proper clothing—and Danvers had made clear what would happen to men who treated them poorly. No one dared lift a hand or belt, and not one whore had sported a bruise in years.

And for years, he'd had to decline their offers of payment. Their gratitude was enough, and, eventually, the wariness that lingered in their eyes would fade.

Pride. He shouldn't feel it, but he did. It was a fine place, Eden. And, though it wasn't as lush as its namesake, the heat suited him.

The interior of Hammond's Saloon was dim, but Danvers had no trouble making out the faces of the men seated around the tables and at the bar. Apparently, they'd already heard of the McCabe boys' approach; their expressions told Danvers they were eager for a kill, eager to collect the bounty on the outlaws' heads.

He'd have to disabuse them of that notion. Mobs, pandemonium, chaos—they were anathema to him. Men couldn't live without order; Danvers provided them with it. And he'd continue to provide it, even if it had to be in spite of them.

His gaze swept over the waiting men, and he delivered his pronouncement in a low voice. "We're just locking them up to await the circuit court's judgment."

Everyone deserved judgment.

The men were disappointed, but the hunger in their demeanor transformed into a willingness to wait. Their conversations resembled the gossip of women.

". . . I hear tell they killed seven men up in Denver . . ."

". . . can bust through a safe in ten seconds. Ain't no jail that can hold 'em . . ."

". . . they call the elder brother Long McCabe, on account of he's almost eight feet tall . . ."

Rumors, suppositions. Danvers sat at the bar and waited for his deputies to return. They wouldn't be persuaded by hearsay; he'd taught them that observation provided facts, and to study well what they saw.

Appearances were rarely deceiving.

From outside the saloon, he heard the heavy tread of booted feet. Danvers was not given to superstition, but the sound suddenly spoke like an omen, the fist of God falling like a hammer against his skull.

He looked toward the batwing doors. Silhouetted against the orange sky was the tall figure of a man, his shoulders as broad as a blacksmith's.

And Sheriff Samuel Danvers was absolutely certain that his little piece of Heaven was soon headed straight for Hell.

CHAPTER 1

"So this cowboy walks into a bar—"

To Charlie Newcomb's relief, a chorus of male groans drowned out the rest, and her automatic *Please, God, kill me now* response died after *Please, God*. There were days she'd rather stab a cocktail umbrella through her eardrum than hear another "walked into a bar" joke.

Thanks to the group of bachelors roosting at the end of her counter in Cole's Hard Time Bar and Grill, this had just become one of those days.

"No, wait. Wait!" Her tormentor's voice was abnormally loud, but Charlie knew it wasn't just the drink. He'd been obnoxious before she'd set the first reduced-calorie beer in front of him. "It's a good one."

"Stevens, you dumbshit, there's no such thing as a good one," someone said as Charlie began unloading the small dishwasher beneath the bar, and she felt an instant of hope. A possible ally existed among the assholes. "Yo, bartender lady!"

Charlie turned, flipping the highball glass in her hand to the rack near her hip. Her ally cocked a dark brow.

"More peanuts, Blondie?" He pushed a wooden tripod bowl

through a pile of shells littering the mahogany surface and loosened his red tie with his opposite hand. "I have to fortify myself for the upcoming bullshit."

Just lovely. "Sure thing," she said. Her sneakers crunched over the floor. How had they gotten the shells on this side? Flicked them over when she wasn't paying attention? Gorillas.

"Okay, so this cowboy, he walks into a bar and sits down, right? And then he realizes that it's a gay bar, but he's real thirsty, right? So he says, 'What the hell, I'll stay anyway.'"

Charlie was better than this Stevens guy if she didn't slam the refilled peanut bowl into his face.

Telling herself that didn't make her *feel* better.

"And so he starts to order his drink, but the bartender, he says . . . Hey, Blondie, hold on. You should do this part."

Stevens's hand came perilously close to hers, as if he intended to detain her. Charlie paused in the middle of scraping the broken shells from the counter into a small wastebasket and gave him a Look.

She'd had to use it before. It was effective, that Look, even on drunks. A narrowing of her eyes, a tightening of her lips, and it said, *Touch me and I'll kill you.*

Or cut off their drinks, which was sometimes the more dire consequence. But Stevens and his friends weren't yet intoxicated—just warmed and loosened.

"Ah," Stevens said, blinking slowly. His hand resembled a quivering mouse when he pulled it back to curl around his mug. "Do you want to do the bartender's part?"

No. But she knew from experience that a Look was one thing; outright rejection, another. Easier just to play along than risk them moving from obnoxious to belligerent.

"All right." She set down the trash bin, wiped her hands on the towel tucked into her lap apron. God, how many of these things had she heard? Not many with cowboys, though. Mostly priests and rabbis. She took a stab. "So the bartender says, 'Before I serve you a drink, you have to tell me the name of your penis.'"

Stevens's mouth didn't move much, but his eyes—slightly red, slightly watery—turned down into a frown. "You've heard this one."

"Well," Charlie said, suddenly wary. The two drinks she'd given him over the past hour weren't usually enough to inebriate a guy his size—but he might have been drinking somewhere else before meeting up with his buddies, and the alcohol was just now kicking in. "Yeah."

"Fuck. You guys, she's already heard this one. That fucking ruins the whole joke. Forget this shit." He tipped up his mug, looked down into it. Empty. "I need another one of these, Blondie. Try not to fuck that up."

The clench of her teeth could have ground peanuts to butter. Like hell she'd serve him more.

"Yo, Stevens. Ease off, man. It isn't her fault." Her ally. His tie now hung limply around his neck, but she managed to restrain herself from reaching over and yanking it tight again when he added, "Listen to her. She's sick or something. Couldn't get off for the night, Blondie?"

His tone was sympathetic, but his assumption scraped her already raw nerves, and the rasp in her voice deepened along with her frustration.

"No." Charlie pointed to the jagged white line crossing the bottom of her throat. She'd ripped out the sleeves and collar of her Metallica T-shirt, and the resulting boat neckline was low; she couldn't believe they'd missed the scar. Unless she was wearing a turtleneck, she usually couldn't get new acquaintances to look at her face. "The Emerald City Slasher."

His eyes widened; so did Stevens's and the others'. "No shit? Thaddeus White, right?"

She nodded. "Seventeen years ago. I was twelve." Hopefully they were too loose and warm to recall that the Slasher had fixated on adult women, not kids.

"How'd you get away?"

"I had to saw through my ankle. Then I crawled to a neighbor's."

"Holy shit." The exclamation made the rounds, and two of the jerks actually tried to lean over the bar for a look at her legs. Did they think she'd pop off a prosthetic foot for them?

A throat cleared behind her. Her savior had come. Charlie turned; Old Matthew's determinedly solemn frown wrinkled his raisin-dark face. "You want to take that break now, Charlie?"

"God, yes," she muttered and limped past him. Just before she reached the "employees only" door, she heard him telling Stevens and company that, when probed too deeply, the memories of the Slasher were liable to send her into a psychotic rage.

Good Old Matthew Cole. He'd likely have them gone by the time she returned—or at least moved to a table in the restaurant.

She grabbed her navy peacoat from the hook inside the break room, slid it on, and dug her knitted cap from the pocket before slipping out through the kitchens. The heavy length of her hair against her back annoyed her, but she didn't untuck it from beneath her collar. Trapped as it was between the coat and the wool hat, it'd be as flat as a one-dollar beer by the end of her break.

But flat could be fluffed; drowned rat could not.

Rain misted over her face and sparkled beneath the halogen security light. Cardboard wilted in the recycler to her left. The lid on the brown Dumpster was up. She grimaced, imagining the sodden garbage, and tipped it closed. The clang shot through the alley, disturbing a yellow-striped cat and echoing in her ears until she reached the gated stairwell to the roof.

The gate was wrought iron, with a metal screen to prevent anyone reaching through the bars to the interior knob. As a safety measure, only the outside knob locked—if someone dropped the key over the side of the roof, they could still open the gate from the inside.

Every Cole's employee had access to the key, but Charlie was one of the few who used it, even when—as now—the air was cool enough to nip at her face, but not enough to make her shiver. Luckily, in Seattle, extremely cold days were as rare as a perceptive drunk.

The top of the stairwell was dark, but the light above the bar's kitchen door shined through the gate, casting shadowy diamonds against the rough brick wall. Charlie ran lightly up the stairs, her feet slapping tinny chimes from the aluminum treads.

In the middle of the roof, a few potted plants edged an Astroturf carpet and surrounded a porch swing better suited to a verandah in Savannah than atop a bar in the trendy Capitol Hill neighborhood. Small firs from a Christmas tree farm flanked the swing's support posts. A white string of lights spiraled around the evergreen branches, though the holidays had passed four months earlier. Steam floated from the ventilation hoods over the kitchen and caught the streetlights in front of

Cole's, then dissipated as it rose. The scent of grease and fried potatoes it carried did not fade as easily.

Old Matthew called the roof garden his little piece of Heaven; when Charlie had utilized the sand-filled planter that doubled as an ashtray at the end of the swing, it had been hers. Still was.

She'd kicked the habit, but the scene was too good not to revisit. Though the old movie theater across the street obscured most of the downtown skyline, there was just enough glitter to offer a lovely view.

The chill from the seat soaked through her black cotton pants, but the canvas awning had kept it dry. A push of her foot sent it swinging, and she fished her cell phone from her coat. For the space of a few seconds, the rocking tempo perfectly matched the ring of the phone.

Jane answered on an upswing. "*Char*-lie."

Charlie's brows rose. She'd heard a couple of men say her name like that, but never her older sister. "I'm just checking to make sure you haven't forgotten about lunch tomorrow."

"Nuh-uh. I wrote it on a sticky. It's stuck on the fridge at home."

"Fridge" was kind of a moan, too. Charlie unwrapped a piece of gum—not the square kind anymore—and folded it over her tongue before she said, "Actually, I wrote it. You just stuck it." At home? "Are you still at the lab?"

"Yeah."

Charlie rolled her eyes. "Did you remember to eat today?"

"Uh-huh. We ordered in. Sushi. And wine." A giggle came through the earpiece. Jane didn't giggle.

"You're with Dylan," Charlie guessed. "Isn't this why you moved in with him? It still shocks me that Legion doesn't dock you both for . . . what's the word? It starts with *F*."

"Fraternization?"

"That's good enough. *With* the regional head, *while* you're at work. Isn't there a policy against that kind of thing?" It seemed like there should be, but Charlie couldn't be sure; both the corporate and academic research worlds were mysteries to her. Jane's descriptions of internal politics, red tape, and the hoops she had to jump through at Legion Laboratories could have been set in another universe.

"Nuh-uh." Breathily. And her ridiculously articulate—if absentminded—sister was spouting two-syllable nonwords.

"Oh, Jesus," Charlie realized. "You're fraternizing him right now. Naked?"

"Almost."

Charlie tried not to imagine that, even though Dylan was . . . well, yummy. All dark hair and eyes and sinful lips. But he was her sister's, and they were so cute together. "Why didn't you say something?"

"I couldn't decide if that would be more awkward."

"Nerd. You didn't have to answer the phone."

"It was you."

"Aw, that's sweet. Except now I feel dirty."

"Imagine how I feel." The dry tone was familiar—it was *Jane*.

Charlie grinned at the phone. "Alrighty then. Try not to be naked at noon."

"I'll try."

That ended on a bit of a scream, and Charlie hastily disconnected. The call time flashed up at her from the backlit screen: fifty-six seconds. Her smile faded.

Adding in the minute it had probably taken to come up here, she had thirteen minutes before she had to return. Shit.

She should have brought a book. Or her knitting bag. How long had she been relying on Jane being available when she needed a distraction? God knew Charlie had been dependent enough in her life; she should have recognized the signs by now.

But she shouldn't be feeling this envy. If anyone deserved happiness, it was Jane. Charlie didn't know if Dylan deserved her sister, but if Jane was happy with him, Charlie would be, as well.

With effort, she forced away the self-pity—that emotion was addictive, too.

She rocked a little harder, let her head fall back against the cushion, and closed her eyes. Why had she let a guy like Stevens get to her? She never had before. She didn't know why she was so tense of late—or why she couldn't shake the certainty that she was constantly under observation. Surely after two months, she couldn't blame her paranoia on nicotine withdrawal.

At least she could be confident that no one could see her for the next ten minutes. Determinedly, she occupied herself with a game of pinball on her cell phone until she heard a swell of laughter and voices.

Charlie left the cover of the swing and looked over the low wall at the front of the building toward the Heritage, where an old-fashioned marquee declared it "James Stewart Month." Groups of twos and threes spilled from the theater's doors, many of them folding their collars up against the rain.

The second show must have ended earlier than usual, or there'd been a problem with the projector—Old Matthew always scheduled her break before any theater patrons straggled in.

Most of the moviegoers turned right, walking down the sidewalk toward Harvard Street and the parking garage. One large group of twenty- or thirty-somethings, males and females in tailored trousers, long, belted coats, and chic haircuts, headed straight for the bar. None of them carried umbrellas, but many Seattle urbanites viewed them with disdain—as if getting soaked honored some sacred Cascadian tradition.

A few minutes remained before Charlie's break ended, but she might as well head back and give Old Matthew a hand.

She walked to the stairwell, hoping Stevens and friends had left—or at least migrated to the restaurant—and hoping that the newcomers wouldn't offer their own variety of condescending bullshit and a pseudo-intellectual discussion of the film over cocktails.

But two steps down, still enshrouded by darkness, Charlie froze. Thoughts of annoying customers fled. She stared through the gate at the wet asphalt in the alley, her heart hammering in her chest.

For an instant, the shadowy diamond pattern at the bottom of the stairs had thickened and congealed into a human shape.

Around her, the soft pattering of rain steadily increased. From Broadway, the rumble of a bus engine was followed by the gassy release of its brakes.

No voices. No footsteps.

It could have been nothing. Someone using the alley as a shortcut. A person who'd just left the bus, or taken in the movie. Someone in the kitchens bringing a bag of trash out to the Dumpster, and she just hadn't heard the door open and close.

But it had been so *fast*. Furtive. And though she hadn't seen anyone cross in front of the gate, the light source was close to the stairs. For someone to have cast a shadow, the person had to have been near as well.

Silently, she edged back up to the landing. It might be nothing, and in a moment she'd call herself an idiot—but better than being mugged or raped in a dark alley.

She looked over the back wall, and her breath caught. A man in black stood directly beneath her. Though the halogen light illuminated his long blue black hair and whitened the skin at his hairline, hands, and the tops of his ears, the depth of the shadow pooled around his feet seemed to enfold him in darkness.

Stopping for a smoke in the rain? Charlie tried to convince herself of it, but he didn't reach into his trench coat pockets for a cigarette. And he was too still—almost expectant. Waiting.

For what?

So absolute was his stillness, Charlie nearly jumped when he leaned away from the wall, turning his head as if searching for someone. His shadow slid like oil, a dark slick spreading the width of the alley.

Charlie looked in time to see a man and a woman melt out of the darkness beyond Cole's street-side corner. Gooseflesh prickled her arms. Their steps seemed sped up, like the cartoonish pace of old black-and-white newsreels.

But there was nothing jerky in their predatory glide, nothing comedic. It was too smooth, too quick, too . . .

Inhuman.

A shiver raced down her spine, drew the skin tight across the nape of her neck. Her breath skimmed in between her lips.

As if he'd heard that soft sound, the figure below tipped his pale face up. His mouth was half-open in a smile. Sharp teeth gleamed.

Long sharp teeth.

Charlie jerked away from the wall and dropped into a crouch. Her legs trembled. Jesus. Oh, Jesus. Had he seen her?

Had *she* just seen fangs?

She was crazy. Fucking crazy. One strange incident two months ago, and now she was imagining vampires.

She squeezed her eyes closed, willing away the vision of his teeth, hoping her blindness might be his, too. They flew open again when the singsongy voice drifted up the stairwell.

"Charlotte . . ."

She was suddenly light-headed, dizzy. Her inhalations were too fast, too shallow. *Hyperventilating*. She was going to pass out if she didn't get ahold of herself.

She forced her breathing to slow, forced herself to think. Had she been panicking like this from the time she'd seen the first shadow?

If so, that might explain why they'd seemed to move so quickly. Her perception could have been distorted.

But he'd said her *name*. How could he know her name?

She hadn't gotten a good look at the other two. Her job put her in contact with a lot of people, and she was on a first-name basis with many of them. Had anyone mentioned a costume party? A rave at a Goth club?

But a casual acquaintance wouldn't know to find her up here, and would only use her nickname.

Still shaking, her breaths ragged, Charlie half-rose from her crouch. She moved quietly to the head of the stairs and peeked around the stairwell housing.

No array of diamond shadows. The stairs were completely dark, the light blocked by the three figures staring up at her through the gate.

Though she could barely see the outline of their features, she was instantly certain she didn't know any of them.

Was instantly certain those smiles weren't friendly.

Oh, God. She turned and flattened her back against the brick wall, frantically searching her coat pocket for her cell. The rough corrugated stone dug into her spine.

An eerie screech tore through the air. She realized what it was at the same time the first ring sounded in her ear.

Cold wrought iron, *bending*.

A hard-edged feminine laugh accompanied another metallic squeal, and Charlie's throat tightened. It wouldn't do any good to shout or scream. She couldn't attain any volume, and nothing pitched higher than a middle C would ever come from her scarred vocal cords. *Come on, comeoncomeoncomeon*—

"Cole's—"

"Old Matthew! There's someone in the alley—"

And now deep male laughter, as if they were relishing her fear.

"Charlie?"

"—trying to get up here, hurry hurry—"

Through the earpiece, she heard Old Matthew calling Vin's name and the crash of the phone to the counter. They'd be out within seconds.

To face these things? Old Matthew was huge, intimidating, and Vin strong and quick, but she hadn't warned them that whatever they were running to confront might be much, much stronger—

A familiar flat clang almost stopped her heart, her breath. The Dumpster. Someone had jumped on top of the lid. And the rough scraping could only be boots against brick.

One of them was climbing the wall.

Charlie shot to her feet, prepared to run. But where? There was no access to street level except the stairs. She whirled in a circle, looking for a place to hide. Nowhere was safe.

The lights from the Heritage penetrated the gray haze of fear clouding her vision. It was only a twenty-foot drop or so. Better to risk broken legs and go over at the front of the building than wait around here for . . .

Her mind shut off before she could contemplate *that*.

Blindly, she sprinted away from the wall and slammed into another. Pain exploded over her cheek. The impact spun her around, she almost fell, but something wrapped around her chest and pulled her back up tight against a surface as hard as the brick, but warm.

What—?

Not a wall. One of them had gotten upstairs.

It was no use, but she tried to yell, kicking her heels against his shins, elbowing his stomach and chest. Her struggles were as ineffectual as her screams, and she hated the desperate whistling noises she made almost as much as she hated this *thing* for scaring her.

"Easy, Charlie. Easy." A male voice. A soft rumble in her ear. "I'll take care of them."

It cut through her panic, and she had a heartbeat's time to see the arm extended over her shoulder, and the crossbow in a large, capable hand. A heartbeat's time to see the dark form launch onto the roof and the shock on his pale face before the bolt thunked into his forehead and he tumbled back over the side.

The female shrieked, a piercing note of surprise and terror. One of the males—probably not the one with an arrow through his brain, Charlie realized—cried a name like a warning. *Gideon?* And then running footsteps, boots against pavement, echoing in the alley . . . so fast. Prestissimo agitato, and the tempo of her heart not much slower.

"Can you stand, Charlie?"

She didn't know. She couldn't think of her legs when her entire existence narrowed down to a stranger's arm and his weapon. The rain beaded on his sleeve, then soaked into the rough weave. There weren't many dark spots on the material, as if he'd donned the coat in the past minute or two.

"Charlie?"

She blinked. "Yes," she rasped, and then he was setting her feet down and running silently past her, a tall form in a long brown duster, the split coattails flaring out behind him. A round-brimmed hat shadowed the side of his face as he jumped atop the wall and went over.

Her stomach quaking, Charlie raced to the edge, looked down.

All of them, gone.

Vertigo struck. The world swam dizzily, and Charlie shook her head. *Not real. Not real.*

She was trying to convince herself of that as Old Matthew and Vin burst through the kitchen door. A shotgun glinted dully in Old Matthew's grip. They rounded the Dumpster.

"Charlie?" Shock hoarsened the older man's voice and twisted his face when he saw the gate. He lifted the weapon to his shoulder, turned in a long sweep of the alley.

It took her two attempts to moisten her tongue enough to reply, to stop the chattering of her teeth. "Up here." It was little more than a whisper, so she added a wave.

She looked into the barrel of the shotgun for half a second, then Old Matthew lowered it. "You all right?"

The weak nod of her head didn't seem sufficient, but she couldn't yet move and didn't want to walk, however briefly, into the darkness. "I'm okay," she said. "I just really have to pee."

"You'd better come down first." Old Matthew's tone was the same he used with weepy drunks.

Not weepy, not drunk—just numb.

Belatedly, she realized her phone was still open. She clicked it shut. Twenty-one seconds.

She forced herself to move slowly away from the safety the sight of Old Matthew's and Vin's familiar faces provided. She wouldn't be dependent on it. She wouldn't—

What in the hell was *that*?

Her legs weakened, and she had to brace her palm against the stairwell wall to steady herself. She shook her head, looked again.

A long white feather lay on the black rooftop, only a yard from where she'd barreled into him. So clean and bright that it appeared to glow, though lit only by dim Christmas tree bulbs and the vapor-scattered streetlight.

"Come on, Charlie girl." Worry had crept into Old Matthew's voice; she must have been out of his view for too long.

She swept up the feather with shaking hands and ran down the stairs, through the dark. And it was crazy, stupid—but once the idea occurred to her, she couldn't let it go.

Perhaps the male hadn't yelled a name, but a word.

Guardian.

CHAPTER 2

When it rained, Charlie preferred the night. Liquid sunshine, gray daylight—they were nothing compared to the glitter caught in the arcs of the street lamps, that beaded against her balcony railing, her windows. The shine of brake lights slicked scarlet on black asphalt; tires lifted a wet spray and splashed through puddles—unremarkable and dirty during the day, but after sundown they became part of a brilliant play of color and sound, and her little enclosed balcony more like a private box at a ramshackle opera house.

Even if the music remained in her head. Her neighbors probably wouldn't have appreciated Bellini at midnight, and Charlie liked to play *Norma* at the volume it deserved.

But the quiet was welcome, too. She tilted her head and listened when, from the adjoining balcony, a door scraped open rather than slid—inexpensive apartments, damp climate.

She hadn't known Ethan McCabe was home, but she was glad for the company. Glad for anything that might distract her from sharp teeth and crossbows and the ache in her cheek.

The wood creaked under his weight. He was looking out over the railing, she realized. Not avoiding the wet, whereas she sat tucked up close to the door, sheltered beneath the roof, with her sweatshirt, flannel pajama pants, and fuzzy slippers as a ward against the cold. Hardly an attractive ensemble, but it hardly mattered.

It was several moments before he said, "I thought you quit."

The tip of her cigarette glowed brightly with the depth of her inhalation. Ethan couldn't see it through the wall that separated their balconies, but the scent would have been unmistakable.

She sent a stream of smoke into the night air, smiled grimly up at the overhanging eaves. "It seemed like the kind of night to start again."

He didn't immediately reply, but she hadn't expected him to. In the two months he'd occupied the apartment next to hers—*occasionally* occupied it—she'd become accustomed to his silences.

During their first conversation, as hidden from her sight as he was now and with only the lazy drawl in his voice to guide her, she'd thought he was slow. It hadn't taken long to discover that "particular" fit him better.

"Seems to me," he finally said, "the only difference between this night and any other is that you're home a mite early."

So did "indirect." He wouldn't ask what had happened, but give her an opening.

And Charlie needed to say it aloud. She couldn't to Jane; her sister knew her too well. She'd recognize that Charlie wasn't joking. She hadn't told the two police officers who'd taken a look at the gate and her statement, or Old Matthew when he'd driven the four blocks from Cole's to her apartment.

She'd seen shadows following them, slinking through the dark streets—most of them, she was certain, the product of her paranoia. Most of them.

"I had an . . . incident down at Cole's." Though she'd tapped it off into a saucer before her last draw, the ash at the end of her cigarette was already a quarter-inch long. Not a leisurely smoke—she was sucking on it like a drowning woman might air. "Three vampires tried to attack me on the roof, but the Lone Ranger arrived and shot them with a crossbow. Or maybe the

Rifleman. I couldn't tell, and I don't know my cowboys very well."

Ethan didn't respond, not even with the slow *Why, Miss Charlie, I do believe you are having me on* he'd given her when, a month ago, she'd told him her voice was a mess because she'd traded it to a sea witch for a pair of legs, and that she lived in Seattle because it was so wet.

He'd never seen the scar. She'd never seen him, but judging by the angle and projection of his voice, she thought he must be tall, with a chest to match.

It was probably fortunate that a wall separated them, because she could have used a chest like that to lean against. Would have *used* it.

So she used a plastic patio chair instead. Her crutches: a chair, a cigarette, and a white feather. It lay on her lap—stiff, but like silk to the touch. When she'd spoken with the police, she'd clung to it like Dumbo with his magic feather.

"My hero had wings," she added when his silence continued. Might as well make it as ridiculous as possible. "Like a guardian angel. And, for a second, I thought he was you."

Charlie knew from experience that almost anyone else who'd found themselves included in such a story would have said *Me?* with a bit of startled laughter.

Ethan only said, "I'm no hero."

"Well, I didn't take you for the type of guy to go flying around looking for vampires to shoot."

"No. Demons need shooting more than vampires do."

Humor had slipped into his tone. His quick answers were usually accompanied by it, and apparently he'd decided to play along. A tall tale to him, truth to her—but his response made it less frightening, easing her tension, and she laughed softly.

It was one of the few noises she could make that wasn't much different before the accident.

Most of her life had revolved around voices. Studying them, perfecting hers. They could be as distinctive as a face, and when she'd heard the first *Easy, Charlie*, it had been familiar. Low, warmed by deep amber tones, and roughened with a hint of oak.

"He sounded exactly like you. The pitch, the resonance. But he didn't talk like you."

"No, Miss Charlie, I reckon he didn't. Most flying men of my acquaintance are Easterners, and liable to talk like a book." Ethan's drawl thickened, and Charlie grinned, reaching forward to stab out the cigarette.

"Anyway, that's why I'm home early." She ran the feather between her fingers. The quill's surface was rounded and smooth, the end a blunt point. "Did you get in tonight?"

"That I did."

"San Francisco again?"

"Yes. And a handful of other cities."

She didn't know exactly what Ethan did for Ramsdell Pharmaceuticals, but she couldn't see why they'd relocate him to Seattle when he spent most of his time in California and the rest hopping around the country—but it wasn't for her to decide, anyway. "Did you eat, or get to the store? Old Matthew sent me home with a box, but I wasn't hungry. I could toss it over."

"I'm settled, Charlie."

"Okay." She tickled the underside of her chin with the tip of the feather, looking at the wall and wishing—not for the first time—that she could see through it.

But perhaps it was best she couldn't. Not yet, not until she was steady. Strong.

With a long sigh, she stood and scooped the pack of smokes from the table. She'd gone through a quarter of them. "Will you do me a favor?" Without waiting for his answer, she held it over the wall. "Will you hide these at your place? I won't buy more if I can get them for free next door."

He didn't respond, but his fingers brushed hers as he took the pack. She closed her eyes. He was warm, as if he'd protected his hands in his pockets instead of exposing them to the cold night air, a feather in one and a cigarette in the other.

"If you ask, should I give them back?"

Her fingers trembled, and she pulled her hand away from his and tucked it against her side. "No. Make me come and get them."

"Well now, Charlie, I don't know whether to hope that you resist, or to pray for an end to our Pyramus and Thisbe routine."

Her teeth clenched, and the frustration that rose up in her wasn't unfamiliar: that feeling of ignorance, of being unable to share in a joke or discussion—or worse, the certainty that she had heard something before, but just couldn't place it. "Hold on, Ethan. I'll be right back."

She didn't close the sliding door behind her. Her computer was on, and luckily the search engine offered up the correct spelling after she put in her mangled, phonetic version. Pyramus and Thisbe. Lovers parted by a family feud, whose only contact was speaking through a crack in a wall.

Damn. She *had* seen this once, at a theater in New York—she'd probably been drunk off her ass, or halfway there.

She grimaced as she scanned the rest of the story, then returned to the balcony. "That didn't end well. Unless you think double suicide is romantic."

Ethan's laughter broke and rolled like muted thunder—a fitting accompaniment to the lights and the weather. "No," he said eventually. "That I don't. Good night, Miss Charlie."

She smiled into the dark; this was a familiar routine. And she was feeling settled now, too—and safe. "Good night, Ethan."

Her smile lingered as she readied for bed, as she placed the feather on her nightstand. The drumming of the rain against the roof, the sighing of the breeze, the swish of the passing cars was a soft symphony lulling her to sleep.

Long before it was silenced, she'd fallen deep.

❧

Charlie needed better locks.

Ethan could have picked them open within seconds, but he didn't require tools or time. He mentally tested the shape of the cylinder in the deadbolt, the simple pin tumbler in the knob, and unlocked them both with an effortless thrust of his Gift.

Though she'd left no lights on, he easily avoided the bamboo trunk that served as a coffee table. Knitted throws in bright colors covered the sofa and the chair in front of her desk. Against one wall, her television was dwarfed by stereo speakers and encased by shelves stuffed with records and CDs. He could read the neatly arranged titles from across the darkened room, but he already knew that classical and opera dominated her collection: she played them often.

It had been her way of introduction two months before, a throwaway comment from the balcony, underscored by Vivaldi: *Tell me if my music is too loud.*

Loud or quiet, it wouldn't have mattered; if he listened closely, Ethan could hear her heartbeat through the walls. The click of knitting needles. The distinctive slide of a feather over skin.

He followed the sound of her deep, even breathing. The fragrance of apple shampoo and cocoa butter rose from the damp towel wadded in a laundry basket at the foot of her bed.

Charlie lay on her stomach, her knee cocked. She'd kicked the blankets off. The left hem of her checkered flannel pajama pants had ridden up, revealing half the length of her sleek calf. The straps of her white top exposed more smooth skin at her shoulders and toned arms.

Despite her ordeal on the roof, her psychic scent suggested that her dreams were soft and pleasant—so different from the tension surrounding her in her waking hours. So different from the neediness, the emotional instability.

She didn't outwardly reveal them, but Ethan often felt both, like a dark itching scab in her psyche. They repelled him almost as much as they aroused his protective instincts.

She began to move restlessly, her wheat gold hair tousled over her pillow, her psychic scent altering, tinged by erotic heat.

Ethan looked away, ignoring the tightening in his gut, his groin. He'd come in for a purpose, but lusting after a human who needed protecting wasn't it.

The feather sat beside her alarm clock; his attempt to vanish it into his cache failed.

With a frown pulling at his mouth, he strode across the room and swept it up. Placing any object into his mental storage space required that he possess it, or obtain permission from the owner. Charlie had apparently formed such a strong attachment to the lost feather that he had to steal it back.

This time, it went easily into his cache. Destroying evidence—and whatever comfort it had offered her.

He couldn't erase Charlie's memories, or the bruise forming across her cheek. A Guardian with a Gift for healing could have taken care of the latter—and had Ethan been prepared for her bolt away from the wall, he could have avoided her slamming into him.

As it was, he'd only managed to keep her from hitting his weapon. His elbow had done less damage, but there shouldn't have been any damage at all.

And there shouldn't have been three vampires ready to do worse. Ethan stifled his simmering frustration. He *should* have caught them, but they'd evaded his pursuit by using the one lock his Gift couldn't breach—a lock formed, not by steel or magnets, but by ancient symbols and magic. The shield it created was damned impossible to break through.

For that reason, he'd use it to protect Charlie. To get to her, the vampires would have to burn down the apartment and flush her out—and Ethan didn't figure they were that desperate.

Yet.

Silence. Surround. Lock. Ethan scraped the symbols into her front door frame, an inch above the cream carpeting. Charlie likely wouldn't notice them or the drops of blood he used to activate the spell, and it would break when she left in the morning.

Immediately, an unearthly quiet descended around the apartment. The symbols not only barred entrance to anyone whose blood didn't key the spell, but prevented all communication. Neither sound, sign language, nor electronic methods of communication could penetrate the shield, from inside or out. Even his psychic senses were useless—a demon could stand on the other side of the door, and Ethan wouldn't know it until he left the protected area. Which he did quickly enough, slipping out into the hall and locking up behind him.

That psychic blindness made him uneasy—as did the symbols' origins. A year ago, only Lucifer had known how to cast the spell. The tyrannical ruler kept his demons ignorant of the symbols' power, so none would dare threaten his position on Hell's throne.

But one demon—Lilith, Lucifer's daughter—inadvertently learned of the spell when she *had* dared to rebel against Lucifer. Ethan had fought in that confrontation, and when the dust had settled, Lucifer had been forced to return to Hell and close the Gates to that realm for five hundred years. Locked in there, as it were, embroiled in a war—and defending his throne against an army of rebels led by the demon Belial.

Though Belial had promised his demons a return to Heaven and their former angelic status, a demon's promises weren't worth the air used to speak them, and Ethan would prefer to see Lucifer's and Belial's armies annihilate each other. Particularly as the Guardians' own ranks had been reduced—not by war, but by an Ascension. A little over a decade before, thousands of Guardians had chosen to move on to their afterlives, leaving less than fifty Guardians in the corps. Five hundred years would hardly be enough time to rebuild the Guardian corps and prepare for the demons' return through the Gates.

As it was, before the Gates had closed, hundreds of demons had escaped Hell, guaranteeing the Guardians plenty of trouble. So much so that Michael, the Guardians' leader, and Rael—one of Belial's demons and a U.S. congressman—had made arrangements with Homeland Security and developed a new law enforcement division, Special Investigations. Located in San Francisco, SI had but three directives: to train novice Guardians and act as an Earth-based center of operations for all other Guardians; to track and slay the rogue demons; and to conceal otherworldly activity from the general human population.

Otherworldly activity, such as magic spells.

And three months ago, only Guardians—and a few vampires recruited by Special Investigations—had known of the symbols. But a demon threat to the vampire population in San Francisco necessitated sharing knowledge of the spell with the vampires, and the use of it had quickly spread to other cities, other vampire communities—and to demons.

Ethan suspected demons had been responsible for the attack on Charlie, but there was only one way to be certain. With luck, the vampires wouldn't have dared leave the safety of their hidey-hole yet. But dawn arrived in less than three hours, and they'd succumb to the daysleep as soon as the sun rose. They'd have to poke their heads out eventually.

Ethan would be waiting.

❦

Son of a bitch.

Ethan clamped his jaw tight and took a cursory glance at the bakery's interior. Excepting the window the vampires had broken to enter the building, nothing had been disturbed.

The faint scent of vampire blood clung to the three symbols carved on the sill with splintered glass. The protective shield had fallen when they'd left, but Ethan dug the tip of his dagger through the shapes. The Seattle police might tie the vandalism here to the destruction of Cole's gate two blocks distant—vampires still had fingerprints and DNA, after all—but Ethan wouldn't leave evidence of the spell for them to find. They likely wouldn't suppose it was something other-worldly, in any case.

Peculiar, that Charlie did. In those rare instances humans spied a vampire's teeth or a Guardian's wings, they assumed it was a person dressed up in a costume. The feather she'd found hadn't been reason enough for the fear and certainty lurking in her psychic scent when she'd passed off truth as exaggeration.

The Lone Ranger. A white hat would never sit easily on him; she'd be a fool to think otherwise. But a reluctant smile tugged at his mouth as he crouched and cast around for the vampires' trail.

The light rain enhanced scent—as did the concrete, slightly warmer than the surrounding air. One vampire had leaned or brushed against the corner of the coffee shop at the end of the block. The odor was mostly human, with an undertone of metallic blood and wet leather. Not a revolting smell, but Ethan preferred green apple and cocoa butter.

He'd taken quite a liking to the combination: sharp and sweet, warm and mellow. It'd be a damn shame if it changed.

And it was strange that it hadn't. Of the nine scientists Legion Laboratories had recruited in the past year—three geneticists, four experts in blood diseases, and two researchers who specialized in artificial blood—only Jane Newcomb hadn't had a close relative transformed into a vampire.

Ethan figured it was pure luck that had delivered Dr. Milliken and her husband to him two months before, and that had let the husband escape the vampires who had attacked and transformed him. Ethan had taken both back to San Francisco, to Special Investigations and the vampire community there—but whatever purpose had been behind the transformation, Dr. Milliken hadn't learned.

If he had to guess, Ethan thought that, given another day or two, the demons who owned Legion Laboratories would have offered her an ultimatum. It hadn't taken long to discover the pattern in the other scientists' families—but after two failed attempts to approach them and offer help, Ethan had backed away.

Something—or someone—had scared the piss out of each of them. Each had been convinced talking with Ethan meant death . . . though he didn't think they were concerned about their own lives. After all, demons couldn't kill humans—but they could kill vampires.

And Ethan didn't know if the vampires who'd gone after Charlie were the same who'd transformed Milliken, but he'd have wagered a trainload of money they were.

Ethan lost their trail a block further on. They'd doubled back toward Cole's, then crossed the street toward a parking garage, where they must have left an automobile. He stood on the darkened ground floor, took stock. A security camera near the exit had been demolished, the cable ripped from its moorings. There'd likely be nothing on the tapes, but he'd make a point to collect them the next afternoon. His Special Investigations badge ought to be good for something; and if it wasn't, he could steal them easily enough.

He turned to go, then halted, his muscles tensing in anticipation of an attack. Instantly, his crossbow and sword appeared in his hands.

The hairs on the back of his neck prickled, and a dark psychic presence slithered across his mind.

Demon. An almighty powerful one, too. Unless Ethan was reaching out with his psychic senses, a demon's psyche typically didn't *feel* like a physical touch. He'd only experienced something similar from Michael, the oldest and most gifted of the Guardians—but the Doyen's psyche hadn't felt like scales on a snake's belly.

A psychic scan revealed nothing, but that meant all-fired nothing: every demon could block a mental probe. Ethan stopped breathing. Listened and watched.

The vehicles formed rows of silent, colorful lumps; outside, a car rolled down the wet street. The garage's overhead lights glared against the windshields, but none were tinged with the glowing crimson of demon eyes.

Ethan had no doubt the demon had deliberately exposed itself. Why wait to engage him, then? Unless it simply wanted to let Ethan know it was aware of the Guardian's presence in Seattle.

A hiss resounded through the garage, formed a single word: *Murderer.*

His fingers clenched on his sword, but the creature had apparently decided to retreat . . . to play with Ethan another day. It had obviously found something in his mind to torment him with—and though demons were notorious for lies, for twisting the truth, there weren't nothing false in the name it had called him.

CHAPTER 3

Ethan flew into San Francisco with the dawn.

On the eastern side of the city, tucked just northwest of an abandoned naval shipyard and the shoreline of the bay, a ramshackle warehouse stood, surrounded by a fenced-in parking lot of cracked and buckling asphalt. For almost a year now, it had served as Special Investigations' headquarters. The fence wouldn't keep demons out—or the neighborhood kids—but the run-down façade would keep both away. Demons, because appearances meant everything, and the appearance of wealth and power was the most critical; and kids because, from outside, there was no indication that the building housed anything worth investigating or stealing.

In the old days, Ethan would have taken one look at the tiny security cameras and infrared sensors posted around the perimeter—that was, if they'd had cameras and sensors in those days—and known it was a building worth cleaning out.

Then he'd have high-tailed it the other way, because folks who went to that much trouble and expense to hide what they had were often too dangerous to trifle with, and more than prepared for someone like him.

But there was no need to break in; even if he didn't have his Gift, he had a keycard. He didn't bother with swiping it. After landing at the back entrance to the warehouse and vanishing his wings, he touched his mind to the wide cylindrical pins anchoring the four-inch-thick steel door into the reinforced wall, slid across the electromagnetic locks, and disengaged both.

Inside, the empty white walls along the corridor hid an array of sensory equipment and defensive measures: face recognition systems, tweaked to detect the slightest alterations in a familiar person's size and form; temperature gauges, to determine if the entrant was a vampire, demon, or Guardian; and hellhound venom-filled darts, to paralyze any unwelcome demon.

At the end of the corridor, clad in his finest butler's gear, Jeeves sat behind a bulletproof shield and watched his approach. Ethan tried to probe his psyche to find out who lay behind that stiff upper lip—each Guardian undergoing training at the facility shape-shifted into Jeeves's form and took a turn guarding the entrance—but Ethan couldn't penetrate this one's shields.

One of the older novices, then, and likely a few decades into his one hundred years of training.

Jeeves's formal greeting was followed by a polite instruction to step up to the retinal, voice, and fingerprint scanners. Even if a demon had managed to fool the sensors to this point, one likely wouldn't have shape-shifted down to such detail.

Ethan could have unlocked the door that slid open when Jeeves approved his identity, but it was simpler to follow protocol—and less likely to bring a phalanx of Guardians down on him. He passed through the security area, then paused when Jeeves met him in the hallway and lowered his shields.

Jake. Ethan glanced past him, into Jeeves's station. It couldn't be left unmanned. "You got a minute?"

The butler's exterior shimmered, changed; the elderly gentleman became a young, T-shirt- and jeans-wearing male, with an erect bearing and dark shaved hair that could have come fresh out of a military boot camp.

Considering that Jake had died in the jungles of Vietnam, the kid likely had been.

"More than that. I'm off." Jake stuck a toothpick between his lips and scooted to the side of the doorway just as another Guardian darted past him, her dark form a blur. "Ten seconds late, Rebecca."

"Fuck you," she said as she shape-shifted. Even if it hadn't been mildly spoken, her response would have been impossible to take seriously, her feminine voice coming as it did from Jeeves's mouth. Her dour gaze lifted to Ethan's face, then narrowed on his grin. "Hey, Drifter. Laugh it up while you can; *she* asked us to let her know when you finally got your ass back here."

Lilith. The former demon and FBI agent now headed operations at Special Investigations. A few Guardians still chafed at the thought of following her direction, but Ethan hadn't any argument with it—particularly as Lilith's partner and SI's co-director, Hugh Castleford, had been Ethan's mentor for a century in Caelum, the realm the Guardians called home. Even if Ethan hadn't trusted Lilith's judgment and two thousand years of experience, he would have Hugh's.

"Well, then, I'll be pleased to accommodate her," Ethan drawled.

Rebecca pursed Jeeves's thin lips. "And you've screwed up the entry logs by failing to swipe your card. There's no record of you at the main door, but there's a record here at security? Red flags everywhere. And guess who has to go in and fix them?"

Ethan adopted his best *aw, shucks* expression. "I'm just keeping you on your toes, Miss Becca. Training and all."

Rebecca spread her arms wide; Ethan could almost hear the starched shirt cracking. "Do I look like a fucking ballerina to you?" A choked laugh from Jake had her glaring in his direction. "You: Shut up. I just learned how to take my sword out of my hammerspace, and I'm not afraid to use it."

Jake held up his hands in surrender, but his gaze centered over her shoulder and on the monitors lining the small room. "You've got a motorcycle coming into the parking lot, Jeeves."

Rebecca turned her head; when she glanced back, Jeeves's smile was a ghastly thing. "Speak of the devil. It's Lilith," she said and slammed the door.

Ethan's brows rose, and he looked from the still-quivering door frame to Jake. "Her *hammerspace*?"

"Her cache." Jake shrugged and moved the toothpick from the right corner of his mouth to the left. "It's a video-game thing. We've been playing DemonSlayer in our downtime."

"Learning a bushel from it, are you?" Ethan asked, his voice dry as desert sand. Though based on a book that accurately described Guardians, the game was riddled with errors—but, fortunately, the public assumed both were fiction.

"There's only so much porn you can download before the thrill is gone." The toothpick bobbed with Jake's unapologetic grin. "Speaking of, that's probably why Becca's ready to snap: I think Emo Vamp always falls asleep right afterwards."

"I can hear you, you bloody bastard." Rebecca's reply came clearly through the door, but this time it was rounded by Jeeves's cultured voice. "And Mackenzie's worth it."

Her vampire lover likely fed from her just before falling into the daysleep, then. Ethan didn't allow his revulsion to show; the thought of the blood and feeding didn't disgust him, but the memory of a vampire's bloodlust, and of how easily it had slipped into his own mind, left a bitter taste in his mouth. He'd done a lot of wrong in his lifetime, but what he'd done to that vampire had been one of the worst.

He'd been a Guardian with a century's training—but the overwhelming need had left him as weak as a human . . . or a vampire.

A hiss of compressed air and the slide of the door preceded Lilith's entrance, and Ethan made a mental amendment as she strode toward them, her long black hair coiled tight at her nape, her dark eyes fixed on his. Lilith was human now, but with the physical strength of a vampire, and "weak" described her about as well as "unsightly" described an Arizona sunset.

And nothing about Lilith was unsightly, either, though Ethan wasn't used to seeing so little of her. Perhaps in deference to the crisp morning, she'd traded in her corset for a high-necked black shirt and a jacket that rivaled his in length.

She didn't stop and offer a greeting; as she passed him, she simply commanded, "Drifter. In my office. And bring your puppy."

Jake made a woofing sound, but Ethan was surprised that *her* dog wasn't trailing at her heels. Lilith's three-headed hellhound could make a demon quake with fear and served as her protection. She rarely went anywhere without it, and Sir Pup's absence likely meant that, wherever Castleford was, he had needed the hellhound more than she did.

Which gave Ethan an advantage he'd have been a fool to squander. Whistling soundlessly, he fell into step behind her.

❧

With its walls painted a rich gold, mahogany furniture, and shelves of books, the office that Lilith and Castleford shared could have fit as easily in a nineteenth-century English manor house—although a gentleman farmer likely wouldn't have had an arsenal of weapons hidden in his library. Lilith sat lightly on the front edge of her desk; Jake dropped into one of the club chairs facing her. Ethan didn't take the seat she pushed toward him with her boot.

Though her psychic blocks were impenetrable, he felt her dark gaze as he moved toward the painting of Caelum that hung against the east wall. Columns and spires of white marble rose against a gloriously blue sky.

"Your pup ain't here," Ethan said.

"Washington, D.C.'s vamp community was wiped out last night," Lilith said. Though her voice was flat, she allowed her frustration and anger to slip through her shields. "Michael took Hugh and Sir Pup with him, looking for evidence. They teleported there just after dawn."

Jake sat forward, inhaled through clenched teeth. "Was it the same as in Rome and Berlin last month? No survivors?"

"Yes. Whoever they are—and however many of them there were—they were methodical."

As they had been in Rome and in Berlin. Ethan could hardly comprehend the organization and planning it must have taken to wipe out every vampire in a city over the course of a single night. "Nothing to show whether it was demons or nosferatu?"

Though demons and nosferatu had once been angels, the nosferatu hadn't been tossed into Hell after Lucifer's rebellion—instead, they'd been cursed with bloodlust and intolerance for daylight. Most demons and every Guardian would slay a nosferatu on sight; for that reason, they usually hid in caves, safe from psychic detection.

But not always—in the past year, Ethan had seen more nosferatu than in the first two decades of his active Guardian service. And, to a one, nosferatu despised vampires. If ever a group would want to destroy the communities, it would be nosferatu.

"I'd wager it was demons," Lilith said, and Ethan's brows rose. She must be certain, then; Lilith didn't speak of bargains or wagers lightly. As a demon, she'd been bound by one—and the consequences for entering into a bargain or wager and then breaking its terms were severe: an eternity of torment, frozen between Hell and the Chaos realm. "Nosferatu would have left a mess, not piled the vampires' bodies up and let them disintegrate in the sun. The demons are trying to keep their activity hidden from humans—but not from us."

"That's still a heap of ash and personal items to be concealing from the local authorities," Ethan pointed out.

"Yes. Michael will take care of that."

Meaning that the Doyen would vanish the evidence into his cache. She wouldn't need Ethan and Jake to go in and help with the physical cover-up, then, but there was still a community missing. So many people disappearing at once would be noticed—jobs and apartments suddenly abandoned, human family members left with questions—and, after Berlin and Rome, Special Investigations had formed a task force to handle the fallout. But neither Ethan nor Jake belonged to it.

"Is this what you pulled us in for?" Ethan asked.

"No. I want an update on Seattle." Lilith stood and shrugged out of her jacket, throwing it across the back of the chair she'd offered him. "Milliken's transformation failed."

Dread digging at his gut, Ethan frowned and watched Lilith round the desk and sink into her high-backed seat. When a human was turned into a vampire against his will—drained, and then forced to drink vampire or nosferatu blood—the transformation rarely took. After a long and painful degeneration, the vampire went out one of two ways: easy, like an old man in his sleep—or violently, driven mad by bloodlust.

"He's dead?" Jake yanked the toothpick from his mouth, glanced back at Ethan.

"Yes," she said. "Colin called me last evening."

"Did he have to finish it?" Ethan asked. If so, it would have been quick and painless; Colin Ames-Beaumont was brutally efficient with his swords.

The two-hundred-year-old vampire led the San Francisco

community with his partner, Savi Murray. Both were connected to SI, and often acted as liaisons between Guardians and vampires in other cities. Ethan couldn't fathom why Savi, one of the sweetest, brightest ladies he'd had the pleasure of knowing, had developed such a powerful liking for her spoiled pretty-boy fiancé—but Ethan had to admit Colin took care of those under his protection. He'd have done everything possible to help Milliken adjust.

"Yes. They'd been watching for the snap, and Savi got Milliken's wife out—but not before she saw part of it. So Dr. Milliken isn't in an emotional state to continue assisting us—though I doubt there's much more she could tell us about Legion than she told you the night you brought them here." Lilith steepled her fingers, pointed at Ethan. "And you came today for a purpose, Drifter, but Hugh and Milliken obviously weren't it. I *can* appreciate a man who waits and listens, gathering as much information as possible before he offers the info that *I* want—but the only man for whom I'd make the effort is in Washington, D.C., sifting through vampire ash. So talk. Now."

Charlie's file was in his cache; with a quick mental pull, Ethan made it appear on Lilith's desk. It contained all of the data Jake had found in various government databases and several financial institutions. "Charlotte Newcomb. Three vampires came for her last night."

Her lips compressed into a thin line before she said, "Is she still alive? Still human?"

Ethan gave a short nod. "They ran when I arrived, and used the symbols." He hesitated briefly, then added, "Charlie knows. Not details, but she was certain they were vampires, and that a guardian angel came to her rescue."

"She would have been a lot more certain if you'd failed and she was sucking blood now." A smile curved Lilith's mouth, but there was little humor in it.

There was less in Ethan's reply. "It's been more than two months since the last transformation. Since Milliken's."

Lilith flipped open the folder, began scanning the pages. "Any reason for them to wait, when they didn't with the others? Is there anything special about her?"

Plenty, but Ethan doubted there was anything a demon might appreciate. "I figured you'd know better than I would. And why they aren't waiting any longer."

"I know Lucifer's demons. Those who used to follow Belial are a bit more individual." She grimaced around the last word.

Jake grinned. "You say that like it's a bad thing."

"It is when you're trying to predict their behavior, puppy." She speared him with a dark look before returning her attention to the file. "Cerberus's balls, this girl is a fucking mess. Overdrafts, maxed-out credit cards, late payments."

"*Was* a mess," Ethan said with an edge of impatience, not moving from his position by the painting. With his Guardian eyesight, he could easily read the page she was holding. "Those are the financials from three years ago."

Lilith darted a glance up at him. "So they are."

Ethan's jaw clenched, and his skin heated slightly. Of course she hadn't missed the date; she'd been trying to draw a response from him, and she'd gotten one. No longer a demon, but still manipulative. Still looking for a man's weaknesses.

Charlie wasn't his. He liked her well enough, but he'd be a damned fool to let a woman like that depend on him or get under his skin.

Apparently oblivious to the smirk that tilted Lilith's lips, Jake leaned forward and tapped his finger against a line item. "A lot of it was this payment—she made it a year after she got out of Mission Creek."

"A five-thousand-dollar fine?" Lilith's brows arched. "And a year at a state correction facility? Was the DUI her first offense?"

Jake nodded. "No other DUIs, but she'd checked herself in and out of alcohol rehab for a couple of years, so the judge took that as a sign that she wasn't capable of rehabilitating herself. And she totaled her rental car, driving into the side of that restaurant, so there were a few other charges thrown on top of it. She was lucky no one else was injured, or she might not have gotten off as easy as she did."

Ethan didn't know it had been all that easy, but he didn't respond. He was hardly one to determine suitable punishments.

"Did you check out the inmates who were in with her? Any hits with Legion?" Lilith asked.

"We ran the names," Ethan said. "There were none."

"Her financials are clean now, though she doesn't have

anything extra," she noted as she hit the end of the file. "Certainly nothing to tempt a demon. Who gave her the money?"

Jake slid his toothpick between his lips again, leaned back. "Her sister, a little over two years ago. The loan got her out of the hole. That's also when Charlie stopped the careless spending and finally got a steady job."

"At . . . Cole's? Hold on." Lilith glanced back at a page. "She's drunk and drives her car through the window of his restaurant, and six years later he offers her a position as *bartender*?"

Another folder appeared in Jake's hand. "Old Matthew Cole. Sentenced thirty-seven years ago for rape and double murder, then had his conviction overturned a quarter century later when DNA evidence showed he was innocent. Legally changed his name to 'Old Matthew' because he said that's what he was when he got out—what the courts did to him, he just wanted to make official. Most of his staff has served time for minor offenses."

"An ex-con turned Mother Hen, with a grudge against the law," Lilith murmured, shaking her head in amusement, then turned back to the first page in Charlie's file and studied her picture.

"We looked at all of Cole's and the staff's associates as well," Ethan said.

"She's attractive, I suppose, if one goes for those blond, sloe-eyed, rock-and-roll, just-fell-out-of-bed types. Don't you think so, puppy?"

"I'd do her," Jake said.

"You'd screw a goat if it looked at you crosswise." Ethan ignored Jake's rueful grin of agreement and stared down at Lilith. Was she trying to rile him again, suggesting such a thing? Demons didn't have a sexual drive; they could perform the act, but couldn't feel physical desire. "A demon ain't likely to lust after her, and it wouldn't make no difference if she looked as she does now or if she were the bearded lady in a traveling wagon."

"No, but they recognize and enjoy beauty. It doesn't take much for appreciation to become envy, which might explain the change. I don't know that her face is so remarkable it'd inspire that much envy, though. She's an odd kind of pretty."

Only the knowledge that Lilith might shoot him kept Ethan

from shaking his head in disbelief and observing that women were far more critical of each other than a man ever would be. Even upside-down and flattened by the photo, Charlie's wide-spaced, heavy-lidded brown eyes, her translucent skin, her plump upper lip, and small, slightly crooked teeth called to the most basic urges in a man: to haul her off to bed and put that mouth to good use, to see her eyes darken and skin flush.

"What about singing?" Jake tossed a silvery compact disc on top of Charlie's picture, and Lilith picked it up. "I don't know anything about this kind of music, and most of her performances took place before newspapers and trade magazines began archiving their reviews online—but those I could find said she was some kind of vocal prodigy out of Juilliard."

Lilith stood, pressed a button on a remote, and a console slid out of the wall. Ethan watched the player suck the disc in, then frowned at Jake. "Where'd you come up with that?"

"Bit torrents. Savi told me about file sharing a couple of months ago, but I only began downloading music last week. And since I was scouring papers for Charlie's info anyway, I looked it up. This was a charity benefit at the Metropolitan Opera in New York, with several other performers—you want track eight," he said when a male began belting an Italian tune that Ethan had first heard when he was human.

Lilith skipped through the CD and, as the initial strains filtered through the speakers, announced, "It's from *Lucia di Lammermoor*." She caught Jake's look and rolled her eyes. "I was a demon, not a Neanderthal. And the most interesting people have always been the politicians, artists, and poets. She's performing the mad scene from the third act, which means she's a bit of a showoff, but a confident one. It's a difficult—" She silenced herself by pressing her lips together when the singing began. She cocked her head, closed her eyes.

Ethan looked away, stared at the thick-piled rug beneath his boots. He'd listened to enough of Charlie's music collection to recognize a fine voice. Her soprano was light and high—but with a strength that swelled through him, left him full of its sound. And pure, he realized—most regular folks and professional singers had rough edges in their voices, edges that had become more apparent with his enhanced hearing. He'd heard nothing this clear since he'd become a Guardian.

Nothing human, leastwise. A voice like that belonged in Caelum—was what he imagined filled the realm before the Guardians had taken it from the angels.

"Fuck me," Lilith said after a moment. She returned to her seat without lowering the volume. "*That's* a gift. Unlocking doors is kid's play next to that. And you said she got off easy? If she lost that voice because of her own stupidity it's no wonder she hit a downward spiral." She looked up at Ethan. "Is she drinking?"

Charlie trilled through a series of quick, high notes that had his gut clenching, his fists tightening. It took a second before he could say, "No. Not a bit."

"But she's bartending. Classic self-flagellation: it serves as punishment because it's a constant reminder, and the temptation of the drink is its own pain—but she tells herself that her resistance just means she's the stronger for it. Maybe that's why the demons haven't touched her; she's doing just fine tormenting herself."

"If their goal was torture, I'd reckon you were correct. But they don't send in vampires for that."

Lilith nodded, her gaze thoughtful. "Let's assume there's nothing about Charlie herself that would have made them hold off, because she doesn't have this voice anymore. But they did, and there had to be a reason for them—or the demon pulling their strings—to change their mind, and her only link to Legion is her sister. Tell me how they came at her."

"During her break. They knew to find her on the roof."

"You've been keeping an eye on her for two months now. Did they come around Cole's before?"

⋅ "No. Not the evenings I was watching." If they had, Ethan would've gotten answers from them long ago. "But Charlie calls Jane most every night."

"So you think that's what tipped them off to her routine. *Who* tipped them off," Lilith said.

"Jane?" Jake shook his head. "I don't see—"

"No. The boyfriend, Dylan Samuels." Ethan brushed the sides of his jacket back, hooked his thumbs at the base of his suspenders. "I figure he's a demon."

Jake's mouth snapped closed, and he glanced warily at Lilith. She set down the folder that had just appeared in her hands and studied Ethan. Her face was expressionless, but if she'd still been a demon, he reckoned her eyes might have been glowing crimson.

"You figure?"

"Yes, ma'am."

"But you aren't certain."

"About ninety-nine percent."

Slowly, she picked up the remote and silenced the stereo. "Ninety-nine," she said flatly. "Why didn't you tell me this as soon as I came in?"

Ethan scratched his jaw, considering. "Two . . . no, three reasons. The first was the one percent, and his human behavior. He's been bedding Miss Jane for eight months now, and from listening in on Charlie's phone calls I gleaned that he's doing it regular-like. He wasn't the person that recruited her, and she isn't rolling in cash, just comfortable—so there weren't no reason to strike up a relationship or continue it as long as he has. And you've got his transcripts there." He gestured to the folder on her desk. "I talked to his professors, a few neighbors. He's got a history that goes back at least ten years, though that doesn't guarantee he didn't just take over another man's identity. I didn't want to alert him to my presence if he was a demon, which meant I had to stay away from him and couldn't feel him out too hard. What I have noted is that his psychic blocks are good."

Lilith was nodding. "But that isn't impossible for humans. Reason number two, because reason number one isn't enough for me not to put a bullet in your eye."

Which would hurt like a son of a bitch, but wouldn't kill him. "It wouldn't benefit me to fly down here and ask your opinion if I colored it with my assumptions first. It took you ten minutes to consider all of the avenues Jake and I have been exploring on and off for two months, and you discarded each one that I did, coming back to the sister. But maybe you wouldn't have bothered had I opened up with Samuels as the demon. And maybe my ninety-nine has increased half a percent."

"Maybe?" She tapped her fingers against Samuels's folder a few times before stilling her hand. "All right. I'll give you that. And three?"

"Sir Pup is three thousand miles east. No matter how many weapons you've hidden around this room, I reckoned it'd be mighty difficult for you to murder me, so it was safe to risk pissing you off."

"Jesus." Jake backed his chair up, as if edging out of the line of fire. "It was good knowing you, Drifter."

Lilith ignored him, tilting her head to the side, her eyes narrowing. "I wonder—do people fall for your 'I'm just simple folk' routine?"

"Yes'm," he said mildly. "Rather often."

She leaned back, and Ethan heard the coil of hair sliding against the seat's leather upholstering. "It's also because of your size. Somewhere around six-three, height doesn't suggest power anymore, but 'big dumb lunk.'"

"I figure I got three extra inches of lunk in my feet then."

"I'd put it in your head," she said, but the sharpening of her gaze told him her thoughts were returning to the demon before she added, "So Samuels is in a relationship with the sister—and any demon is arrogant enough to think the control he has there is sufficient. Why transform Charlie if he's got the sister in hand? It'd be a blow to his ego to resort to that."

"But he did," Jake said.

"Yes. Which gives us several possibilities: another demon wanted to strike that blow, maybe someone higher up at Legion, and he directed the vampires to go after Charlie; or, if Samuels is directing the vampires, something happened at Legion that changed his priorities—so that a blow to his ego was the lesser of two evils; or, Jane is starting to suspect something's wrong, and he wanted another level of control over her. But there's always the fourth possibility, which is the unknown factor that usually fucks everything up." She glanced up at Ethan. "Did they know you were in Seattle?"

Remembering the surprise in the vampires' psychic scents, Ethan shook his head. "No. But the vampires do now. At least one demon does, too."

"And your cover with Charlie is blown. Does she still trust—"

"She doesn't know it was me that saved her." And Ethan preferred to keep it that way.

Jake turned in his seat. "You shape-shifted? Are you sure she was convinced by it? You're the worst—"

"She didn't see me clearly." Only heard him. If he ever had to use the one false shape he could successfully hold, he'd be

certain not to talk much. He looked at Lilith. "The way I figure, there's about seven vampires being held at Legion, and
about seven scientists working there under coercion."

She nodded and picked up the small pile of files, tossed them
at Ethan. He vanished them into his cache the moment they left
her fingers. "You've been going to Caelum each day, getting
your assignments from Michael. I want you in Seattle full-time.
I'll clear it with him. Whatever Legion is doing, finding out
what it is needs to take precedence over everything else. Everything but keeping Charlie Newcomb out of the vamps' hands."

"Yes." It needn't be said. A Guardian's first duty was always protecting human life.

"I'll be sending Jake up in a day or two as your backup."

Surprise lightened Jake's psychic scent, and he said softly,
"Sweet, sweet freedom. You are a goddess, Lilith."

Ethan frowned, his brows drawing together as he looked at
the novice. A Guardian's heightened senses left him vulnerable to sensory overload in the first years of his active service.
Cloistering the novices at SI had helped with some of the
young Guardians' adjustments, but the Enthrallment still hit
them, especially when they left the warehouse.

"You still Enthralled? You won't be much good to me outside if you're spinning."

Jake shrugged. "I've gone out several times without being
overwhelmed."

"It doesn't matter," Lilith said. "Once he's there, he's going to stay in one place. I just want him to act as your base of
operations and SI's contact, if it all goes to shit. Particularly
as they know you're there now."

Ethan nodded. "I'm agreeable to the help, but the apartment I've got isn't equipped for that. Does SI have a location?"

Lilith leaned forward and punched in a number on her phone.
"No, but Ramsdell Pharmaceuticals picked up a property when
Colin and Savi visited the vampire community a few months
back. Knowing Savi, everything Jake could possibly use—and a
couple of things he'd never think to use—should be ready to
go." A smile widened her lips when the vampire answered. "Ah,
Colin, you gorgeous freak. You aren't in your daysleep."

"Not today, my dear Agent Milton, but I've little doubt
I'll soon wish I was. What do you want?"

"Your house in Seattle."

"Dare I ask why?"

"Drifter needs it."

Ethan stepped nearer the desk, uncertain how well the speaker would pick up his voice. "I'm going in after Legion."

"McCabe," Colin said. "Lilith told you about Milliken?"

"Yes. How is the doctor?"

"Once she's stable, I'll find her a position at Ramsdell. Savi thinks she'll recuperate faster if she's busy." Colin paused. "Don't bring me any more turned against their will. Savi's not resting easy."

No, Ethan imagined she wasn't. Seeing a man cut down might have given anyone nightmares, and he supposed that was one of the benefits of not having to sleep. "I don't aim to."

There was a long sigh, and a sound that Ethan thought might have been a swipe of fingers through hair. "Very well, McCabe. But I'll not be pleased if you bring in a bloody herd of cows and let them chew on the furnishings."

Lilith raised her gaze to Ethan's. "Come now, Colin," she murmured. "Drifter's taste in women isn't *that* bad."

"I daresay his taste is nonexistent. Don't use your Gift, McCabe. I'm sending the access codes to Lilith. Savi prepared a few surprises for unauthorized entrants, and the system looks for discrepancies."

"He warned you, so he must like you," Lilith mused a moment after the vampire had disconnected. "Did you call him beautiful?"

A wry smile pulled at Ethan's mouth. "I believe I said something of that nature when I met him." Encountering the vampire for the first time had been a bit like being Enthralled; struck by the impossible perfection of Colin's features, Ethan hadn't managed his tongue well.

The effect had eventually faded, and it was easy to find it amusing now—at the time, his involuntary response had infuriated him.

"That's nothing." Jake stood up, retrieved his CD from the player. "I tried to kiss him."

Lilith pursed her lips, her eyes alight with interest. "I don't suppose you'd reenact it with Drifter?"

They left her office on her sigh of disappointment, but Ethan's good humor fled when he felt the hesitation in Jake's psychic scent, then the younger Guardian's quick blocks.

Ethan stopped in the middle of the hallway, turned. "Spit it out."

Jake's jaw clenched briefly and regret darkened his face. "I found the data you requested."

Ethan's gaze fell to the paper that appeared in his hand. He swallowed past the sudden chokehold on his throat and read the header as he unfolded it. "Arizona State Library?"

"In their microfiche. There wasn't much. Just this short mention, from a Wilmont newsletter dated August 1886."

The month after he and Caleb had ridden into Eden. Ethan frowned, shook his head. "Wilmont? That's east of Tucson. I told him to head west."

"That's why it took me so long to find it. I was looking in the wrong direction."

Jake was correct; there wasn't much. Just a single line: *Caleb McCabe, murder and thievery. Hanged.*

Ethan vanished the paper before it crumpled in his fist. The goddamned fool. He should have gone west.

CHAPTER 4

"So, you remind me about lunch, but it's *you* who forgets—Jesus, Charlie!" Jane abandoned her superior tone when she finally opened the door wide enough to see her. "Get in here. Did you put ice on it down at the gym? Did you forget to duck or forget to weave?"

"Neither." Charlie self-consciously lifted her hand to her face. A dark bruise flared from cheekbone to jaw. "I ran into a wall."

Jane rolled her eyes, grabbed Charlie's hand, and pulled her down the hall toward the kitchen. Charlie dragged her feet on the hardwood floors, smiling for the first time since she'd woken—late—and found the feather gone. She'd looked for almost forty-five minutes before giving up, missing her regular workout routine—though her frantic search through her blankets and throughout the apartment had left her almost as sweaty, and halfway to tears.

She hadn't predicted Jane would assume the bruise came from kickboxing, but it saved Charlie from making up a story she'd believe.

With the feather missing, Charlie wasn't quite certain *she* believed the story anymore.

"Ice isn't going to work," she said when Jane pushed her onto a chair at the dining room table and headed for the freezer. "This is from yesterday." •

"Oh." Jane tossed a handful of ice into the sink and wiped her hands on her jeans. "Then why were you late? And I called you about five times this morning."

"Really? I didn't—" Charlie pulled out her cell and frowned down at the display. Five voice messages. She'd checked before leaving her place. There hadn't been any calls then, and she hadn't felt it vibrate on the bus ride from Capitol Hill to Queen Anne, or on the short hike up Jane's street. "Okay, weird. The radio station was out, too, because my alarm didn't work. I woke up to static around eleven thirty." She glanced back up at Jane. "Did you cut your hair? Without me?"

Jane's hair had been on the verge of shaggy last weekend. Rich chestnut highlights streaked through the brown strands now, and they perfectly framed her small, pointed chin and large green eyes.

"Yes." A light blush stained Jane's cheeks. "Sorry. I'd planned to wait for our usual salon day, but Dylan purchased a couple of hours at a spa and arranged the time off from work as a gift—"

"No, it's okay. I didn't mean—" Charlie shook her head, immediately feeling like a bitch. "I was just surprised."

"You like it?"

"You look like an elf. But it's cute."

"Cute? I was hoping for ravishing."

Charlie dragged her fingers through the thick, messy tumble of her hair. "That's me. You can have cute."

"Thanks a lot. Your roots are starting to show."

"I'm trying to convince everyone that I have hidden depths."

"You'll have to grow it out at least another inch to even *begin* to persuade anyone."

There was only one response to that: a *fuck you* combined with the flip of her middle finger, and then wondering how a minute in Jane's presence turned them into giggling thirteen- and fifteen-year-old girls.

Those had been the best years. Before their parents' divorce—before they'd been separated by a continent and too wrapped up in their own obsessions to find each other again. Before their father had brought them together again to announce that he was dying; before Charlie had destroyed her own life, and brought another year of separation on them.

And if not for Jane slapping her awake when she most needed it, Charlie knew they'd be separated now.

Jane pulled two diet sodas from the fridge, set one in front of Charlie. "We're in trouble today."

With her drink halfway to her lips, Charlie stopped and stared up at her sister. "What does that mean?"

"Dylan's gone. He had a meeting."

"Oh, no. Did he leave something for us to eat? Or are we going out? And maybe a movie?" Charlie asked hopefully.

Jane grimaced. "He left instructions. And shopped for ingredients while I was sleeping this morning. If we didn't at least make the attempt . . ." She trailed off, and her expression seemed caught between pleading and stricken.

"You'd feel bad." Charlie would, too, but not as bad as—

"Food poisoning would be worse. We can make sandwiches. Something we don't have to cook."

Jane pointed to the grid of yellow stickies on the refrigerator. "I thought of that. But one of those was supposed to remind me to buy bread."

"Oh, God," Charlie groaned. "Okay, you're smart, and I can mix drinks. I suppose we can try."

After a fortifying chug of her soda, she joined her sister in the kitchen—and then stared in disbelief at one of the drawers Jane pulled open. Each spatula and serving spoon was perfectly aligned. A glance in the icebox revealed the same: everything neatly stacked and labeled.

With such organization, they might actually be able to cook whatever he'd planned for them.

"You know, Jane," Charlie said. "I've thought for a while that you spliced and diced DNA to create Dylan, because he's too good to be true. Now I'm convinced of it."

"You should see his closet." Jane threw a wry glance over her shoulder, then stood on her toes to retrieve a pan from the rack above the island.

A roasting pan. Charlie frowned, some of her apprehension returning. "What are we making, anyway?"

"I can't pronounce it." A wave of her hand directed Charlie to the recipe lying on the counter. "Something with duck, I think."

"Canard rôti au thym et miel, sauce airelles et pommes de terre rôties," Charlie read aloud, and managed not to wince as her voice butchered the fricatives. "Roasted duck with thyme and honey, a cranberry sauce and roasted potatoes? Is he crazy? I was thinking macaroni and cheese or spaghetti. I can do those."

"I don't think Dylan's ever had mac and cheese."

She scanned the directions. "This is going to take a couple of hours. I won't be home until—" Almost dark. Closing her eyes, she fought the wave of panic that rolled through her.

"Oh. Are you going to be late for work?" Jane sounded almost hopeful—glad of the excuse.

Charlie shook her head, determined. She *could* be out in the night; no one was watching her, no one was waiting. At least not here. "No. My shift doesn't start until eight."

"Maybe we can turn the oven up to a higher temperature. I'm too hungry to wait that long." Jane slapped a paper-wrapped duck on the island. "How's work, anyway? Old Matthew?"

"Both good. Except for the assholes that make a mess with the peanuts. And Legion?"

As they did each time she spoke of her research, Jane's eyes lit up, and her smile creased two dimples in her cheeks. "Good. Actually, fantastic. I've never seen anything like the blood samples we've been getting, Charlie, and the implications for medicine are astounding—spontaneous cell regeneration and repair. And not just trauma usage, which is intuitive, but reversing any degenerative disease. But though we've successfully replicated the blood composition, we can't force it to *behave* in the same way as the original." Jane continued, peppering the rest with jargon; the duck lay naked in the pan and they had unloaded most of the contents of the fridge when Jane halted mid-sentence and glanced at Charlie. "Okay, I got a little carried away."

"You lost me at 'platelet storage lesion.'" Grinning, Charlie waved away the apology. "You're talking about changing-the-world stuff. You have a reason to be carried away."

"I could save it for Dylan, because he has to love every-thing I say. Or for everyone at Legion—but most of them have been so tense lately they're just as likely to snap my head off. At least you don't mind when I . . . Do we really need all of this butter? Our arteries are going to clog overnight." Jane arched a brow. "And I said 'clog' just for you."

"Bitch. I'd look that up, but I don't know if it starts with a C or a K." She waited until Jane stopped laughing before she added, "I don't see why we can't use half the amount."

"You decide how much. I trust your math skills more than mine. The very thought of your accounting course makes me break out in hives."

"I like it." Which had surprised Charlie two years previous, when she'd begun taking the online classes offered by the University of Washington, mostly to fill the afternoon hours. And, she had to admit, so that Jane wouldn't think she was as directionless as she'd felt. She'd been a late registrant, and a business class had been the only one open—but she'd taken to it. Not easily, but she enjoyed the challenge. "That laptop you gave me is making a big difference, too. I think I might have killed myself if I went through another term with the dial-up on my old piece of crap."

"Well, don't get too attached to it. In six months I'll re-place my new one, and if I don't give it to you, I'll just throw it away."

Charlie shook her head; the computer Jane had just bought was worth about five months' rent. "That's stupid."

"I know." Jane shrugged. "But Legion's confidentiality clause says it has to stay within my household. So I just con-sider you part of my household."

"Aw," Charlie said, though if her hands hadn't been cov-ered in butter, she might have given in to the emotion that swelled up in her and hugged Jane embarrassingly tight. "I don't really need it, though, and I'd have to redo my settings."

"Oh, the horror," Jane said, rolling her eyes.

"Fuck you. It took me forever just to set up online banking this week. I don't want to go through that again." She paused, took a long breath; it always made Jane uncomfortable when she brought this up. "And if you send me your account info, I can transfer my payment to you each month instead of writing the check out."

Two bright spots of color appeared high on Jane's cheeks. A half-inch-thick potato peel unwound beneath her knife. "You don't have to do that, you know."

Charlie waited until Jane looked up, and steadily held her gaze. "Yes, I do."

❧

Charlie's resolve to walk the four blocks to Cole's—boldly and unafraid—faded with the setting sun.

At seven thirty, she swallowed her pride. She might be crazy worrying about vampires, she decided, but she wasn't an idiot: the twisted gate at Cole's wasn't a figment of her imagination. And there was no sense in going alone when she could just ask Ethan to take her.

It didn't occur to her until she was on the balcony, calling Ethan's name over the wall, that a normal person would have knocked on his front door—and that if he wasn't outside, he couldn't hear her voice. But he either had very good timing or hearing, because a moment later his door slid open.

She pressed her hands against the wall and rose up on her tiptoes as if the extra three inches might let her see over, and only succeeded in looking at a spot on the next piece of vinyl siding. "Ethan?"

"Charlie."

That voice, so warm and smooth, and with a hint of amusement. Her fingers curled, her nails rasping faux wood grain. "Remember I told you last night I had an incident?"

The amusement vanished. "Yes."

"I'm still a little jumpy." She drew in a deep breath. "Okay, I'm freaking out. So I wanted to ask a favor."

"You want your cigarettes back?"

"No." Yes. Yes yes *yes*. Her eyes squeezed shut. "Though I guess we won't be Pyramus and Thisbe anymore. I was hoping you'd drive me to work."

"I would, Charlie, but my automobile is in storage."

Startled, she blinked her eyes open. "Really? I thought I was the only one who didn't drive much." And she'd never heard "automobile" drawn out so long, like a word that sat foreign on his tongue. Had he exaggerated it, knowing that his drawl made her laugh and hoping to ease her anxiety a bit?

It worked. She sank back down to her heels, waited for his reply.

"I've got no need for one here. But I'll be happy to walk with you."

The anxiety returned full-force, but underscored by giddy excitement instead of fear. "Okay. All right. I have to be there at eight, and I'm almost ready. Go and get dressed, Ethan, and I'll be at your door in five minutes."

"Get dressed—?" His chuckle roughened the night air. "Am I to wear something special?"

Her skin heated, but she wasn't going to admit that she'd been babbling like a schoolgirl with a crush. "No, I just assume when people are alone in their apartments, they walk around naked. I know I do."

He was silent for a long second. "Well now, Miss Charlie, I wish you'd told me that two months ago. I might have come on over for a cup of sugar."

She grinned, but only said, "Five minutes," as she backed into her apartment, her pulse racing. A check in the mirror. Jesus, the bruise made her look like a hooker who'd been slapped by her pimp. But slathering foundation on it would just make it worse, not to mention hurt like hell, so she left it alone. Her brows and lashes were naturally dark, but she touched up both. Her hair was good . . . great, actually, even with brown at the roots. She'd leave her hat off as long as possible.

Her coat still smelled like burnt duck, but only when she sniffed it up close. Ethan wouldn't be *that* near her.

And she didn't usually wear jewelry, but she selected a two-inch cross dangling at the end of a long black cord. It had been a part of a Halloween costume, and was supposed to hang between her breasts—but she wound it around her neck like a choker.

A lot of women wore similar necklaces; Ethan probably wouldn't think anything of it.

The knock made her heart stop, and she forced herself to walk slowly to the door. He hadn't waited, but maybe his apartment was a mess, just like most guys', and—

Tall.

Charlie was used to being level with a man's face, if not his eyes. She had a large frame, though she'd pared down and hardened her soft singing weight at the gym, and she was above average height.

But Ethan was *tall*. And not at all as she'd imagined, when she had let her mind wander that way. She'd seen urban cowboy, blond, with a big hat and a bigger buckle, Wrangler jeans and pointy-toed boots.

She hadn't pictured short, melting-chocolate-brown hair—thick and uncovered—that just brushed his forehead. Eyes the color of fine whiskey, caught between amber and caramel. Shoulders broad enough to carry a woman easily, hips lean enough to wrap her legs around.

He wore boots, but with a rounded toe and sturdy like a construction worker's. The rough weave of his brown trousers caught at her memory, but Charlie couldn't focus below his waist long enough to pin it down, not when his face had those roughly hewn planes and angles, like he'd been carved from oak, and his jaw looked strong and absolutely lickable.

"Hello, Miss Charlie," he said with the voice that matched his eyes. A scar cut through the left side of his thin upper lip, and crooked his smile just a little.

"Hi," she said, and for the first time was glad that the rasp in her throat hid her croak.

His gaze fell to her cheek. His jaw clenched, and oak hardened to stone before he met her eyes again. "You all right?"

"Yes." Beneath his tan corduroy jacket, she saw the edge of brown leather suspenders.

She should have been bold. Should have been unafraid.

She was in so much trouble.

❧

Charlie couldn't think of a single thing to say. It wasn't like her; there was always *something* to talk about. But she walked the first two blocks in silence, Ethan a huge presence next to her. The problem with a man that tall was any glance up at his face was obvious; she couldn't steal a look.

She stared into the familiar storefronts that lined Broadway instead, watched the passing cars, fiddled her hands in her pockets and cast her gaze everywhere but at the one thing she wanted to study.

Narrow shadows lurked between the buildings, tiny slices of darkness that the bright streetlights couldn't penetrate, and she felt her apprehension returning. Even someone of Ethan's size might not protect her from what she'd seen the previous night.

Her guardian angel had been big, too, but she thought Ethan must be bigger . . . though it was difficult to tell. Her protector had held her above the ground, but it could have been one inch or ten.

And she'd probably be similarly speechless if her guardian angel showed up, though out of awe rather than attraction. What would she say to such a being? *Thanks, nice shot*?

Would she even want him to show up? She'd almost convinced herself that it had been her paranoia and imagination; his appearance would just be a confirmation that he *had* been real . . . and so were vampires.

Nervously, she glanced away from the shadows, and squinted against the headlights of an oncoming car. Their glare recalled her to another kind of fear: the gut-wrenching instant of certainty that her voice would fail her when the curtain rose and the shine of the spotlight in her eyes rendered the audience dark and faceless. But that was a fear that never penetrated; her confidence in her ability was too strong to let it take root, the knowledge that the music was hers. And the terror always fell away with the first note, until the world narrowed down to the composition and the lyrics.

But she had no confidence in this, no knowledge. No certainty that what she'd seen was real, let alone something she could master. And it settled deep in her, until the night hid a creature with fangs, and even the long slide of Ethan's shadow on the sidewalk concealed a horror that was waiting to grab her and—

"You suddenly take up religion?"

The question seemed to jump out of that darkness, unexpected and low, and Charlie barely stifled her scream. Her heart pounded. She stopped walking and looked up at Ethan, found him watching her with his brows drawn.

"Religion?" she echoed.

He raised his hand to his throat, and she automatically mirrored the action. Her palm met cool metal, and she gripped the cross tight, the edges digging into her fingers.

Her fear drained away. She'd protected herself; she wasn't completely helpless. "I'm not taking up anything," she said with a lift of her shoulder and a brief smile. "It's to scare away the vampires."

The scar paled when his mouth thinned, but the taut line quickly melted away with humor. "I don't reckon a bit of jewelry would frighten them, Charlie."

It was ridiculous how easily his voice heated her from the inside, and she was suddenly all too aware of the kiss of crisp air over her belly and breasts. She tucked a strand of hair behind her ear, and surreptitiously checked out his reflection in the darkened window of the antique store behind him.

Very, very nice.

"Garlic, then?" This time, she could look at him without worrying her interest would be—pathetically—obvious. People looked at each other when they talked. Of course, she usually didn't have to tilt her head quite as far to see someone, but the line of his jaw and the crease that formed at the corner of his mouth when he smiled made the effort worth it. "Silver? A wooden stake?"

"Now, Miss Charlie, you ought to know that the best way to slay a vampire is by removing his head or slicing his heart in two," he said. "It's mighty difficult to do either with a stake. Messy, too."

"Killed a lot of them, have you?" She stole another glance at the window. Lord, but she'd have liked a bite of that. Though his trousers sat low on his waist and didn't have any distinctive tailoring, the strength of his body defined his shape better than the finest clothes could have.

And she obviously hadn't been with anyone in far too long, if a man's ass could get her this excited.

Maybe it was the suspenders. They'd thrown her off-kilter.

"I've slain some," he said, and slipped out of his jacket with a roll of his shoulders. The collar of his burgundy shirt curled at the edges, soft and worn, and the top button was unfastened. Everything about him spoke of ease and comfort—even the way he'd tucked his hand into his pants pocket and slung his jacket over his wrist made the corduroy drape over his hip like a long lazy cat.

It wasn't a pose that screamed vampire slayer, but nevertheless, the sheer confidence he exuded was reassuring.

"Most of the legends are wrong, Miss Charlie."

She met his gaze again, but couldn't read his expression. "Which legends?"

"They have reflections, for one," Ethan said with a long, uneven smile. "As sure as I do."

Her embarrassed laugh was slammed by fear, smashed into the shape of words. "Some of them don't," she said, and gave in to the sudden urge to glance over her shoulder, to make sure nothing was sneaking up behind her, invisible in the window's reflection, and Ethan unaware he was supposed to be looking out for creatures like that.

"You sound awful certain," he said slowly.

The street was empty.

Of course it was. What had she come to, that she was scaring herself, imagining real vampires who weren't there?

There or not, paranoid or not—she didn't want to wait around until one showed up.

"I'm going to be late," she said, and walked out from under his sharpening stare.

He caught up with her an instant later, matched the rhythm of her steps. For a few seconds, there was only the beat of their feet in sync, the thudding of her heart in her ears. He must have been shortening his stride, but she wouldn't have known it to look at him; it was as long and easy as his drawl.

Finally, he said, "So I reckon there's a story behind that certainty? I'd sure like to hear it, Miss Charlie."

And that was perhaps the most direct request she'd ever heard Ethan make. She tucked her chin down, pushed her hands into her pockets. It would only sound ridiculous. Stupid.

Which made it safe to tell.

She kicked a piece of gravel on the sidewalk, watched it rattle away before she said, "Well, about two months ago, I was working at the bar when a hush falls over the people in the restaurant." It hadn't been silent; Cole's was never silent, but she had heard the quiet even over the music. "So I look up, and there's a guy walking into the lounge. And he's so incredible to look at that it's like I've been kicked in the chest. Or just narrowly missed being hit by a car."

Ethan made a choking sound. His mouth was tight, but she thought he was holding back laughter. That was good—just Charlie, making up another story.

The muscles knotted low in her back relaxed, and she fell into her tall-tale mode, the effortless rhythm of it. "It takes me a few seconds to realize that he's got a chick with him. And even if I hadn't seen their rings, it would have been obvious that they're *together* together—but they don't get a table."

"You looked for his ring?" Ethan paused at the edge of the curb, the traffic light washing the scar on his lip with pale green.

Charlie would have expected a crooked nose to go along with that scar, but the lines of his face were strong and firm. And, like the rest of him, straight and long—not thin or wide, but just medium. Despite his height, there was nothing lanky about him, no awkward angles. He was in perfect proportion, even if all of the portions were oversized.

"Well, yeah." Was *all* of him oversized? She closed her eyes so she wouldn't cast a measuring glance that way as she hit the crosswalk button. Then pressed it a few more times, though she knew it wouldn't make it go any faster. "A guy looks like that, you check for one."

"And if he doesn't have one?"

"You look hard, then run away as fast as possible." Even though Charlie was certain Ethan wasn't attached, she'd double-checked for his. And she hadn't run, but she'd known for a long time she wasn't the highest note in the register.

She stuffed her hands back into her pockets when the cross-walk signal finally changed. "Anyway, most couples come into the lounge, they get a table of their own—but these two belly up to the bar and start talking to me. And he's got this lovely British accent." She shook her head, still disbelieving her reaction. "It actually takes me a couple of minutes to say anything that doesn't sound idiotic, because he's so . . . so . . ."

"Almighty beautiful that your sense tucks its tail between its legs, but it's your tongue that runs away," Ethan drawled, his smile the widest she'd yet seen, and she grinned in response.

"Yes. He's too pretty *not* to look at. But I'm trying not to stare, because I'm sure his wife gets enough of that. Luckily, that kicked-in-the-chest feeling went away after a few minutes, and she doesn't seem to be offended. If anything, she seems to be laughing at him for it. It's difficult to be certain, though, because every time she smiles or laughs she does this." Charlie lifted her hand to cover her mouth.

"Like a vampire hiding her fangs," Ethan said.

There wasn't much teasing in his voice now, but Charlie tried to drum up a smile—this was supposed to be a joke. "Yeah. At the time I was thinking she might be shy, but she hadn't seemed the shy type. So I thought maybe she used to have braces or funky teeth and hadn't broken the habit of covering them."

She fingered the cross again. It had taken her a long time to get over the instinctive need to hide her scar when someone's gaze rested too long on her neck. Now she was more likely to call attention to it, make them aware of what they were doing.

Except with Ethan she hadn't—and she thought now that she'd deliberately covered the scar with the necklace. Hiding it—or just not wanting to know if he was the type to stare?

She glanced up at him, realized he was waiting for her to continue, and picked up where she'd left off. "And before I know it, I've told them about my parents' divorce, my dad's leukemia, my mom's latest marriage to the composer in Paris, and about Jane and Dylan." Her voice wouldn't convey her bemusement, so she added, "It usually doesn't go that way. Typically, it's all about the customer, but I had no control over that conversation. He did. But they were fun to talk to, so I didn't even think about how weird that was until afterward. After the other thing."

They were at Cole's now. Iron bars striped the front of the glass doors and the restaurant's large, street-side windows. Melody led a group of four past the hostess podium, a clutch of menus in her hand, her hips swaying in time with Janis Joplin's earthy voice.

Charlie checked her watch. "You want to come in? Protecting me from the bloodthirsty undead deserves at least a drink, and I've still got about ten minutes."

Ethan studied her for a long moment, his face impassive. Faint lines radiated from the corners of his eyes. It was difficult to determine if they were wrinkles or tan lines. If it was from the sun, it had been kind; he wasn't at all weathered.

How old was he? Mid-thirties?

His nostrils flared slightly and he looked away from her. "I'd best not, Charlie."

"All right." She concealed her disappointment with a smile, shifted awkwardly on her feet. What should she do now? Shake his hand? A thank-you kiss to his cheek? She probably couldn't get up that high.

And what the hell did *I'd best not* mean?

Dammit. *She'd* best not make herself go crazy wondering, or make an embarrassment of herself by asking him. "Another time, then. Thanks, Ethan."

Her hand was on the long iron bar that served as a door handle when his voice stopped her. "You'll finish your story when I walk you home?"

She averted her face to hide her relieved smile. "I can do it now. There's not much more." Tucking her coat a little closer around her body, she stepped up onto the bench seat and sat on the top. She wasn't on level with Ethan, but at least she didn't have to crane her neck up so much this way, and she didn't think he'd sit.

"So I was talking to them, and wiping the area next to them to look like I was busy. The bar is dark wood, sealed with a varnish, and I always keep it clean. Shining. Anything sitting on it reflects—not perfectly, just a gleam. And that's when I notice that even though his hand is on the bar, there's no reflection. Her hand and sleeve do, her glass does, his glass does . . . but not him or his clothes."

Ethan didn't respond, just studied her face with that steady, quiet expression. Charlie dropped her gaze to her hands, then to the side. The ashtray at the end of the bench had a single butt crushed into the sand. Whoever it was had probably sat alone in the cold, sucking down the cigarette as quickly as possible before returning to his party.

She touched her fingers to her lips and forced herself to meet Ethan's eyes again.

"So I'm thinking that it's strange, but it's not frightening— until I have to turn around to use the cash register. There's a mirror on the wall back there, mostly hidden behind the shelves of bottles. And I can see *her*, I can hear them talking, so I know he hasn't gone to the restroom or anything . . . and then his glass lifts into the air."

Even now, the thought of that floating glass made her heart skip and race.

As if Ethan heard it, his gaze fell to her chest. "Were you frightened then?"

She shook her head. "I was trying to convince myself that

I hadn't seen it. And it's not like they were drinking blood. He had an orange juice, for God's sake—she was teasing him about it. It was only after, when I couldn't stop thinking about that glass, that I realized what he was. What *they* were. But even then . . ."

She pulled off her cap, stuck her hand into her hair to fluff it, and smiled weakly. She had completely lost the pretense that this was just a story. Was Ethan now thinking she was mentally unhinged? He was watching her too closely, his eyes too assessing.

Why was it that nothing about him was direct but the way he looked at her?

"Then he gave me a hundred-dollar tip, and they left," she finished in a rush, then glanced at the time and hopped down from the bench.

Ethan blinked. His grin was slow as he opened the door for her. Music and the heavy odor of steaks and fries rolled out. "Well, now, Miss Charlie—that may be the strangest part of your tale."

A tale. Relieved that he'd taken it in the way she'd intended, she returned his smile. "Why strange?"

"In my experience, vampires that comely are as tightfisted as they are vain."

That was an odd bit of humor, yet strangely accurate. "Oh. Well, he technically gave it to me—but only after she said something to him. Otherwise I'm pretty sure he wouldn't have thought to leave anything at all. Probably wouldn't have even paid for their drinks."

That had him rolling into laughter, and Charlie's brow creased as she watched him. There was obviously a joke here that she didn't understand, but she liked the sound of his amusement too much to let it bother her. His laugh was deep, his head hanging low as he bent into it. On impulse, she rose up on her toes, pressed her lips to the firm corner of his mouth.

Then swept through the entrance with a mumbled thanks, unsure if she should be flattered or mortified that such an insignificant kiss had shocked him silent.

CHAPTER 5

If Charlie had turned around, she'd likely have settled whatever internal argument that had set her psychic scent spinning with uncertainty. Ethan held the door wide and watched her walk across the dark-tiled floor, wishing his Guardian sight could burn through the coat concealing her curves.

The most unexpected blows always came from the front—Ethan had learned that long before he'd become a Guardian. Though a man couldn't see the hit coming from behind or from the side, he knew it might. Not *when*, but expecting that eventually it would, and so he was always bracing himself against the surprise.

But even a light blow could knock a man off his feet when he'd been watching for it, because he figured he was prepared.

Apparently, Ethan had figured wrong with Charlie.

Her picture and the few glimpses he'd had told him he liked the look of her. Plenty of conversations over a wall had revealed her easy and entertaining way with a story that could draw him in or set him laughing. He'd gotten real familiar with her voice—the low rasp that often had him wondering about the sounds she'd make if he was in her deep.

But those things hadn't warned him about the way she could size a man up with a glance from beneath her lashes, making him hope that whatever she saw pleased her. Hadn't warned him about the way her hair fell in a soft wave against her jaw when she ducked her chin to smile—or that when she pushed it back, exposing the vulnerable skin at the side of her neck, he'd want to unwind the necklace she'd used as protection, place his mouth on that spot, and tell her that he'd provide it for her.

And he hadn't known she could guard her expression as well as the wall had. Had Ethan been human, he'd never have wanted to face her across a poker table—a tell was easier to spot when it was a twitch in a blank mask. But hers wasn't a studied or artificial expression; the emotions she chose to show were genuine enough—they simply weren't all of what she felt, forcing him to read her psyche instead of her features.

When he had, her interest had slipped like warm velvet across his mind. He'd sensed it before, but it had been nebulous—light curiosity about the man who lived next to her—and easy enough to ignore. Now it was strong, and reaching out with his mind as he was, her interest felt like a touch as real as the kiss that had Ethan's fingers clenching on iron and his eyes staring after her.

Charlie didn't glance back, though he watched until the black-haired hostess returned to her podium and narrowed her eyes at him, as if wondering why a man would remain outside looking starved instead of coming in and eating his fill.

Ethan let the door fall closed, leaving him frowning at his reflection through the bars. Abruptly he turned away from it, vanished the jacket in his hand, and walked around the back of Cole's to examine the twisted gate.

The lock was intact, but even a vampire could have broken it with a hard twist of the knob, or pulled the gate's metal frame from its seat of brick.

They'd intended to scare her first, then. It didn't surprise Ethan that a demon would recruit vampires with a streak of mean. And like a horse or a dog with a rabid temperament and an eagerness to hurt, there was but one option: put them down.

Ethan had destroyed a few animals when he was human, and he reckoned he felt worse for them; they didn't know any better. Anything that had once been human did.

And Charlie had been well and frightened. Her fear had dogged her several times during their walk. Each time, she'd managed to push it away—leaving Ethan torn between his relief that she wasn't relying on him, the sting to his pride that she thought he couldn't defend her, and his unexpected need to reassure her that he would.

But a conflicted man was a distracted one, and he wouldn't be doing right by her if he allowed his ego to get in the way of protecting her.

As it was, Ethan hadn't sensed the vampire nearby until they'd been standing outside Cole's. Ethan didn't figure this particular vampire was any danger to Charlie . . . but chasing him down might be exactly what Ethan needed to cool the heat she'd created in him.

Ethan walked quickly down the deserted alley, picking up speed. His duster appeared on a thought, and his forward motion created its own wind, the coattails flapping behind him. He'd have to cross two blocks to reach the vampire, and he was moving faster than a human could; he ought to get up top.

And although Ethan was certain no one watched, it was best not to perform impossible feats. It was easy enough to change his direction, take a leap at the alley wall and push off with his foot, using the momentum he'd gained to launch himself to the roof of the opposite building. Every human who'd ever watched a martial arts movie had seen a man run up a wall and flip away from it; Ethan had taken that to an extraordinary level, but not outside the realm of human belief.

Wings would have been.

Crossing the street took only another leap. No one was likely looking up—and in the dark, they would mistake whatever they'd seen. The next block down, Manny's red boat of an automobile idled off a side street, its wheel rims shiny as spit. A human was in it with him.

Ethan propped his foot on an air-conditioning unit, rested his elbow on his knee, and settled down to watch and listen.

Luckily for Manny, the person in the car with him didn't sound all that young. The first and last time Ethan had found the vampire passing something off to a boy not much past puberty, Ethan had rolled him over hard. Guardians had to respect human free will, even when the decisions humans made were foolish. If they wanted to rot their brains with the shit

Manny sold, that was their choice. But Ethan figured kids didn't know any better—and if he couldn't stop the humans from selling to them, at least he could stop Manny.

Hell, there were plenty of reasons to beat the vampire, but not enough reasons to slay him. And, at any rate, it was Ethan's own damn fault Manny was alive. He'd been the one to transform the vampire twelve years before, when he'd heard the screams coming from an alley in Tacoma. Only the nosferatu's focus on Manny and its bloodlust had allowed Ethan the easy kill; but the nosferatu had already fed well, and Ethan had had to use the nosferatu's blood to transform Manny into a vampire.

A Guardian wasn't meant to judge, but there were times Ethan reckoned he'd have done just as well to let Manny bleed to death in that alley.

But those times inevitably led to wondering whether Michael had thought the same of him, transforming him to Guardian in an oven of a jail cell. And so it was best not to wonder at all, and just get the job done.

And if the vampires who'd come after Charlie belonged to the Seattle community, Manny might prove a useful source of information. Until a few months ago, he'd remained on the periphery of the vampire community. Aside from his two female partners, Manny had only associated with Vladimir and Katya, the heads of the Seattle community, acting as their enforcer.

A community's leaders meted out punishments and executions to vampires who threatened the secrecy of their kind or who fed from humans, but not every leader liked to get blood on his hands. As one of the rare nosferatu-born, Manny was the strongest vampire in the city, and he'd taken on those duties in return for modest payments.

But when Vladimir and Katya had been killed three months before, Manny had taken their position—likely by virtue of his strength, as Ethan doubted Manny had been the one to murder them . . . and whoever had wasn't stepping up to claim their place.

Manny hadn't been all that successful winning over the community, but perhaps he intended to change that. Money would give him a more solid foothold than strength alone. Maybe that was why he was selling out here. Ethan hadn't seen him in this part of the city before, but Manny might be thinking to expand his territory.

The transaction didn't take long, and the human finally slid out onto the sidewalk. Nineteen to twenty-two years old, buzzed blond hair, undershirt, and oversized pants with the crotch hanging down near his ankles. Ethan shook his head; the only difference between this kid and fifty others Ethan had seen come out of Manny's car was the brand names on their skivvies, and whether they cinched their belt around their ass or below it.

The kid looked up and down the deserted street before strolling off, and Manny climbed out of his car. The silver medallions banding his black hat winked as brightly as his wheels. The brim cast a shadow down to his hooked nose and over a mustache that hung like a skinny dead ferret down the sides of his mouth.

Ethan waited until the kid disappeared around the corner before clearing his throat.

The tail end of the ferret twitched back to life. Manny's eyes widened briefly and met Ethan's before the vampire dropped into his seat. The white reverse lights flared as Manny shoved the gear out of park.

Ethan leapt from the roof and slammed to the ground in a crouch, getting an up-close view of the Cadillac's rear license plate. He reached just beneath and behind the bumper; once he got a good grip on the frame, he braced his elbow against his knee and lifted.

The vampire was stubborn—Ethan had to give him that. Manny sat for a good thirty seconds with his rear tires spinning wildly, the rubber grabbing for purchase an inch above the road. Finally, he eased up on the accelerator and fired a barrage of curses over his shoulder.

Not trusting that admission of defeat, Ethan called for him to shut it down, then waited another minute until the engine cut off.

The air reeked of fuel. Ethan rounded the automobile; Manny grinned at him through the window and pushed down the little plastic lock.

Ethan braced his hands on top of the car, leaned down. "You planning on playing all night? Or do I haul you out?"

With barely a touch of his Gift, the lock popped up, straight as a toy soldier. Manny glanced uneasily at it, then slowly opened the door. His polished, pointed boot swung to the ground.

"Drifter. I didn't know it was you, man," he said as Ethan stepped back to give the vampire room to stand. Even at full height, Manny had to tip his head back so far the brim of his hat was near vertical. "All I seen was some huge white dude jumping off a roof, and I didn't want to be hanging around here when the cops come to scrape up the mess."

Chrome glittered over his front incisors, and matching wire wrapped the upper length of his fangs, making for a smile as pretty as the automobile's radiator grill.

Ethan angled his head, looked Manny up and down. There wasn't much money to be had as a two-bit dealer, pimp, and former enforcer, but considering the sparklies the vampire sported, Ethan wouldn't have guessed it just to look at him.

"You dealing out here now?"

"No, man." Manny plucked at the third button of his striped shirt, the cotton as crisp and stiff as his black jeans. "I was just sitting here, and he just walked by."

That fit what Ethan had caught from Manny and the kid; the transaction hadn't been planned, but a chance meeting.

"Are your girls working over here?" Ethan asked, though he doubted it. Capitol Hill wasn't Angie's and Cora's style. "Maybe drinking from their johns?"

Offended machismo poured from Manny's psychic scent. "I'm man enough for both of them." When Ethan refrained from commenting on that, Manny pulled at the button again. "Come on, Drifter. Why are you hassling me? I haven't done anything."

Ethan's gaze fell to Manny's fingers. "You're awful twitchy for someone who doesn't need to be hassled."

Manny's hand immediately dropped to his side, and he gave a short laugh before it, too, dropped away and left a hunted expression in its place. His voice had an edge of a whine to it. "I just came by to see if what I heard about a dead man walking was true."

Ethan frowned. "What dead man?"

"Just some dead white guy." A passing car's lights caught the flash of chrome teeth and gleamed off the silver ring on his middle finger. Manny was absently rubbing the band with his thumb, spinning it around. Another tell, but Ethan wouldn't call the vampire's attention to this one.

"You, me, we're all dead men walking," Manny added with a grin and a shrug.

Now, that was just nonsense. Was Manny thinking to distract him? The ring went round and round. Ethan's gaze narrowed, and he inhaled deep. "Put your hands on the hood."

"Aw, man—" Manny's lips pressed together, and he turned around.

Ethan quickly patted him down, pulled the small bag of sweet-smelling marijuana from the vampire's front pocket, and vanished it into his cache. Unfortunately for Manny, vampires couldn't carry or hide items the same way. Another sniff led Ethan to the giant trunk. He popped the lock and dug out what he figured was about five thousand dollars' worth of goods from beneath the spare tire.

"You Guardians are worse than the pig cops," Manny said with an expression more resigned than angry.

"And here I thought we were such good friends, Manny, considering that I saved your life and all." Ethan slammed the trunk closed. He confiscated Manny's stash each time they met up; this couldn't account for the vampire's jumpiness. "You hear of any vampires—one female, two males, black hair, a lot of black leather—talking about being in this area? Maybe hunting down a human girl?"

"You're describing half of the community, Drifter. Them white boys like to go around looking like dead freaks."

Not all of them, but too many to make those that had gone after Charlie remarkable. "Any word about demons, maybe vampires who are thinking of working for them?"

Manny shook his head. "The only thing everyone talks about is how nervous they are."

"Why is that?"

The vampire's eyes hardened into weasely little beads. "Well, we've been hearing about these other cities being wiped out. Then you Guardians come in with your Rules, and talk about these demons." His fingers started working the ring; the whine came in again. "It was better back when only I knew about you, Drifter—Vladimir and Katya never had to deal with everyone wanting to know what you Guardians are planning to do, what you are, what all of us are. And then comes that fancy vampire up from San Francisco, talking about changing the way things are done, telling us we should align ourselves with you Guardians—though you've never given *me* anything but shit."

Ethan didn't figure Manny had earned anything but shit. "Maybe you ought to talk to that fancy vampire."

"Vladimir and Katya did. No one got anywhere, except they got dead. So I don't think I'll be rushing into that, Drifter." Manny looked away from him. "Was that fancy boy the same one that girl was talking about?"

Ethan stiffened. "What girl?"

Manny grinned. "I thought I could hear you coming, so I went on over to take a look. Fine bit of ass there. You should get a piece of that."

Manny's grin slowly faded under Ethan's stare.

Ethan didn't disguise the menace in his voice. "You get back on your side of town right quick."

He didn't wait for Manny to slink away, but Manny was fast enough that Ethan had just turned from him when the squeal of tires split the night.

Halfway back to Cole's, Ethan caught the presence of another vampire. And another. They were mostly shielded— he couldn't get a strong fix on their location.

He'd have to wait for them to come for Charlie. Going out and hunting them would only leave her vulnerable to any he hadn't sensed.

And he'd gone off half-cocked once in his life, hunting down men who'd transgressed against those Ethan considered his. But although Ethan had handed some of them what they'd deserved, he wasn't certain it had been worth it in the end, and he'd lost more than his life.

Now he knew that Caleb had lost, too.

Hell and damnation, he could have done without reading that newsletter. Over a hundred and twenty years had passed since that hellish week in an Eden jail cell; he'd known his brother couldn't have been alive. His grief had settled down— but discovering Caleb hadn't made it out west was still tearing at his gut.

But Ethan would be damned if his brother's death meant his sacrifice was nothing, if it meant the demon had won.

Caleb had always claimed there were two things worth living for: good drink and a pretty woman. Ethan figured he could have one for his brother, and keep on protecting the other.

❧

"So they must have used a crowbar on that gate, huh?"

Charlie nodded without glancing up. She didn't need to see Vin to know he'd be leaning against the bar, the cork-bottomed drink tray balanced on his splayed hand. That stance had accompanied every question he'd tossed her way that evening.

"Yeah, must have," she agreed. And she didn't want to talk about it anymore. "What do you need?"

"G&T and a Riesling. Table ten—take a guess."

Charlie glanced over his shoulder. Table ten was in the restaurant, but she had a clear view through the lounge's entryway. Two men faced each other across the red vinyl booth. Both well fed and groomed. One sported silvering auburn hair, the other lighter with just a touch of red—a father and son, maybe. Surrounded by Cole's rock-and-roll memorabilia, with the Stones trolling about a little yellow pill, their conservative suits, spit-shiny shoes, and dark overcoats looked wildly out of place.

She guessed, "The gin and tonic for the uptight blond." And he apparently needed it. The younger sat with his feet placed firmly together, his back rigid.

Vin shook his head, his choppy blue bangs brushing his eyebrows, the diamond studs in his ears winking. "That's zero for three tonight, Char. Junior wanted the wine—and your number."

Charlie sighed and returned the Riesling bottle to the small refrigerator under the counter.

"I didn't think he was your type, but he said he knew you."

She frowned and studied the blond's profile. It was vaguely familiar, but—

He swiveled his head, met her eyes, and it clicked into place. She forced a bright smile and returned his wave. "Shit," she muttered between her teeth when his fingers waggled in a beckoning gesture.

"Old boyfriend?"

"One of Jane's." What was his name? Patrick? Paul?

Something with a "P." "About five years ago, I think. Will you tell him I'll come over in a second?"

Better to go to him than wait until he approached her. If he was chatty, she could use work as an excuse to get away.

"Will do." Vin placed the glasses on the tray, the tribal tattoo around his lower biceps peeking out from beneath the edge of his sleeve.

She watched him deliver the drinks, and delayed as long as possible by wiping down the counter. Five years. She didn't want to deal with this tonight, didn't want to lose the sweet buzz left over from her walk with Ethan by dredging up the past with a guy whose name she couldn't remember.

Peter? Or maybe the "P" had been in reference to something else . . . his job? A professor? Five years ago, he wouldn't have been old enough. A politician—?

She snapped her fingers in triumph. "Mark Brandt!" It was as close to a crow as she could produce.

Her lone customer at the bar—a precise elderly gentleman in a tweed coat—raised his graying eyebrows. He was probably wondering if she'd been taking a few drinks and talking to herself as a result.

Her smile aggravated her sore cheek, so she kept it brief and nodded to his glass. "Another?" A swallow of their best single malt remained in the bottom.

He shook his head. A quiet one. Charlie was used to it— some of them wanted to talk all night. Others never opened their mouths except to pour in more liquor.

"I'll be right back if you change your mind." She hoped he would now, so that she could put Mark Brandt off for another minute, but he only responded with a slow dip of his neatly combed head.

Strange that he didn't seem as out of place here as Mark did, she thought as she crossed the lounge. But then, Mark was on the wrong Capitol Hill; he probably looked on edge anywhere he wasn't amid movers and shakers. No one at Cole's came close to qualifying.

But he'd been nice enough, she remembered. Full of admirable ideals and ambition. Jane had dated him for six or seven months before he'd relocated to D.C.

Jane hadn't been hurt, so Charlie didn't have to hate him.

Mark stood as she approached the table. "Charlotte!" He

took her hand in a two-fisted shake, his smile exposing his square, even teeth.

Well, he'd perfected the politician bit. His kiss to each of her cheeks was overkill, but maybe it was a D.C. thing. Hopefully he wouldn't realize her grin was more amusement than greeting. "Mark. It's been a long time."

He pulled back, and his gaze dropped to her cheek before darting back up. "Not so long that you've forgotten me," he said, smiling again. "How are you? You look well."

That was sweet of him, but it said a lot that even with the bruise, she very likely *did* look better than when he'd last seen her. "I'm doing okay." She shrugged and glanced at his companion. Mid-fifties, as good-looking as Mark with his regular features and healthy frame. His pale blue eyes were scrutinizing, assessing.

Almost like a cop. Charlie shoved her unease away.

"Charlotte—my father, Bill Brandt." Mark slid back into his seat. After a quick look from the older man, he added, "*Senator* Bill Brandt."

Charlie said something she thought was appropriate, but dipped her hands into her pockets so she wouldn't have to shake his. On the table, their drinks sat untouched. She rocked back on her heels. "So—how is D.C.? Are you visiting long?"

"A few weeks." Mark drummed his fingertips against the back of his opposite hand. "I'll return to prepare for summer session. I'm legal counsel to Senator Gerath."

There was no mistaking the pride in his voice, but Charlie had no idea who that was. She shifted her weight, tried not to appear as ignorant as she felt. What could she say to that?

She grasped for something, anything, and was relieved when she remembered it was an election year. "You must be busy preparing for his campaign then."

"Gerath was Ohio's incumbent in 2006. He'll serve another six-year term before running again," the senator put in with austere tones. "It was a highly publicized race."

She darted a look at the elder Brandt and said lamely, "That's right."

Mark's hands clenched. "But there are other campaigns to support, Dad." He turned back to Charlie. "We'll be swamped until November."

Politics, she didn't know; overworked customers, she did. "Is this a vacation before the long haul?"

"A working vacation. Dad's reconnecting with the constituents before heading back to D.C."

"At Cole's?"

Mark's bland smile appeared again, similar to those she'd seen on hundreds of political ads. "The Heritage Theater. An out-of-town interest has been making noises about buying it, so we're raising the possibility of it being listed as a historical marker, hoping to keep it local."

Considering that the current owners had giant sticks up their asses and looked down their noses at anyone who worked for Old Matthew, Charlie wouldn't be sorry to see it change hands.

But she only threw out another rote bartender's response designed to keep the conversation going. "You must have seen the first movie while you were over there, then—*Destry Rides Again*?"

Mark looked to his father, and Brandt said, "We left early. My son doesn't appreciate the classics. Too much black-and-white."

A slight flush colored Mark's cheeks, and Charlie said, "I don't like the end of it. Frenchy dies." At Mark's blank look, she added, "The Marlene Dietrich character—the singer in the saloon."

Mark nodded vaguely. "Ah, yes."

Brandt leveled his pale gaze at Charlie's throat as he said, "Mark tells me that you used to sing."

Her back stiffened, but she didn't let her expression change. "Yes."

"One of those grunge groups?"

Mark apparently hadn't told him much, or the details had gotten smashed. "Not exactly," she said with a tight smile.

"Dad—"

Brandt held up his hand. "I'm not saying there's anything wrong with that kind of music, son. It brought Seattle a lot of attention and more money. And Miss Newcomb isn't offended."

"No." Not insulted, but even if she wasn't being paranoid and he *had* deliberately provoked it, he likely couldn't read the frustration in her voice. Not many people heard emotion over the rasp.

"And how is Jane?" Mark finally took a drink of his wine—more of a gulp.

Had he fortified himself before asking that question? "She's good. Just Jane. Working, scatterbrained. You know."

"Yes." He wiped at a drop of wine on the edge of the glass and absently rubbed the moist pad of his finger around the gently flaring rim. A low wavering note sounded beneath his voice. "I heard that she was the brain behind the breakthrough in artificial blood production at the University of Washington a little over two years ago. Is she still there?"

Charlie's brows rose. Did he read medical journals in his spare time? He couldn't have known Jane was involved, otherwise. Though the research and conclusions had been hers, and she'd authored the article, the UW Medicine department heads had stood in the limelight during the brief media flurry surrounding the announcement. It was one of the reasons Jane's decision to leave UW had been easy for her.

"No," Charlie said. "Legion made her an offer last year."

The elder Brandt's hands fisted on the table, and he exhaled sharply.

It didn't surprise her. Legion Labs had been the center of an ethics controversy six months earlier, when a Californian congressman with financial ties to the corporation had pushed for government funding on one of Legion's research projects.

Charlie glanced at the senator, saw the disapproving twist of his mouth, and couldn't resist. "They aren't Microsoft or Boeing, but they do bring in a little money to the local economy."

"Not the kind we want."

"It must be nice to choose the kind of money you want," Charlie said. Those pale eyes narrowed, and she turned back to Mark with a smile. He was downing more of his drink, so she took pity on him and offered the information first. "I think Jane's close to announcing her engagement to someone at Legion."

Mark's jaw tightened. Poor guy. An asshole for a father and a torch for her sister. "I'm not surprised," he finally said. The force of his drumming fingers against the tabletop increased, then he lifted his gaze to hers. "Well, I'm not in Seattle long, but I'd hate to lose touch again. Do you think we can go out for a bite sometime this week, catch up?"

Catch up? Wasn't that what they'd just done? Or did he want to invite Jane and Dylan on a double date—or worse, spend the meal pumping Charlie for information about her sister?

But when she opened her mouth to decline, she saw the senator's pinched lips and decided she could at least shoot him down out of his father's sight.

"It's possible that I could arrange some time off," she said. Could, but wouldn't—and she might as well set up her rejection now. "I do have finals coming up, but I could probably squeeze a few hours in before you leave."

"Fantastic!"

She wondered how many votes that smile would garner in the next forty years, and obligingly wrote down her home phone number. Charlie rarely answered it; anyone she wanted to speak with had her cell number. Only debt collectors and telemarketers called at her apartment—none of the former lately, but she was still wary enough to screen the calls.

She passed Vin on the way back to the bar, widening her eyes in a silent *Thank God that's over* that had him looking at the Brandts and grinning. In the corner of the lounge, Joel sat at his usual table, with the perfect angle on the television and his laptop open in front of him. Charlie eyed the amount of ice and alcohol in the glass of the woman whose rigid smile and frequent glances at her watch suggested that she was on an awkward date, and the much lower level in the glass of the guy who wasn't impressing her. Most likely, the woman would be leaving soon, and he would be wanting another drink.

The elderly gentleman at the bar was still nursing his. He didn't sit primly, as Charlie would have expected of someone his trim size, but with the easy sprawl of a large man accustomed to taking up space. His right foot rested on the brass rail in front of the bar, the low heel of his shiny black boot hooked casually on the rung of the stool.

This time he nodded when she asked if he wanted a refill, and he murmured a thanks when she tipped a splash into his glass.

He picked up his drink, and gestured toward the restaurant with it. "I would venture that the young man only takes wine when his father dines with him."

Charlie blinked, then realized he must have heard Vin speaking to her earlier. "I think you're probably right."

She studied him, tried to place his accent. Definitely educated. It reminded her of New York upper crust, but slightly more formal in its delivery. And although there was no hesitation in his speech, he spoke like an actor after a session with a voice coach, testing the shape of each word before it left his mouth.

"I'd have pegged you for a port," she offered. "Or a cognac."

A brief flash of humor and surprise crossed his face. He leaned forward, rested his forearms on the bar. "You are not altogether wrong. My father preferred port. And in his last year of life, he preferred to have quite a lot of it. It was a much more dignified drink than *this*."

Charlie couldn't imagine what his father had to do with his drink, but she held her tongue when he raised his glass and downed the two fingers' worth in a single swallow.

Either he was no stranger to the bottle himself, or he had a throat of steel. Not a wince, a flaring of his nostrils, or a watering of his eyes.

"But I've always thought its only threat to a man's dignity is when he's had too much to please a pretty woman," he added with a smile. "I'm not likely to get there."

His tone was flirtatious—and though it invited her to play along, she only asked, "Another then?"

"Yes." His fingers circled the heavy-bottomed glass, the tip of his thumb a scant distance from his middle finger. "What would you have taken the father for?"

Remembering the senator's pale gaze, his disapproving frown, she said, "I'd have said he doesn't drink. Ever."

"He ordered one."

"But he hasn't taken a sip. He probably came in, thought: Okay, I'm going to connect with my voters, seem like a regular guy. And a place like this, a regular guy gets a drink, so he did. Only, a beer's *too* regular, wine's too formal—or sissy—and whiskey might give the impression he takes his drink too seriously." She stopped. Had he recognized the senator? He hadn't even blinked when she'd mentioned voters, and was only nodding thoughtfully as he looked down into his glass.

"I see it a lot," she added, and he glanced back up at her. "People keeping up appearances."

A wry smile creased the corners of his mouth. "But appearances are almost always deceiving," he said, and downed half the whiskey in his glass.

"Yes." She watched him, feeling the first hint of unease. He was taking them too fast. With her chin, she gestured behind him, hoping to turn his attention from his drink. "Take Joel over there. Tonight, alone, he's a screwdriver and he's got the local news on. But every so often, he brings in someone he met online and orders a German beer from the tap. And although he's the sweetest guy, he's completely different in front of them: changing the channel to ESPN and pulling off some macho act. And they don't ever come back. I can never decide if it's funny or sad," she finished softly.

Maybe both. Her brow furrowed as she watched Joel's thin, pale face brighten at whatever he read on his laptop screen, then his smile as he typed a response.

So many expectations set up, and then destroyed. Did he really think the front he put on was what they wanted? Or did he sabotage himself, unable to bear the idea that when they met him in person they would be disappointed in what he really was—so he gave them something false to be disappointed in?

After two months chatting over a wall, had Ethan been disappointed?

She hadn't even realized how she'd built up her own expectations until she'd finally been on the verge of meeting him—and maybe all of the expectation had been on her side.

She should have looked back.

Suddenly a little depressed, she glanced away from Joel and found the gentleman's gaze fixed on her. A shiver ran over her skin, pricking the fine hairs on her arms. His eyes were bottle green, clear and hard as glass, and surrounded by dark brown lashes untouched by the gray that peppered his hair.

Perhaps his drink fit him, after all. Though the rest of him suggested it, that emerald stare was not at all grandfatherly. Nor had it been dulled by age or the whiskey.

And the intensity of it was oddly . . . sexy.

Jesus. She dipped her head, turned away. Her hands made jerky little movements at her waist. She tugged at her apron, pretending to tighten it, and trying to tamp down the unexpected and inappropriate attraction.

Customer. Old enough to be your father. Probably an alcoholic.

And with an expression that reminded her of Ethan's when she'd first opened her door.

She closed her eyes, breathed out. That must be it. She found a lot of people sexually appealing—but in a vague way, appreciative of their looks or personalities. They rarely provoked a physical reaction.

Ethan had. And so seeing something similar in this man must have triggered the same response.

The long fingers of his left hand were tracing a spiraling pattern on the bar. He'd propped his elbow up, settling his chin against his fist as he studied her.

Definitely reminded me of Ethan, she decided with a smile—although she'd have bet anything Grandpa had had some moves back in the day, too.

Steady again, she tried to get back to where she'd started—or to start over, rather, since his opening hadn't been the usual. "So, what are you in for? I'm guessing it isn't the same reason as Joel over there."

He shook his head, the corners of his mouth lifting. "You don't have to play this."

Her brows drew together. "Play what?"

"Keeping me talking, now that I've started, in the hope that I'll slow down." Ice clinked as his large palm engulfed the glass; he tipped it at an angle but didn't bring the tumbler to his lips. "In the hope that I'll leave here not wanting it so bad. But I'm not drinking for myself, Charlie."

He met her gaze when she looked up from his whiskey, and her stomach performed a long, lazy flop. "I've heard that before," she said. Her throat was dry, her rasp more pronounced.

For an instant, everything in his face stilled. His gaze flicked over her shoulder. Then he blinked and the easy manner fell over him again.

"From whom did you hear it before?" His voice had rolled up a little stiff; she hadn't noticed how casual it had become until the formality returned.

Formal—but not distant.

She grabbed for a story, any story to keep him going. "A guy who used to come in here. After spending the day tossing fish over at the Market, he was in here every night, drinking a bottle of top-shelf tequila that he always said wasn't for him." She arched a brow. "He never got drunk, either."

He was silent for a long moment. Then he said, "That couldn't be healthful for a body."

"It wasn't, and before long he was in the morgue. And guess what they found when they cut him open?"

"A petrified liver the size of Texas," he said dryly.

She pressed her lips together, shook her head. "A trout. It seems one day this guy had been working, but the fish was still alive, not quite drowned in the air. And when he tried to catch it, it wriggled through his hands, straight into his mouth and down his belly. But it didn't die, just swam around in there."

Though the corners of his eyes were twitching a little, he only nodded. "I suppose something of that nature is bound to happen."

"Particularly in a city where fish tossing is a huge tourist attraction," Charlie agreed with a straight face. "But this guy didn't appreciate that he could become a Seattle icon—and he knew that drinking water wouldn't drown the fish. So he tried to poison it with the tequila."

The dry note slipped into his voice again, and he tugged at his shirt collar. "Poison is never a certainty. Sometimes they keep on living."

"The fish certainly did—he got hooked on the tequila, until he needed it so bad the guy had to keep on coming in for that bottle even after he realized he'd failed to kill it. So when they performed the autopsy on him a few days later, they found the fish going through DTs so hard his flippers were buzzing."

She held out her hands, let them shake in demonstration, but didn't let herself think of the rest—didn't let herself remember how horrifying it had been: the sweats, the sharp, churning nausea, the blinding headaches and disorientation, and the unrelenting, bone-deep thirst.

"You almost had me." Though he narrowed his eyes, he was smiling. He pulled at his collar again, then unfastened the top button with fingers that seemed too large for a man of his size. "But fish have fins, Charlie. Not flippers."

"Well, I'm not very smart. I just know it started with 'f.'" Charlie grinned. "In any case, it's the truth. They got the fish out, sobered him up, and he's working at a sushi bar in Pioneer Square. Everyone calls him Trembling Tom."

He didn't give in to his laughter, but he bent forward, raising his hand and rubbing the side of his brow. His smile widened and formed a slash beside his mouth that might have been a dimple in a softer face.

Her first impression of him had been a neat and precise man, but now she revised it. His coat stretched a little tight across the shoulders, the sleeves edged a little high on his wrists.

Or maybe not. Vin appeared at the end of the bar, and by the time she filled the order and returned, everything seemed to fit just right—though he was still bigger than she'd first thought.

He'd lost the light mood, too, frowning down into his scotch, his expression that of a man telling himself he shouldn't be doing something, but not quite convincing himself of it yet.

Charlie laid her forearms on the bar, leaned in. "So I'm guessing the remainder of that drink isn't for a fish."

"No." His brusque response seemed to end it, but after a moment he pinched the bridge of his nose and said abruptly, "My brother. I thought he'd had a second chance—maybe had a family. A woman to hold on to. Unlike your friend on the computer, he had a way with them."

She worked it over, chose her words carefully. "You hadn't heard from him in a long time?" Hopefully, it had just been that—his brother getting in touch, and the shock of discovering he was in bad circumstances.

"No. And won't again, I figure."

Dead, then. And the news had been recent and unexpected. He didn't sound like a man who'd had time to get used to the idea.

She watched him finish off his drink and hoped he would hear the genuine sympathy in her voice, see it on her face when she said, "I can't give you another, not right away. But if you want some coffee or—"

"No." He stood, took a beaten leather wallet from inside his jacket, slipped out several folded bills. He didn't throw the money to the bar, but held it out. "The balance is yours. For the story."

She deliberately let her fingers rest against his before sliding the money from his grasp. His hand was steady as a rock, his gaze clear and focused, but drunk didn't always show. "You aren't driving?"

His smile was slow and warm. "No, Charlie. But I'm grateful for your concern." He leaned forward.

Oh, Lord, did he have moves. Smooth and quick. His mouth pressed softly against hers. Charlie stood frozen, her forearms crossed on the surface of the bar. He lingered for the space of a breath, then pulled away.

For a long second she couldn't respond, couldn't do anything but stare into his eyes. Thin lines of amber striated the green, like a starburst of gold on a field of emerald.

Finally she shook herself, licked her lips—and tasted alcohol.

His gaze followed the movement of her fingers as she wiped away the smoky flavor of the whiskey before she could begin to want more. His voice roughened. "I apologize, Charlie. That was awful forward of me."

She should have been enraged, or upset, or—something. But she only said, "I stole a kiss from someone tonight, too."

"I doubt he thought it was thievery." He looked at her for a long moment. "And I'm hard-pressed to feel true shame for stealing one from you. That was also for my brother—I'd have died for him to have something so sweet." He glanced over her shoulder. His face hardened, his eyes cooled to emerald again. "I'd have killed to give it to him, too."

She was too breathless to form a strong farewell when he turned, and she watched him walk through the lounge with her heart pounding far too quickly. She'd completely misjudged his size when he'd been sitting: as he passed the hostess's podium, he was a head taller than Melody. And unless he'd been standing on the brass rail, he must have been at least six foot two or so to lean over the counter and kiss her.

She blinked when he finally moved out of sight, and glanced down at the five twenties in her hand, then at the ice melting into the pale amber liquid at the bottom of his glass.

Definitely not a port.

CHAPTER 6

That had been about the most damn fool thing he'd ever done.

His mouth a hard line, Ethan stared out over the city, contemplating the speed with which he'd lost his hold on that shape.

Usually, he could shift into his father's form for much longer. He looked down at his hands, concentrated on an image of them smaller. They shrank, sure enough, but it was a damned unsettling feeling.

He was just too comfortable in his own skin; putting on someone else's itched something terrible—and the added distraction of Charlie's soft lips hadn't helped him a bit.

Her lips, the deceptively sleepy look in her eyes when she studied him, the deadpan expression she used when telling a story, the remembered pain that—for an instant—had flared bright beneath the tale.

And her voice. He'd been just fine until he'd started speaking with her.

He could list a hundred different distractions—but, hell, he couldn't truly blame her lips. Truth was, he'd been feeling awful sorry for himself, thinking about Caleb. Her laugh and her smile had done more than the alcohol could toward soothing that hurt, so he'd reckoned her mouth would be even better. But kissing hadn't eased anything.

It only made him think of having more, and that was a dangerous notion. When a man was hungry, one or two bites only whetted the appetite—and he could get real used to being full.

He took a long breath, pushed away the memory of her lips before he got too fuzzy. He couldn't drift and clear his head now—he'd wait until he returned to Caelum. But a few hours up here on Cole's roof would help; he could keep watch for the vampires without taking in too much else.

He could well understand Charlie's attraction to the little roof garden. He liked the city, but solitude was difficult to find—and with senses like his, even more so.

A Guardian blocked out the noise, the scents, and the psyches, until he only heard what felt normal and let the rest fade into the background. But after a few days without drifting, Ethan had to work at blocking them out. For most Guardians, blocking was easy—only in those first Enthralled years did the enhanced senses trouble them.

They didn't trouble Ethan all that much anymore, but it did get to weighing on him, until he was fuzzy and jittery as a human on a couple of nights without sleep, and it became harder to ignore sensations—particularly those he enjoyed.

The buildup happened to all Guardians; Ethan just had to rid himself of the weight more often than others did. More often than even a novice did.

And since he'd been coming around Charlie, he'd had to drift even more frequently than usual. There wasn't nothing about her that didn't grate or stroke or tickle a nerve. With the rasp of her voice, her music, and her sweet-smelling lotions, she put his senses on high alert—and she filled them up almighty quick.

Now that he'd been looking at her, too, he suspected that interval would shorten.

With a deep sigh, he pulled his long jacket in from his cache. The night air was cool, and the contrast of temperature only provided another distraction. He didn't get cold, but he felt the difference; when he was fuzzy, he felt it all the more. It was best just to prevent as much sensation as possible from slipping through.

A psychic sweep of the area picked up the vampires again, still indistinct. It might be they weren't aware of his presence; vampires' minds weren't near as powerful as Guardians' or demons'. Even if a vampire attempted to probe Ethan's shields, he wouldn't necessarily realize Ethan wasn't human.

Still, Ethan wouldn't rely on psychic detection—with enough practice, a vampire or human could form damn good shields, too.

His eyes narrowed when the senator and his son left Cole's. Now, there were two men with shields that could shame a novice Guardian. It wasn't all that unusual for humans who made a habit of guarding their thoughts and responses to have strong psychic blocks; someone in government certainly would. Ethan hadn't given either of them more than a cursory scan after they'd called Charlie over, but he'd attempted to look deeper once Jane and Legion had been included in the conversation.

Considering the son's history with Jane, that inclusion might have been nothing more than coincidence—but Ethan didn't trust coincidence.

There wasn't much suspicious about them now, though. They walked in silence toward a sleek black Town Car, and Ethan was certain it was disappointment that slumped the younger Brandt's shoulders.

Charlie had handled him real well. Just looking at her, it would have been difficult to see how awkward she'd felt, or that she had no intention of meeting with young Brandt later.

Difficult, but apparently not impossible. Standing at the door of his car, the senator said, "She won't return your call."

Mark Brandt glanced back toward the restaurant. "She might."

"Don't be a fool, son." He unlocked his door with a remote device. "This indirect route to Jane will lead you nowhere."

If using his Gift wouldn't have alerted any nearby vampires to his presence, Ethan would have locked the car door again, simply to observe the senator's reaction. Ethan couldn't get through his shields, but a man's response to an unexpected obstacle spoke loudly enough.

"The direct route got me nowhere, too," Mark Brandt muttered.

The senator's jaw clenched briefly. "Then create another path."

That silenced the younger man, and Ethan watched them drive away. Coincidence or not, it was best to have Jake look up the Brandts, see if they had any connection to Legion.

His cell phone was in his cache. He turned it on, then frowned at the display. A moment later, the lighted screen went dark. Well, shit. He'd forgotten that he'd vanished it the last time because of the bothersome beep that signaled the low battery.

Charlie's laughter suddenly hit him, made him look around. The roof was empty. Her voice struck again, and he realized she was talking in low tones with someone inside the restaurant.

Hell and damnation, he'd been *listening* for her.

With a shake of his head, he pushed it away. She should have been background noise. He only listened for what was necessary, or the influx of sounds would drive him mad—right now, that meant a furtive footstep or a whisper. The ring of a blade or the chambering of a bullet.

Protecting Charlie was necessary—but it was best that *she* wasn't.

❧

Charlie almost dropped her cash drawer when she turned around and found Ethan sitting at her bar, twenty minutes after Cole's had closed. She'd been thinking that he'd fallen asleep at home or forgotten, or had been waiting for her outside after they'd locked the front doors. She had no idea who had let him in—and she didn't realize how a tight band of anxiety had wrapped around her chest until it let go.

He watched her fumble with the drawer, an easy half smile curving his lips. "I didn't mean to startle you."

A few quarters slid to the floor, landing soundlessly against the anti-fatigue mat. "I wasn't surprised. I do this every night." She took a deep breath, steadied the drawer between her stomach and the register. "I have to go in the back, finish up. It might take me a couple of minutes."

"I don't plan on going anywhere."

And he did look like he'd settled in, turning on the stool and letting his gaze roam the lounge. She glanced in the mirror; the movement of his head flexed the tendon that ran from behind his jaw to the hollow of his throat. She wanted to run her fingers over his collar, compare the softness of the fabric with the smoothness of his skin. He still wasn't wearing his jacket, though it was past two o'clock in the morning. But then, maybe someone as big and rangy as Ethan didn't get cold; he probably generated his own heat.

Sighing, she bent and retrieved the quarters, then headed through the employees' door. Hot or not, it didn't bode well that he seemed to find Vin putting the chairs up more interesting to observe than he did Charlie.

In his office, Old Matthew was muttering numbers to himself and working his way through a stack of one-dollar bills; she quietly slid her drawer on the desk next to him so he wouldn't lose count, and continued on to the employees' room. He called her name on her way back through.

Old Matthew's office was an explosion of paperwork that he always claimed was completely organized, but he'd brought her in more than once to help him search for a paper he'd mislaid. The one-way mirror on the back wall looked out over the lounge; through the silhouettes of bottles and shelves, Charlie saw Ethan pick up a pink packet of sugar substitute from the bar, read the back, and shake his head.

"Charlie, take a look at this."

She tore her gaze away from Ethan. Old Matthew had rocked back in his chair, holding a pair of bills over his head and squinting at them under the light. The tiny loops in the black kufi she'd knitted for him at the beginning of winter were a little loose and faded now; he wouldn't care that it was becoming worn, but she made a mental note to pick up yarn for another.

He gave her the cash, his big fingertip sliding down the edge. "See the ink here?" Purple had soaked into the side of the twenty in a long blotchy streak. "It's from a security packet, the kind they use at banks. During a robbery, the teller will stick this in the bag with the cash. When the packet explodes, it marks all of the bills in the bag."

They were old-style twenties, with the small portrait of Andrew Jackson. Charlie didn't get them often, but enough not to bother looking twice when she did. "These were from my drawer? Should I not have taken them?"

"No, no—I needed to talk to you, but I'm not pulling you

in about this. I just thought it was interesting. When they get the guy, the money is taken into evidence—then eventually destroyed, because there's not much usable left after that packet goes off. But these are in sequential order; they haven't been in circulation, though their print date was over fifteen years ago. So he'd been caught, just got out, and went back to wherever he'd stashed the money—or had been holding on to it until he thought it safe to spend." He slid the bills back into her drawer, and his face wrinkled around his grin. "I don't care if he spends it here, as long as he doesn't plan on taking any. And I'd bet dollars to donuts he knew just how to distract you."

Blood rushed to her face. Old Matthew hadn't missed the kiss through the one-way. But though he was laughing at her, her embarrassment couldn't last—and she didn't let herself acknowledge the disappointment that the kiss hadn't been about her at all, but a way of getting the marked money into her hand.

"He was slick," Charlie agreed. A glance at the one-way confirmed that Ethan didn't look impatient or bored—only watching the floors being mopped in the lounge, a slight furrow on his brow that told her he probably wasn't thinking of the nightly cleaning. "What else did you need to talk about?"

Old Matthew unpinned the schedule from the corkboard behind his desk, flipped it to the second page. "Do you still need the time off next week?"

"Yes." A hard little knot formed in her stomach; the semester had been a difficult one. She'd asked for three days to complete a project and study for finals—days that she desperately needed. "I thought Robbie was okay to cover my shift."

"He is." Old Matthew glanced up at her from under his thick brows. "You still planning on using Cole's as a model for your project?"

"Yes."

"How about you get started early on that? Working back here part of the evenings, helping me with some of the paperwork to give you a better feel for it."

The knot unwound, and her smile tugged at her cheek. "Is it the bruise?"

"Charlie girl, if I wanted ugly up front, I'd have Robbie tending the bar all the time." Old Matthew's teeth were very straight and white against his dark skin, and his grin was broad. When her laughter faded, he added, "No. Truth is, I've been thinking about this since you first mentioned the classes. I've just been too set in my ways to do anything about it yet."

"About what?"

He waved his hand at the mess around his desk. "I'm starting to feel trapped in here with all these numbers, seven days a week, year-round. This wasn't all that I wanted to be doing when I started her up—and you don't want to be slinging drinks forever."

Once, it hadn't mattered what "forever" consisted of. Now she knew this wasn't all she wanted—she just didn't know what "all" was yet. But she said, "I like working the bar—"

"Charlie girl, liking isn't *living*." The frown that passed over his face left it looking more careworn than normal when it receded. "You can get comfortable enough in any situation; that doesn't mean you should accept what you've been handed and stay there."

"Yeah." There was no other response to that. "Would this be a permanent thing?"

"If it suits both of us. 'Assistant manager' sounds like a pretty nice title to put on the résumé, whenever you figure out what it is you're doing after you're done here. We can work you up to that, and I can start taking off a few nights a week."

Uncertainty held her throat tight, and Charlie slipped on her jacket so the silence wouldn't be so big. He was right, it would be a step forward.

So why was she hesitating? Was she depending on the comfort of the familiar?

"All right," she said with a jerky nod. "We'll try it out."

A look through the one-way made her recognize how long she'd been talking to Old Matthew: Ethan was on his feet, eyeing the door.

Old Matthew was looking, too, a slight frown wrinkling his brow as he turned back toward her. "One more thing, Charlie—I didn't have to answer any questions about Betty last night."

His shotgun. He could legally carry it, but she'd heard enough stories to know that didn't mean the cops wouldn't give him grief about it. "They didn't ask if you had a weapon," she said, "and I didn't feel like volunteering it."

"What put your back up? Did they give you any trouble when they questioned you?"

"No." She shifted her bag to her right shoulder. Ethan was prowling the length of the bar now. "It's just the way they look at you, you know? Because they have your name, your history, everything—and probably thought that I was up there drinking, imagined someone coming after me, and just fell down the stairs and hit the gate so hard it twisted like that."

Old Matthew's wide shoulders were shaking, his head moving back and forth, his laugh deep. "Oh, Charlie girl, that's how they'd be looking at *me*, not a pretty white gal. Wondering if I really did kill that couple, and got out because everyone's turned into a bleeding-heart liberal. And thinking that even if I didn't do it, I probably did something so that I deserved the time. Or they're looking at Vin, wondering if he's swinging by a chop shop every night on his way home." His amusement had turned hard. With a deep breath, he pulled off his kufi, swiped it over his bald head. "You okay getting home?"

Charlie tipped her chin toward the one-way. "Do you see the size of the guy out there? He could take Betty on and come out smiling."

"He a cop?"

Charlie blinked, startled. Old Matthew had a shrewd sense of those things; he could always make a cop. "No."

"Health inspector? He's got that look. Seeing everything."

She could understand why he'd gotten the impression; Ethan had stopped walking the length of the bar, was staring at the mirror as if he could see right through it. Good Lord, but she could feel the intensity of that gaze down to her toes.

"He's in pharmaceuticals." When Old Matthew frowned at her, she quickly added, "Not a drug dealer."

His face lightened. "All right. Good night, Charlie girl."

She was in the hall again before her own good-bye had left her lips, and every thought scattered when she swung through the lounge door. Ethan was waiting for her, holding his hand out, his face without expression.

Except for those eyes.

"You ready?"

She nodded, speechless again. Maybe there would come a day when she wasn't struck dumb when she opened up a door and found him standing there, when she could come up with a topic and chat with him as easily as she had over the wall. But for now, she only slid her palm into his and let him lead her to the front entrance.

He paused outside, looking up and down the street. Even this late, there were still quite a few people on the sidewalks.

Late. "Sorry—" She had to catch her breath in surprise when he pulled her forward again. He wasn't matching her stride anymore, and she was almost race-walking to keep up with him. "Sorry to keep you waiting," she finally got out. "I hope you didn't have to wake up."

An image of him in bed, sleep-rumpled and warm, ballooned through her mind; his flat response quickly deflated it. "No."

She could really use a little help in this conversation. And a slower pace; if she didn't visit the gym every day, she'd probably have been huffing by now.

"Old Matthew just wanted to talk to me about some new stuff I might be doing." Counting drawers and ordering supplies wasn't all that thrilling, though. "Important work back there, you know—investigations into bank robberies, thwarting bad guys."

Unease prickled the length of her spine. They were off the main street now. Ethan had stopped at an intersection, turned his head to stare down the empty sidewalk behind them.

Her breath shortened. Someone was moving in the darkness near a residential building.

But she'd been so paranoid lately that someone was *always* moving in the darkness.

She closed her eyes and kept on talking. "That'll be me: bartender by night, FBI by day—" Ethan's forward motion almost yanked her off her feet, pulled her out of her fright like a cartoon character who'd left her shadow behind. She ran along beside him and almost stumbled over the opposite curb. "The, uh, white collar division."

"You like numbers, Charlie?" He looked behind them, his nostrils flaring, his lips forming the beginning of a snarl.

"When they add up." She darted a glance over her shoulder, panic starting to fill her belly with jittering bugs. *Nothing there, nothing there.* "When they don't, not so much. Ethan—"

"I'm not all that fond of shit that don't add up, either." He suddenly stopped walking, and slowly turned. "And I don't like five against two."

Her stomach dropped to her feet. Five figures slunk out of the dark. In the arc of the streetlights, their skin was pale—then concealed by shadows again as they came closer. Not as fast as they had the night before, but like a pack of wolves edging up on their prey, not wanting them to scatter too early.

Ethan's jaw hardened, and he breathed out long through his nose, a heavy sound of resignation. She couldn't read any fear in his face—just determination. "But I reckon five against one will suit me just fine."

Did he think he was going to fight them? But the incredulous thought had barely formed when his arm came around her waist. The world tilted, whirling and spinning, her cheek against his neck, her fingers clutching at his arms.

It stopped, and her bag thumped against her back, finishing its swing. She staggered into Ethan's chest—she was on her feet, but not steady.

"Can you stand, Charlie?"

She blinked. A silver-and-black telephone box hung near her left arm. Ethan filled up the booth, hunching over her.

The material beneath her fingers was roughly woven—not soft as she'd expected his shirt to be. She looked down, saw the brown sleeves. A long knife appeared in his hand.

She jerked away, the back of her head rapping against plastic as she crowded herself into the corner. "Oh, no."

No no no. He was so big. Huge. She thought she'd be grateful, awed—but she was only afraid.

His face was set as he turned and dug his blade into the trim beside the door. The flashing point of the dagger scratched metallic shrieks from the aluminum. Shadows surrounded the booth, flashes of dark and pale.

Charlie slid to the floor, wrapped her arms around her shins, making herself as small as possible. The scraping stopped, and it was suddenly so quiet she could only hear the thudding of her heart, her crazy breaths.

Then a flutter of movement as Ethan crouched in front of her, his knees filling up the space on either side of her legs. The brown coat pooled around him, his boots longer now, a smooth shine the length of his shins. Buckles winked dully at his ankles.

"Charlie." He ducked his head into her line of sight, forced her to meet his eyes. Hard and sharp, like shards from amber stone. She looked away from them, letting her gaze fall to the holsters hanging low on his hips and anchored with braided leather around his lower thighs. "You've got to stay put, Charlie, you hear me? Don't you open this door, don't you leave this booth for anything—until either I come get you or the sun comes up. For *anything*. Promise me that."

Shivers wracked her body; a cold breeze snaked around his legs, seemed to wriggle its way through every thin point of her clothes and skin. Outside, a shadow formed a human shape; a white hand tapped soundlessly against the plastic, then a face looked in, grinning.

She'd seen that face before—for just an instant. An arrow had been through his forehead.

"Charlie?"

She met Ethan's eyes. "I promise."

♦

There was no escaping Charlie knowing now. And he'd lose this opportunity to make these sons of bitches talk by running with her.

A man played the hand he was dealt, but Ethan had learned to carry an ace or two up his sleeve. And a Guardian against a vampire was like having a whole goddamn deck full of aces.

With a burst of speed, he caught the first vampire. A male, yelping like a coyote when Ethan got hold of his collar. Ethan pivoted, slammed the vampire flat against the pavement, intending to keep him down with his boot against the vampire's neck until he handled the others.

Ethan heard the crunch of the vampire's skull against concrete, felt the sudden blandness in the male's psychic scent that wasn't unreadable, like psychic blocks or the spell, but just empty.

Hell and damnation—he'd slammed him too hard. Until the vampire's brain healed, he wouldn't talk any more than a vegetable would.

Footsteps came up fast behind him. Ethan looked under his

arm, snatched the attacking vampire's wrist before he could take off Ethan's head with his sword. A tight squeeze had the vampire dropping his weapon. Ethan caught the sword before it hit the ground and swung the vampire by his broken wrist, whipping him up hard against a wooden storefront. He clamped his hand around the vampire's throat, lifted the bastard until he dangled.

The muffled pop warned him, but even Ethan couldn't move quick enough to avoid the bullet. Pain exploded in his upper back, tore into his chest like a blacksmith pounding a hot iron stake through him. His muscles screamed as he turned and re-placed the vampire's sword with his crossbow.

Ethan fired. The vampire holding the gun dropped, the weapon clattering to the sidewalk, the bolt between its eyes. Gritting his teeth against the agony in his back, Ethan trained the crossbow on the vampires circling the booth.

Charlie was watching them wide-eyed, and he could see by the rise of her chest that she was breathing erratically. Her lips were trembling.

Then she flinched and raised her arms protectively when a female with long dark hair and wearing half a cow in leather lifted her gun. The pings of the bullets against the glass were no louder than the silenced shots.

Charlie lowered her arms and stared. Her gaze shifted to Ethan and he nodded once, letting a smile touch his lips. She might not understand magic was at work, but the results were unmistakable: they wouldn't be getting in, and couldn't hurt her through the spell.

Her mouth widened in a relieved grin, opened in a laugh that he could see but not hear.

Still watching her, still watching the vampires circling the booth, Ethan replaced the crossbow with his own sword, pressed it to the neck of the vampire he held before loosening his grip.

Using his lungs brought blood up to his mouth; he swal-lowed it down and ignored the burning in his back and chest.

"Let me make this real simple." His tone was low enough it made speaking less of an effort, dangerous enough they wouldn't know how much it was hurting. It was better the vam-pires thought a bullet had little effect, or they'd soon be shooting more at him. "Anything happens to Charlie, any more humans are turned against their will, and Sodom and Gomorrah is going to look pretty next to what I'll do to Legion."

In the booth, Charlie rose to her feet. Her palms flattened against the window panel. Not cowering anymore, though she took a startled step back when the female snarled at her and made a lunge at the plastic.

Rabid dogs, just looking to frighten her.

Beneath Ethan's hand, the vampire's throat worked as he struggled to speak. "You Guardians talk a lot, but you don't help us. Don't give us anything we need."

That sounded like a line a demon would feed them. Ethan smiled a bit, and even without fangs he reckoned it looked as lethal as a demon's. "Well now, you just tell me what Legion is giving you, and perhaps—"

The female rushed around the booth, snapped at Charlie again. The vampire's movement must have looked near instantaneous to Charlie, as if she'd appeared from thin air; Charlie stumbled back against the opposite side of the small space.

Her surprise crackled through the air like summer lightning. *Son of a bitch.* She'd rubbed up against the blood on the symbols, wiping them clean.

And the vampires realized it the instant he did. If they got in there with her, reactivated the spell with their own blood, Ethan wouldn't have a chance in hell of helping her.

The female was on the wrong side of the booth—her companion went for the door.

Put them down. This wasn't a risk Ethan was taking again, not with these vampires. He let go of the one he was holding; his sword slid through the vampire's neck before his feet hit the ground. Two quick slices as he ran past the vampires lying motionless on the sidewalk meant they wouldn't be getting up again.

The female turned to flee; Ethan set his sights on the male at the door and let her go. He needed one left alive to deliver his message to Legion.

Unless Legion was coming to him.

That scaly psyche he'd felt the night before crawled over his skin, and it was getting closer, stronger. A demon posed a real threat to Ethan, and he wouldn't be protecting anyone if he was gutted or dead.

Time to get Charlie out of there.

❧

It was so unbelievably fast.

One second Charlie was stumbling away from the pale woman, crowding into the corner again, and calling herself an idiot for being startled. And the next second, the door was opening and the vampire who'd had an arrow lobotomy was coming through.

Then crimson arced in a horizontal line across the booth panels beside Charlie, sprayed her face in a cool mist. The vampire's head slid forward off his neck, his body slowly crumpling before it was yanked away from the open door like a marionette.

Ethan. His maroon shirt black and wet, his skin dripping red. Charlie wiped at her face, stared at the blood on her fingers. They began to shake.

"Easy, Charlie." She heard the urgency in his voice but couldn't make herself take the hand he offered her. "You're all right." He glanced down; the stains on his skin and clothes disappeared. The itchy slide over her cheeks was gone, her fingers clean again.

The body at his feet vanished, then the head.

Ethan swallowed hard. "Charlie, there's something worse coming."

Worse? But it must be: Ethan stiffened and looked to the side; a female's scream ripped through the air.

Charlie leapt toward the door, and his arms circled her, brought her in tight. White flashed behind him, soft and bright and beautiful. His wings unfolded, and pressure made her head swim, her chest ache, her stomach drop, like driving down a hill too fast and realizing nothing was going to stop her until she got to the bottom. The edges of her vision blurred, but she looked down and back, the ground like a dark blank sky lit by the stars of streetlights and two glowing red eyes.

❧

Having to fly hadn't helped Ethan heal any faster, but the gunshot wound had subsided to a dull ache by the time he was over their apartment building. The speed with which he'd launched himself into the air meant Charlie had lost consciousness, but Ethan reckoned it was shock that kept her out until he settled onto her balcony. He rid himself of the wings and held her lightly across his lap, her head on his shoulder.

He made himself pat her cheek instead of stroking his fingers over her skin, murmuring her name over and over so that she wouldn't startle so bad. That he'd brought her to a familiar location would help, but they couldn't stay long.

He'd vanished each of the dead vampires and their weapons into his cache before the demon had arrived, but the female hadn't yet been dead when he'd gotten Charlie away. And there was blood to clean up, bullets to collect, evidence to destroy.

The fifteen-second altercation had left far too much for humans to find and wonder about.

Charlie stirred, her lips gently parting—and then she was sitting upright, her eyes wide. She looked around, and he felt the instant she recognized her surroundings, but her bolt toward the sliding door wasn't out of fear.

She didn't make it, and he held his palm under her ribs, keeping her steady and off the floor as her knees collapsed and she bent, heaving into the corner. Nothing came up, though it clamped hard on her body.

A normal reaction, he told himself. But he still worried as she straightened and tugged listlessly at the balcony door. She didn't comment on how easily it opened, though she must have remembered locking it. He couldn't sense much from her, but she wasn't blocking; sliding into her emotions felt a little like touching the mind of the vampire whose brain he'd smashed.

He followed her inside, past the tiny dining room table and the vase filled with blue marbles in the center of it. Her coat dropped to the floor.

"Charlie."

She halted in the short hallway, but didn't turn to look at him.

"We can't stay here. They've become aggressive enough; you wouldn't be safe."

Her hands clenched convulsively at her sides. The rasp

didn't conceal the dullness in her voice. "Are my smokes still over at your place?"

"No." His jaw tightened, and he considered smashing the vase against the wall, scattering those goddamn marbles all over just to wake her up, but he pulled the pack in from his cache instead.

Touching the mental space only pissed him off more; the vampires' bodies felt like grotesque lumps in his mind, on his tongue.

She took a cigarette from him, put it between her lips. Patted her pants pockets. "I need to get my luggage?"

And he didn't like that she formed it as a question—looking for guidance, having him tell her what to do, not making any decisions.

"No." He vanished the pack of cigarettes, and she blinked. The sweep of her dark lashes was echoed by a brush of curiosity and surprise. "Just tell me what you want me to take."

She pulled the cigarette from between her lips and rubbed her forehead with her scissored fingers. "Am I coming back?"

"Well, I don't rightly know, Miss Charlie. I reckon that's up to you."

Her brows drew tight, as if she wasn't quite certain she'd heard the frustration beneath the drawl.

"Should I give notice to Jenkins?"

The landlord. That vase was in immediate danger, and he figured every other breakable within reach was, too.

"Not tonight."

She took a deep, trembling breath. Resolve stiffened her psychic scent. "We'll take it all." Her thumb tapped the end of the cigarette, and she glanced up at him. "How?"

He sized up the table with a look, pulled it into his cache. The vase fell, and he vanished it just before it hit the vinyl flooring. A small banquette stood by the sliding glass door; her lighter lay in the wide-bottomed bowl that sat next to a small potted cactus.

"You need that lighter, Charlie?" He pointed. "And I can't take your plant, because it's alive."

She flicked the cigarette in the same direction. Her hair slid across her shoulders as she shook her head. "No."

Too easily, he saw himself wrapping its apple-scented length around his fist and taking a long, hard taste from her mouth, so he vanished everything but the plant and moved on to the next room.

"My music," she said, coming to stand next to him as the furniture in her living room and the little desk in the corner vanished. He used more care with her CDs, taking them one at a time and reading the titles as he did. They disappeared from her shelves like rows of falling dominoes.

They crowded into the small bathroom, and she wasn't watching her things vanish anymore, but was gazing up at him, wonder and fascination flushing her cheeks. Countless bottles of lotions littered her cupboards and sink, razors in pretty colors and curved to slide over a woman's contours with nary a nick. Her skin would be soft and smooth under a man's hands.

And her psychic scent wasn't empty anymore, but filling up with something that made him even more uneasy: awe.

He wasn't a goddamned hero, and if she looked at him like he was one it'd keep her as helpless as shock might: depending on him to make all her decisions, deciding what was right.

And he particularly didn't like how all-fired good it felt when she looked at him that way.

Damnation, but she'd riled him up with that zombie routine, and worse now that she'd come out of it. It wasn't like him. His temper was slow to heat and cooled off quick, rarely reaching more than a simmer. But she'd not only got his temper going—she'd gotten the rest of him, too.

He strode past her and cleaned out her bedroom before she had a chance to stand in the room with him, her appreciation and scent and that golden soft skin tempting him into something he ought not to be even thinking. Not with a woman like her, not in circumstances like these.

"You got anything else?"

"No." She touched her fingers to the cross at her neck. Her voice was hoarser than usual. "What are you, Ethan?"

"Not that." His gaze fell to the necklace. "But if you've been to church I reckon you've heard the story enough. Part of it, leastwise."

Worry darkened her eyes. "I haven't."

"Well, Miss Charlie, you're in good company, because I haven't sat on a pew for a hundred and thirty years."

She began to smile, but it froze midway. "You're serious."

"That I am." He scanned the apartment, the surrounding

area—and didn't detect anything, but he wasn't going to wait until more vampires showed up or give the demon a chance to follow them. "But I'll tell you the rest of it when we're secure."

Her nod was jerky, a touch of fear flickering deep. She followed close behind him, out of her apartment and into his. He didn't have anything to collect but the cell phone charger plugged into the wall outlet.

A thread of doubt colored her psychic scent. "Did you already get all of your stuff?"

"There wasn't nothing to get," he said, and continued out to the balcony. He looked back, saw her standing in the living room, taking in the emptiness. "You ready?"

She hurried out, stepped up close to him. Forming his wings pulled at the bullet still lodged in his back, but he was glad of the distraction when she wrapped her arms around his neck, when she gasped and laughed in startled delight as they caught air.

This time, though he went straight up, he didn't have to go so quickly. He slid his arm under her knees, shifted her weight. It was easier for him to maneuver—and more comfortable for Charlie—if he carried her cradled against his chest rather than hanging. Her breath puffed against his throat, formed a cloud of vapor that slid instantly away with the wind as they ascended.

"Ethan." His name vibrated through her chattering teeth. "Do you have my coat?"

He didn't need to gain any more altitude; they were high enough that no one looking up would see them. He hovered, his wings beating steadily. "You've got to hang on to me."

She nodded, her arms tightening and holding her face close to his. He slowly lowered her knees, let her take her own weight. Draping the coat around her shoulders was awkward, the wind threatening to rip it away, the wool flapping and twisting.

Until Charlie wound her legs around his waist, held on with one arm, and stuck her other arm through the sleeve. She switched sides and quickly repeated the action before bringing her eyes even with his.

Her hair was blowing against his face, caught in the seam of his lips. Her thighs tightened at the sides of his hips, and she lifted her hand to his mouth, dragging the strands away with a curl of her finger. "Thank you, Ethan."

He gave an abrupt nod. "It's what I do."

Charlie regarded him steadily, but he didn't dare sink into her emotions to discover if anything more than gratitude lay behind that expression. After a long moment, she sighed and laid her cheek on his shoulder. Her hand trailed over the frame of his wings on its journey back around his neck.

Ethan pushed her legs down over his hips and slipped his arm beneath her knees before she felt how much he'd wanted her to lay her lips against his again.

In gratitude, in awe—for any damn reason at all.

CHAPTER 7

Ethan had a heartbeat.

Charlie wasn't certain why that reassured her so much, but the deep sound and even rhythm of it did. After a few moments of listening, she braved her face and eyes to the freezing wind created by his flight. Seattle stretched out below them—then abruptly the city lights were gone, everything below them dark as they crossed Lake Washington.

Giant residences lined the opposite shoreline. She knew of the area, though it had been a long time since she'd been invited to anyplace like it, and that hadn't been in Seattle. Eastside was home to the billionaires of the tech industry or the likes of Senator Brandt.

And, apparently, Ethan. Instead of heading farther inland, he skimmed above the placid water before landing on a wooden dock. She swayed in time with the lapping of the water against the floats until her knees adjusted to the motion. Moonlight whitewashed the stairs that led up the hill and gleamed in the windows of the lodge-style house. Tall firs broke the peaked line of the roof's silhouette.

Ethan was looking up at the large, rustic home with the

same appreciation—and, she thought, a little bit of surprise. She saw him glance at the address placard tacked to the dock post, check it against a piece of paper that appeared in his hand, and shake his head.

"You don't own this?"

"No." His hand captured hers. The trees cast shadows across the upper half of the stairs, leaving it too dark for her to see—but he had no trouble navigating the steps and the flagstone path that led to the lakeside entrance. "Ramsdell Pharmaceuticals does. I just figured it'd be . . . fussy."

She blinked quickly. The job hadn't been a lie? Did he live a normal life at the same time he fought vampires—and whatever he considered to be worse?

"What was coming back there at the phone booth?"

"A demon." The door opened at his touch. Though he had them folded tight against his back, his wings brushed the sides and top of the door frame. He paused just inside, consulted the paper again, then moved to the security panel situated between a giant picture window and a framed landscape painting.

A demon. She didn't know much about them, only what she'd seen in movies and operas, but she had a good idea what the opposite of a demon was.

Charlie stared up at his profile, then at the wings arching above his head. She'd touched them—soft down had covered a heavy frame of bone and muscle; the flight feathers had been like silk. And though she longed to run her hands over them again, now it struck her as shameful that she'd done it without permission . . . and possibly blasphemous that she'd touched them at all.

And she wasn't even sure what she was blaspheming.

She tucked her hands into her coat pockets. More than touching—she'd stolen a kiss from him. Thought of doing things a lot less innocent than that.

The alarm light switched from red to green. Ethan studied the security panel as if he expected it to give up a secret, then finally turned toward her.

His eyes narrowed. "Whatever you're thinking that put that fire in your cheeks, you unthink it. I got a pile of mattress stuffing on my back, but it don't mean I'm wearing a halo."

His reading her so easily only made her embarrassment

worse, but she said in the strongest voice she could muster, "Okay."

The sound in the room was strange; large and open, with vaulted ceilings lined with beams—their voices should have echoed, come back hollow. Instead the tones remained full without bouncing back. Perhaps the amount of wood and the thick rugs softened the echo, or they'd placed sound dampeners in the walls, like the shell of a concert hall.

The furnishings were light in color and sparse; paintings filled the walls, but it was too dark to see details on the canvases.

Ethan was looking, too, but whatever he saw on one wall made him smile a little. It turned into a grimace when his wings vanished. He cocked his right elbow and rotated his shoulder in a wide circle before holding out his hand to her again.

"I've got to go back, Charlie, see what I can about the demon and anything he left behind."

Charlie swallowed hard. "All right."

His palm enfolded hers, and she realized how cold her hands were from the flight and the unheated house. "You'll be fine here. Take a look at this." He led her to the door, placed his fingers about halfway up the frame. "You see these markings?"

It was dim enough in the room that she couldn't see anything, but when she trailed her fingertips down the wood, she could feel the scratches on the smooth surface—and remembered how Ethan had scraped something into the phone booth. "So, these will keep vampires out—unless they're invited in?"

Had she accidentally invited one into the booth?

"An invitation doesn't mean anything," Ethan said. He let go of her hand, and a dagger flashed in his. "It's a spell. You put your blood on each one of these symbols—there's three of them—from top to bottom, like this." He stabbed the pad of his thumb, touched it to the frame three times.

Charlie's breath caught. The house had been quiet, but now it was silent; she hadn't been listening to the lake, the wind, but she heard their absence better than she had their lapping and sighing.

"This one's on a main entrance, so it locks down the

entire house. There ain't nothing that can get in, not demon or vampire or human—and you've got nothing to worry about but an earthquake or fire."

"But—"

Ethan wiped at the frame with his sleeve, and the sound slipped back in.

Charlie's lips parted in realization. "Oh."

His smile edged just a bit higher on the right side when he looked down at her. "I ought to have warned you."

She almost said, *That's okay*, but then she remembered the vampire's face and his fang-filled grin. "You should have," she agreed, and watched him poke his thumb again. "Will my blood do that?"

"Yes. But if your blood activates the spell, I can't get back in. The spell will stay up for as long as a person's alive inside—but only the one who cast it can go in and out. So if you go out while I'm gone, you'll be able to get back in, but the spell won't be around the house anymore—you got that?" At her nod, he continued, "You won't be able to call anyone or communicate through the shield it creates. Nothing gets through; not television, not e-mail, not radio."

"Nothing at all?" Charlie frowned, wondering why that tripped a memory for her.

Ethan shook his head. "I could stand outside the window and write a note on a paper, but you wouldn't be able to read it. You'd see it, but couldn't understand it."

"Oh. Well, that's normal for me." She gave up trying to remember what had pulled at her memory. Everything was coming at her too fast; she could feel herself withdrawing again, going numb, and he hadn't even told her what he was. She took a deep breath and admitted, "I need some time to process all of this, Ethan."

"You'll get time. If you like, you can claim a bed and sleep. I'll be a good hour or so."

She looked back into the large, open room, the moonlit water outside the window, the distant sparkle of the city. "I think I'll stay in here."

For a long moment, Ethan's gaze was steady and firm on hers; then his brow furrowed like a man facing a puzzle. "I don't see a single electric light switch, or I'd turn them on for you. I suspect they're integrated into the computerized system that runs the house, but I neglected to ask the details—and I don't want to go selecting the wrong button."

Charlie shrugged. "I like the dark."

"Yes, but you ought to have something—" He blinked. "Well, hell."

She turned as Ethan strode past her, the tails of his coat brushing her legs. There was no sign that his wings had penetrated the brown fabric, but it was marred by a small hole high on his back. Charlie frowned, followed him.

The main part of the room had a sunken floor. Charlie stood at the edge of the two steps leading down; Ethan had her favorite lamp, the one that had been next to her bed, and was plugging it in and setting it on a small table. The stained-glass shade washed the room with soft blues, reds, and golds.

It was comforting, familiar—and she had to admit, better than the dark. She folded her arms over her chest, and wasn't sure if she wanted to laugh or start crying.

Ethan came to stand in front of her, his left foot on the first step. "You'll be all right, Miss Charlie."

She swallowed hard, nodded. "Are *you* okay? Did they shoot you?"

"They got me, but it ain't no trouble." He showed her his thumb. "I heal quick."

The wounds he'd made with his dagger were already gone—not even a trace of pink remained. She held herself tighter to keep from touching his hand, raised her gaze to his face, let it settle on his lips. Her brows drew together. "But you have a scar."

His smile held a hint of teasing in it. "A souvenir from when I was human," he said. The lines at the corners of his eyes deepened. "I keep it because womenfolk can't resist taking a better look; and once they're in close, they're like bears on honey."

Laughing relieved some of the pressure that had been building up in her chest, left her slightly light-headed. Ethan was watching her, grinning in full now, and Charlie could easily believe that any woman near those lips would be tempted.

She was probably too close.

Her laughter faded, her breath came hard. He didn't move away when she leaned toward him. For an instant she was unbalanced, at too far an angle over the stairs—but she braced her palms on his wide shoulders and caught his upper lip between hers, a soft brush before simply holding her mouth against his.

It was easy, so easy to stand there with his breath heating her bottom lip. But Charlie knew herself too well, and this felt too good. She wouldn't be satisfied with a little taste—she'd want more.

And although his lips moved under hers, Ethan wasn't kissing her back; he just wasn't smiling anymore.

She pulled away, her hands falling to her sides.

Ethan blinked his eyes open, and a vertical line formed between his eyebrows, as if he was surprised to see her standing a foot away.

"Well, I'll be going—" He shook his head, blinked again, and looked down at his hand. "You'll be—" His jaw tightened, and he glanced up at her. "Son of a bitch."

Ethan simply straightened, shifting his weight forward and up, his left foot still on the first step but now he was towering over her. His fingers speared into the hair at her temples, his huge hands cupping her face and tilting her head back for the claim of his mouth.

Heat surrounded her: his palms curving around her cold cheeks, his chest against hers. Her fingers slid beneath his jacket, across the softness of his shirt and the hard muscle it covered.

Oh, Lord, and his *mouth*. Hot and wet, and he didn't wait for her to recover from her surprise but used the insistent pressure of his lips to guide hers apart. He sipped, licked, and his warmth stole through her, sliding down to her belly and seeping into her blood like a sweet kiss of Drambuie, leaving her flushed and dizzy and all too ready for another drink.

But this couldn't be bad for her. The shuddering drag of her breath when his mouth left hers wasn't harsh to her ears, but the most luscious sound she'd made in years, the emotions unmistakable. Need. Desire. Wonder.

Ethan spoke roughly against her throat, and she didn't hear the words clearly but her answer was yes. Her necklace loosened—disappeared. She thought of the scar, then banished it from her mind.

Demons and vampires could never hurt her as badly as

she'd hurt herself. And she'd done enough wrong in her life, fucked up so many times that she didn't know how she deserved to be here now, with a man with wings and a laugh like whiskey and who kissed as if he wanted to swallow her down—but she'd be grateful for it every second of the rest of her life, even if she never encountered anything like him or anything miraculous again. And now she only wanted to crawl onto him, lean on him, and hold on to this wondrously *alive* feeling—

Ethan froze. He lifted his head to stare down at her, his eyes like amber stone. His thumbs swept across her cheekbones—and then he abruptly let her go and turned away from her. "I'd best go."

His voice was as hard as his expression had been. Reeling from the change, she didn't know what to say, tried to read his profile instead—but it was inscrutable. "Ethan?"

A round-brimmed hat appeared in his hand and he jammed it on his head, shadowing his features. "Don't rely on me, Charlie. I'll keep you safe. But don't be thinking it's more than that, or that I'll be anything more than someone who protects you."

But he'd wanted to be. A man didn't kiss like that unless he craved it. Her chest tightened, and she struggled to understand the point behind his warning. "Because you're unreliable?"

Maybe there was a kindness in that—cautioning her that nothing would come of a relationship with him except disappointment. But Charlie wasn't looking for anything permanent, and she'd never been idiot enough to think she could change someone.

He drew in a long breath. "No. I'm steady enough—but you'll throw yourself into relying on me."

She couldn't comprehend it for a long moment, and just stood there, blinking stupidly. Then it hit her and she stepped back, wrapped her arms across her roiling stomach and curled in on herself a little, like a pill bug.

He was right. But she hadn't known he could see her so well . . . that all of her weaknesses were exposed to him, and so revolting that although he might want her enough to kiss her like he had, he didn't *want* to want someone like her.

"Charlie—" He lifted his hand, then let it drop back to his side. And that was only more devastating—that he could be sorry for hurting her, but he realized that if he softened the blow it'd just be worse in the end.

"You'd best go, Ethan," she rasped, and his fist tightened as if a response lay just beneath his skin—but he walked to the door without speaking a word.

Though she'd seen him for the first time that night, already his shape and features were familiar, so easy to apply to the faceless man she'd known for two months.

But she didn't know him at all. Didn't even know— "Should I be calling you Ethan? Or is your real name something else?"

He didn't turn around, but stood with his hand on the doorknob. His voice was quiet when he finally said, "They call me Drifter."

The door closed behind him; the house loomed silent and cold around her.

But at least it wasn't dark.

❧

The demon had drained her.

Ethan studied the position of the female vampire's body, unease twisting through him. The demon had left her on her back in an alley, her blank eyes staring up at the stars, her booted feet at an angle up against the brick wall, as if she'd just laid down and propped her feet up to watch the night sky.

Ethan had told Charlie the only way to kill a vampire was cutting through its heart or taking its head, but that wasn't quite right—it was just the other options weren't so practical.

They could be burned, but Ethan didn't know many vampires who'd sit around while their flesh roasted. So those who died that way, it was usually accidental—in a house that caught fire while they were in their daysleep. A demon might trap and burn them alive, but it took a lot of effort to make certain they didn't find another exit. Easier to just use a sword. More merciful, too.

But a demon wouldn't care for that, and he certainly hadn't been merciful with this one. Ethan wouldn't have felt the least compunction against slaying her, but he'd never have considered something like this. Her neck had been opened down to her spine—but a vampire healed quick. Not as fast as a Guardian or demon, but enough to keep from bleeding out, even if an artery was severed. The demon must have kept slicing it open—taking a good five minutes to finish it.

And he'd held her upside down, like an animal hung for slaughter. Bloody handprints circled her ankle. The back of her opposite boot had a bit of splatter, too, and her nails some flesh—Ethan reckoned she might have gotten a few good kicks in, but the blunt heels wouldn't have done much damage and the demon would have barely felt the scratches.

The rest of her blood was in a dark pool beneath her.

It just didn't make any kind of sense. A public place like this—she wouldn't have been able to scream, but the demon had been taking an awful risk that someone might happen on them. And if torture had been on his mind, he'd have been better served carrying her to a different location and taking his time doing it.

Unless he knew Ethan would be returning, and wanted the Guardian to find her this way.

He could examine the body later, but it was best to record the scene. Michael or Lilith might recognize something about the demon—like serial killers, they often repeated their patterns.

He snapped pictures, shaking his right hand out before repositioning the camera each time. His arm was going stiff—the bullet was working itself out, passing through a muscle that was tightening him up.

Ethan was crouching for a shot of the spatter on the wall when the female's body and blood disappeared from in front of him.

Hell and damnation. He replaced the camera with his crossbow and palmed his sword in his left hand. Stepped back from the wall.

He felt the demon an instant before it spoke.

"I'm oddly impressed, Guardian. I thought Michael had whipped the killer out of all of you."

It perched on the edge of the roof, looking into the alley. Except for the membranous black wings that stretched behind him, he was in human form: a pretty-boy face, black hair and eyes—and wearing a fancy suit that Ethan reckoned had been bought for a hefty penny, instead of being made by the demon.

Ethan couldn't say he was all that surprised. "Samuels."

The demon's eyes narrowed slightly. The psychic probe it sent toward Ethan was slick and powerful, but easily blocked.

And it was nothing like the scaly psychic presence he'd felt earlier. Now *that* was unexpected, but Ethan didn't let it show, just backed up another step to give himself a better angle with the crossbow. The bolt's wooden shaft had been soaked in hellhound venom; even a small dose would paralyze a demon, and in trace quantities, it slowed them down right quick, made them easier to slay. The bolt was coated with more venom than a bullet would be—and with his arm gimped up, Ethan would need every advantage he could get.

The demon's lips curled into a smile. His teeth were human, too. "I prefer Sammael."

"I'll make a note of it. I imagine Miss Jane might like to hear the truth of it, as well."

Well, now, that was interesting: mention of Jane got the demon's eyes flaring, though his smile just widened. "You're favoring your right side, Guardian. I wonder if you could even pull that trigger before I take your head."

"I reckon you might get a bit closer than normal, but whether I kill you where you are now or up at the end of my nose don't matter much to me." He paused as something changed in the demon's psychic scent—an instant of recognition and anger—and then it was gone. Ethan dug at him again, looking for a repeat of the demon's break in control. "And then I'll just fly right on over to Miss Jane's, maybe dandy myself up to look like you—"

Sammael dove at him, his sword flashing. The bolt only nicked the demon's shoulder, ripped through the sleeve of his suit. Bad aim, but Ethan was as proficient with his left hand as his right, and he blocked the demon's first blow.

Ethan smelled blood—the bolt had broken the demon's skin. Then his own blood, as Sammael's blade darted in and caught his sword arm, slicing into his wrist, through a tendon. Ethan's weapon fell.

Grinning again, the demon slithered back—but the venom must have slowed him down, because Ethan followed him quick and slammed his bleeding fist into the bastard's smiling face. Bone crunched.

Slowed . . . but Ethan didn't get a chance to do it again. Hissing, the demon leapt back and up, perching once more at the edge of the roof, blood dripping over his mouth and chin. Within a moment, the dripping had stopped, and his nose began regaining its shape. Two pistols appeared in the demon's hands, and Ethan eyed them warily. He didn't want to have to scamper off like a rabbit. But they weren't pointed at him yet, just spinning on the demon's forefingers like he was a gunslinger showing off.

"I smell Charlotte on you, Guardian. Have you put your hands on her?"

"Shucks, no," Ethan said, smiling. "Just my mouth."

He imagined if he'd said the same of Jane, he'd have a bullet in him now. But though the demon stiffened and disgust rippled through his scent, he didn't stop spinning his weapons.

"You know I will not kill Charlotte, but give her immortality."

"All well and good, if she asks for it. But I don't figure your vampires were planning to give her the opportunity to refuse."

"Perhaps not." But knowing the vampires would have broken the Rules obviously didn't displease the demon. "Perhaps I ought to ask her very nicely: 'Charlie, your worthless, pitiable, self-destructive existence sickens me. Why not donate your body to help protect my kind from those who would destroy us?'" Sammael's eyes gleamed, black and human again. "I *could* offer her a choice—and with it, a purpose; but I doubt she is capable of understanding or accepting that. And so I must use the vampires."

"Five less than you used before." Ethan's wrist had healed up, but he didn't yet reclaim his sword. He could pull in another from his cache, and Sammael might be bolder in his offense—and more careless—if he thought Ethan would depend on the ancient pistols holstered at his thighs. "Tell me: Did you leave Miss Jane home alone? I just might go calling on her."

The demon moved, but not into an attack. He stood and stared down at Ethan before saying, "I will not allow you contact with Jane."

"Considering that Charlie's with me, and Jane will very likely want to see her sister in the near future . . . well, I sure do hope you attempt to deny Jane's free will and try to stop her." Ethan didn't know what—if any—immediate consequences there were for a demon who hindered a human's free will now that the Gates to Hell were closed and Lucifer locked behind them, but he figured something must have been keeping the demons from doing it the past year.

The demon's eyes narrowed. "You have no idea what you're up against, Guardian—or who you are dealing with," he said, and his grin was sharp and wide. He launched himself up into the sky with his teeth gleaming.

Well now, *that* had finally been a response that Ethan could have predicted. Demons were masters of spouting lines that could have been straight from a penny dreadful.

Ethan took another look at the alley floor, hoping the demon had left something behind, but it was clean. Mighty peculiar, that Sammael assumed Ethan had killed the female vampire. If Sammael was associated with the other demon, was communication at Legion breaking down? And if Sammael hadn't known of the other demon, was it one of Lucifer's demons coming in to give trouble to Belial's?

Odd to think that demons had loyalties, but the civil war in Hell had been raging for almost a millennium; it might be that—even with the Gates closed—Lucifer's and Belial's followers continued their struggles against one another.

But Ethan wasn't going to figure it out standing here. A look at the sky told him dawn was coming in less than two hours—and he wouldn't be able to speak with Savitri Murray once the sun rose.

His phone was dead, but a mental search through Charlie's things confirmed that hers was in the big embroidered bag that she carried around.

He ought to have left more of her belongings with her—a single lamp wouldn't bring much comfort while she was alone, and the terrible hurt he'd put on her wouldn't have made the empty house easier to bear.

Goddammit, he shouldn't have kissed her back. If he'd just kept his hands off her, there wouldn't have been any need to say what he had.

"Drifter?"

Even the bright sound of Savi's voice didn't lift the heavy weight in his gut—but it was joined by surprise. "How the blazes did you figure that?"

"I've recently added 'omnipotent' to my growing list of superpowers," she said. "That, and you're calling from Charlotte Newcomb's cell phone to my unregistered number—somehow I doubt that she dialed it by accident. And the security feed from inside the house went dead about forty-five minutes ago, sending up alerts all over the place, so I checked out the exterior video. Two entered, but only you left, and I know Charlotte isn't calling me from inside the house. She makes a kick-ass margarita, by the way."

"Pours a mighty fine whiskey, as well—and Charlie also noticed that your fiancé can't see how pretty he is." Vampires could see their reflections, but a curse had robbed Colin of his.

"Ah." Savi went quiet for a second. Probably considering that, chewing on her lip, her eyes wide. "Sorry," she finally said. "We weren't very careful. Most people don't pay attention, or they rationalize it away when they do."

Just as they did when they saw fangs, or a Guardian's wings. "Well, it don't matter much, since she knows more'n that now. We ran into a spot of trouble."

"I thought you might have. What do you need?"

"I've had Jake working on Samuels's data—"

"But you want me to go deeper."

"Yes."

"I'll try. Can you get me something from inside Legion? I haven't been able to worm my way in. They've got a demon Brian Dorsett working for them, or something."

Ethan had no idea what that meant, but he gleaned that she hadn't been able to hack into Legion's computer network. "I'll do what I can. It ain't a matter of waltzing on in."

"Yeah, no shit. Anything else you need?"

"There's two more I want you to look at: Mark and William Brandt."

She confirmed the spelling, then said in some surprise, "The senator? What are you looking for—anything specific?"

"Anything that don't feel right."

The sound that came through the earpiece sounded an awful lot like a little girl muffling her giggles. After a second, she said, "Sorry. There's probably going to be quite a bit that doesn't feel right—he's been in politics a long time."

Ethan smiled slightly. "They ain't all demons."

"No, just the one who's funding SI." He could almost see her lips pursing in frustration as she referred to Rael, the demon congressman who had ties to both Special Investigations and Legion—and heard her sigh as she let it go. "Okay. Is that it? Because I've got a complaint to lodge against your pupil."

"Jake?" Since Hugh Castleford had taken over the novices' training, Ethan wasn't officially Jake's mentor anymore, but everyone still went to Ethan whenever Jake pulled something stupid. "What's he done?"

"He kicked me out of the poker game tonight."

Ethan scowled. Though her shields were as good as his, Savi's expression gave away her hand every single deal. She was a terrible player . . . and rich as a nabob. And whatever the novices won from her in the occasional game she sat in on, Ethan usually cleaned out from them within a week or two. Running Savi off was the most damn fool thing he'd ever heard. Unless— "Were you counting cards?"

"Maybe." There wasn't a hint of apology in her voice. "I've dropped twenty thousand on that table in the past three months."

"And we surely do appreciate it, Miss Savi."

In the background, her partner Colin Ames-Beaumont sounded mighty amused.

"Stop laughing, you ass," she said. "Or I'll use *your* money next time." Then Ethan was the one chuckling as the vampire's laughter pulled up lame. "Anyway, Drifter . . . I heard about your brother. I wanted to say I was sorry. Is there anything Colin and I can do?"

Ethan's throat closed up. Hit from the side, and he hadn't been expecting it at all. It took him a second, but he finally managed, "I reckon not, Miss Savi." Hell and damnation, his voice was about as hoarse as Charlie's had been when she'd told him to go. He closed his eyes and pushed it away. "Aside from you telling me how to sweet-talk the computer running your house."

"Oh, god. Don't tell me you couldn't get the lights on before you left."

"All right."

Her laughter sounded again before she said, "It's on the wall panel in every room—and there's also a remote control. There's a lighting menu, and the heat is under environmental control. Your temp is less than 106 degrees, so you won't be electrocuted when you adjust the settings. And I wouldn't move any of the paintings downstairs, although the ones upstairs are okay." The humor suddenly dropped from her tone.

"Drifter—if Charlotte saw Colin, knew what he was . . . did you get a chance to explain about the portraits?"

"The port—?" His teeth snapped together, and he sucked in a sharp whistling breath between them. Son of a goddamn bitch.

He was in the air less than a second later.

CHAPTER 8

She'd gone in search of a bathroom, but found a puzzle instead. In the master bedroom, silvery moonlight illuminated a life-sized painting of the gorgeous blond vampire.

Charlie shivered inside her coat, her heart thumped madly in her chest, and her instincts screamed at her to run—but she stayed and tried to figure it out.

Because the woman he'd come into Cole's with was pictured there, too, and the expression on his face wasn't anything like a vampire's should have been. Not cruel or cold—there was something so tender in his eyes, in his smile, that it made Charlie's heart ache just to see it, made her feel like an intruder on a moment that was beautiful . . . and private.

And they were standing in the midst of what must have been Heaven.

It was depicted on other canvases, too—in bright blues and whites, columns and temples of marble, so huge and perfect and impossibly lovely that it made her dizzy to look at them for too long.

She unsteadily made her way downstairs to the living room, sat in the corner of a sofa and drew her legs up. The lake sparkled and the trees swayed, and slowly it came together.

Ethan had moved in not long after the vampire couple had spoken with her at the bar, asking about her family. Ethan, who didn't have anything in his apartment—he obviously didn't live there. So she had been paranoid, but someone had been watching her . . . or watching *over* her.

But why? How had he known she'd be attacked? She couldn't think it had been random. The first time, maybe—but the second? And they'd known her name.

She closed her eyes, ran it all through her mind in a quick, erratic rhythm, waiting for it to settle into a tempo that she could follow.

Vampires who'd wanted to hurt her. A demon. Ethan, and his wings. Blood all over her hands, his face—but there were some vampires he didn't kill, and apparently trusted. Vampires who'd asked so many questions about her family.

Vampires. Ethan. *Blood.* Her family.

Blood. Her sister.

The click of the door shot through the silence of the house. Her eyes flew open; Ethan already stood in front of her, his hat and wings gone, his face tight and his gaze wary on hers.

"It's about Jane, isn't it?" Her voice was loud—not to her ears, but from the inside, like she was speaking underwater or holding her ear to check her key.

His taut skin twitched a little around his eyebrows, his mouth. "Yes."

She slid off the sofa; her legs were solid beneath her now. "Is she safe? Can we go get her?"

Ethan hesitated, then said, "She's safe. There's a shield around her house, too."

"Someone's been watching her? Like you—oh, my God. Dylan." Charlie's relief didn't last; her eyes widened and she laughed a hard, sour note. And to think she'd liked Dylan— liked how friendly and smart and fun he was, and how much he adored Jane. And Jane was crazy in love with him; if everything had been a lie, this would kill her. "I *knew* he was too fucking perfect. So he's an angel like you, and in order to get close to her he—"

"No. That's not how it is, Charlie. He's not a Guardian."

Ethan stood still as she stalked toward him. "That's not how it is at all."

"No?" She pushed against his chest. The muscle under the heel of her hand might has well have been stone, and Ethan a mountain.

"No." His response was as firm as the rest of him.

Firm enough that she believed it.

"Well . . . well, fuck." Her fists were curled. She'd wanted to get up in his face and scream at him, but now she just felt out of control. She shoved her hands into her coat pockets. "Then how is it? Do they want Jane to cure them?"

"I don't rightly know what they want from her, but I don't reckon it's a cure, because there isn't one." His voice deepened with something that sounded like weariness. "But it wouldn't surprise me if the demons were telling them something of the sort, making promises so that the vampires fall in line with their plans."

"What plans?"

"Hell if I know, Charlie." He lifted his hand like he meant to rub it over his face, to make action match his tone, but he winced and let it drop back to his side. "Are you mad enough to cut me open?"

"I'd rather punch you, actually." No, not really. Just punch *something*. Ethan was simply a convenient target. "I don't understand why Jane and I got pulled into this. Whatever *this* is."

Ethan nodded. "I owe you some explaining." He seemed to smile at her snort of agreement, though his lips didn't move. But she saw it at the corners of his eyes, the slight lift of his brows. "And I'd be much obliged if you'd help me out while I'm doing it. How strong is your stomach?"

Blinking quickly didn't make his question make any more sense. "What?"

"The bullet's giving me some trouble, and it's coming out too slow. I can't protect you like I should if my arm don't function when I need it. But if the bullet's out, it'll heal up quick and clean."

It took her two more blinks. "You want me to get the bullet out of your back?"

"I reckon it'll hurt like a son of a bitch if I go in through the front," he drawled, and she closed her eyes, pressed her lips together. "Now, Charlie, don't you start laughing and lose your mad, because if you're angry it'll be easier to use a knife on me. Though I must be all kinds of a fool, hoping you're riled up before I give it to you." He paused, and the drawl slipped away. "But only if you feel up to it, Charlie."

That was the voice she'd heard from him the night on the roof. Still slow and long, as smooth and warm as a sip of scotch, but without an exaggerated flavor to it. "You'll tell me who you are? What you are?"

"Yes. But we'd best do this in the kitchen."

Charlie looked down at the pale rug, realized that they were moving to avoid staining it with blood, and wasn't sure if she *was* up to it. But Ethan was already walking that way, so she hurried after him. He stopped just inside the kitchen, in front of a security panel. Light flooded the room.

And maybe her stomach wasn't all that strong, because it began roiling when he laid a knife on the butcher-block island top and pulled a ladder-back chair in from the breakfast nook. He straddled it, crossing his forearms on the backrest.

She took a deep breath, stepped up behind him. The hole in his coat centered above his right shoulder blade. Charlie gingerly touched the skin showing through the tear. "Right here?"

"Yes." His muscles shifted under her finger, and she looked up to see him tilting a black felt-tip pen her direction. "Mark it, so you won't have to cut more'n once or twice." He turned his head in profile to her, his brows drawing together. "That hole pisses me off more than getting shot, Charlie. I don't have a talent for creating my own clothes, particularly something that fits me this well. You got that marked?"

"Yes." She couldn't say anything else. His jacket, suspenders, and shirt disappeared, leaving his broad shoulders naked and exposing tanned skin over long, rangy muscles. Her fingers itched to run the length of his back, from the short thick hair at his nape to the tight ridges of flesh hugging his spine and narrowing down to his waistband.

But she didn't want to touch him like *this*.

The knife gleamed wickedly on the countertop.

"Forgive my blushes, Miss Charlie. I'm so awfully modest and bashful." He grinned and rested his chin against the top of his shoulder, watching her sidelong. "And you'll have to pardon any groaning I do. It's not becoming for a man to cry, so we groan real loud instead."

"I know you're trying to make it better, Ethan, but you're just freaking me out. Do you want a drink or something first?" She could make a drink, that would be nice and comfortable—

"I doubt Colin and Savi keep any around—liquor doesn't do anything for me, in any case. Nor would medicine or painkillers. I'll talk myself through it."

And her, too, she hoped. "How deep is it?"

He rolled his shoulders, grimaced. "About two or three inches. Just dig in there until you hit lead and then use the tip of the blade to wiggle it on out."

Oh, Jesus. "That doesn't sound like a good plan."

"It's likely not, but—" He sat up straight, and his jacket was suddenly in his hands. He lifted the sleeve up from the rest of the bundle; from the wrist to the elbow, it was dark with blood. "That's mine, Charlie. Nearly lost my hand to a demon. Now, I can reattach it, or wait until I return to Caelum and get a Healer to fix me up, or eventually grow another one—but next time it might be my head, and I can't put that back on. And *next time* might be the moment I let the shield down around the house, because there's no way for me to know if a demon's waiting for us when the spell is up."

Demons, spells, being constantly prepared to defend himself . . . Charlie could barely imagine life at that level or think in those terms.

But she had to now, didn't she?

"All right. All right." She shrugged out of her coat, tossed it onto the island. The ivory-handled knife was as cold as her fingers, and gooseflesh crawled over her body—but Ethan's skin was smooth, as if he didn't feel the chill in the air. "Do we need to sterilize this?"

"No. Just quick and deep, Charlie. And soon, before I turn yellow and embarrass myself."

"Just hold on a second, Ethan. Jesus." She thought his lips twitched before he turned, facing straight ahead. "I need a towel. Or five. You've got some of—"

A rainbow of her neatly folded hand towels appeared on the island.

"My tweezers, too."

After a second, Ethan said, "They in something?"

"A brown makeup bag. It's got a fleur-de-lis design all over the outside. Yeah, that one." God. *Just wiggle the bullet on out, Charlie.* He was crazy. She wiped off the tips of the tweezers and laid them next to the towels. "Are you ready? You'd better start talking. You said you're a Guardian—what does that mean?"

"You ever play DemonSlayer?"

"The video game? No." She held the blade over the black circle she'd made on his skin. Just stabbing wouldn't let her work in there; she needed an incision.

"Good, because it's mostly bull*holy fucking whoreson*—!" His jaw clamped together and he dropped his forehead to his arms; his knee lifted and he slammed his boot against the floor.

Charlie felt the vibration in her feet, and she stared in shock at the deep wound she'd made, the blood pouring from it. She'd convinced herself it wouldn't really hurt him. For God's sake, he'd been *shot* and she hadn't heard him complain about the pain, just the inconvenience. "Ethan—"

His voice was muffled against his arms. "Get in there, Charlie, or it'll close up and you'll have to do it again."

He was right; it had bled hard the first second, but it was already slowing. She grabbed a towel and her tweezers. "Guardians?" she prompted.

"Yes." He hissed when she probed the incision, and she thought she heard wood splinter. "You've heard about Lucifer and his rebellion in Heaven?"

"I think so." She couldn't see anything inside the wound, and looking at it was just making her sick; she closed her eyes and gently felt around for the bullet. She'd forgotten what a distinctive odor blood had. "Lucifer and his followers were turned into demons and thrown into Hell—but Lucifer decided to trick humans into wearing clothes instead of leaves, so he turned into a snake and made Eve eat the apple and then humans were eternally screwed."

His back shook under her hand, like he was holding in laughter. "I don't know if the snake and the apple is true—but the demons did begin tempting humans, and angels remained on Earth to stop them. Except it wasn't long before humans started thinking the angels were gods, and the demons got almighty jealous." He sucked in a long breath. "You'll have to open it up again. Deep as you can. Poke around in there, Charlie. You don't need to be gentle, because it'll only hurt for a second—I can hardly feel the cut you made now. And you aren't doing any damage."

"Okay." Charlie wiped the blood from her hands, the tweezers, then his back—cleaning the work space. "It's all over your pants."

"I'd take them off and sit here in my skivvies, but—*sonofabitch.*" He gripped his knees, the muscles and tendons in his hands and arms standing in sharp relief. *"But I ain't wearing any."*

He'd probably meant that to be teasing, instead of sounding like it had been ground between two jagged stones.

"Sorry," she murmured, and swiftly got the tweezers going. When the steely tension in his back eased, she said, "So the demons were jealous?"

"Enough to wage another war against the angels. Only this time Lucifer had creatures from Chaos, a dragon and demon dogs and such, and they just about slaughtered the seraphim—that's the angels—until humans began fighting with them. I felt it there, Charlie."

"Yeah, I found it." She bit her lip and held her breath as she carefully dragged the tweezers against the bullet, searching for the edge. "So the demons started killing people, too?" She made a frustrated noise in the back of her throat. "It's slippery."

"You'll get it." Her probing must have been hurting him; his thumbs were working circles on his thighs, though the rest of him was still. "Demons can't kill humans—it's against the Rules. No killing or hurting them, no denying them free will."

"Why?"

"Used to be, they got dragged back to Hell by Lucifer, then Punished or destroyed."

"Used to be?"

"The Gates are closed now. But that's another story, Charlie, and not nearly so old. This one, the men who joined in the battle turned the victory back the angels' way."

"How?"

"One of them—Michael—killed the dragon."

"Got it," she breathed, and slowly began to draw the bullet out. She lost it, and fished back in, trying to work under it instead of squeezing this time. "Damn. It's going to take a second, though. And then what?"

"And then the angels gave Caelum—their home—to Michael, gave him a Guardians' powers, and left him to recruit others."

"When did all of this— Oh, shit, here it is."

The slug landed with a plop in her cupped hand, and she held it over his shoulder, grinning.

Ethan whistled low and picked up the mushroomed bullet between his thumb and forefinger. "A forty-four hollow-point—unfortunately, only the light cartridge behind it. If they'd used a Magnum round, it'd likely have punched right on through, made it all a bit easier for me." The slug vanished, and he slanted a glance up at her. "Thank you kindly, Miss Charlie."

The darkness of his lashes only made the impact of his amber eyes more intense, knocking the wind out of her. She swallowed, forced a reply. "Sure thing. Just give me another minute, and I'll get you cleaned up."

Herself, too. Blood covered her fingers, pooled in her palm. She didn't want to look down and see how much was on her shoes and pants.

"It ain't necessary, Charlie. I can . . ." The rest of it was lost beneath the sound of the faucet, and by the time she'd soaked a towel with warm water and lathered soap into it, he'd apparently decided to let her help.

His elbows were resting on the seat back, his posture easy, his booted feet flat against the floor. He tensed beneath the first swipe of the towel over his skin. His right boot slid back a couple of inches, his heel lifting, and she paused, remembering how he'd reacted on the first cut. But the incision had healed; only a four-inch pink line remained against his tan, and that was fading quickly.

The triumphant haze of getting through the operation without fainting was fading, too.

"That didn't hurt, did it?" It wasn't really a question. And now she recalled how he'd vanished the blood from her hands in the booth.

"Not a bit. I suspect there's more hurting to come, though."

She wasn't so slow that she couldn't interpret *that*. "Yet you're still sitting here," she said, and wiped another section of skin clean. Efficiently, though she was tempted to take her time, to make that hurt just a little worse—maybe even bad enough he'd want to relieve it.

"Well, Charlie, I just ain't man enough to walk away when a pretty woman offers a warm bath."

A dark emotion grabbed at her throat. She'd been pretty enough to kiss, too. And apparently pretty enough to get his dick hard, but she'd bet that if she walked around the chair and took any of that for herself, he'd push her away and tell her it was for her own good.

She let the towel drop to the floor. "But I don't think I'm woman enough to keep nurturing a man who doesn't need it."

She backed up to the island, lifted herself up onto the wooden surface, and kept her hands clenched on the edge of the counter. Her fingers were screaming to do something, and she'd have done just about anything for a cigarette—anything but ask Ethan for one.

Even something as innocent as asking for her knitting seemed too much a giveaway of her hurt, so she just squeezed the wood instead.

Ethan's gaze lifted from her hands to her face. "Charlie—"

"So you can fly, and you heal fast," she interrupted, because she sure as hell didn't want to talk about anything else. Didn't want to hear him say again that she was needy, or to think about how easily he saw into her.

Didn't want to think about how simply knowing that she'd aroused him had created an ache that centered much lower— and was much warmer—than the one in her throat.

She was good at wanting things that she shouldn't . . . and equally good at denying herself them.

Ethan watched her carefully as he stood. A blue cotton shirt appeared in his hands. "Yes. I can run quick enough a human can't see it, lift a city bus if it needs to be lifted."

A thin scar bisected his navel horizontally, rippled across the left side of his abdomen. She swung her legs out so that she had something to stare at besides his stomach. Her shoes were spotless; so were her pants. Considering how much blood had spilled, and how close she'd been to him, that was impossible. "And you make stuff disappear."

"If I can get my head around it, I can store it. Blood doesn't feel good, though." He slid into his shirt, frowned at the length of the sleeves. He met her eyes again as he rolled up the cuffs. "If I have the opportunity, I choose to clean it off in the normal way."

She didn't know if that was an apology or an explanation, or just an excuse—but it helped that he offered one. "Do you drink blood?"

"No. Don't eat, don't drink, don't sleep."

"That must be nice," she said.

"What's that?"

"Not to need anything. Then it wouldn't hurt so much when you didn't have it." Or when you had to give it up.

His lips tightened. "Well, the lack of sleep is more difficult than the others. Close your eyes, Charlie—I'm about to make new britches, and I don't always get it right the first time."

She did, but an image of his body appeared behind her eyes anyway. "Where'd you get that other scar?" Not as a Guardian—he'd said the one on his lip was from when he was human.

"Which?"

How many did he have? "Here." She lifted the hem of her shirt a couple of inches and ran her finger in a quick line over her stomach.

She heard him swear lightly and fabric rip before he said, "A saloon in Cheyenne. I'd tracked . . . hell if I remember his name, but he'd swindled a nice bundle out of some society matron in New York. A little dude, and I never expected he'd pull a— Now, Charlie, what about that is so almighty funny?"

It took her a second to stop laughing, but she finally managed, "Dude?"

His voice suggested that he was smiling again. "Ah, well, a 'dude' back in my day was a fancy man who had no business being out west. And I'm decent now."

Indigo denim jeans—not formfitting, but falling straight from his hips, like the old-fashioned Levi's she'd seen miners wearing in pictures. His suspenders looped the length of his thighs, and Ethan had his head bent, working a metal button on his waistband through the end of the leather strap. His shirt was still unfastened, exposing a wide swath of skin. Dark hair roughened his chest, arrowed down the center of his stomach.

Nothing about that visual was decent; it embodied some

kinky fantasy Charlie hadn't even known she'd had. She picked up her makeup bag, began digging through it to distract herself.

"You tracked him—you were a cop?" Old Matthew hadn't been wrong, after all.

He shook his head. "I was employed by a detective agency."

"Like . . . like . . ." Dammit. "It starts with 'P.' "

"Pinkerton's?" He glanced up from his buttons, and she nodded. "Similar to it, yes. I worked with Pinkerton's for a spell, but they mostly wanted thugs to hassle unionizing workers. So I moved on to a smaller agency where I could be put to better use."

She leaned to the side and turned on the faucet in the middle of the island, rinsing her tweezers. "You're big enough to be useful as a thug."

"But I'm more useful thinking like a thief and murderer." His eyes narrowed. "What's it with you and letters? 'Starts with "P." ' "

"I remember the sound I associate with the thing easier than I do the actual word or name." She kept her focus on her hands as she dried the tweezers and replaced them in the makeup bag. Hopefully, the threat of a unibrow would overpower the memory of where they'd been. "They teach you that in conservatory—mnemonic devices so that you don't forget the lyrics, or where to come in. Except words don't pull so easily for me. Not unless you set them to music." She pursed her lips, finally glanced up at him, and was glad he wasn't staring at her throat. "I can't spell, either."

"Hell, Charlie, 'reckon' and 'ain't' trip off my tongue like I was born saying them, but the truth is, my ma would have whupped me something fierce if she'd ever heard me speak like this." He smiled when she laughed, and it softened his face, as if mention of his mother had struck a sweet memory. His fingers began working up his shirtfront. "But it served me well to start, and I don't figure I'll stop anytime soon. My ma ain't going to protest, at any rate—and I can sum up my human life by saying that I was born on Beacon Hill in 1854, where I learned to talk a certain way, but by the time I died thirty-two years later in a no-account Arizona town, I had speaking habits that would make my parents roll in their graves."

That didn't add up to as little as he claimed, but though she was curious, Charlie let it go. She didn't like to talk about the details of her life, either. And when she did, she just twisted them up into barely believable stories.

Ethan had already heard several of them.

She waited a beat, then said, "There's a painting up in one of the bedrooms."

His hands stilled in the middle of tucking in his shirt, and then he finished it and slowly drew his suspenders up. "I figured you'd seen the one in the living room. Savi at the poker table with the novices—and me."

Charlie slid off the island. "I missed that one." Of course, by the time she'd come back downstairs she hadn't been seeing much at all.

She heard the pad of his feet as he followed after her; in the hallway, it changed to the tread of boots. "I'd have told you, Charlie, but—"

"I wouldn't have believed you."

She looked over her shoulder in time to see the quirk of his lips. "For that reason, too," he said. "But mostly we don't tell anyone unless it's necessary. And I'd hoped we'd clear all of this up without it ever coming to the point where I had to tell you."

"But you'll show Jane and Dylan what you are tomorrow—in case they need evidence?"

The painting was huge, but in shadow—her lamp was across the room, and one of the wooden posts that divided the living areas blocked the light. Charlie stopped in front of it, and realized that Ethan hadn't yet responded.

She looked around for him, saw him at the wall panel. She had to blink at the sudden illumination; his features were grim as he made his way to her side.

"You do plan on telling them?" If he didn't, Charlie would. She just didn't know if she could convince them.

"We'll show Jane," he finally said. "In the morning I'll drive us on over, and we'll talk to her."

"Okay." The tension drained from her. "Drive in what?"

"I've got that truck stored away. Haven't used it in a decade or so, but it should run." It took her a second to realize he meant *stored* in that place he vanished things to, not somewhere in the city—but before she could wrap her head around the concept of it, he began to point out the participants in the painting. "You've seen Savi. Jake's to her left—you'll meet him tomorrow—and Becca, Mackenzie, Pim, and Randall on the other side."

Ethan was depicted at the far left, leaning back in his chair, his long legs in an easy sprawl and his thumbs hooked into his suspenders just above his waist. Though his expression didn't show it, everything about his posture suggested that he was heartily enjoying himself.

She made herself study the others. The small, dark woman from Cole's had been caught in a laughing pose, and her fangs gleamed. No one else had his mouth open, though a couple were smiling. There weren't any drinks on the table—or any snacks. "Are they all vampires?"

"Just Savi and Mackenzie. The others are novices—Guardians in their first hundred years of training. Used to be, they were taught in Caelum, but now a human man is overseeing their training so we've moved the novices to San Francisco. This is only a handful, though."

"You're training vampires, too?" Charlie glanced at the woman's fangs again and barely repressed her shudder.

"Yes. They're not all as bad as those who came at you, Charlie. Mostly, they live in the cities, forming communities and working like the rest of the folk. They were once human—and just like humans, some are worth knowing, and some you just want to acquaint with the end of your sword."

"But they drink blood."

"They do, but from one another—and not from humans, unless they intend to transform them. Communities have strict rules against that."

"Not the Seattle community, apparently." She turned away from the canvas.

Ethan was still looking at the painting, nodding slightly, a frown creasing his brow. It smoothed away when he glanced down at her. "For the most part, they do. But the remainder is why I'm here. The demons are mucking the community up; I intend to set it straight again."

And . . . what? Everything would go back to normal? "I hope you do," she admitted. "I don't think I want one sucking on my neck."

His grin was sudden. "To be truthful, Charlie, though there

are several vampires that I consider friends, I'm not all that eager to have them sucking on me, either."

Cold lips, pointed teeth, blood . . . this time she couldn't halt her shiver. "I can imagine it doesn't feel very good."

"No, I reckon not." His humor vanished as quickly as it had arisen. "You ought to take a few hours of sleep. I'll be waiting for Jake, but we'll head out to Jane's first thing after he arrives. It's best that you're sharp."

The last thing she felt like was sleeping, but time alone to process everything would be welcome. Time alone . . . in a room filled with paintings of Heaven. "Is it okay if I take the big bedroom?"

"Don't matter none to me." His long legs ate up the distance to the stairs, and she followed slowly. The suspenders formed a large Y on his back. "I'll put your things in there."

"Can you remove the painting of . . ." What had their names been? "Colin and Savi? I don't feel comfortable with it."

Ethan paused in the doorway to the bedroom, and the portrait vanished from the wall. "A bit naked, aren't they?" he said quietly before entering the room.

"Yes." He didn't mean unclothed—both had been dressed. "A little too personal. What did you call that place? It's real?" She nodded to one of the other paintings.

"Caelum." The corner of his mouth tilted up, and his voice was gently teasing. "It's real—and it's Latin, so it starts with 'C,' not 'K.' "

She leaned her shoulder against the door frame, dipping her chin to laugh. And although she usually felt uncomfortable when anyone but Jane ribbed her about that quirk, this time the embarrassment didn't come.

Her laughter ended on a sigh when she caught sight of another painting, a different angle. "And you've been there?"

"For a hundred years I lived there, and since then I drop by about once a day. Sometimes less, but at least once a week." He fell into silence, and when she glanced at him, she found him watching her face. He seemed to straighten up, and said abruptly, "Where would you like your things? What do you need for the night?"

The room didn't have much furniture—just a bed and a wardrobe. "How about my dresser over in that corner, and then dump the junk from my bathroom on the bed, and I'll put it up. My iPod, too." She paused. "My computer doesn't work if the spell's up?"

He shook his head. "It works, but won't have online access."

"So I can't even send her an e-mail until tomorrow—okay, then, I won't need it." She ran her fingers down the buttons of her coat, trying to think of anything else she would use. Her gaze ran to the en suite bathroom.

Oh, Lord.

Her cheeks flooded with heat. "Do you have super-hearing, too?"

"Yes." Ethan turned from the wall panel; she heard the soft sound of electric air heaters blowing to life. His brows drew together when he saw her expression. "Ah, hell, Charlie—I don't listen."

"But from your apartment you could hear . . . what?"

"Most everything in that building. If I listen close enough now, I can hear you digest your food. But I tune it out—it's just life, and I can't listen to all of it. Most of it I don't want to hear, anyway."

She stared at him, and despite his assurance, her mortification only deepened. For two months he'd lived next to her. And not just the *living*—she hadn't had any men over in a long time, but she took care of herself. Had plenty of fantasies, and a few had included a faceless Ethan making his way over the wall. Had she ever said his name aloud?

His hands were jammed deep in his pockets. "I swear that whenever you did anything intimate that I couldn't tune out, I left."

Oh, thank God. Relief swept through her, but his eyes closed and his jaw firmed.

"Don't look at me grateful, Charlie. A man can only take so much before he thinks about unlocking a door that isn't his to open."

She would have probably let him in. Even now, with that big bed behind him, she was thinking that she'd like to lose herself in that: the slide of skin, the intoxication that passion could bring. It would be that hot between them, that good, that numbing—their kiss had been evidence of it. His mouth would be all over her, and he'd be gentle, fucking her sweet and slow, until he lost control and then it would be deep and hard. He was so big, so strong, the craving in him just beneath the surface. But if he let it out, let it take over him, take *her*, she could just float along with it.

It wouldn't make a difference, though: the sun would rise, he still wouldn't want to want her, and they'd have to go convince Jane that vampires existed and were crawling the night.

She sighed. No, it wouldn't all go away—but she would have loved for him to take her there for an hour or two.

"Charlie—" His voice was strained. His fists drew the denim tight across his groin. *Oh . . . Lord.* Her gaze flew to his face, to his eyes—so intense they seemed to be glowing. His throat worked before he said, "I won't unlock that door."

She didn't flinch beneath that stare or the rejection his words contained. "I don't remember asking you."

"No." Ethan rubbed at the back of his neck, his expression changing to one of chagrin. "No, that you didn't."

But he obviously wanted it, too. Was considering it. His body had reacted as if he'd been thinking the same thing she had—*oh, Jesus*.

Horror clutched at her chest. "Can you read my mind?"

"No." His hand dropped to his side. "Your emotions. Some images, if you think them hard enough."

That wasn't much better. "Can you *not* do it?"

"Most times. You project a bit, but I won't look unless it's necessary." Ethan moved toward her, and his focus shifted to the right. "You can also use these, Charlie. The spell will close off this room, give you time alone when you need it."

She turned. His long fingers were tracing the symbols on the door frame. He was so close she could feel the warmth of him.

"We'll key it with my blood, however, so I'll be able to come in if I need to." He met her eyes. "But I won't, unless there's trouble."

This time, his words didn't feel like a rejection—just reassurance that he wouldn't invade her privacy. "All right." She shifted her weight, glanced around the room again. "I guess that's it, then."

"I reckon so." The drops of his blood glistened crimson against the pale yellow paint. "You need anything, you come and get me."

"I will."

He nodded once. The crooked smile tilted his lips. "Good night, Miss Charlie."

Good night, Ethan. The familiar response poised on her tongue, but the weight of the evening held it there.

Nothing was the same. Nothing would ever be the same again, and she couldn't be dependent on what used to be.

She crossed her arms over her chest, hugged herself tight. "Good night, Drifter."

CHAPTER 9

He'd built a right solid wall between them again. Ethan spent the next couple of hours thumbing through *Billy Budd*, but he had read it almost to pieces in the eighty years since Castleford had brought the novella to Caelum, and he didn't look at the words so much as contemplate all of the reasons he shouldn't tear the wall down.

That he couldn't come up with many was likely an indication of how fuzzy he was getting.

Dawn had come and the sun lifting well into the sky when he broke the spell around the house. He breathed slow and long until the flood of sounds and psyches faded to a hum.

Charlie still hadn't come down when the click of heels on the deck outside told him Jake had gotten a ride. Ethan went on out, leaving the French doors open behind him; Selah leaned against the railing overlooking the lake, the breeze blowing her pale blond hair around her shoulders. Jake had his hands linked behind his head, whirling in a circle and looking mighty pleased with himself.

"This your doing?" Ethan said as Selah turned to face him and set her elbows against the rail.

"I told him the teleportation would make him dizzy. It didn't, so I believe he's celebrating by trying to get there himself." Her bright green skirt fluttered around her slim legs. A Guardian for two and a half centuries, Selah had assisted Castleford in mentoring Ethan—and lately she'd taken to dressing like a fashion plate. "Or maybe he's celebrating because Lilith had him convinced that Colin's house was on an isolated pig farm outside of Puyallup. Are you well, Drifter?"

"Ain't got nothing to complain about." But her blue eyes were too direct, and she'd known him too long. Hoping to distract her, he quickly asked, "And you and yours?"

She'd recently taken up with a vampire, but as much as Ethan wanted to direct her attention from himself, he hoped she wouldn't dwell on it. Women in love were apt to go on and on about their partners, and though Ethan liked her vampire well enough, he could get along just fine without hearing about how Marsden was so almighty considerate or his eyelashes or whatever it was that had captured Selah's fancy.

"Good. We're both good." Selah paused in a delicate way, and Ethan's stomach wound up tight. "I heard about your brother. Do you need—"

Ethan reached out, caught Jake by his collar mid-spin. "You take out an ad?"

Jake's grin was only slightly apologetic. "I *might* have said something at the poker game last night when Becca asked where you were."

"Novices these days, I swear," Selah said dryly.

Ethan let him go, frowning, but couldn't work up a good talking-to. Jake was sixty years old, but Ethan figured his personality had been fixed at twenty. Or at twelve, on even-numbered days.

And Selah was delicately quiet again, running her fingers along her beaded necklace. "Drifter, are you certain you don't need anything?"

From the house came the sound of a door opening, Charlie's breath and heartbeat. Maybe they wouldn't note that Ethan's sped up a bit.

"Some kind of breakfast for Charlie wouldn't be out of order," he said. "Anywhere you teleport downtown, chances are you'll land in a coffee shop. And I'd be much obliged if you'd make me up a new jacket."

Selah did instantly, tossing the long coat toward him.

Ethan vanished it, and he added, "I've also got pictures I'll be sending Lilith, but if you run into Michael, tell him to have a look, too. I found something I wasn't expecting, but I'll outline the details in an e-mail." If any demon was near enough to listen, he wouldn't hear what Ethan had to say about the one who'd killed the female vampire.

Selah nodded, a line of concern appearing between her brows, and then her gaze shifted behind him. Jake inhaled audibly, then released it with a soft sound of masculine appreciation.

Guardians just don't smell that good, Jake gestured with one hand when Ethan pinned a hard stare on him.

They didn't—Guardians didn't have much odor at all. But if Jake was still suffering from Enthrallment, too much scent could twist him up. *Don't you go sniffing and lose your head,* Ethan signed back.

Charlie might have been pleased to know that her psychic shields were tight when she came outside. Ethan wouldn't have had much trouble getting through, but awareness—and wariness—had lent them some strength. An unconscious reaction, but with time and practice she could deliberately raise and lower them.

She sure as hell didn't need any practice concealing her expression, however. Though she must have been feeling something in addition to the friendly curiosity that she showed, Ethan couldn't find a hint of anything more.

Except that she was cold. She pulled the sleeves of her thin hooded sweatshirt down over her hands after Ethan performed the introductions. He glanced at Selah, and another—smaller—jacket came flying his way.

"It'll disappear in a couple of hours," he said as Charlie slung it around her shoulders and pulled her mass of wheat gold hair from beneath the collar. "Unless you're a Guardian, they don't stay long."

She opened her mouth, then closed it and shook her head with a small smile. "All right."

Disappointment slipped through him. He'd have bet anything that she'd been set to make up a story about vanishing clothes, but she must not be feeling comfortable enough to tell it. "You hungry?"

At Charlie's nod, Selah asked, "How do you take your coffee?" and Charlie recited a list of preparation details and flavorings that had Ethan wondering if he'd been deprived as a human, drinking coffee so bitter that even fine white sugar couldn't sweeten it, instead of something that sounded like dessert.

Selah teleported an instant after Charlie finished.

"Ah," she said, blinking quickly.

"You all right?"

"Just . . . surprised." Her dark gaze moved to Jake, who'd taken a seat at the deck's dining table, then to Ethan. "I think I'm going to sit, too. Why didn't you do that last night?"

"I can't teleport. It's her Gift. Some Guardians are Healers; others teleport or talk to spiders or play with metal. Other abilities, too, mostly depending on what they did when they were human." Ethan scooted Charlie's seat out, then tucked it under her before taking the adjacent chair. Fortunately, it wasn't one of those tiny café sets, and he could sit without rapping his knees beneath the table every time he breathed.

"What can you do?" she asked when he was settled. In the daylight, Charlie's brown eyes were a bit more hazel, the sun bringing out the green. Her loose tumble of curls looked as if she'd just lifted her head from her pillow, but he knew she usually spent a good fifteen minutes styling her hair just so.

Ethan figured it might take him about thirty seconds of hard loving to get it to the same state.

He cleared the roughness from his throat. "I fiddle with locks."

Jake snorted. "He's being modest. He does a lot more than fiddle. Which reminds me . . ." A large roll of blueprint paper appeared on the table. Jake leaned back and grinned. "I got the schematics for Legion's security system. A custom design—but you're already familiar with most of the components."

Hell and damnation. He'd planned to lead up to this. Ethan glanced at Charlie; she lifted her gaze from the schematics to his face, and kept her eyes steady on his, but he could hear her fingers rubbing the fabric of her jacket, each stroke rough and irregular.

"What's your Gift, Jake?" she asked softly.

The novice was eyeing her uneasily. The maturity of a

twenty-year-old, but still sharp and observant. "I dunno," he said slowly. "I haven't gotten it yet."

"That's too bad. Do you have my phone, Drifter?"

His jaw clenched. He'd given her that name, knowing it would act as mortar in the wall—he hadn't expected that when she used it, it would go on so thick. "That I do. I had to make a call last night. If you're charged for it, you'll be reimbursed."

"Thanks." Though her expression didn't change, an agitated flush spread over her skin. Unlike her tone and her features, she couldn't control that—and Ethan was glad of it, glad of any indication of her emotional state. She picked up the phone from the table. "Is there anything I shouldn't say? Something that I don't know yet about *my sister*, or that might put *my sister* in danger?"

Pissed off, for certain. "Just see if she's home. And if not, when she will be."

"And if she's at Legion?"

Jake groaned quietly, as if he'd just realized what Ethan had yet to tell her.

Don't ever try to pass on your woman-handling skills, Jake signed.

That decided it for him. Ethan didn't figure that Charlie wanted—or needed—to be handled. After the initial shock of the vampire attack had worn off, she'd taken every blow he'd landed on her—even given him back some.

He'd rather have laid this one on a little easier, though.

"I reckon you shouldn't tell her she's working for a passel of demons," he finally said.

The flush fled her skin, left her pale. "But they can't hurt her, right? You said demons can't hurt people."

"No, but if they lock a door, it's going to be mighty difficult for her to get out. Pins and tumblers don't have to respect free will. And I can open it up, but fighting my way through is something entirely different. Nor can I force her to leave, because I'm bound by the same Rules the demons are. And they can lie real well, make her think staying there is for her protection, so she'd have no reason to go with me." He leaned forward, softened the next words. "Particularly if one demon is someone she already trusts. Loves him, even."

Ethan saw it coming. Saw it in the way she trapped her bottom lip between her teeth, as if in denial, waiting for him to continue and change the meaning. How she let it go when her brows drew tight with acceptance and worry. Heard it when the rubbing of her fingers stopped.

And when her fist came at him, he could have avoided it, but he just eased back so the impact wouldn't hurt her hand so bad—or his chin. Even seated, Charlie managed to put a mule kick of force behind it.

The long coat swirled around her when she stalked into the house. A few seconds later, he heard the faint tones of Jane's voice . . . a recording for voice mail.

So Jane was Charlie's boiling point. A threat to her sister, or someone denying Charlie information needed to protect her, and she went off violently—though she never had when the threat was personal.

Interesting that Sammael's reaction had been the same. What did that say about the demon's feelings for Jane?

"That was one hell of a jab," Jake mused. He'd gotten his toothpick out, and was grinning around it.

Ethan nodded, sucking in his bottom lip and tasting blood. She'd busted it pretty well. And he imagined that if she could, she'd be tearing Sammael apart right about now.

"One hell of a woman, too," he said quietly, and had to admit it wasn't just the fuzzy talking.

❧

Jane wasn't home.

Charlie had been praying that it was just the shield around the house that kept her calls from getting through the cell and land lines, and when she saw Jane's hybrid car at the curb, her hopes had risen. But Dylan's Lexus SUV was missing from the driveway, and Ethan confirmed a moment later that no one was inside.

"So what do we do? Wait?"

Ethan parallel parked on the other side of the street, somehow maneuvering the big truck into a car-sized spot. About two feet of bench seat separated them, but when he cut the engine and turned toward her, it seemed half that distance. "I don't see as we have much other choice. Looking for them at Legion would be like traipsing into a snake pit, and if they've taken off somewhere else for the day, there ain't no way to get ahold of her but the phone."

Charlie sighed and looked out the window again. A missing phone wouldn't make Jane suspicious; it would be just another item that she'd misplaced. "Would Dylan have taken it?"

"Yes. He must know we'd be attempting to contact her. He'll likely be screening everything possible—her e-mail, all phone calls, any letters." Ethan repositioned his legs, resting his right boot near the stick shift, stretching out his left to the accelerator. "If they return and you go up to her, ask to talk with her alone, will she go? Even if he tells her not to?"

"Yes."

"Then we'll wait."

Dammit. Charlie propped her elbow on the armrest and began chewing at her thumbnail, staring at Jane's driveway and mentally urging her sister home.

"Charlie."

She turned; Ethan was holding out a white coffee cup.

"This might be a bit more flavorful than that." He nodded toward her thumb. "Be careful with it—nothing changes in my cache, so it's as hot as when Selah brought it back an hour ago."

"That's . . . weird. But thanks." It *was* hot, and without an insulating jacket; she had to pull her sleeves down over her hands to hold it. Her knuckles ached when she curled her fingers around the cup, but his mouth didn't seem any worse for her hitting him. "Sorry about . . ." She gestured to his chin.

"I could've moved out of the way, but I figured I brought it on myself."

She mulled that over, the cup just under her lips so she could inhale the hazelnut-scented steam. "I guess you probably thought that if you'd told me last night, I'd drive myself crazy between then and this morning. Or maybe do something stupid like try to run over here before dawn and save her."

"It was the bit about fretting. Maybe not sleeping and working yourself into a bundle of nerves before coming here, so Jane might be more concerned about you than listening to what you were telling her. I never thought you'd be so foolish as to come here alone."

"Okay, then I really am sorry for punching you. I just *said* it before." His deep chuckle filled the truck cab, but it faded when she locked her eyes with his and added, "I did sleep well—longer than I thought I would, considering. But I'd rather you let me worry, next time. I know you have a job to do, keeping me from getting killed—I'm grateful for that. And I'll listen to you, because you know more about this than I do. But I'm not so emotionally fragile that I need to be protected from the truth, especially when it's about Jane. *And* it takes me a while to work through things, so the sooner I find out about them, the more thinking time I have."

Ethan looked at his hand resting along the top of the steering wheel. His jaw worked for a second before he turned back to her. "All right, Miss Charlie. If it's something that pertains to you, I'll lay it out straight."

"Thanks."

So that was settled, but Jane's driveway was still empty. Restlessness began twitching at her fingers, her legs. A rustle had her glancing across the seat—Ethan was unrolling the blueprints Jake had left on the table.

Ethan dipped the paper and looked at her over the top. "You all right if I study these for a bit?"

"Yeah." The truck had a tape cassette player. Her iPod was at the house. Jane's driveway was *still* empty. "Do you have anything else in there that keeps you busy?"

"Books—mostly westerns and adventure novels, but a few others, as well. I might have something you'll enjoy."

"I can't sit quiet enough to read right now. What else?"

"Manuals for just about every security system and lock made in the last century, a harmonica—"

"Really?" She tried to imagine that, but only got as far as thinking about his lips and tongue sliding over the mouthpiece.

He nodded, the corners of his eyes wrinkling into a smile. "All of your things, too. And some playing cards . . ." He bent the paper a little farther. "You play poker?"

She shook her head.

"That's a shame, Charlie. A damn crying shame." The blueprints vanished. "But it ain't nothing we can't fix."

❦

By half past three in the afternoon, Charlie was starving, her ass was numb, she desperately had to use the bathroom, and

Ethan had won most of her miniature unicorn collection. She'd forgotten they'd been in the back of her closet, but Ethan seemed thrilled by every porcelain figurine that accumulated on his side of the cab, examining each before adding it to his pile and claiming he hadn't seen such a fine herd of horseflesh in over a century.

And despite her worry for Jane, she couldn't remember when she'd had a better time since she'd been a kid and she and Jane had been saving all of their extra money to purchase them. Ethan was patient and teasing as he talked her through the rules of the games, just as quick with a joke as he'd been across the wall, and as slow as he'd always been when the conversation veered to other topics.

It was a combination that was potently sexy, and several times Charlie had to stop herself from simply staring—or leaping across the bench seat and having her way with him on their makeshift card table. Luckily, she could easily distract herself by asking him about being a Guardian—and, as soon as he mentioned Special Investigations, having him explain its role, as well. His job at Ramsdell had been a cover, she learned; Ethan spent most of his time traveling to different cities, tracking down demons, and slaying them. His brief accounts of several fights had her alternately laughing and horrified. And after the first few stories, she realized that he probably glossed over the worst of it.

She had one unicorn left on her lap when Ethan folded the cards together and vanished the deck. His unicorns went, too, and he looked over at the house, shaking his head. "This would have been too easy, Charlie. I'd wager anything that Sammael won't return before dark."

The anxiety that had been lurking in the back of her mind sprang forward again. She clenched her teeth and breathed deep, trying to control the frustration and fear racing through her. How could Dylan block every single method of communication? Maybe she couldn't call Jane once the spell went up, but what about— "Can we leave her a note inside so that she'll try to sneak out and call me?"

Ethan shook his head. "She wouldn't be able to sneak if a demon's in the house, Charlie. And as soon as the sun sets, I'll have you back at the lake with Jake, and the house shielded."

"Even if she can't get out tonight, she'll know that I need

to speak with her as soon as possible. So she might call as soon as she's alone in the morning."

Ethan narrowed his eyes, as if he was considering it. "If she finds a note without you there to explain it, first thing she'd do is take it to Sammael, get his opinion."

"Maybe, unless I say on the note that she shouldn't. I could leave it on her fridge, the stickies—okay, no, Dylan would see it. Or her bathroom, tucked in her birth control, because he'd never look there, and she takes it right before bed. And I really, *really* want to visit that bathroom."

He grinned, then opened his door. "I don't suppose we'd lose anything by it."

Although Charlie had a key, Ethan got her in just as quickly—without setting off the alarm or entering the code into the system. Her note filled four stickies. Ethan carefully read it through before she folded the stickies up tight, put them in the birth control compact, then stood the last little unicorn on the top of it.

Butterflies were rioting in her stomach and her hands were trembling when they got back to the truck, but the helpless feeling had passed. It wasn't much, but it had been *something*.

"I'm going to throw up," she announced as he pulled into the street, but a few blocks later she pointed out a Burgerville and ordered a cheeseburger, rings, and a shake at the drive-thru.

And then everything in her froze when Ethan's battered leather wallet appeared in his hand. She watched him pay with an old-fashioned twenty and take the grease-stained bag.

She waited until he'd driven out of the line. "Can I see that?"

He looked from her face to the wallet, and his eyes closed. "Damnation. It's not what you're thinking."

"What am I thinking?" she asked quietly.

"Hell if I know . . . that I've been lying to you about everything. That I kissed you to get that money into your hand. That I've been using my Gift for thieving. Just whatever it is, it's not how it really is."

She opened up the wallet. Most of the bills had faint ink stains. If Old Matthew hadn't pointed them out, she'd never have paid attention to them. "Then how is it? Is it stolen?"

"That it is. And after he'd been convicted, this was scheduled to be destroyed. I took it before it went into the incinerator."

"Why?"

"Because it was the most harmless way of obtaining resources—it wasn't taken from anyone, hurting their business or their life, and no one ever missed it." He frowned and glanced over at her. "Before Special Investigations, Guardians didn't have an Earth-based center of operations, but we had to work here, sometimes acting like humans—and having that human cover meant we needed money. But we don't have jobs, or inheritances, or any of the material things that we had when we were human. I got six thousand dollars of usable cash out of it, divided it between five Guardians, and I've been spending my portion for fifteen years. And I won't feel a lick of guilt for it, Charlie—except that it's upsetting you."

"No, that makes sense, I just . . ." She shook her head. "That was *you* at Cole's?"

"Yes. Mostly, I was there to watch over you."

He didn't say what the other part was, and she slowly unwrapped her burger. Even with her emotions spinning, she was hungry, and it gave her a reason to be quiet as she thought it over.

They were crossing the floating bridge over Lake Washington when she realized that she wasn't getting anywhere just thinking. "So you can change shape?"

"Not all that well," he said wryly.

Then she hadn't been crazy, thinking he'd grown while he'd been talking to her. "And you *could* rob banks, if you wanted to."

He glanced away from the road. "Well, sure I could. Getting through locks has always been my one thing—what I do best. Are you asking me to get you something, Charlie?"

She dipped her head, smiling as she took a bite of an onion ring. His gaze dropped to her mouth, and he looked forward again with a deep sigh.

"I'd be willing to do just about anything for one of those," he said. "But I promise I won't steal any from you."

She set the fast-food bag in the middle of the seat, and he reached in. "Take all you want. I shouldn't be eating them, anyway."

He finished the first one and went back for another. "Now that's just crazy talk. There ain't no one that shouldn't be eating these, even if they don't *need* to eat."

She grinned, shook her head. "No, that's just it . . . I love them. So I don't let myself eat them, because I'll overdo it." The low afternoon sun glittered like gold over the lake; water stretched out on both sides of them, the hills on Eastside rising green in front, the bridge a straight gray ribbon.

"You worried about your figure?" Ethan sounded so incredulous that a short laugh escaped her.

"Well, I like thinking that I'm someone who's strong, who looks as if she's got it together—but I guess it *is* crazy talk, because my body is just the result of me knowing how needy I am." The glare off the water was starting to hurt her eyes, so she blinked down at her cheeseburger instead. "I don't eat stuff I like—or very much of it—because I'm afraid I'll eat too much. And I go to the gym every day so that I have somewhere besides knitting to put the energy. They teach you that in Mission Creek, and some of the other rehab places—finding a hobby or outlet. I guess knitting wasn't enough."

She glanced up at his profile; his brow was furrowed, his jaw slowly moving as he ate another ring, his right hand loose on the steering wheel.

"And I like hitting stuff," she added.

"Hell, I enjoy it, too. And being the 'stuff' ain't so bad, neither." He made a show of rubbing his jaw before he added, "I've seen pictures of you singing, Charlie—you were all soft and curvy. In my day, whether you were like that or as you are now, you'd have had men lining up to court you. Women didn't obsess about this so much then."

She almost snorted strawberry milkshake through her nose. "That's such bullshit," she said, laughing. "I've seen those . . . those . . . what do you call them? They're pictures of women, and they've got the foofy hair, and the ladies are wearing dresses and corsets so tight and waists so tiny I could break them in half. But they all went by the same name, because of the guy who started it. You know, the . . ." Dammit. She couldn't even get a sound to associate. God, she *hated* this. "What were they called?"

"The Gibson Girl?"

"Yeah. You can't tell me women didn't try to look like that, too." She suddenly didn't feel like laughing much anymore, and neither was she hungry. The paper crackled around the burger as she wrapped the rest of it up. "You want this?"

His jaw was clenching, his hands tight on the wheel. "No. Goddammit, Charlie, you knew what it was. Just because you don't have the name on the tip of your tongue, it doesn't mean you're lacking brains."

"I never said I did. It just pisses me off, because I start to feel sorry for myself, and I can't stand that."

Tall firs lined the drive down to the house, shadowing the interior of the cab, but she had no trouble making out his surprise.

"I ought to go back to reading you, Charlie, because I sure as hell can't figure you out otherwise."

"It's not that hard. You know everything about me, don't you? Probably even know my shoe size."

"No, I can't say as I do know that."

"But you know about my singing, if you've seen pictures."

The house came into view below them. The drive wound down from high on the hill, and the lake spread out behind it, the city in the distance. She could fall in love with this place, far too easily.

A careful note entered his voice. "What's that to do with it?"

"Well, for example, I can play the piano—but although I'm proficient, I don't have a real talent. But my singing . . . it was *amazing*. And I studied, and practiced, and worked my ass off making it better—but compared to what I saw some of the others at Juilliard go through, it came easy to me."

The truck halted in front of the house, but Ethan didn't make a move to get out. "So it was your one thing."

"Yeah." Charlie propped her elbow up on the armrest, stared blindly out of the window. "Maybe if I'd had to work a little harder at it, I'd have been more careful about keeping it. Because it sure was nice having *something* that came easily. And not just anything, but the one thing I really, really loved, because having it made up for everything else I couldn't do. But I did this instead." She waved her fingers at her throat, then turned to frown at him. "And I'm starting to feel sorry for myself again, so—"

Two feet of bench seat was apparently nothing when a man had a reach as long as Ethan's. His hands slid around her waist and he hauled her against him so quickly that she prepared herself for an onslaught on her mouth, but the first touch of his lips was soft and searching.

That sweet heat slipped through her again, warming and melting her from the inside, leaving her skin hot and tight. He groaned, and it sounded like a denial, but then his big palm curved up from her stomach, and the light brush of his fingers over her breast was followed by a possessive stroke of his tongue past her lips.

And it imploded, the burning ache sweeping from her skin to her core. His fingers tangled in her hair. He shifted, turned until he was half-lying on top of her, never relinquishing her lips. The seat cushioned her back, but there was nothing soft about Ethan's body above hers.

She could hardly breathe, he was so heavy and he was practically fucking her mouth with each deep lick, and then blazing a hot trail of need to her womb when she returned the penetrating thrust and he caught her tongue in a suckling kiss.

Jesus. Excitement tore through her in an erotic wave, pushing her hips up, arching her back. Her fingers clenched on his waist. He was tilted awkwardly, his legs still beneath the wheel, but she pushed her foot over his thighs to grind closer, trying to kick and pull and do *anything* to have him big and hard between her legs.

A flat, loud honk split the air. Ethan jerked his head up and away from her, turning to check each of the windows.

"The horn," Charlie gasped. "I hit it."

His eyes closed and his head dropped forward. His hips rocked toward her, giving her the pressure she'd wanted so, so badly, in just the right place.

"God Almighty," he groaned as she pushed her foot against the door and rocked him again. "I just meant it to be a little kiss. But I'm so fuzzy I can't keep my hands—ah, not like that, Charlie—"

"Then how?"

His lids were heavy as he stared down at her, his fingers cupping her jaw and his thumb running across her moistened lips.

She rolled her hips beneath him. "How?"

"Not like this." His scar whitened as he pressed his jaw tight. "Not this at all."

He had to be joking. But he wasn't; he sat up and began un-tangling her legs.

Her stomach aching, she shook off his hands and scooted away. "I don't understand you, Drifter. You tell me not to want you, not to rely on you for anything but protection, that I'm too needy, and then you kiss me here and in the house and in the bar, *knowing* how much I—"

She couldn't continue. Hurt was ripening into anger and she began thinking that the knuckles of her left hand could use a good taste of his face, too.

The window beside Ethan's head shattered. *Oh, fuck fuck.* Her heart thundering, Charlie jumped for her door handle and turned to look, expecting vampires and demons and anything but the steel door crumpled around his elbow and hanging drunkenly in the frame.

Ethan was staring straight ahead, frustration in every taut line of his body, in his hard profile.

Goddamn him. It was one thing if he didn't want her, but he was breaking doors and had an erection the size of a tree. "Why don't we just fuck and get it over with? I'll bend over the tailgate, and it'll be done, and I swear I won't ask for any-thing more from you and you won't be sitting there with your dick busting through your pants."

He didn't say anything, didn't look at her. She picked up her milkshake and threw it at him. If he wouldn't acknowl-edge her then he sure as hell wasn't worth the pain of hitting.

Ethan simply plucked the cup out of the air and set it up-right on his knee without turning his head. "Now, Charlie, let me just ponder that image for a minute."

You bastard. But the words wouldn't pass the constriction in her throat. She quietly pushed open her door, certain she'd never felt so stupid and *dismissed* in her life. The air was pun-gent with the fragrance of pine needles, the fresh scent of the lake, but she couldn't breathe it in deep.

Metal screeched behind her; then Ethan stood in front of her, blocking her exit from the cab. The edges of his lips were pale. "That was a damn fool thing to say. I meant to set you laughing, and then lay it out straight. Not put a hurt on you like this."

Her fists clenched. "Are you in my head?"

"No. No, I could feel this without looking into you." He

caught her chin when her cheeks flared with heat and she'd have turned away. "I'm the one who ought to be embarrassed, Charlie. I ain't doing right by you. But bending you over the tailgate won't be doing right, either."

Oh, Lord. She'd said that? "I actually meant the . . . the . . ." She waved her hand at the front of the truck. Then the visual struck her, and she ground her teeth together before the laugh escaped.

He brushed a strand of hair from her face and seemed relieved by what he read there—his shoulders not so straight, his muscles not so rigid beneath his clothes. "I'd give anything to bend you there or just about anywhere, but I suspect the one relying on someone else and needing too much would be me."

Charlie closed her eyes, unsure if she was being slow, if he wasn't making any sense, or if she was rattled by his proximity. Their position was too intimate, the height of the seat putting them almost on eye level, his big body taking up too much space in the door. She'd been half-outside when he'd appeared in front of her—he only had to step forward and he'd be between her legs.

But he had "indirect" perfected, so she'd bet it wasn't just her. She met his gaze again and said, "This isn't laying it out straight, Drifter."

His jaw tightened for an instant, then he was shaking his head. "All right. I ain't good at storytelling, so I'll just say that what I told you at Cole's was mostly true. And that in order for a man to become a Guardian, he's got to sacrifice his life to save someone else's."

What had he told her at Cole's? Her brow furrowed, until she realized she was holding the two encounters separate in her mind.

Oh, Lord—he hadn't told her as himself, but as the older gentleman. "Your brother's life?"

He nodded, tension carving lines beside his mouth. "I figured he got out. There's no way he could have been living, so I didn't expect—" He paused and lay his forearm on the top of the door frame. His gaze searched her face. "And I'm losing you again, most likely because I can hardly think straight about it myself."

She'd seen and spoken with enough grieving customers to recognize it in him now. "It's okay. I'll catch up."

He swallowed, looked down at his boots. After a minute he said, "We'd gotten into a spot of trouble, Caleb and me. And there wasn't a way out of it—even before we rode into Eden. But the opportunity came for me to make a bargain, and for him to get out." He lifted his head. "Not just out of Eden, Charlie, but to get to California or Oregon, and start over. When the two of us were together, no one could mistake us for anyone else. But Caleb alone? He could get by. And it was a chance for him to get back to the life he should have been living. So before I took the poison, I made him promise he'd give up what we'd started. Made him swear he'd do right again, have a family." He reached up, touched his lip. "Fair had to beat the promise out of him."

Charlie's stomach was a hard knot, and she didn't understand all of what he was talking about, but she nodded.

"We had no inkling that Michael would know when someone sacrificed himself like that—and Caleb never could have known that I became a Guardian, because the sheriff had let him go before the poison killed me, before Michael showed up. So Caleb took off with that promise, and me dying in a furnace of a jail cell so he'd have another chance . . . and he went right on back to thieving. He got himself hanged a month later." His thumbs slipped in low on his suspenders, and his throat worked a couple of times. "I got the news yesterday morning."

Gingerly, Charlie ran her fingers along his left suspender until her hand rested against his. A light touch, a connection that wasn't asking or taking anything.

He seemed grateful for it, though; he turned his wrist to cup her hand in his palm. "I can't help but think that maybe my sacrifice didn't mean anything to him. Leastwise not enough to quit, to do what he'd sworn he would. So it's tore me up some, Charlie. It would feel awful good to slip into your arms, and I want you so bad I'm damn near dying for it. But I don't know that my head's on straight after the blow Caleb laid on me. And I don't know if I'd be taking what you're offering for wanting you or because I'm hurting. I just know I ain't going to use you as a salve."

Charlie understood *that* all too well. "All right," she said softly.

His fingers flexed around hers. "All right?" His brows lowered over his eyes with his frown. Had he expected her to argue, to talk him into letting her fuck his grief away?

She looked away from that piercing gaze, tilting her head so that her hair hid her expression. She didn't know exactly what she was feeling; exhaustion, sadness, grim amusement, and resignation all seemed to be playing their notes within her, but she didn't want to put on a show with any of them.

But he probably knew this about her, too, so there was really no reason not to explain. "Mine crept up on me instead of hitting me fast, but after a while, it was the same—so that if I didn't have a . . . a salve, I couldn't function, and I'd start planning my day around just getting it," she said quietly, and had to swallow before she continued. "And you tell yourself that it makes you feel good—but really, you're just getting by. Because you feel like shit with it, but you *really* feel like shit without it, so you need it to get through the day. And after a while, you're desperate to get through the day without it, but know that stopping will feel worse than going—and you don't know if you're clinging to it as much as it's clinging to you. But you're constantly looking for a way to get rid of it without hurting yourself . . . but there's no way. And eventually you hate it as much as you need it."

She tugged lightly on Ethan's suspender before meeting his direct gaze with a sincerity she hoped he couldn't mistake. "So I never, *ever* want to be anybody's salve."

CHAPTER 10

He'd figured Charlie all wrong.

Ethan watched the tight curves of her waist and hips as she trotted up the stairs, the lean length of her legs. She'd called her body the result of her dependency, but it was evidence that he'd overlooked when he'd been focusing on the inside and avoiding what he'd perceived as a weakness.

The emotional neediness was there; he hadn't been mistaken in that. But like the fool who missed the forest for the trees, he hadn't seen the whole right in front of him: Charlie knew herself so well that she'd created a layer of pure steel that was physical and emotional, keeping those tendencies contained. She'd channeled weakness into strength, and he'd wager anything that if she found herself being trapped by her need, she'd chew her arm off escaping it—knowing that the brief agony of loss was better than a slow starving death.

Had it been her lack of shields? He hadn't had to expend any effort getting in. He'd noted how well she chose which emotions she revealed, but only considered it relevant as to his need to get into her head to read her. Maybe that was why he'd missed seeing how strong she'd built the gate that led into her emotions; it had swung open so easily to admit him, he'd never imagined that she'd built an impenetrable lock on the other side.

And when she'd closed it, she'd surely gotten a part of him caught up in there.

Part of him? Hell, she'd gotten him so worked up that the slide of his breath over his tongue was like kissing air. And the memory of the sympathy in her eyes as he'd spoken of Caleb, her soft touch against his hand, was fuzzing him up, making him want to reach out for more.

Making him a right useless son of a bitch.

The security room was at the center of the house, a sleek and modern heart buried in the rustic design. Jake didn't turn from his computer when Ethan came in, but remained hunched over the keyboard, furiously typing away.

"I didn't hear a thing," Jake said.

Which, Ethan figured, was a fair indication of how much he *had* heard. Living in Caelum, surrounded by Guardians with enhanced hearing, twisted a man's conception of privacy; Jake hadn't yet reverted to a human way of thinking. "It don't matter much to me, but it does to Charlie. So you just keep on saying that, should it ever occur to her that you might have listened to anything that went on outside."

Jake straightened up, face forward. "Sir! Yes, sir."

Ethan bent low, braced his hand on the desk, and waited until Jake broke his smart-ass military pose and looked at him. "And now that you know it matters to her, I reckon that if you don't close up your ears next time, I'll have to skin you. And I'll do it real slow."

A grimace pulled the boy's face tight, and he had the sense to thread his apology through his psychic scent. "I never did like the tattoo on my ass."

With a sharp nod, Ethan said, "I don't much care for it, neither. You got anything new on Legion or Sammael—or a response on those pictures I sent Lilith?"

"Not a thing, and Lilith says that neither she nor Hugh recognize the MO. But they'll call around a few vampire communities while she's waiting for Michael to pop in."

Ethan suspected there wouldn't be much. The heads of too few communities trusted SI enough yet to give out that kind of information. And in any case, vampire remains were easy to get rid of—it only took a moment in the sun to reduce them to ash. The communities might have had similar murders taking place without anyone knowing exactly how they had occurred.

And there was no reason to have Jake hanging around waiting for something that wasn't likely to come in. "Is there anything else pressing on your time?"

"A big ugly negative on that, as well. Have you got something for me?"

"That I do. There's about an hour and a quarter until sunset—I need you with Charlie for an hour of it, or I won't be any good to her by tomorrow. You'll shield up my room, and make certain to fetch me if you have the faintest notion of trouble."

Jake's brows shot up. "You can drift here? With everything around?"

"Well, sure I can." And a good thing, too. If he'd had to wait for the sterility of Caelum to settle down and release the buildup, he'd never be venturing far from a Gate. Ethan turned toward the door, then paused. Between the vampires, her sister, and their encounter outside, Charlie was fairly wound up as well.

"Charlie likes to hit stuff," Ethan added. "And I'd be much obliged if you gave her something to aim at."

❧

When Jake had knocked on her door and invited her to a round of sparring on the deck, Charlie hadn't been certain it would be a good idea. Going up against a Guardian seemed a pointless exercise—and that he'd known to ask her at all was just another reminder of how long they'd been watching her. It was frustrating, she decided, to be both grateful for and resentful of that surveillance.

Ultimately, it was that same frustration that led her to change into her sports tank and yoga pants, and make her way down.

Jake must have heard her coming, but his face was pensive until he saw her, and then he broke into a wide grin. "First rule of Guardian Fight Club is," he said, hopping down from the deck railing, his jeans changing to a pair of track pants, "you don't talk about Guardian Fight Club."

That was cute, though by all rights, nothing about him should have been. Young, yes—but he was tall and whipcord lean with muscle. Yet his exuberant energy and the way he was bouncing into his footwork, mock-punching the air, made her want to rub his shaved head.

"I've heard that before," Charlie said, and set her cell phone on the table.

"In a theater? A real live theater?" His eyes widened and he tossed her the roll of tape that appeared in his palm.

Charlie shook her head. "No, there was this guy I knew . . ." And she was already losing him. His brows were drawing down and she thought he looked ready to pull a DVD out, sit her down, and educate her. "Never mind. And yes, I've seen it."

He fell quiet as she began wrapping her knuckles, but when she glanced up she realized it was only because he was keeping himself from exploding with laughter.

"What?" she asked warily.

"I was trying to put you at ease, going to play it innocent and naïve, see how long it took you to catch on. Instead we ruined each other's jokes."

"Oh." She wound the tape around her hand a few more times. "Maybe we should have a signal, so we know whose turn it is to pull a story over on someone else. Obviously it won't work on each other."

"You're a smart lady, Charlie. I team up with you, and I might be able to pull one over on Drifter for once."

"You can't now?" She jogged in place, rolling her shoulders. Lord, but this deck was incredible. Stretching and warming up in a gym that was lighted and clean, but always smelling slightly of body odor and sounding of thin carpeting and exercise equipment, couldn't compare to the lake, the sun, the wind through the trees.

"Not only was he my mentor for a while, I've been playing poker with him too long. I can't bluff him for shit—pardon my language."

She shot him an incredulous glance, but his embarrassment seemed genuine—and his flush was so *cute*—that she decided not to point out that she worked in a bar and often said worse. "Where is he now?"

"Drifting, so you don't have to worry that he can hear our diabolical plan. It's like meditation," he added when she cast a puzzled look at him. "Deep breathing and focusing on an inner point, until all of the buildup just drifts away."

She pulled her arm over her head until she felt the burn in her triceps. "Is that why they call him Drifter?" She'd assumed he'd gotten his name by never staying in one place very long.

"Well, the spaghetti western bit doesn't help."

That response had come quick, and Charlie smiled to herself. Jake was apparently a talker, one of those gregarious types who couldn't keep something to themselves if their lives depended on it, and she was suddenly very glad she'd come down. Ethan's description of the events surrounding his brother's death had left a lot of holes and raised more questions—but she wouldn't ask him to revisit those memories just so that she could catch up.

Jake might be able to provide some answers. And if she started him out by showing that she was already in-the-know, he'd probably be less likely to balk at sharing personal information.

"He said the western bit was something he'd adopted."

"Did he?"

Responding with a question was never good—so maybe Jake was more careful with information than she'd thought. Or maybe just aware of when someone was manipulating him; he'd quickly recognized her tall-tale mode. A glance beneath her lashes confirmed the cuteness had dissolved into pointed, sharp attention.

"Yes," she said.

He regarded her with that expression for a long moment. "Drifter tells me that your privacy is important to you."

Dammit. That sounded like a polite way to tell her to mind her own business. She sighed and nodded. "It is."

Jake rubbed his palm over his head, in much the way she'd imagined herself doing only a few minutes before. His grin appeared again. "The thing is, I'm the kind of guy who's a big believer in equality, and I got him a lot of information on you. And I don't suppose there's anything I could tell you that you couldn't just look up in a history book, anyway . . . or by digging around a few obscure archives and rifling through copies of personal letters. Some of it, like his name on a list of graduates from Harvard Law School, 1878, you can find just by searching for it online. And his brother's name is there, two years later. You ready to start?"

Not if it was going to interrupt his recitation of Ethan's history. "Can you talk while . . ." She looked him over as he stepped in close, his hands at his sides, and she frowned. "Are you just going to stand there while I punch and kick you?"

"Basically. Anything else would be picking on you—but don't worry, I'll give you a workout. And we'll make a wager: when you hit anywhere on my body or head, you win."

Charlie bounced up on her toes, flexing her fingers, her eyes widening. "Win what?"

Her enthusiasm seemed to amuse him; he closed his eyes like he was fighting a laugh and turned his head to the side. *Sucker.* Pulled in by the same tactic he'd attempted to use on her. "A few details that you can't find in history books . . ." He huffed out a breath when her fist connected with his ribs. "Hot damn!"

"Sorry," she said as he rubbed his side. "Okay, not really. He told me he was born on Beacon Hill." Many of the wealthy opera patrons in the Boston area had Beacon Hill addresses; she'd been there a couple of times, and the houses were old, but not all of the money was. Ethan might have been from either. "A good family?"

This time, Jake was ready, and he blocked her without effort, simply sliding his flattened palm in front of her fist, using his forearm to brush aside her kicks. "His mom, yes—his dad, no. McCabe, Sr., worked himself up through a law firm. Made a nice name for himself, but when the war started, he enlisted. The Civil War," he clarified when she paused for a second.

"That was . . ." She blew a strand of hair out of her face, tried desperately to remember. "1860? So Drifter was six?"

"Yes. Does this ever make you feel like saying, 'Wax on, wax off'?"

Only a strange gravity beneath the question kept her from rolling her eyes, and she said carefully, "It might have twenty years ago. Why?"

Jake ran his hand over his hair again, but this time his expression was troubled. "The only exposure I've had to pop culture is the magazines and books the others brought back through the Gate. So I'm figuring out where it all fits, what's passé and what's relevant, so that when I go active duty I can pass as someone who *hasn't* lived forty years on Caelum—or sound like a hippie."

"Ah." What had Ethan's adjustment been like? Even with news coming in from outside, Charlie imagined going from the 1880s to the 1980s would be even more difficult than adapting to all of the changes in four decades. "Well, okay—for someone like me, I've just heard the Karate Kid thing too many times. But if you said something similar to Jane, she'd probably laugh her head off."

In fact, Jane had done exactly that when Charlie had made a similar joke not long after she'd first begun visiting the gym.

Jane. Charlie's fists clenched as anxiety grabbed hold.

"Just a second, Jake." She didn't have much hope that Jane would answer, but she used the cell phone and left yet another voice mail. She closed the phone, noted the time, and realized she had another call she needed to place. A heavy weight settled in her stomach. "I'm not going to make it to Cole's tonight, am I?"

"Probably not."

She'd done this before, at all of the crappy little jobs she'd had before Cole's, before Jane had given her ultimatum and Charlie had been forced to decide between her self-pity and her sister. With Charlie's voice as hoarse as it was, no one had questioned whether she was really sick—at least not the first few times. And she hadn't cared when they'd eventually told her not to bother coming in, only felt a vague sense of relief that they weren't depending on her anymore.

She certainly hadn't felt the horrible guilt and disappointment that tore at her when Old Matthew answered and she lied her way through his concern, assuring him she'd be better tomorrow.

Goddammit. She made her way back to Jake, anger and dread dragging at her steps. What if this hadn't been settled by tomorrow? And even if they got Jane away from Dylan, would they be staying in Seattle?

Aside from Jane, her job and the offer Old Matthew had made to her were the best things Charlie had going—and she was about to fuck it all up.

"Just let me know when you're ready to talk again," Jake said quietly.

Her hair was in a sweaty tangle around her face, her shoulders and back aching, her calves and thighs screaming when she finally eased up and began to shake it out. She hadn't landed a single blow past his blocks, but it was more relieving than frustrating—she hadn't had to hold back, hadn't had to worry about hurting anyone or pushing anyone but herself too far.

"Okay," she said, her chest heaving, "talk."

"Okay," Jake said. "So his dad got out of the Confederate prison camp in 1864, and a few years later he bought a big place near what would spring up as Leadville, Colorado, and moved there."

She moved in on him again, but lighter now—just cooling down. "How long was he a P.O.W.?"

"Not sure. And everything after that is sketchy until after Drifter and his brother graduated from Harvard—but that's just likely because they didn't attend any public schools, so there's no record."

Remembering what Ethan had said about his mother's re-action to his speech, Charlie put in, "I think his mom might have schooled them at home."

Jake nodded. "It wasn't unusual. And after Harvard, Caleb went into a practice in Denver. Drifter was already working for a couple of different agencies, tracking down criminals who'd fled west, or who just hid out in the smaller towns. There's quite a few mentions in various papers of him bring-ing in outlaws, swindlers, that sort. Then around 1885, it all seems to go to hell."

"How?"

"His mom died. Killed, actually, because there was a murder trial not long after. The defendants were acquitted. Then Mc-Cabe, Sr., dies, and although the papers aren't specific about this, there's just enough to make me think it was suicide. Then reports of 'The McCabe Boys' start showing up—the trains and banks they've hit, the rewards on their heads, news of the bounty hunters and lawmen they've killed while evading cap-ture, the jails they've broken out of when they did get caught."

Charlie stopped dead, stared at him. "You're serious?" *Please, let him be pulling something over on me.*

But a solemn expression had settled over his features, and she couldn't find a hint of a joke behind it. "Yes. But it wasn't until 1886 that Drifter's death is finally recorded—then Caleb's, right after."

She let that sink in. The ache in her chest wasn't just from the exercise or frustration now—she wanted to see Ethan, hold on to him for a long, long time. *A spot of trouble,* he'd said. And he'd given up his life to get his brother out of it.

"So, I can't tell you what Drifter was like when he first got to Caelum, or anything much before 1968—and even then, I only saw him a few times before he was assigned as my mentor in the early nineties."

"I—" Imagining the span of Ethan's lifetime was knocking her loopy. Charlie huffed out a breath, tried again. "I'm slow adjusting to thinking in these time periods, but I'll catch up."

"I understand. I still can't fathom Michael's age, and he's God-knows-how-old." He laughed a little, but Charlie had just gotten the joke when he added, "Anyway, when I first met Drifter, he was with another Guardian, a really pretty young . . . Hot dog, that had your back behind it. Are we going for another sweaty round?"

"Sorry," Charlie muttered, and reminded herself that she was cooling down.

His grin flashed, all too knowing for her comfort. "Anyway, it was nothing serious. I think they were just fu—" Jake cleared his throat. "Friends."

"Fuck buddies." Which was all Charlie would have asked for. Impossible for her now. Not just his determination not to use her as a salve, and her determination not to be used as one—there was no chance that she could keep that emotional distance from him.

Her sister, her job, the most fascinating man she'd ever met . . . Charlie's life was just getting more and more fucked by the second.

At least she had too many endorphins running through her to feel sorry for herself right now.

"Yes. Until she Ascended with the others, and then I think it's just been random human women, because I'd have heard if it was a Guardian. Back in the eighties, there was a rumor about things going sour between him and a vampire, but I don't know if it was legitimate, and I only knew him by his coat and his height then." Jake turned his head. "Do you think you're even? Because he's lowered the spell around his room."

No. She wanted to hear more about the vampire and about where he lived on Caelum and what Ascending was. But she only nodded and said, "I think so. Thank you."

He streaked into the house, leaving Charlie alone on the deck. The sun was setting over the city, painting oranges and purples in long strokes across the sky and the water. The air was cool, and now that she wasn't active, it pricked gooseflesh over her sweaty skin.

She tried to keep the fear from her voice in her final message to Jane, just convey a sense of urgency, but she wasn't certain she managed it. When she hung up, only the knowledge that the phone was the one way Jane could reach her prevented Charlie from throwing it into the lake.

"She'll be all right," Ethan said softly, coming to stand beside her. He leaned his elbows on the rail, clasped his hands, and stared out over the water. "Sammael cares for her. I don't rightly know how corrupt it is, but he's protective. He won't allow her to be hurt."

"If he's the one telling the vampires to kill me—"

"Turn you into one of them." His gaze lowered to his hands. "They're looking to transform you."

Her breath hitched. "Either way, he's got to be one sick and twisted motherfucker not to realize that hurting me would hurt Jane pretty damn bad, too."

Ethan nodded, a tiny smile kicking up the corner of his mouth. "He's a demon, Charlie, which means he's both sick and twisted—and since it pertains to you, I'm laying it out straight. This is why I'm not taking you with me at night, even if it means it won't be as easy to get to Jane. I don't want you out there, because the vampires can hurt you. The demons can't."

A short laugh escaped her, and she shook her head. "Well, as much as I'd like to hang outside her window and wave until she sees me, I don't want to become a vampire target, either."

He glanced at her. "That's not a half-bad idea. And I reckon I've seen enough of you to try it for a minute or two."

That didn't make any sense, but her body was making it very clear that he hadn't seen as much of her as she'd have liked. Not just the cold—every nerve seemed aware of his presence. The slight brush of her inner thighs as she shifted her weight was enough to have her attention zinging low, and her gaze settled on his mouth.

But that was done with. And though she couldn't be immune to him, it wasn't anything a little self-denial and a lot of self-gratification wouldn't ease.

"Are you feeling okay now?" She searched for any difference, but he looked as easy and relaxed as he had their first walk to Cole's. "After drifting?"

His smile deepened, and he turned toward her. He was wearing almost the same clothes as when the vampires had attacked—the jacket, brown trousers, knee-high boots, and holsters. His shirt was a deep blue now, but it still looked eminently touchable. "Has Jake been running his mouth again?"

"I won a bet," she said.

"You ought to be careful making wagers; if they're ever with a demon, it can land you some serious trouble." His gaze ran over her face, down to her chest. He turned back to the lake. "You worked him over pretty hard?"

She touched her hair, wondered how matted and stringy it looked. "Yes."

"That's good. That's real . . ." His lips tightened, and he swallowed. "I'd best go. You ought to get inside, so I can lock the house down. I'll try to bring Jane back to you tonight, Charlie."

"Thank you." She bumped her hip against his thigh, smiled up at him. "For sending Jake to be my punching bag, too."

His nod was abrupt, but his attention lingered on her mouth. "I sure wish I—" His jaw clenched. "Hell and damnation. Don't lay your hands on me, Charlie."

Frozen, she watched his head descend, felt his warm breath, the light brush of his lips against hers.

He immediately stepped back. "That's all I meant to do before."

She closed her eyes. "I guess drifting did work, then."

"It cleared a few things for me, that's for damn certain," he said, low and forceful. Startled, she glanced up and his amber gaze locked with hers. "The first is that I won't be torn up forever. I hope not much longer than it takes to fetch Jane for you, get you both settled again. Then we can see where we're at, and if it's still agreeable to you, maybe scratching this powerful itch we've got. Most likely, we'll be scratching a long time, and more'n once—but we'll figure that as we go."

Her breath caught in her throat and a slow lick of anticipation curled deep. "I'd like that," she managed. "And you don't have to worry that I'll let myself need more from you."

Or ask for more, if she couldn't stop herself from needing it.

"I only recently figured that, too."

She couldn't interpret the wry note in his voice, so she said, "What's the other thing?"

"That I ought to staple Jake's lips shut before he heads back to San Francisco." His grin was slow. "But I've since added another realization to those: you look awful good when you're all sweaty."

She returned his grin. He was such a tease, but she could give a little back, then wait for the rest. "If you'd ever peeked over that wall, you'd know that I look better sweaty and *naked*."

Ethan groaned, dropped his head into his hands. "You hush, Miss Charlie."

CHAPTER II

A few minutes after sunset, Ethan went out to the deck and formed his wings. Charlie watched him through the French doors until he flew too high for her to see, then she took her time through her shower, fixing her hair, and dressing in her favorite gray pants and a blue camisole.

Even Ethan probably wouldn't think dried perspiration was sexy.

Tired, but not at all sleepy, she searched for Jake. When she found him in the attic entertainment center, she decided that there wasn't a room in the house that she didn't love. Huge triangular windows bookended the room, offering a view of the lake on the west and the dark rise of the hill and drive in front of the house. Thick rugs welcomed her bare feet, a fireplace and the facing wingback chairs invited long reads and cozy chats.

Jake had sunk into the deep cushions on the sectional sofa. Demons and angels fought across a wide-screen television, and he muttered to himself when his character received a hit from a demon that sent blood flying and his life indicator shrinking.

"Is that how they look?" Horns curled beside the demon's head. She had crimson skin and fangs, but no tail, no trident.

"Not exactly," Jake said, leaning to the side as his character rounded a corner. "They shape-shift to look like people. They look like people when they're demons, too, but they have more snake and goat to them. The whole scales and cloven feet thing, you know . . ."

The rest was lost in another mutter and a furious clatter of buttons, and Charlie smiled to herself and moved to the east window. Ethan's truck was gone.

"You guys would make a killing as a moving service—" She broke off, looked closer. Two pinpoints of light were moving through the trees. "Jake, I think a car's coming."

The room went dark, and Jake was beside her an instant later, touching her arm before her scream could escape. "I did that, Charlie. I can see better if I don't have the reflection to look through."

He didn't say anything about someone else not seeing in, and she fought the urge to creep away from the window, to find the nearest bed and hide under it.

Squinting, he leaned toward the glass. "It's a little car . . . a Toyota. Can't see the driver yet."

Aside from the illuminated landscaping at the front of the house, Charlie couldn't see anything but the headlights. "Jane drives a Toyota."

"Jane doesn't know where we are," he said, but there was uncertainty in his voice. "Unless Drifter did get ahold of her, and bought her some time to come here."

"Would he do that?" The question rattled from between her teeth.

"He might have thought he'd be coming right after, or getting here first to tell us she was headed this way."

But because Ethan wasn't there, it could mean that driver wasn't Jane—or that he was hurt somewhere, or still fighting Dylan.

She didn't let herself think of any other option.

"It's Jane," Jake said softly. "*Maybe.* Let's go on downstairs, Charlie."

He turned off the lights along the way; an automatic pistol appeared in his hand. Charlie hung back from the front entrance until he gestured her closer, then she stood to the side of the large double doors, trying to look through the beveled glass. The driveway wavered in front of her.

Jake's jaw was tight. "SI's got temperature sensors being developed so we can tell demon from human through the spell, but aside from a few prototypes, they aren't ready yet. I wish they were."

"Me, too." Charlie rubbed her arms. "Can vampires shape-shift?"

"No. Yes. One, but she's—" Jake stopped, flashed a nar-rowed look at her. "You're thinking that if it's a demon, you can go out there and you won't be in danger."

She'd been approaching the idea in a vague way, but when he put it in those precise terms, it didn't sound dumb. "Yeah."

"Over my dead body. And it would be, because Drifter would kill me. In any case, without psychic abilities you wouldn't be able to tell until you touched her." He held up his empty hand, wiggled his fingers. "Hot skin. Feels like you're touching someone with an extremely high fever."

Charlie stared out the window, trembling. How had Jane not noticed something like that?

"Damn," Jake muttered. "It looks like she's injured."

"What?" She scrambled to his side. Her heart had already been racing; now it was pounding so hard it made it difficult to breathe. The headlights were swinging into the drive . . . definitely Jane's car, but Charlie could only see the silhouette of her sister inside. "How bad?"

"There's blood on her forehead and her shoulder, and she's driving a little erratically." A calm seemed to settle over him, and he looked down at her. "Okay, Charlie, this is what I'm going to do. I'll put a new set of symbols on the door frame, key them to my blood, then remove Drifter's. Then I'll go out—and if it's her, I'll bring her in. If it's not, I'm going to call Drifter and SI. I might have to run, but you'll be okay in here."

He bent to scrape the door, and she leaned over him, star-ing through the window.

"I understand—oh, Jesus! *Jane.*" Her nails dug into his shoulder. Jane stumbled past the hood of her car, the front of her white shirt crimson.

A dark form darted through the shadows behind her.

"Oh, my God. Jake, hurry!"

Jake stood up, swore, and aimed through the glass. "Vampire. And—shit, I don't have a shot. Change of plan, Charlie—I get him away from her, you get her inside and use the symbols. Drifter showed you how?"

Charlie was already nodding frantically, tugging at the door handle. Locked. "Okay, okay—"

Jake pulled her hand away from the deadbolt, stabbed the pad of her forefinger with his dagger, and said grimly, "So you're ready as soon as you get back."

Then he replaced the knife with a sword and twisted the lock.

The door swung open on a visual more horrific than anything Charlie could have imagined, and worse for the silence of it: her sister on her stomach, the vampire holding her to the ground with his knee on her back and using her hair to pull her head up, exposing her throat. Jane's mouth opened in a scream, the vampire leaning forward to tear at her neck.

Then the scene was replaced by Jake's back as he ran through the door. Charlie followed him . . . and it was all wrong. Sounds rushed in, but there was no screaming, nothing human except the strange whistling noise that Charlie was making.

Only two steps past the door, she slammed into Jake. He was turning, his hands on her arms to spin her around, shove her back inside.

The side of his head caved in. She felt the splatter of his blood the same instant she heard the suppressed burst of gunfire.

He vanished.

Charlie was still spinning, but Jake's hands weren't there to guide her into the house. She hit the solid wood beside the door, crumpled to the porch.

Get inside. But she was dizzy, looked the wrong way. The vampire lifted himself off Jane. Jane . . . who held two pistols in her hands.

Charlie blinked, and now it was Dylan climbing to his feet, a startled expression on his face. "I wasn't expecting him to teleport. A shame, that. His head would have left a nice message for Michael."

Get inside. She crawled forward. Dylan's shiny shoes appeared in front of her. He crouched, looked into her face, and his expression was so sympathetic, so familiar, that for an instant she wanted to reach out to him.

"A message that they need to receive, because they've been lying to you, Charlie," he said quietly. "Let me take you to Jane, and we'll get all of this sorted out. She can explain everything to you."

God, how she wanted to believe him. She'd eaten dinner with this man, laughed with him, seen the love with which he'd treated her sister.

But Jake's blood was on her face, her hands . . . her finger was bleeding. *Get inside.*

She staggered to her feet. "Move out of my way, Dylan. You can't keep me from going in."

"No, I can't." He stood, smooth as a snake rising from his coils. Cold hands gripped her arms from behind. "But Mr. Henderson, my associate, can. Let's take a ride."

His SUV appeared next to Jane's car. Charlie kicked backward, heard a satisfying grunt before Henderson twisted her wrist up high, almost brought her to her knees.

Tears filled her eyes, and she walked forward obediently, the pea gravel rough under her feet. The SUV's alarm chirped when Dylan pointed his key at it, and the blinkers flashed.

They were going to turn her into a vampire.

Fuck this. Ignoring the agony in her right arm, she slammed her left elbow into his belly.

She didn't get another blow in. Henderson simply lifted her, squeezed her tight. Dylan turned, frowning.

"Mr. Henderson, I told you that if you hurt her at all, or if you touch her wrong, I wouldn't be pleased."

Charlie stared at him in disbelief, but the arms around her loosened. Not enough to get away, despite her struggles. Henderson shoved her into the backseat, took a place beside her. His hand covered the opposite door handle before she'd done more than move an inch toward it.

Dylan slid into the driver's seat, turned to smile at her. "Now, that's a good girl. You learned that you can't beat him much more quickly than I thought you would."

Terror was setting in, leaving her cold and shaking. "Where's Jane?"

"Safe at home with me."

She didn't try to make sense of that; she'd never been good

at word games, and she suspected a demon was a master. "Where's Drifter?"

Dylan was right—she couldn't physically defeat them, but Ethan could.

He *would*.

"McCabe? I don't know." Dylan's eyes changed, the whites and irises glowing a brilliant scarlet. Horror crept into Charlie's veins and began a morbid dance with fear. "But I hope he comes soon. I've got a message for him, too."

۶

Shape-shifting into Charlie's form and waving at Jane through the window might have been a bit more successful if Jane hadn't been so devoted to her work.

The light in her upstairs office was likely keeping her from seeing him when he did take the opportunity of darkness and a street empty of traffic to hover at her window. The remainder of the time he spent in the small fenced backyard, watching the demon.

Sammael didn't appear all that concerned that a Guardian was outside the house; he lounged on the recliner in the unlit room, reading the Sunday paper, tipping it down now and then to cast a shit-eating grin at Ethan through the sliding glass door.

Until the grin slipped, and confusion flitted over his features, his focus moving behind Ethan.

Ethan spun around, caught Jake before he landed in a bleeding heap at his feet. His breath sucked in hard through his teeth when the sight, the smell hit him.

Oh, Christ Jesus. The kid's head had been shot to hell.

Jake's brain couldn't be much good, but it must be functioning enough that he'd teleported here—his Gift manifesting in a moment of pain, terror.

A hard shake and roaring Jake's name roused him. His lids opened a slit before closing again.

"Jake, goddammit! Is Charlie still in the house and the spell up?" Ethan's voice roughened, tore at his throat. "*Is Charlie in the house?*"

No verbal response—but failure and urgency filled the kid's psychic scent.

God Almighty.

A bone in Jake's chest snapped as Ethan grabbed him up tight and launched into the air. Couldn't leave the kid behind in the yard—Sammael would be out within a second to kill him.

"You get to a Healer!" Ethan had to shout over the wind, the torrent of his wings. "You anchor yourself to Michael or Dru, just like you did to me, and you teleport yourself to them. Or else you sink deep and stay underwater, and put your mental blocks up until it heals. You understand me?"

Jake's psyche had barely shifted to indicate that he did understand when the lake appeared below them.

Ethan let him go, and was halfway across the expanse of the water before the kid hit the lake's surface.

❧

The scene that had taken place at the house was as clear as if had happened right in front of him. Jane's car, the heavy footprints in the gravel that intercepted hers, the blood on the ground. Ethan bent and sniffed, just to make certain: demon blood.

He didn't vanish any of the evidence. Human and vampire blood laying dead and heavy in his cache felt bad enough; demon and nosferatu blood tended to creep around his mind, like a bit of the creature still existed in the tiny drops.

And though he was certain Charlie had been in the vehicle whose tracks led away from the driveway, he took an extra second to check the interior of the house—Charlie wasn't hiding in any of the rooms. The second set of symbols scratched in the frame near the front entrance and Charlie's bloody handprint on the porch told their own story.

It was the same ploy Charlie had suggested—just showing up outside the window—but given a demon's touch. She and Jake hadn't had a chance.

But there might still be time to get to her. Sammael wouldn't want to force the transformation on her, but wait until he'd been able to manipulate and convince her to accept it—whatever it took to convince her.

Most likely, that would be Jane.

Less than ten seconds after arriving at the house, Ethan was in the air again, flying over the northbound road and mentally testing the occupants of each car, forcing his rising panic into cold determination, sending his probes in an ever-widening search. If her mind was open, he'd find her quick. And if she was projecting . . .

He prayed it wouldn't be pain.

❧

Charlie couldn't tell if Dylan's glowing eyes watched her in the rearview mirror—there were no irises or pupils to judge the direction of his gaze.

The vampire sat next to her, blocking every attempt she'd made for the door or Dylan's head. The demon was driving fast, but she'd have risked jumping out at speed to avoid what Henderson had in store for her.

His hunger was almost palpable, and when he wasn't avoiding her fists and elbows, he stared at her hand, her neck.

"Mr. Henderson," Dylan said. "Heal her. There's no need to torture yourself before it's time to transform her."

Henderson's cold hand clamped around her wrist. She kicked and pulled when he opened his own thumb against his fang, but couldn't stop him from spreading his blood across the cut Jake had made on her finger.

She frantically wiped it off on her pants the second he let her go.

Dylan looked over his shoulder, flashed an affable smile. Then the blood disappeared from her clothes, Jake's blood from her hands and face. "That won't do anything to you, Charlotte, except heal it. Take a look."

Charlie set her jaw, stared straight through the front window.

"Vampire blood can heal just about any injury. It can't cure naturally occurring diseases or cancers, but it can give anyone suffering them some strength, take away some of the pain . . . so you can see why Jane might have such a vested interest in re-creating it, modifying it for medical use." A hard note slipped under Dylan's friendly tone. "Of course, maybe you *can't* see why, considering that while she was caring for your father as he wasted away, you were knitting him a scarf from prison. Didn't even get to the funeral, did you? But I bet that bright red yarn looked great in the casket."

Bastard. Her lungs drew in tight on themselves, her throat closed.

"And Jane worries about you, Charlotte. A lot. She's told me several times how she wondered if you'd pull your life together. Do you know how much pain you've caused your sister?"

She met Dylan's eyes in the mirror. She'd already beaten herself up for all of this; she wouldn't let him do it again. "Yes."

His brows shot up. "Well, that's good. And you should know how happy she is with what you've done in the last two years, though—" Dylan's lips pursed, and he bobbed his head as if he was agreeing with himself. "No, I simply can't see why she's so pleased. And I think that if she's going to worry, it should be about something worthwhile, not whether you'll get your little degree and go on to live a little life."

Charlie swallowed the hurt and betrayal ripping at her chest. *Of course* Jane had spoken about her to Dylan. The betrayal here wasn't Jane's, but the demon's.

"Don't you want to be a part of something great? You and Jane, working together? Initially, Jane may not agree with the way I've gone about it—but once she sees the big picture, I think she'll come around, too." Dylan's voice softened, and a whimsical smile curved his lips. "She's a visionary. She's what humans *should* be: intelligent, modest, kind . . . and dedicated to improving the world. She's perfect."

"Jane, perfect?" Charlie echoed wryly, trying not to expose her disgust. He really did love her sister—but it was so corrupted, ugly. "I don't think so. Live with her a few more years, Dylan."

"I intend to."

He slowed for a red light and Charlie jumped for the door again, but Henderson yanked her back against his side. They were nearing the bridge that would take them back to Seattle. Once they were in the city, it would be more difficult for Ethan to track them down.

Did Ethan even know that she was gone? He had those psychic abilities, and had said she projected . . . Could he feel her terror now?

And he'd also told her he could get images if she thought them hard enough and wanted him to see them.

Charlie closed her eyes, pictured the bridge, and focused on him seeing it with everything in her.

"That's a good idea, Charlotte. It'll bring him right to us. I'll add my own to it."

Henderson stiffened beside her, and Dylan laughed softly.

"Mr. Henderson is a vampire, so he can't see what I'm sending, but he gets the *feel* of it. And I'm afraid it's making his bloodlust worse. Isn't that true, Mr. Henderson?"

"Yes." The response was strained.

·Charlie turned her head, really looked at Henderson for the first time. A little pale, yes—but otherwise normal in just about every way. Khaki pants, an unbuttoned cotton shirt over a Henley, deck shoes. His light brown hair and soft green eyes might have been pretty if she'd seen them across the bar.

He glanced away from her, his mouth set in a thin line.

She hoped she wasn't mistaken that she read guilt in that avoidance. Maybe she'd been appealing to the wrong person; Dylan couldn't keep her here. Only this vampire did.

"Please don't do this, Henderson."

Dylan sighed. "Charlotte, I told you there's a big picture. Healing people is only part of it; that will help bring order, because fear of death drives men to irrational acts. The rest of it, however, will have to be done by example. But it's difficult to be an example—or *make* examples—when you can't obstruct human free will. That's where vampires like Mr. Henderson come in."

She tried to meet the vampire's gaze again. "So you're going to be his hired thug? Listen to him—he's an insane, twisted asshole. And you don't look like the type of guy—"

"What *you* don't understand is that Mr. Henderson and every other vampire has abilities and gifts that a normal human can't comprehend. It's a blessed existence. But there is a drawback: bloodlust. It's an affliction that forces them to . . ."

"Fuck," Henderson said in a low growl.

"Mr. Henderson!" Dylan's eyes flared brightly, illuminating the steering wheel and dashboard with crimson. "Charlotte, it's better not to mention in polite company, but vampires, being forced to feed from each other, are forced to engage in other acts with their partners, as well. The bloodlust isn't always so powerful, but when a vampire is as hungry as Mr. Henderson is, it just takes the other vampire desiring him to leave Mr. Henderson absolutely no choice in whether there is consummation. And whether the bloodlust forces full consummation or not, he'll still experience . . . arousal." Dylan's mouth curled with disgust. "No one should be forced into an intimacy that they'd rather experience with a loved one, should they?"

She didn't know what to say. Agreeing with anything he said seemed like surrendering to *all* of it.

"And vampires can only survive on blood from a living, non-animal source. But if Legion re-creates the property in living blood that nourishes them, and we can manufacture a substitute that they can drink from a bottle . . . that's *freedom*. And that's what Mr. Henderson here is looking for; that's what so many vampires need. And that's why Jane will continue her research even after she discovers the source of the blood . . . because she won't want to see you so dependent on it, and forced into intimacy every night by the one who feeds you. None of the other scientists have their relatives, that's for certain."

Charlie touched Henderson's hand. It was clammy beneath her fingers, and she barely suppressed her shudder. "Do you really believe him? Any of this? He's a *demon*."

"He has to, because the stakes have recently been upped. We aren't the only demons in town—we're just the only ones looking for a way back to Grace. Setting humanity on the right path will help us get there." Dylan narrowed his eyes, his focus seeming to shift inward. "Well, I'll be damned. Your hero is on his way, Charlie. This should be fun."

Ethan. She closed her eyes and sent him the image of the SUV with all of her might.

❧

The horrific visual of a nosferatu thrusting his huge body between Charlie's legs, his fangs tearing at her neck, had slammed into Ethan only an instant after he'd felt the faint brush of Charlie's mind—but the wavering image of the floating bridge had been enough to send him speeding toward it.

The traffic was heavy approaching the bridge; he spotted the black SUV at the same moment the image bloomed behind his eyes. Hope and relief lay beneath Charlie's fear, but they changed to horror a few seconds before Sammael's voice traveled the same distance:

"I guess we've no choice but to start now, Mr. Henderson. Just make certain not to touch her wrong."

God Almighty, *no*. Ethan dove. He'd be seen, but it didn't matter much. Charlie's hoarse cry filled his ears—his name.

And then nothing.

He hit the SUV's roof, used the ski rack to pivot and kick at the windshield. His boot slid down the glass like it was buttered. His wings dragged with the speed of the vehicle—he vanished them, swung around and grabbed hold of the driver's door handle. His arm wrenched with the force of his pull, but he might as well have been trying to move a mountain.

The demon's eyes gleamed brightly inside. The symbols had been scratched into the dash next to him, and three drops of blood reflected the crimson light.

A hand slapped soundlessly against the window behind Sammael, grasping and frantically searching for something to hold on to.

Charlie. The vampire's fangs were in her throat. She was still fighting.

Taking unwilling blood was painful for a vampire, and judging by the tightness of the skin, the strain around his mouth, Charlie was resisting awful hard. But the bastard was trying to overcome it, using the pleasure of the feeding against her, trying to make her succumb. His hand moved beneath her shirt, covered her breast.

She couldn't have heard Ethan shouting her name, or the horns honking around him. He blasted his Gift at the spell, felt the lock *there* but nothing to move, no magnetic connection to break, no tumblers to push.

He didn't know how it worked. *He had to know how it worked.*

Still, he pushed harder. *Harder*, until his Gift was erupting through his mind and darkness edged the center of his consciousness. Around them, doors and trunks unlocked and popped open, spilling items across the road. Brakes screeched and cars swerved, tires squealing. A crash of metal, then another. Blood dripped from his nose; he'd busted something in his brain pushing so hard, but the Gift was still there and he kept at it.

The spell protected the wheels, but he called in his guns and scrambled across the roof, firing two clips at each tire, praying for any hole in the shield, that his Gift had weakened it, that *something* would give.

His prayer wasn't answered. The bridge stretched out ahead of them. Sirens sounded in the distance.

His chest heaving, Ethan hung over the side and looked in through the window. Charlie was laid out on the seat, kicking weakly at the opposite door. The vampire was on her, his hand slipping beneath her waistband, his mouth at her neck forcing her chin back, and she was looking at Ethan upside down.

Her eyes locked with Ethan's, pleading.

"Charlie." His throat was raw from shouting her name, salted and scraped by fear. "Charlie, please hold on."

Her eyelids drifted shut.

CHAPTER 12

"Mr. Henderson, I told you not to . . ."

It faded. She couldn't really hear Dylan now, just that awful sucking sound, the slow throb of her heart in her ears. Her legs and arms were heavy; her body had forsaken her. Weak . . . and reacting to the vampire's frigid touch as if he was a lover.

But Ethan was out there. His face pale and tormented when he'd looked in at her, his eyes feral, desperate.

Jane, smiling and her ponytails swinging, a unicorn rearing in her outstretched palm . . .

Charlie didn't realize she'd had any breath until Henderson jarred back, then fell heavily against her, knocking it from her lungs.

"He's going to push us over the edge!" Dylan's laughter was a rollicking study in sharps. "He must care for you, Charlie. This just gets better and better."

"Charlotte, you will never improve if you do not practice." Her mother runs the scale on the piano, a key to each syllable. "You cannot rely on your voice, no more than a woman can rely on beauty or health. It can go at any time."

Her father, grinning over the top of his paper. "Jane's brains won't go."

Jane, rolling her eyes and making a face behind their parents' backs.

The seat rose up beneath her, tipping her upright before she fell against the ceiling, her legs tangling with Henderson's. She slammed back down to the seat. Lights flashed, red and white. Rolling again.

Spinning. Going too fast. The scream of metal. The broken windshield, the broken window with its iron bars. Glass in her throat. Blood. So much blood.

"It's unfortunate that you didn't listen to me, Mr. Henderson, and you touched her, because I could have helped you. When I lower this shield, he'll have an instant to decide which one of us to go after—but he'll be in such a tear to save her, he won't even look at me. His choice is already made, and I'll let him make it."

Staggering into the apartment she shared with Jane, finding the contents of her bedroom stacked by the door in boxes and trash bags. Her fingers clenching on the arm of a grunge musician whose name she could barely remember. But Jane's face still so clear—tormented, and as white as the powder in the little plastic bag on the table next to her.

"I can't do this anymore, Charlie. You're going to have to make a choice."

Sound slowly filtered in: the lap of water. A male's panicked plea, a demon's cold reply.

And Ethan, calling her name.

❧

Ethan had lifted objects heavier than the SUV, but not moving as fast as the vehicle had been . . . and he'd never caught one midair.

Even quadrupling the size of his wings and the burning rage that possessed him couldn't stop it from falling to the embankment alongside the head of the bridge, but he slowed it enough that the impact against the ground wouldn't rattle Charlie around too much inside.

The vehicle wasn't damaged, and Ethan quickly rolled it upright.

The shield around it vanished.

A tug at the rear passenger door sent it flying behind him to crash against a concrete support post. His crossbow was instantly in his hand, and the bolt through the vampire's forehead less than a second later. He tumbled out to lie motionless on the rocks at Ethan's feet.

Sammael scrabbled his way on top of the vehicle, perching in his human form, his dark eyes alight with interest.

Ethan paid him no mind. He softly repeated Charlie's name as he leaned in and slid his palms up the length of her legs, over her torso, pulling her clothes back into place. Her only injury seemed to be the bite at her neck, but he could hear the struggle of her heart trying to pump too little blood through her body.

Even a Healer couldn't repair that.

Ethan's breath shuddered painfully from his chest. No choice then, but the one she had left to make.

He held her against him, sitting her up as best he could at the edge of the seat, then bent to haul the vampire from the ground, shoving him to the floorboard between the seats. A slice of Ethan's knife on the vampire's wrist got the blood flowing, and he smeared it over the punctures on her neck.

"Charlie." A gentle shake got little response. "I need you to wake up, Miss Charlie."

"Look how her toes are twitching," Sammael said. "She's still trying to kick."

Only knowing that if he didn't do this soon he couldn't finish it at all kept Ethan in that spot, hanging on to Charlie rather than tearing the demon apart.

His stomach twisted as he laid her down and reopened the slash across the vampire's vein. The blood dripped into her mouth, and he watched the convulsive swallowing of her throat with his heart pounding a sickening beat.

Humans shouted on the bridge above, sirens wailing over them.

Ethan sat her up, cupped her face in his hands, put his nose to hers. His voice was hard, loud. "Charlie, *wake up*. You got a decision to make."

A ragged inhalation passed her lips. Her eyes opened.

"That's good, Charlie, that's just fine." He curled his fingers, rhythmically stroking her cheeks. "Listen: you've got vampire blood in you. It's what's keeping you alive, but it's not much. I need to know if you want me to complete the transformation, or if you want me to let you go."

Ethan felt the bewilderment in her psychic scent and closed his eyes so she wouldn't see his own uncertainty. A woman shouldn't have to make this decision, not like this; and if her choice wasn't the answer he needed to hear, a man shouldn't have to make the decision whether to honor it.

He fought down the roar of denial that was pushing its way up from his gut, then he looked at her and laid it out straight. "Charlie, if you don't become a vampire, you'll die. And I need you to choose, because if I force this on you, it'll go wrong. But you got to choose quick."

Her lips trembled, and terror chased the confusion from her eyes. "Ethan . . . I don't want to be . . ." Her fingers pressed weakly into his forearms. "Please." Her gaze searched his, frantic, beseeching. "*Please.*"

She wanted another option, but there wasn't one. "You'll be alive." He brushed her hair back, traced her jaw with the side of his thumb. "You'll be strong. Or you'll be dead."

A harsh, broken sound ripped from her, and she slapped her hands over her mouth. His throat aching, Ethan wrapped his arms around her, held her in. Her feet beat his shins, but she wasn't trying to get away. She was fighting something different now—but she couldn't much longer.

"Your brother kicked like that," Sammael said quietly, his voice sliding lower, deeper.

"Charlie, you have to—" Ethan's lungs seized up. He jerked back to look up at the demon, but didn't *see* the sheriff. No . . . no, but Ethan heard him. Samuel Danvers. He hadn't forgotten that slimy, self-righteous voice, not in one hundred and twenty years.

Sammael was pursing his lips, his gaze turned inward as if in remembrance. "They made the rope short because he was so tall. But he was heavy, so they thought it might break his neck anyway. It didn't, and he just hung there, struggling, his feet kicking. Until all they did was twitch. Just like Charlotte's."

Charlie. She was quiet in his arms now, her head tilting back. Ethan met her eyes; beneath the sheen of horror and pain, realization swam to the surface. "Caleb?" she whispered.

His nod was abrupt. His breath was rough. "It's past, Charlie, it don't matter now. I need to know—do you want to live?"

Her mouth pressed into a wavering line. After a long moment, she nodded.

Relief hollowed his chest, but that small gesture wasn't enough. "You sure? There ain't no going back."

Tears slipped over her cheeks, but she nodded again, harder, determination filling her psychic scent. "Yes."

He didn't give her time to reconsider. She gagged on the first taste, but he held the vampire's bleeding wrist against her lips, urged another swallow. Used his left palm to rub her back, trying to soothe the shuddering revulsion that was tearing through her.

Sammael dropped to the ground, looking in but staying a safe distance away. Ethan eyed him warily, but didn't take his hands from Charlie.

The demon smiled again. "I don't intend to stop you. She's drinking fast. By the time the rescue crews make their way down, we should be finished." He tilted his head, as if to get a better angle. "It took a long time for your brother. The poison would have been faster—I remember how you squirmed as it tore out your guts. You should have let him drink it, too. It'd have been kinder than the hanging."

Ethan sliced open the vampire's wrist again, his jaw set, but when Charlie was back to drinking he couldn't hold it in. A man could only take so much, and fierce pleasure rose up in him. "You didn't keep up your end of the bargain."

Which meant that as soon as Ethan killed the demon—slow—Sammael's soul and face would be frozen in Hell, his body dangling in Chaos and eternally devoured by dragons.

That suited Ethan just fine.

"No, I didn't renege. We let him ride out, gave him a month's worth of supplies, and not a single one of my deputies or I went after him. But you didn't say anything about my flying to the next town and alerting the law there, telling them he was running off west. Of course, once he realized they were after him, he tried to throw them off by going back the other way." Sammael chuckled, shaking his head with amusement. "Didn't get far, did he?"

He'd gone west. The demon couldn't know how welcome

that was. Ethan held back his smile, bent his head to rest his cheek against Charlie's temple. Pressed a kiss to her hair.

Her fingers flexed on his arm—stronger now. Then a hard, painful clench as the first wave of the transformation hit her.

Sammael formed his wings. "Well, that's done. You've still got to pay for Eden, McCabe . . . but I'll give you time to ruminate over this failure."

"I'm much obliged," Ethan said. He let the vampire's arm drop away from Charlie's mouth and called in the crossbow, but Sammael was already flying high, quickly moving out of range.

Astonished human shouts rent the air.

Damnation.

He laid Charlie back on the seat; she immediately turned and curled in on herself, her eyes closed and her hands over her ears, her body shaking. The vampire he'd stuffed between the seats was jerking around a little now.

Charlie had likely experienced enough violence for one night, and her daysleep—the dreams—would be coming soon. As it was, it'd be plenty difficult getting her stable before she fell into them.

"You are one lucky son of a bitch," Ethan muttered as he hauled the vampire out of the SUV, then flung him as far as he could over the water. A splash told Ethan he'd got three hundred yards; if the vampire went down deep and avoided the sun, and if the humans didn't think to drag him up, he might just live through the next day.

He returned to the vehicle and pulled Charlie against his chest, frowning. Convulsions were hitting her hard—he'd never seen them this hard. Most transformations were smooth.

The change was obviously taking hold—her skin was cooling, and the points of her fangs were visible between her open lips—but she was panting, whimpering, her palms tight to her ears, her eyes squeezed shut.

He vanished the SUV into his cache, and walked beneath the bridge's expanse so they wouldn't be seen. Cold water crept up to his knees.

"You all right, Charlie?"

She flinched, and it struck him: she wasn't yet accustomed to her hearing. The sirens, the shouts, even his voice must have been like a jackhammer, a jet engine in her head.

She'd been projecting despair, confusion; now that sank into absolute devastation.

He dropped his words below a whisper; just as well, because his throat felt so swollen he could hardly speak. "It won't always be like this. You'll adjust quick." A body had to adapt; no one could function with the senses always on full. "We're going under the water. Don't be afraid, because you don't need to breathe, and you can't drown. But it'll cut out some of the sound until we're away from the noise up above. Until then, just think of your favorite song, and you think it hard."

"Okay," she replied, her teeth chattering. But then a second later: "I need Jane."

He took off his jacket, wrapped it around her before picking her up again. She couldn't be cold, but it might offer her some comfort.

"All right. We'll go to her tonight, do whatever it takes to see her." No reason not to. Sammael had accomplished what he'd intended, and Charlie had little to fear from the demon now.

But Ethan was looking forward to bringing a hell of a lot of fear down on the demon.

There weren't nothing he could do for Caleb. But Charlie— he'd do right by her. He'd do right by her if it took his last breath, the last beat of his heart.

He waded out, was up to his waist when she suddenly stiffened, her hand flying up to her mouth. He delved into her emotions quick, looking for the source of the panic.

Her fangs had scraped her inner bottom lip. Blood scented the air, glistened on her fingertips.

Need tore through her . . . through him. Not sexual, not thirst—but something more powerful, and feeling an awful lot like both. His cock hardened, his balls drawing up tight.

"Oh, God," she whispered, staring at the blood. "Oh, God."

Then, as if mesmerized by it, she brought her fingers to her lips and slowly licked it off.

Instantly, he craved the long swipe of her pink tongue over his flesh. Heard the pounding of her blood, scented the perfume of her body's arousal. Imagined sliding into her as her fangs penetrated his skin.

Ethan pulled out of her head and dove, his heart thundering.

But the frigid water couldn't cool the heat rising in him, or the dread.

She'd need to feed, and soon. And Ethan could no more tolerate the idea of someone taking from her what she didn't want to give, than he could the thought that her bloodlust might take him over and bring more hurt on her.

But, *by God*, he'd do right by her.

CHAPTER 13

Ethan had been correct: she adjusted quickly. It wasn't so bad if she didn't listen to the sounds; they faded into the background, helped along with a little mental push from Pachelbel. When she paid attention, however, she could hear the water from her shower draining through the house's pipes, the slow rhythm of Ethan's breath beyond the bathroom door.

Incredible—especially considering that he'd said vampires had much less range than Guardians or demons. How much of an adjustment did *that* take? The full hundred years on Caelum?

She ran the water in the sink to brush her teeth, and she couldn't detect the sound of his breath anymore, just his voice. She'd told him what Dylan—Sammael—had said about creating bottled blood. Now he was on the phone, relaying it to his contact at Special Investigations, a woman named Lilith. Although Charlie couldn't distinctly hear the other woman, she sounded upset—apparently not at Ethan, however, because his responses were as easy as usual, even when he described how Jake had teleported to him and the events at the bridge.

And those events hadn't been so bad. Once she'd conquered

the instinct to breathe, the trip through the lake had been surreal . . . almost enjoyable. She could see in the dark. Flying was as amazing as before, and she hadn't had to turn her face from the wind. She was strong and fast, but she wasn't stumbling around and breaking things—as if expending human-level effort was a habit that her body recognized.

She wouldn't be taking many more hot showers, though. It hadn't hurt, but she'd immediately begun perspiring from the water, the steam. After a few seconds under the warm spray, she'd had to turn it to just above tepid.

A drop of blood fell to the basin, and Charlie looked down in dismay, then at her bleeding lip in the mirror. The need swept through her, but the thirst receded as soon as she rinsed out her mouth and the wound healed.

That wasn't so bad either, then. Her fangs were sharp, but only extended to her lower gum line when she held her teeth closed. Long, but not unmanageable. When she'd been singing, she'd always been aware of the placement of her lips, teeth, and tongue; she just had to be more conscious of her mouth until it became second nature again.

And the need the blood had created was like the flare of a match head: bright and hot, but dying quickly. The odor might briefly render her almost senseless, but the blood had had no effect when she licked it from her fingers. It hadn't even had a taste . . . and it had been nothing like the revolting sensation of drinking from Henderson's cold arm.

She couldn't taste anything—not the toothpaste, not the salt of her skin, not the water from the tap.

She didn't like that as much, but it wasn't so bad.

And at least I'm still alive.

The moment the thought squirmed into her mind, Charlie wanted to scrub it away. She'd told herself that same thing for six years after losing her voice; it hadn't helped any, and she certainly hadn't been *living*—just getting by.

She wouldn't do that now.

When Charlie left the bathroom, Ethan was standing beside the bed, nodding gravely at whatever the woman was saying to him.

He finished the call and slid the phone into the pocket of his jacket. His gaze traveled the length of her as she pulled on the lightweight hoodie she'd laid out on the mattress.

He met her eyes. "You all right, then?"

She nodded, attempted a smile—but had to look away from that searching gaze. On the wall, Caelum's towers and spires gleamed beneath a painted sun.

The sun. She wouldn't see it again, except in pictures and on television. "Tell me one really, really good thing."

And hopefully nothing trite about living forever. She'd already figured that out . . . but it wasn't so reassuring when she didn't know what life was going to be like from now on.

Ethan was silent for a moment, then said, "You'll be able to land a hit on Jake now and then."

Her smile felt real when she glanced up at him again. Good Lord, he was tall. And this close, his shoulders seemed as wide as a mountain. "He's really okay?"

His expression lightened, and some of the stiffness eased from his posture. "Yes. We can heal from just about anything."

"I guess that's pretty good, too, if you happen to be shot in the head."

He echoed her blithe tone. "I reckon it is."

She almost bit her lip to hold in her laugh, then remembered she'd probably cut herself with her fangs and let it out.

His gaze fell to her mouth, lingered there. "Unless you're laughing, I imagine you'll be able to conceal them in public. Your upper lip is nicely . . ." He trailed off. "Well, it starts with a 'P.'"

"Pouty," she offered, and touched it with the tip of her tongue.

Ethan cleared his throat, looked over her head. "I'm much obliged, Miss Charlie. 'Pouty' sounds just fine. I sure as hell wasn't going to call any part of a woman 'plump' out loud, no matter how pretty I think that part is."

She grinned. Once, "plump" might have described her in quite a few places—but she doubted it would ever describe any part of Ethan.

While she'd been in the shower he'd cleaned and dried his clothes—using some Guardian ability, because he'd never left the bedroom. His thumbs were tucked in his suspenders again, and his jacket opened to reveal his holsters, the gun belt slung at an angle across his hips.

It was an absolutely masculine pose, and strong, and made her want to step into that warm space against his chest and hold him to her . . . or grab that belt and tug him down to the bed. But Henderson's hands had been cold, and she'd been disgusted when he'd touched her, and she didn't know if she could survive the same reaction from Ethan.

"Are we going to see Jane?" she asked instead.

He nodded, but a troubled look crossed his features. "We need to talk some first, Charlie. Sammael will attempt to drive a wedge between us, try to turn you against me. And not everything he says will be a lie—but whether true or false, he'll twist it so it frightens you more, or serves him better. And he'll hit you with it fast, keeping you confused. And, in turn, keeping Jane confused so it's harder for her to decide."

"So you're giving me time to think it all over."

"Yes. She has to come of her free will, Charlie. I can't force her. And getting her to come will mostly depend on you."

"All right." She drew a long breath. "What will he think frightens me?"

"Considering what he said about Jane doing anything to keep you from being forced into intimacy, it'll be the feeding. He's going to ask you who you'll be taking blood from, remind you of—" Ethan's jaw clenched and his lips paled around the edges. "Of how Henderson touched you."

Her legs wobbled. Charlie sank down on the bed, shoving her hands into the pockets of her sweatshirt. Her feet dangled over the side; her polished toenails looked like cheery squares of blood against her skin. "Was the thing about having to feed from a living source true?" she wondered dully. "I have to find someone to drink from?"

And depend on them to provide it to her.

"It's true, Charlie, but you won't have to look far." He lowered to his heels in front of her, tilted his head to look up into her eyes. "I'll be feeding you."

For how long? She stared at his throat, remembered the cold lips, the humiliating arousal, the painful bite. "Why would you?"

"You'll need me," he replied easily, and anxiety pinched her lungs, kicked at her stomach. His brows drew together, and he shook his head as if he was confused by her reaction. "If this is about what I said before, about not wanting a vampire sucking at my neck, I was speaking of something that's past—and I'll share it with you in a moment—but I'm determined it won't matter here." He lifted his hands to the mattress beside her legs, smoothed his palms along the coverlet. "I'm willing, Charlie, and we were already headed in this direction."

She closed her eyes, swallowed hard. She'd be an idiot to reject his offer; it wasn't as if she had many options.

And before her transformation, there was no doubt they'd have ended up in bed. But it had been equal then: she'd wanted him, he'd wanted her. She wouldn't have starved and wouldn't have been forced to turn to someone else if he *hadn't* wanted her.

But Ethan didn't need anything to survive.

"We don't have to tumble into the bed quick, Charlie. I reckon you've got more adjustments to make, need time to become accustomed to the bloodlust. I can give you that time."

She looked down at him in surprise, met his earnest gaze. "How?"

"You can't physically force me. So when Sammael starts talking about how you'll be bedded against your will, you know you'll have a choice."

Bedded. How could he make such an old-fashioned term sound like a sexy, heated promise? It'd be good between them . . . but would the feeding change it? Change *her*?

"I do think I need a few days to get used to . . ." She waved her fingers at her mouth, then slid her fist back into her sweat-shirt pouch. Maybe more than a few days.

He nodded slowly. "There's a couple of other things, Charlie, but I'd like to get something settled first." He rocked forward, coming up off his heels and onto his knees, his chest pressing into her shins.

She automatically moved her legs apart to make room for her feet. Her breath was shallow. "Settle what?"

His fingers encircled her wrists and he tugged her hands from their pockets. "Why it is, now that you're a vampire, that I don't want you touching me . . . unless you can't help it."

"Ethan—" Her throat closed, and she tried to pull away.

"Drifter," he said softly. "Unless you're touching me, and we're in a private moment like this." He slid his palms over hers, locked their fingers together. His skin was hot.

No, his was a normal, human temperature. Hers was cold.

"It wasn't just that you didn't want Henderson to touch you—your instinctive reaction was to draw away from him, your skin tightening up with gooseflesh. Isn't that so?"

"Yes." Her hoarse whisper barely carried the response.

He rested their linked hands on the mattress beside her knees. "I ain't human, Charlie. Cold and hot don't feel uncomfortable or disgusting—they're just another sensation that I have to block out. But I can't block *you* out so easily. Not when you were human, and certainly not when there's a twenty-degree difference between us."

He was right; she could feel every inch of his bare skin. Even with her attention centered on his words, she was completely conscious of the heat of his fingers between hers.

"I hold myself tight, Charlie. A distraction means I ain't protecting you as well as I should, or that a demon might have an opportunity to take my head." His thumb stroked hers, sending shivers of awareness across her skin. "Sammael will try to say I'll be feeding you out of obligation or guilt—and if you don't know what I've been thinking in private moments, I reckon you might believe him, because I've been running hot and cold with you. You have good reason to doubt how willing I am."

She knew how deeply he wanted her. She'd felt it in his kiss, his hunger in the truck. But that was *then*, and she was unsteady enough to need it now. "What are you thinking?"

"That for two months, most every time you've said my name, I imagined hearing it with you beneath me." He spread his fingers, pinned her hands to the bed. "And now that I've had you call me Drifter, knowing that it put a wall between us, I don't figure I'll be able hear my given name from your lips without wanting you under me, or on your hands and knees while I work into you from behind, or with your legs around me and your back against a door."

Oh, Lord. Her calves squeezed his sides as she instinctively tried to press her thighs closed—but whether she was trying to dam the need building within her or encourage it with more pressure, she didn't know.

Her breathing quickened, and she'd have said his name then if his voice wasn't pouring over her again.

"And I'm thinking that I've never seen your titties naked, but I know their shape, and I know your nipples won't ever again tighten up as they did on the deck tonight. Not from the cold, leastwise." His palms moved rhythmically against hers, rocking her fingers against the silk coverlet. "But they will when I put my hands on them, or my mouth, or maybe just when you think of my hands and my mouth."

Not just tight . . . aching. He hadn't touched her anywhere but her hands and with his voice, and her nipples were *aching.* "They are now," she whispered hoarsely.

His throat worked, and his response was rough. "And I would slide my hands on up over your skin to feel them, but I reckon I ain't man enough to stop there. Because my heat would make you sweaty, now that you're a vampire, and feeling you all wet would make me think of touching, tasting you where you're even wetter."

Jesus. Charlie whimpered and rolled her hips, scooting forward against the mattress, only an inch, seeking more sensation, some kind of relief. "Ethan—"

"Because there are some things it's just crazy talk to say a man shouldn't eat." Without releasing her hands, he brought them to her knees and pushed her thighs farther apart. Raw desire abraded her nerves, left them frayed and quivering with anticipation. His amber gaze held hers, glowing with intensity. "And I'd be feasting a long time, Charlie, making you ready for me, making you wetter for me. I'm a big man, and I'd want you needing me so bad it'd hurt more for me *not* to be inside you than it would to take me in."

Charlie stared at him, unable to speak. Her breathing was too harsh, her arousal too sharp. He couldn't mistake it; the air was heavy with her slick, heady scent.

Ethan groaned her name and closed his eyes, laid his forehead on the mattress's edge between her knees. He let go of her hands to slide his up the length of her thighs until they clasped her waist. She leaned forward, ran fingers through his hair, then down over his collar. The back of his jacket was coarse under her palms, his muscles as taut as a steel string.

And he held her there, his body motionless until the electric charge between them faded to a hum, until she finally heard him draw a breath.

He turned his head, lifted it to lay his cheek on her knee and slant a rueful look up at her. "Hell, Charlie. I don't know that once you put your hands on me, I'll actually make it inside you."

Her fangs poked her bottom lip when she grinned, but she controlled the pressure and they didn't break skin. "I guess it's a good thing we've got super-speed then."

His laughter rumbled against her leg. "I reckon it is." After another long moment and a deep sigh, he sat back on his heels again, swiped his hands through his hair. "I didn't mean to take it that far. We've still got to get to Jane's, and there's something more I need to tell you."

Charlie checked the clock at the side of the bed; it was two in the morning. Sunrise came just before seven. "Maybe you should tell me on the way. And it might be easier if we're not *here*." She patted the mattress.

He nodded. "We'll go out the front, take her automobile with us."

"She'll probably want to fly, if you can carry two."

"I can, but it leaves me without hands to defend us."

"Oh. Okay, the car then." Charlie tied her sneakers and glanced at the clock again, her brow furrowing. "The other day, my radio alarm didn't go off and my cell phone didn't work. Did you put the spell up around my apartment?"

"That I did."

"You stole my feather?"

"That I did."

"Can I have—"

It appeared on her lap before she could finish. She stroked her fingers down the length and tucked it into her sweatshirt pouch. Her throat felt oddly thick; she hadn't thought she'd be this glad to get the silly thing back. "Thank you."

Then, because Ethan's expression was changing from amusement to a deeper, searching look, she quickly added, "You were telling me the other things?"

"Yes, well—" He glanced behind her, toward the bed. The skin across his cheeks tightened, his lips thinned. "We'll fly slow."

❧

The city sparkled as she'd never seen it before, each square window perfectly outlined, even from across the lake. Charlie soaked in the vision of it before rubbing her palm lightly against the down-covered frame of Ethan's left wing. It flexed beneath her fingers with each powerful stroke.

"The other thing?" she reminded him, although she was certain he hadn't forgotten, and slid her arm fully around his neck so she wouldn't be a distraction.

Ethan didn't glance away from the air in front of them. "It may be that Sammael doesn't know this, but rumor ain't an imaginary many-tongued chimera, and so it's equally possible that he does. There was a vampire. A woman, about twenty years ago."

She studied the wooden line of his jaw. His voice wasn't giving much away, but she'd have bet anything that talking about this was difficult for him. "Jake said something about her. You loved her?"

"Didn't know her from Eve. Didn't know her name. Still don't."

The wind was stinging cold tears from her eyes; she wiped them away. "What went wrong, then?"

"I did." He swallowed hard, and her gaze dropped to the muscle that ran from behind his ear to the hollow of his throat. Hunger flicked a teasing tongue across her fangs. "It was my first year back on Earth. The worst part of the Enthrallment had passed, but it still hit me now and again." He glanced down at her. "You'll get the same. Days where you'll be all right, then a sound or a scent just gets in you, overwhelms you."

"Worse for Guardians, though?"

"I reckon." The flap of his wings and the distant buzz of the city filled the brief silence. "One night, we ran across a vampire defending herself against a demon, but she was losing quick."

"We?"

"My mentor—Hugh Castleford, they call him now—and I. Hugh took on the demon; I was just to get her to safety, watch over her until Hugh finished up. But she'd been hurt pretty bad, had bled out some, and she needed to feed. So I offered myself on up." A rueful expression crossed his features. "Was more than willing to offer myself up. She'd fought like a warrior, was strong, beautiful, and she smelled something wonderful."

"And you wanted her?"

His eyes closed; when he opened them again, they were flat and dull, like a water-worn stone. "Yes. She began feeding—then the bloodlust grabbed hold of her. I should have known that the way she was responding wasn't *her*, Charlie. Hugh taught me well—I knew what happened to vampires when it hit them like that. Sometimes, when they're not too hungry, they can feed without it ever taking them over. But my blocks were down, and her hands were so cold and she looked and smelled so good, and she was sending me the pleasure of the feeding . . . and I just wasn't thinking with my head. What she was feeling got into me, too, mixed with the Enthrallment. I pretty much *lost* my head."

Charlie was shivering; she wasn't cold. "It's that strong? The bloodlust—it's that overwhelming?"

"Yes. I thought she was eager enough, and I didn't have any inkling that something was wrong until after. I didn't physically hurt her—but then she told me the demon had just killed her partner of over a hundred years. And she'd thought that, because I was a Guardian, I would feed her without taking anything. And the way she looked at me, Charlie . . ."

He fell silent again. Charlie tried to speak, but shame was clawing at her lungs, guilt holding her tongue in a bitter grip. They were unfamiliar, unexpected—and heavy.

Panic followed, weighing down on her chest, and she tugged at Ethan's hand, frantic.

"Son of a bitch." He drew up vertical, hovering high above the edge of the lake. The shame and guilt vanished; her fear receded. "Charlie . . . Charlie—*they're not yours*. I opened my shields a bit and projected. It's easiest to do that when we don't have the words to express something."

"Okay." Her breath came hard. "How can I tell?"

"I'll do it again, slow. It's not yours, and you'll feel the difference." He held her gaze, and something slipped into her, light but firm, with lilting, hopeful notes playing at the surface. Apology. "Most vampires say it's like a scent or a taste, probably because those senses are—"

She shook her head. "It's more like a sound. This is almost like . . . a clarinet, accompanied by a flute."

His brows lifted. "That's rare, but some Guardians were the same way. Most of those were musically inclined, too. For me, it's scent and feel." The wind picked up around them again as Ethan flew forward. "Blood, I've heard described as light or electricity for vampires drinking it. Could be your perception will be different there, too."

"It didn't taste like anything." She pulled a strand of hair out of her eyes, and averted her gaze from his neck. "My blood."

"No, I don't reckon it would, even if you could still taste food. It isn't necessarily the blood that feeds you, but the psychic energy it carries when it's taken from the living source—and that's what vampires taste when you drink it." He paused. "Leastwise, that's what we figure. And you wouldn't taste your own psychic energy, any more than you'd taste a candy if your tongue was made of sugar."

Jane had been studying vampire blood. Charlie hadn't understood all of Jane's description, but she couldn't remember her mentioning anything about energy—just artificially replicating the blood, and its healing properties. "So Legion intends to . . . what? Replicate psychic energy?"

Ethan's brows drew together, and he shook his head. "I don't rightly know, Charlie. First, they'd have to measure it—and so far as I'm aware, it can't be detected by scientific instruments, only by living beings who are sensitive to it. And once vampire blood is outside a body it can still heal or transform a human—but it doesn't carry that psychic energy."

"Would Legion be trying to measure it *inside* the body then? Trying to find a way to detect it?" And using vampires as test subjects. Charlie closed her eyes, felt slightly sick. Jane would never be a part of that.

His voice was troubled. "I hope not, Charlie; but if so, I hope the vampires are there voluntarily. But with demons, it's impossible to be certain. They'll stoop lower than most people want to imagine." They banked northwest. Capitol Hill slid by far below them. Ethan took a long breath, seemed to gather himself, and said, "Regarding that vampire, Charlie . . . if Sammael knows, he'll use it. He'll claim that I'll never be able to give you a day, let alone the time you need to adjust—and that I'll succumb to the bloodlust again."

Trepidation rolled through her. Not that they'd have sex—she wanted that, wanted him. But she wanted a choice just as much, so that when she'd adapted to life as a vampire, she could accept him because of that desire. *Not* because her body and the bloodlust forced her to. "Will you succumb?"

"No. I swear it. You rile me up pretty good, Charlie, but I ain't an Enthralled novice."

He opened his shields to underscore his words, and his

determination filled her with a strong, steady beat. How strange and amazing, to sense his emotions that way. To immediately recognize them—though there must be nuances she'd have to learn to decipher. These were in broad, single layers; but emotions were rarely uncomplicated.

"All right," she said softly.

Jane's neighborhood slept below them. Charlie opened herself to the sounds—the sparse traffic, the televisions and music, a few voices—and pushed them away before it became too much. So many families, couples, lovers.

She closed her eyes, shut out the vision of her sister's perfect house, and thought of Ethan's brother. "You're going to kill Sammael, aren't you?"

Ethan took a long second before answering. "Probably not tonight. But eventually, it'll come to that. He'll kill me, or I will him. I admit I'm looking forward to slaying him, and if an opportunity arises, I'll take it."

Tears pricked behind her eyelids. When she finally stopped thinking of Sammael as Dylan, and when she could separate the demon she'd met from the man she'd thought she'd known, Charlie imagined that she wouldn't regret it either.

Except for one thing.

"Jane loves him. I know who he's pretending to be isn't real, but her feelings are."

"Yes." His arms tightened around her. "She'll need you."

"Yes." She turned her face against his shoulder. What would she do if it was reversed? How would that tear her up, leaning on a sister who was with a man who'd brought such pain . . . however good his reasons for doing it? "I don't know how she'll take it, if you're feeding me and she still loves him. I don't know if you being around will hurt her."

Ethan's jaw looked as hard as the knot of dread in her belly. He didn't reply until they were hovering over Jane's eerily silent house.

"Well," he finally said, "if it comes to that, then it's fortunate that I'm real good at sneaking through windows in the middle of the night."

CHAPTER 14

From their positions behind the sliding door, Sammael and the second demon could likely smell the gasoline fumes, but they probably thought a Guardian was too sissified to light it.

Charlie obviously had no doubts. She took one sniff and backed away from Sammael's fancy SUV, unease rolling through her psychic scent. "Are you sure Jane won't be trapped in there?"

"Yes. The security system has a fire alarm, and it'll blare something fierce when smoke starts moving in—the spell can't stop air, smoke, or fire. And Sammael will wake her up if it doesn't ring loud enough." Ethan yanked his sword out of the gas tank and stood. He'd shoved the SUV as far onto the backyard patio as it'd go, and the driver's side was almost flush with the glass sliding door. "My most pressing concern is how big a chunk Lilith's dog is going to take out of my ass when she has to find a way to cover this up, too."

Eyes narrowed, Charlie backed up another step. "Are you enjoying this?" She sounded on the edge between falling into laughter and flying into a temper.

God Almighty, she sure was something. Despite everything

that had come at her, how bad it had knocked her around, she'd gotten right back on her feet. Not perfectly steady, but fighting. And he figured it did him good just to look at her, to hear her voice, to breathe the same air.

"I'm enjoying it a bit," he said easily. "Now you step back a little farther. A spark won't set you aflame, but this much heat will leave a burn on you." Him, too, but it wouldn't pain a Guardian as much as it would a vampire.

She was across the backyard within a blink. Ethan vanished his jacket; no need to singe it.

He pulled her pack of cigarettes and her lighter from his cache. "You want a smoke, Charlie?" he called softly over his shoulder.

"Thanks, but I'm trying to quit."

Ethan grinned. Mostly amusement filled her reply now, and that was just fine. "I used to roll my own cigarettes." He slipped one between his lips, tossed the rest through the missing passenger door. Charlie's blood stained the seat's leather upholstery. "It was more manly that way. Out west, only dudes smoked store-bought. But the rest of us, we rolled our own, and used live rattlesnakes as suspenders."

Charlie was choking on her laughter; Sammael was frowning at him through the window, starting to shake his head. The demon at his side was smaller in stature, not as pretty, and was backing away from the door.

Now, that was interesting. Appearances mattered to demons. He was likely subservient to Sammael, then.

"You cover your ears, Charlie. It ought to just flare up pretty good, but if it blows, it'll set them ringing. And when they lower the spell, the alarm will." He glanced back; her hands were tight on either side of her head. "You ready?"

She nodded, and he cupped his palm around the end of the cigarette, lit it, and took a long drag. It burned his throat and lungs like hell, but he kept smiling into Sammael's now-glowing eyes.

Then he vanished a good amount of gasoline into his cache and dumped it onto the SUV's backseat. Even if nothing else roasted, that seat would.

"All right then," he said, and pitched the cigarette in after the fuel.

His jacket was in his hands again less than a second later,

and he wrapped it around Charlie, used it and his body to shield her from the rush of superheated air. The sky lighted up, orange as a sunset. Metal squealed as it warped. Glass shattered—the SUV's windows. The sliding door had likely done the same, but he wouldn't be hearing it.

From beneath his jacket, Charlie whispered, "Holy shit."

That about summed it up. His arms tight around her, he formed his wings and took to the air, avoiding the wavering column of heat rising from the burning vehicle. The side of the house was catching, too, little runners of fire climbing the shingles like ivy.

A light winked on in the upstairs bedroom. That'd be Jane, jolted out of bed by the alarm. Sammael was likely already in there with her. And not doing anything a human couldn't do yet, Ethan figured, because the demon would be confident he could continue his charade indefinitely. He'd hold on to that human identity, not wanting to scare Jane away.

And it was far too hot for a human to escape through the back, so they'd go out the front door.

Ethan set Charlie down on the opposite side of the street, vanished his wings again. Neighbors would be coming out before too long, or peeking through their windows. He put Jane's little car by the curb, and didn't suppress the tiny shudder of relief that the demon blood inside was out of his cache, as well.

A tug on his jacket spun Charlie out of it, and he steadied her without taking his gaze from the house. Shadows moved behind the closed drapes on the first floor, coming toward the door.

"All right," he said, slipping his coat on. "When she comes out, you yell for her, get her attention. They can't hold her back."

"I can't yell."

He darted a glance at her. No, she hadn't on the roof that first night, either. At the time, he'd thought her fear had kept her quiet, but he reckoned now she'd have broken a few windows if she'd had her voice. Maybe a few eardrums, too. "I'll get her attention, then. You just wave her on over."

Her fingers clenched on his arm when the door opened, and Jane ran through in a pair of flannel pajamas, holding on to Sammael's hand and with a big bag in her other hand. She slowed and backpedaled, watching the house and looking away from the street.

"That's Jane. It ain't a demon," he assured Charlie. "Cover your ears up again."

He hadn't done this in over a century, but it just took two fingers against his tongue and a blast of air from his lungs—and his whistle was loud enough it about broke his own eardrums.

Jane spun around. A line appeared between her brows, her mouth turning down with surprise. "Charlie?" She stepped toward them, pulling Sammael along with her.

Where was the other demon? Must be still inside—Ethan couldn't hear the alarm yet, so the spell was up. It'd fall just as soon as they all left.

Jane took another step, and Ethan met the demon's eyes.

That wasn't Sammael.

"Jane, darling, hold on a minute," the demon said.

"Come on, Jane." It was a rasp, but Charlie's frantically gesturing hands spoke it louder and better.

Jane looked away from her sister to frown at the demon. "The alarm's off, Dylan." She tugged her hand, but he didn't release her. "Why can't I hear the alarm?"

"I can't let you go, Jane." He held her hand tight, though she pulled at it again. His voice was almost pleading. "I can't let you get away from me."

Ethan sucked in a hard breath. The demon was denying her free will. There wasn't much Ethan could imagine would make a demon do that—unless he was compelled by a bargain with Sammael to keep Jane from leaving with Charlie.

That sure as hell would explain the subservience. A demon might be destroyed or Punished for denying a human's will, but many would consider the punishment for breaking a bargain worse than death or torture. And with the Gates closed, maybe this one wouldn't face the consequences for going against Jane's will for five hundred years yet, so it seemed a better alternative than facing Sammael's immediate vengeance.

Jane yanked on her arm, and when she couldn't get away, got up in the demon's face. The woman had a powerful temper on her.

"Charlie wrote me a sticky, Dylan, about silencing spells

and vampires and demons, saying that you can't stop me if I want to go. I thought it was a joke—but *I can't hear the alarm.* So you've got about one second to prove her wrong, and then I'm walking over there."

"Just do it now," Charlie muttered, but apparently she wasn't going to wait for Jane's second to pass. She made a move forward. Ethan put his hand over hers, keeping her from approaching the demon.

"That's not Sammael, Charlie," he said softly. "I don't rightly know if he'll come after you to keep Jane from going, even if Sammael has told him not to hurt you. I reckon he's got a lot to lose right now."

The demon met Ethan's eyes again. "He'll kill me, Jane. If you leave with him, he'll kill me."

Jane had turned her head to look at Charlie, but at that statement her gaze lifted to Ethan's face, then returned to the demon's. "Him?"

"Just stay with me of your free will until he comes out, so I can live. You're an extraordinary woman, Jane, and you can save me just by waiting with me for another minute. I love you so much."

The demon was awful good at the kicked-puppy bit, with his eyes big and swimming with tears, his voice pleading; if Ethan was in her shoes, his heart would have been about breaking.

Ethan called out, "That ain't Dylan, Jane."

She turned to look again, but not at Ethan. Her gaze sought Charlie's, and when Charlie shook her head, her eyes wide and pleading, Jane's face set with determination.

She pulled hard, and the demon didn't let her go.

The hairs on Ethan's nape prickled. The air hummed like something had rubbed out a static charge . . . something big and powerful that didn't feel like Sammael, or anything else he'd ever encountered.

The demon felt it, too. He half-turned, glanced back at the house, the begging posture dropping away.

So did his human form. Taloned hands and feet, black horns curling away from a still-human face—human but for the scarlet scales.

Jane screamed, and this time, the demon let her slip away without a fight. Swords appeared in his hands, and he turned round and round. Ethan watched him, his heart pounding, and ran with Charlie to Jane, then backed up slowly as both women sprinted to the car. He palmed his sword in his right hand, his crossbow in his left, and made certain it was loaded with venom-soaked bolts.

"Dylan?" Jane whispered in disbelief, and the alarm split the air.

Ethan glanced away from the demon, saw Sammael at the front door, his face twisting with surprise . . . and fear.

Sammael hissed a few words in the demon tongue, and his own weapons appeared. His gaze searched out Jane, and his face softened. "Don't be afraid. You need to close your eyes. And you need to get away from Charlie."

Ethan frowned. The women had their arms around each other and were leaning against Jane's small car. Nothing was going to be separating them, and surely Sammael wasn't fearing that Charlie was going to bite—

The being came in from nowhere. Teleported. Ethan swore and backed up a step, and for an instant shock held him motionless.

Black feathered wings.

No Guardian but the Doyen could create wings like that; a demon couldn't either. Only white feathers or the membranous wings that demons and nosferatu wore.

But this creature wasn't Michael, the only other being Ethan had ever seen with those wings, and one of the few Guardians who could teleport.

He'd *never* heard of a demon teleporting.

And although it had crimson skin and eyes that were fully obsidian, the rest of it looked human. Metal plates formed a skirt like a Roman centurion's armor, and they clinked with its movement.

Quick—quicker than Ethan—it went after the demon who'd been impersonating Sammael, had him hanging upside-down with its hand circling his ankle.

Its psyche felt like scales on a snake's belly.

"God Almighty," Ethan whispered, and threw himself in front of Charlie and Jane, blocking their view just as the creature's sword slid through the demon's neck.

No torture. Just a simple, clean kill, and the demon's head dropped to the ground. The body and the head vanished.

Sammael slowly circled the creature, wariness in every step, as if he was trying not to draw its attention.

Charlie's fear was leaking through her shields. "Drifter?" Her voice was below a whisper. "What's going on?"

The creature's uncanny black gaze settled on Ethan. But the interest in its psychic scent was all wrong, not on Ethan at all . . . but behind him. Its eyes turned red, began shining.

Ethan's gut twisted up tight. A demon. Some kind of demon . . . and it had tortured and bled out a *vampire*.

"Charlie," he said hoarsely. "You and Jane get away from here." Her bag was in his cache; he dropped it at her feet, then dumped a pile of weapons on the Toyota's backseat. The demon tilted its head, as if sizing Ethan up. "You take the car and put the symbols on the dash, and drive in any direction you want. Before dawn comes, you find a place, pay for it with a credit card, and put the spell up around the room. Don't let the sunlight touch you. You'll be in your daysleep until evening, and I'll find you when you wake up. Or if I don't come, you use the number I dialed on your phone last night."

"If you don't . . . ?" Her voice shuddered to nothing. "Drifter—"

"*Miss Charlie.* Go." He wanted to look back, to see her. But hearing her scramble around the car, opening the passenger door for Jane would have to do.

The black-winged demon moved. Ethan let the bolt from the crossbow fly, then raced across the street to meet its sword an instant later. His blade broke under the force of its swing, pain tearing up his arms. He immediately brought in another, just managed to keep his head on his shoulders.

The crossbow's bolt was embedded in its chest.

The venom hadn't slowed it a bit.

Get the shield up around the car. He didn't have time to shout the warning before dodging yet another attack from the demon's sword. He was quickly losing the distance he'd gained. Jane wasn't even inside the vehicle yet, her human speed nothing in comparison to Ethan's, or even Charlie's.

He heard Charlie urging her in, ducked a swipe of a blade, and saw Sammael's gaze fix on the women.

The winged demon's attack was elegant and brutal. A feint, then a strike low. Pain tore across Ethan's stomach in a burning line. The scent of blood filled the air, and Charlie's cry; she must have seen it slice his belly open.

This thing was going to have him dead before she was in the car.

Like hell. Guns weren't much good short-range, too easy to knock off the aim, but Ethan called in a pistol, got a shot to its face before its foot caught his arm. That slowed it a little, but the ache in Ethan's forearm told him a bone had snapped.

He fell back a yard, two, tried to gain a moment to re-assess, to think. He didn't get one.

Jane's voice barely registered through the haze of pain, but Sammael's psychic wave of indecision did. Then resignation, when she shouted again. "Dylan—for God's sake, *help him*!"

Ethan dropped, flattened himself against the pavement to avoid the winged demon's whistling blade. No way to get up in time—

It suddenly fell back, its swords flashing.

Ethan blinked, and rose up on his knees. Sammael was meeting it strike for strike, forcing it away from Ethan and the women.

He dared a glance back at the car. Charlie was pulling the driver's side door closed; her frightened eyes met his through the window. "Come with us."

He shook his head. "Go," he said, then turned to focus on the battle in front of him. Sammael was still fighting, but although the creature had lost ground, surprised by Sammael's attack, it was bearing in on him as it regrouped.

Tires screeched as Charlie tore onto the road, barely missing Ethan's leg. The shield was up a moment later.

That wouldn't be enough; they had to get the creature out of public sight, keep it occupied long enough that it couldn't follow the vehicle.

"I could use some saving here, Guardian," Sammael growled. "Unless you *don't* want them to get away."

Ethan didn't consider himself an easily surprised man, but that did it. "Well, I'll be damned," he muttered, and jumped to his feet.

And if not damned, probably stabbed through the back within a minute.

CHAPTER 15

"What are they doing?" Charlie tried to use the rearview mirror to see, but Jane had turned to look through the window, and her head was blocking the view. In the side mirror, she only saw the glow from the fire in Jane's backyard. They were going to turn the corner in a second, lose sight of Ethan and that . . . whatever it had been. "Jane! What are they doing?"

"I can't—they're going too fast . . . Oh my God, how can they move that fast?" Jane's voice rose shrilly, then abruptly lowered. "It looks like they're pushing that thing back toward the house."

"Both of them? Together?" Ethan had been injured, bleeding across his stomach, but he'd seemed strong when he'd told her to go. She hoped she'd done the right thing by listening to him. "Does Ethan look okay?"

"Yes. Yes, they're both fighting and—oh, *Jesus*. There are knives and guns and swords back here. What the fuck is going on?"

Charlie drew a quick breath through her nose, prepared to answer her . . . and the scent hit her, rich and dark. Blood.

Her body tightened; her fangs began to ache. She'd been

careful when she'd poked her finger and cast the spell, inhaling only through her mouth. She'd forgotten that Sammael had bled in here as part of his ruse to get her out of the house.

She focused hard on the road, not breathing, and pushed the need away.

It didn't recede as much as it had the last time.

They rounded the end of the block; from farther down the street came flashing lights. Probably a siren, too, but she couldn't hear it through the spell.

"Turn around, Jane," she rasped. "Don't let a cop see you up out of the seat like that."

No driver's license, and a pile of weapons in the back. She didn't want to be pulled over now.

Jane seemed to realize it at the same instant. She sat, buckled up. "Let me drive, then."

Charlie shook her head. "I've got some stuff to tell you, and I don't think you'll be able to concentrate on the road."

Charlie thought she'd be lucky if *she* could. She controlled her breathing, ignored the hunger.

A high, rising note slid into her. Fear. Light and elusive, barely a touch; she stole a glance at Jane. Her sister was staring at her mouth.

"Oh, my God, Charlie," she said in a small voice, and the fear shifted into disbelief, dread. "Smile at me."

Charlie looked through the windshield again, her lips pressed together. The taillights of a car farther down the street wavered in front of her, and she wondered if she'd ever see red lights again without thinking of Sammael's eyes, the vampire sucking at her neck.

She'd never been this terrified in her life. Would have given anything for Ethan to appear beside them, so she could stop and lean on him, fly away and put off telling this to Jane for as long as possible.

But Jane wouldn't be put off. She reached out as if she meant to push back Charlie's upper lip.

Charlie caught her wrist, then met her eyes. They were wide with surprise—and though Charlie felt the shudder that raced through her sister's body, Jane didn't yank her hand away.

Jane swallowed. "Your skin is like ice," she whispered.

Charlie let go of her wrist. "And your hair is sticking up in the back." But she couldn't hold it in, had to wipe at her cheeks, use her sleeve to clear her vision.

Jane seemed to attempt a smile, drawing her feet up to the edge of the seat, wrapping her arms around her shins. Her gaze remained on Charlie's face, her voice thick. "Are you okay?"

"Yes. No." She lifted her hands and spread them wide before slapping them back to the steering wheel. "I don't know, but I think I will be." If Ethan was all right. If Jane handled the news about Dylan as well as she had her sister being a vampire. If the blood in the car didn't turn her into a ravenous animal by the time they got . . . wherever they were going. "We're about to hit I-5. Should we go north or south?"

"South." Jane was still studying her. "Were you bitten?"

Charlie touched the side of her neck, thankful that the bite marks had long since healed. "Yes."

"Was it that guy? Ethan?"

"No. He's not a vampire." She immediately regretted saying the word out loud; now there was no way to take it back. She rushed on, "He tried to stop it."

"A vampire," Jane echoed, then put her face between her knees, slid her hands up to link them behind her head. Charlie recognized the pose—it had been the same the night their dad had told them about his leukemia. Jane had curled herself up like that. Charlie had gone for a bottle—but she would have gone for one that night, regardless. Just as she had every night.

"Yes," Charlie said.

"And you didn't want it." Jane's voice was muffled.

"No."

A low, heavy beat rolled into her, its tempo increasing. Anger. Jane lifted her face from her knees, and her eyes were glinting with it. "Who did it?"

Charlie held her gaze, and it took two attempts to push the answer past the terrible ache in her throat.

"Dylan."

❧

Sammael didn't stab Ethan in the back. Instead, the bastard just up and left.

Ethan only had a moment to glance behind him, to register his disbelief that Sammael was waving good-bye to him with the arm the black-winged demon had just severed from Sammael's shoulder. Then the winged demon was coming at Ethan again, and he couldn't think of Sammael anymore.

They'd managed to get it into the house—the empty house, as Sammael had apparently taken those few extra moments to clean it out before coming outside—and once they'd gotten the demon into the backyard and up into the air, they'd covered ground fast. Ground *and* water—they were far out over Puget Sound. Almost to Port Townsend, Ethan figured. Small islands formed dark spots in the water, a few lights sparkling from houses and boats.

Awful pretty, but Ethan didn't want to be killed here, and he'd have to be a fool to think he could beat it alone. He dove, folding his wings against his back. The demon came after him.

Son of a bitch. Ethan was willing to look a yellow-bellied coward if it saved his life, but this thing wasn't letting him run. He turned, tried to keep ahead of it, but it was gaining on him. Rolling onto his back, falling headfirst, Ethan pulled in his last loaded pistols from his cache and fired them past his feet.

Though his aim was true, the bullets didn't slow it down.

Fear clawed at his chest, but he forced it into icy purpose. He wasn't going to die like this, not knowing if Charlie was all right and without warning the other Guardians about this thing. He rolled again, banked toward the city. He couldn't shake the demon out here in all this open air, but downtown he might have a chance, maybe getting into a building or underground, putting up the spell and waiting it out.

If he made it back to the city. He was looking ahead, flying as fast as he'd ever flown, but he could feel it closing in.

How much time had he bought Charlie? Five minutes, ten? Enough to get her onto the highway? He ought to have made certain she'd be cared for and taught to master her new abilities, that there'd be someone she could feed from.

His eyes narrowed. Far ahead, a small dark form was flying toward them. Sammael, returning? The bastard's arm would have healed by now. Leastwise, enough that it wouldn't fall off.

No, not Sammael. Jake, in an erratic, up-and-down flight path.

The kid was projecting the spinning, whirling emotions of a novice in deep Enthrallment. Even when he didn't have a lotus-eating smile on his face, Jake hadn't experience enough to fight the demon, and he hadn't had any opportunity to learn his Gift. And if he was flying, he must not have been able to teleport to Ethan.

Goddammit. Jake obviously intended to help, but it'd be an all-fired miracle if they weren't both killed in about ten seconds. At least Ethan hadn't had to care if the black-winged demon had gutted Sammael, except that it meant Ethan wouldn't have had the pleasure of doing it himself.

He needed more time. Ethan glanced back and dropped his truck out of his cache above the demon. The heavy vehicle slammed onto its back, flipping it over in the air.

That only bought a few seconds, but it was enough for Ethan to adjust his course to intercept the novice. He called in his swords again, holding them flat against his body to avoid unnecessary drag. Little choice but to grab Jake, tell him to haul ass, and then try to keep the demon off the kid for as long as possible.

He didn't hear it, but he saw Jake mouth his name as he drew in close.

Below them, a light twinkled. A ship plowed through the water—long, dark, and solid.

Well, hell. He wasn't going to die just yet.

"Dive!" Ethan shouted and gestured the command at the same time, vanishing his swords.

Jake looked confused for about a second, then he was heading down. Ethan caught up with him. "Get rid of your wings!"

Jake was yelling something, probably that they were going to smash pretty hard against the water if they didn't let up.

It's a boat, Ethan signed. *We'll crash in through the side, get the spell up.*

"It's a *tanker,*" Jake shouted as his wings disappeared.

"Well, I figure it's too late to stop now!" Ethan straightened out his body, increasing the speed of the dive, using minute movements of his wings to align himself over Jake's back.

"How the hell did you ever become anyone's mentor?" Despite the bluster in Jake's voice, fear was cutting through his Enthrallment.

As soon as Ethan got hold of the kid's sides, he pulled him in tight against his chest and vanished his wings. A glance behind them confirmed the demon was still coming. "I reckon this is going to hurt *real bad*!"

"You think?" Jake screamed back at him.

"That tanker looks awful big, Jake, and that steel damn solid," Ethan said, his voice low and dangerous now, deliberately winding up the kid's fear. "If you don't want to be scraped up with a shovel and my teeth embedded in your tattooed ass, you better picture us in a real happy place, and you better picture it hard!"

Then he was twisting, turning, and slamming into a plastic floor. It cracked beneath his weight, but held. Ethan didn't open his eyes. His head was spinning, nausea churning in his stomach.

That was the roughest teleportation he'd ever had, but damn if it didn't feel fine to be on the verge of heaving up his lungs rather than having his stomach laid open again.

"You did good, Jake. You all right?"

"Yeah." He couldn't hear Jake moving either, but the groan that accompanied the word told Ethan it was for a different reason: utter relief. "I think you're my hero, Drifter."

Well, damn. Ethan rolled onto his back, pulled his phone in, and concentrated on dialing the tiny buttons while his head was whirling. Charlie's number went straight to voice mail. She'd had her phone on, so that meant she was inside the shield. He left a short message, telling her again to use her credit card, and to be under cover when the sun rose.

She'd be hungry by dawn, and feeling it bad by nightfall.

"How is she?" Jake asked quietly. "I heard you flying over the lake, but it sounded like you were having a private conversation, so I stayed behind. Then when I got there the house was burning, and it was just, 'Fire, pretty' and I lost it. I saw you take off fighting, but I didn't think I'd catch up to you."

Ethan stared up at the low wooden ceiling. "She's sucking blood."

"God damn." Jake was silent for a minute, which was about fifty seconds longer than Ethan would have expected. "I don't know what to say."

"That's just fine." Ethan clenched his jaw. "Because I'm grateful to you for teleporting us out of there, and what happened to Charlie is my own damn fault, but I don't reckon I'll have anything civil to say to you for a day, maybe a week."

"All right." Ten seconds passed. "Was that a demon?"

"I don't rightly know." Ethan stood, keeping his back hunched so he wouldn't rap his head, and waited for his legs to steady. Unease rolled through him. Life-sized dolls surrounded them, some dressed in leathers and moccasins, some in chaps and ten-gallon hats. Most of them were smiling. "Where in damnation did you bring us?"

Jake lifted his head and grinned like a fool. "Disneyland."

❧

Jane cried for almost two hours. She'd listened quietly as Charlie had told her everything that had happened—then she'd broken.

After the first bout of sobbing had passed, she'd silently wept while staring out the passenger window.

Charlie thought exhaustion brought it to an end, because the pain was still deep, steady, and discordant when Jane's tears stopped. There was too much emotion mixed up in there to hear correctly: grief and disbelief, denial and—even now—what Charlie thought must be love. But that was complicated, too, with its own set of notes, and Charlie was having difficulty sorting through them.

And it didn't help that she was starving.

She'd spent most of the last half hour not thinking of her sister's pain, but imagining ways of easing the burning need inside her: Pulling off at the next exit and taking a drink from a gas station attendant. From a waitress.

From Jane.

They passed a blue road sign advertising food and lodging. Jane sat up, wiped at her face. "Why don't we pull off here?"

Woodland. A small town, but it was right off the highway, so there'd probably be something open.

"Okay," Charlie said. "Are you hungry?"

"No. Are you?"

"Yes." Charlie bared her fangs, clicked her teeth lightly together a few times, but couldn't quite hide the truth behind it. "We should pick up a few things first. Food for you tomorrow. A book, because there won't be any TV."

"What will you do?"

Ethan had said something about daysleep. "I think I'll sleep. But I don't know what that means."

"If you're hungry, will you attack me while you're unconscious?"

"I don't know." Her hands tightened on the steering wheel. "Maybe I'll lock myself in the bathroom."

Jane was silent for a tense moment. "Why don't you just take some of my blood—"

"No."

"I don't care. And if you can heal me, it's no big deal—"

It burst from her. "Except I'll end up screwing you!"

They stared at each other, until Jane clapped her hands over her eyes and bent forward. "Oh, *Jesus,* Charlie!" Her amusement was light and sweet, like the trill of a piccolo; her laughter was much heavier, deep and rolling.

Charlie grinned, turned back to the road. "Shut up."

"I guess I don't love you *that* much!"

"Fuck you. Yes, you do."

That only made Jane laugh harder, but by then Charlie was having a difficult time controlling her laughter, too.

Yet a sour note lay beneath it, and not until they'd shielded themselves in the little motel room did Charlie realize what it was: desperation. They'd needed the laugh, but the edge of hysteria lingered longer than the amusement did.

The bed frame sat on the floor, with no room beneath it. The small closet had no door. If she locked herself in the bathroom, Jane wouldn't be able to use it.

And Charlie wanted nothing more than to sit down and cry.

Nothing more than to suck someone dry.

At least Ethan had called. His message had been brief; he hadn't said how he was doing.

But he was alive. Her phone hadn't recorded the incoming number to return the call, but she thought if she hadn't heard from him, she probably *would* be sobbing by now, not just feeling like it.

"Take the bed, Charlie," Jane said, closing the drapes. She'd had four messages from Sammael on Charlie's phone; Charlie had had to convince her not to listen to them. Now resignation and grief hung around Jane, tinged by uncertainty and fear. "I won't be able to sleep, anyway. And it's almost dawn."

"But what if—"

"Do you think that flimsy little door will stop you?" Jane waved at the bathroom.

Charlie shook her head, and shoved her hands into her sweatshirt pouch. Ethan's feather slid between her fingers.

A tingling began at the back of her neck. Instinct drove her to the bed, and she dug under the blankets, making certain she was covered. The sun. She had *felt* the sun coming up, and now it was dragging her down.

Clutching the feather to her chest, hunger burning in her fangs and cramping in her stomach, she fell into sleep.

And kept falling, into dreams that were stained with crimson: Jane's blood, Ethan's blood, and a demon's red, red eyes.

CHAPTER 16

Just about everyone at SI was watching him careful, talking gently as if they expected him to start bawling at the least little upset. After Becca rolled up her usual snarky tone and asked him quiet-like if he was doing all right, and she'd heard about his brother, and was there anything they could do to help him locate Charlie, Ethan began to look forward to the bite Lilith's dog was sure to take out of his hindquarters.

Except when he walked into Castleford and Lilith's office, both she and Sir Pup grinned at him. Her three-headed hellhound had just as many sets of wickedly sharp teeth, but it was Lilith's gleaming smile that had him pausing, suddenly wary.

Ethan caught Castleford's eyes. "Should I turn tail?"

"That will depend on what you have to tell us." Castleford closed the book he'd been holding and dropped it to his desk. "But as of this moment, no."

Lilith slung her leg over the arm of her chair and leaned back, still grinning. "A winged man landing on top of a moving vehicle on a busy street. A man in a duster crawling around the top of said vehicle, shooting at the tires. A man sliding down the front of the hood, disappearing underneath the vehicle, and then—by all accounts—lifting it and tossing it over the side of a bridge. And, somehow, that same vehicle, which disappeared from the scene at the bridge, being involved in an arson fire at the home of a wealthy medical researcher." She extended her leg, glanced down at the toe of her boot. "This should be a mile up your ass right now, but I haven't had to come up with so many lies so quickly in decades. So I'm having far too much fun."

"*Far* too much," Castleford echoed dryly. "She's had the novices claiming to be eyewitnesses, and they're feeding bloggers, reporters, and the investigators so many conflicting accounts that no one will be able to piece together the truth of what happened. Fortunately, we've only seen one photo so far, taken from a cell phone—you on top of the SUV, but no wings or guns."

"You look ridiculous," Lilith said. "Like something out of a bad action movie, so we're playing that angle, too—kids making a home video, an unauthorized film shoot—though it would have been better if you'd been wearing a hat. And we'll buy costume wings, toss them into the lake. Maybe a hang glider, too, because we've been running with that on the personal blogs. And speaking of movies . . ."

She trailed off and looked at Castleford, who crossed the room and sat against the front of her desk. Ethan had difficulty seeing the young, monkish Guardian he'd known in the human man before him, but the patience in Castleford's gaze and the deliberation which underpinned Castleford's every movement were as familiar to Ethan as the weight of his holsters, the heft of his wings.

Michael had transformed Ethan, but this man had made him a Guardian.

And the concern he read in Castleford's psychic scent worried him more than Lilith's grin. One, that it was there—and two, that Castleford was letting him read it.

Castleford held Ethan's gaze and asked, "How is Charlotte Newcomb?"

"She's adjusting. But she's a vampire, and she'd rather not be," Ethan said quietly.

Lilith sat up, turning her computer monitor to face him. "Savi called us directly before dawn, told us she'd just taken a look at this video, then sent it to us by e-mail. It's copied to you, so it'll be in your inbox, as well."

The images were from the security feed from the front of the lake house. Jane's car arriving, the vampire streaking out of the shadows. The angle changing as Savi chose the feed from another camera, and Charlie was trying to crawl past Sammael into the house, then being forced toward the SUV.

Castleford slid on his glasses, tilting his head as he studied the monitor. "She chooses her hits well—going for the least expected and the most impact in vulnerable points—and she learns quickly what doesn't work." He paused. "Did she fight all the way?"

"Yes." Ethan watched with his hands clenched, his jaw set. When it looped back to Jane's car driving in, he managed to say, "Fought the vampire, leastwise. She chose the transformation at the end, but only because she didn't want to die."

Castleford frowned, glanced at the video again. "When the choice is between life and death, it's a fine line between free will and force. Sammael must have known that she'd choose the change, that she'd force herself to drink."

"He was good: the setup, the vampire," Lilith said, then turned off the monitor. "But it shouldn't have happened."

"No," Ethan said, his voice rough.

Castleford turned to Ethan. "Lilith and I can speak with Jake, or you can."

Ethan's brows drew together, and he glanced between them. "You're putting this on *Jake*?"

"No." Lilith frowned, and laid her hand on Sir Pup's neck when the dog lifted one of his giant heads from his forepaws. "Newcomb was yours. We're putting it on you—all of it, including Jake."

"And everything we have to say to him would be more meaningful coming from you," Castleford said.

Well, damn. Ethan pulled the sides of his jacket back, hooked his thumbs in his suspenders, and studied their faces. "Does this mean I'm mentoring him again?"

Lilith offered a demure smile that Ethan figured was pure evil. "Only demons Punish their own kind. Guardians are too good at punishing themselves when they fuck up. Any attempt to top that guilt is an exercise in futility."

Castleford slanted her a wry look before glancing back at

Ethan. "He's been training for forty years. We need more Guardians active and can't wait the usual century before getting them there. Jake is skilled; he just hasn't had to use it."

That was where Castleford's troubled feeling was coming from, then: partnering the novices up and putting them out would teach them quicker than just training, but it'd also put them at a greater risk. But it was also true that their Guardian numbers were too low, and a change had to be made.

And Jake's teleporting Gift would protect him somewhat; if he got in serious trouble, he could get out of it easier than most novices. For the same reason, Selah was often the one who accompanied Michael when he needed a Guardian to assist him with something he couldn't handle alone.

Ethan nodded slowly. "All right then. I'll have him split his time between training here and working out there with me. Once he's mastered his Gift, it'll be easy enough for him to do both."

"Teleportation," Lilith said, pursing her lips. "I was sure his Gift would be making rainbows or something equally useless. Now, Drifter—" Her eyes narrowed, and Sir Pup got to his feet. "You've felt us out, seen where we're at. You've got two seconds to start talking."

That was two more seconds than she'd given him last time; she must have heard about Caleb, and was going easy on him for it. "You got any inkling of where Michael is?"

Castleford and Lilith exchanged a glance.

"It's that bad?" Lilith asked.

"I don't rightly know," Ethan said. "But I ran into something that looked an awful lot like him, but with crimson skin. And it teleported in."

Castleford's brows pulled in tight, and he said with a slight shake of his head, "Like Michael? Took his form?"

"No, though they were roughly the same size. I'm speaking of the wings, and before they went red, the eyes."

Lilith's expression didn't change, but beside her, Sir Pup whined softly and licked her hand with his left head. "Black?"

"Yes."

Castleford half-turned to look at her, then picked up her phone. "Selah hasn't been able to anchor to Michael for a day now," he told Ethan as he dialed. "We'll try again."

Ethan nodded. If Michael had his psychic shields up full,

Selah couldn't locate him and teleport to his location. Lilith sat quietly, stroking one of Sir Pup's heads while Castleford spoke with Selah. It didn't take long to get the same answer.

"She still can't," Castleford said, and his gaze was curious as it ran over Lilith's face. "You've heard of something like this before?"

"Heard, yes. I have no idea how much of it was lies, or exaggeration."

"You heard it from demons?" Ethan guessed.

A smile tilted her lips. "Yes, from one of Belial's demons not long after I became a halfling. And it was an old story then."

Ethan frowned. Lilith had been transformed into a demon over two thousand years before, about the same amount of time Guardian history had been recorded in the Scrolls. "What was it, then?"

"The only other beings I've heard of having the black wings are the nephilim," she said, and a flicker of recognition crossed Castleford's face. "Another one of Lucifer's experiments—the nephilim were the offspring of demons and humans."

"I remember reading something of them in the Scrolls several hundred years ago, but I'm certain there was no mention that they'd been born of humans," Castleford said slowly. "And demons aren't fertile—was it done through a ritual?"

Lilith shrugged. "I never got the details. I don't even know that the demon who told me had the details, or was just passing it on."

"How could he not know?" Ethan asked. "Demons have been around since The First Battle, and I ain't ever met one with a faulty memory."

Lilith arched her brows. "Three weeks ago, you tracked down a demon living in Toronto and slew her. *You*—a Guardian with little more than a century of training—killed an ageless demon. And I don't know for certain, but I can guess the reason why has a lot to do with Lucifer."

Ethan figured most everything in Hell had to do with Lucifer. "How is that?"

"Every demon was once an angel," Lilith said. "But only Lucifer has any real knowledge of the symbols, and how to use the magic. If *He* didn't take the rebelling angels' knowledge when He transformed them into demons, then Lucifer must have been the one to take it from them."

Ethan nodded. "To keep them under control."

"Yes. He always removed anything that might threaten his throne." Lilith's fingers were drawing blissful sighs from Sir Pup; half of his fur had become scales, reminding Ethan that Lucifer experiments had created hellhounds, too. Creating another form of demon wouldn't be all that different. "And perhaps he took the demons' memories, too," Lilith added, "or at least blocked them. If he did, I suspect he has altered them more than once. Lucifer wouldn't have wanted anyone to remember his failures, and the nephilim must have been one of those."

"If it was a nephilim, it was almighty powerful," Ethan said. "I ain't sure I'd consider it a failure."

"If it was *one*, it was a nephil. And according to the demon who told me about them, they were an enormous failure," Lilith said, her lips curving. "Apparently, the nephilim rose up against Lucifer, and it took the combined efforts of Belial's followers and Lucifer's to stop them."

Castleford leaned forward a bit, shaking his head. "Belial and Lucifer have only been at war these eight hundred years. How far back does their rivalry go?"

"As far as anyone remembers." Her gaze turned inward, and she rose from her desk to retrieve a bottle of water from a small refrigerated cupboard. She tossed another to Castleford, then a chunk of meat to the hellhound. "Which, again, tells me that Lucifer took something from the demons. How can they not know when it started? Yet to listen to a demon, it would seem that Belial has always wanted to return to Grace, rebelling against Lucifer's rule—but at one point, Belial must have been one of Lucifer's followers, too."

She returned to her seat. "And that is why I don't know how much of the story is propaganda—I was one of Lucifer's halflings, and it would have served Belial's demons to spread rumors about Lucifer's weaknesses and make us doubt his power. Because doubt was akin to betrayal, and a halfling's betrayal inevitably sent them to the field."

The frozen field suspended between Hell and Chaos. Ethan

hadn't ever seen it, except for images that Selah had once shown him—and judging by the way Lilith's face tightened at its mention, her hellhound's whining growls, Ethan reckoned he was lucky he never had experienced it firsthand.

Castleford was watching her as well. "What was the story he told you?" he asked quietly.

Lilith seemed to shake herself and then shrugged. "That the nephilim were the second of Lucifer's experiments. The first, the grigori, were destroyed." She looked between Ethan and Castleford. "He didn't say why or how, except that they didn't please Lucifer. The nephilim did please him, however—for a time."

"That time must have been until they stopped serving him," Ethan guessed. With Lucifer, some things were that simple.

"Yes. And although the nephilim's numbers were small, they brought Lucifer's forces to their knees . . . until Belial stepped in to assist him." Lilith's mouth twisted in a wry smile, and she glanced at Castleford. "Whether Belial truly stepped in or was forced into service . . . ? Considering the source, it's difficult to say."

"Yes," Castleford agreed.

"And they managed to imprison the nephilim—though where or how, I have no idea," Lilith said. "I've never seen any evidence of it—but there are many parts of Hell that were closed to me, or where I wouldn't have dared to venture."

Ethan frowned. "Why imprison them rather than destroy them?"

Lilith shook her head. "Perhaps they couldn't—or, if that imprisonment included Punishment, Lucifer might have preferred they experience an eternity of torture." Her brows drew together. "And the demon went on about a prophecy—in which the destruction of the nephilim would herald Lucifer's fall from the throne, Chaos breaking open on Earth, and the world saved by the sons of Belial—the standard doomsday bullshit that always looks best to those who believe it. So it might have been he didn't really know what happened to the nephilim, but just told me the version that flattered Belial."

"If it's bullshit, then why do you even mention—"

Lilith answered before Ethan could finish. "Because if Belial's demons believe it, then they might act as if it's truth.

And if this was one of the nephilim, Belial's demons will be doing anything they can to kill them."

"It ain't going to be by fighting them," Ethan said. "Sammael rabbited awful fast."

"And you tried to run, too?" Castleford asked. There was no reprimand in the question, only curiosity.

"I would have if it had let me. Jake's the only reason I ain't in pieces at the bottom of Puget Sound. That, and after Jane Newcomb yelled at Sammael, the demon assisted me a bit."

Both Lilith and Castleford sat back, their faces reflecting their surprise.

"Fuck me," Lilith said. "Does he *love* her?"

"I reckon." Ethan didn't know if that would make it all easier, or more difficult. "And it wasn't us that the nephil came after—not at first, leastwise. But once it got wind of Charlie, it sure was eager to get a kill. I figure it was what tortured that other vampire, as well."

Castleford looked at Lilith. "Did the demon who told you the story mention anything about vampires?"

"No. I don't think vampires even existed then," Lilith said, her voice dark. "And that adds another question: Is this nephil connected to the vampire massacres in Berlin, Rome, and D.C.?"

If it was, Ethan sure as hell wouldn't be leaving Charlie alone in Seattle. He made to turn toward the office door, but halted when Castleford's gaze narrowed on him, and the other man frowned thoughtfully.

"You're wondering about Sammael," Ethan guessed, figuring Castleford must have read something in his tone when Ethan had been talking about the demon. When Castleford nodded, he explained, "He's the one who gave me the poison."

Lilith sat up a little straighter, a line forming between her brows. "And your brother?" she asked.

"Sammael saw him hanged." Ethan glanced down at his boots, then up at Castleford again. The other man was studying his expression and would know Ethan wasn't lying. "It won't get in the way of protecting her. I'll do the job."

Castleford regarded him a moment longer. "All right," he said finally.

Lilith's grin was back in place. "I suppose it doesn't hurt

that 'doing the job' means that you'll probably chop Sammael's head off."

Just the thought of slaying the bastard had Ethan smiling with grim satisfaction. "That it doesn't," he agreed.

❧

Ethan found Jake in the tech room at the back of the warehouse. The light shining in from the single, small window high up on the wall glared on his computer screen, but Jake didn't look as if he was paying attention to it, anyway. He was sitting low in his seat, his hands tucked in his pockets.

Lilith hadn't been mistaken; Guardians did tend to beat up on themselves better than anyone else could.

"You got the video?"

Jake nodded without looking away from the computer.

"Pull it up," Ethan said, and crossed the room to stand beside Jake's chair.

With a deep sigh, Jake hauled himself up and fiddled with the mouse until the video was playing.

Ethan let it run through. "There's two things you ought to have done different," he said finally.

"Only two?" Jake's reply hung somewhere between sarcasm and surprise.

"You had to go out. If that had been Jane, and you'd watched a vampire get on her like that without doing anything, I'd be feeding your head to Sir Pup. And having Charlie assist you was a good idea, because with Jane's throat ripped up, there wouldn't be no way for her to get inside by herself."

"But?"

"You ought to have had Charlie wait inside until you made certain it was Jane. You had to think quick once the vampire showed, and I reckon if you'd had another second, you'd have realized that. But you often don't have seconds, so you have to think quicker."

Jake nodded. "How would I have communicated it to her through the spell?"

"Charlie's smart enough to figure that you taking off and running for your life was a damn good indication that it wasn't Jane. Have a bit of faith in the people you protect—they want to keep themselves safe just as bad as you do."

A blush spread over the kid's cheeks. "Yes, sir. What's the second thing?"

Ethan called in a sword, laid it next to the computer. "It takes less than a second. Next time, you leave weapons for her. Give her something to defend herself with if it all goes to hell. It may be she won't have a chance to use them, but a little chance is better than none. A gun might have given her a second to get back into the house; a dagger might have let her get away once the vampire got hold of her."

"All right." Jake was silent for a moment, then he looked up at Ethan with a startled lift of his brows. "That's it?"

Ethan frowned. "You want me to lay my fists into you? I'm willing."

"No. No, I just—" Jake shook his head. He turned back to the computer. "Charlie's debit card is showing a purchase at a 7-Eleven, and a pending charge at a motel in Woodland."

"You see that she's reimbursed for that." Ethan leaned down to look at the name of the motel, and nodded. "All right then. You got anything else in?"

"No, but I checked your inbox, and Savi sent you some preliminary info on Senator and Mark Brandt. She flagged one part—said she didn't know if it mattered, but Mark Brandt works for Senator Gerath."

Ethan remembered the younger Brandt mentioning that, but it hadn't meant anything to him then, either. "Why the flag?"

"Because Gerath is on the closed-door senatorial committee that formed SI. The same committee that Rael, our friendly demon congressman, had to testify in front of before they approved funding." Jake pulled up a document on-screen. "And look here: the elder Brandt was firmly against the research contract that Congressman Stafford—Rael—pushed through for Legion about six months ago, though Brandt supported a similar contract two years previous."

Ethan read through the page, and remembered the senator's comment about Legion's money not being the kind he wanted. At the time, Ethan had thought it political bluster—but Brandt, Gerath, and the demon Rael all belonged to the same party.

With a narrowing of his eyes, Ethan said, "So maybe young Brandt has been breaking confidence as legal counsel to Gerath, telling his father about Special Investigations, what's going on here. And Senator Brandt maybe knows that Stafford is a demon, and—considering that he's connected to Legion—was against the contract to keep from funding demon activity."

"That's my guess," Jake said.

"So how does Jane Newcomb fit? What were they trying to accomplish by contacting her?"

"You don't think it was just the son looking up an old flame?"

"Oh, he was partial to her—but the father was pushing him, too. And the coincidence is just too damn big." Ethan stepped back, shook his head again. The senator was trying to block Legion; normally, Ethan would have approved. But something just wasn't sitting right. "You forward this on to Castleford and Lilith, I'll ask her to feel out Rael about Brandt and Gerath."

"Done. Are you heading back up to Seattle?" Jake slipped the question in above the clacking of the keys.

"Only to Woodland. I'll be stopping at the Gate, visiting Caelum first." And getting himself as clear as he could; Charlie would be feeding from him later that night, and she'd be hungry. The bloodlust would hit hard—he didn't want to go to her without a few hours of drifting. "You're wondering if you're going back with me."

"Yes."

"No. Not today, leastwise," he said when Jake's shoulders slumped. "I'll be bringing Charlie on down. So I'd be grateful if you could ready one of the rooms upstairs—I figure SI is the safest location until I can get her settled elsewhere."

Ethan ignored Jake's wide-eyed stare. The rooms were small and utilitarian—more to give novices time alone than for living in. In some cases, however, they'd been used as temporary lodging for vampires who were visiting or undergoing training. "I've got her things," Ethan added, "but maybe you could order flowers or something pretty to put in there."

Jake turned back to the computer with a wide grin, and a moment later the screen filled with a webpage advertising flower delivery. "Right. A room for Jane, too?"

"If you want to order two bouquets, go on ahead. But I reckon it'll only be Charlie."

Jake blinked up at him. "Why?"

"Because Sammael helped me when she told him to—and because she loves him almost as hard as she does Charlie. And Sammael is twisted in his thinking, but he ain't a fool—he knows what matters to her. I figure she'll convince herself that discovering a blood substitute will save her sister long before Sammael gets a chance to do the same—and she'll believe that Sammael will change for her."

"You're serious."

"Yes." Ethan nodded slowly, heaviness settling in his chest as he thought of what Charlie's response might be. "I'd wager anything on it."

Jake snorted. "That doesn't mean anything. You'd put money on a pair of deuces."

"That's true enough." Even if his odds were low, Ethan would lay down money and bluff his way through. "But I wouldn't put one cent on Jane not returning to Seattle within a day or two."

CHAPTER 17

Charlie woke with a scream paralyzed in her throat and the cold metallic flavor of blood in her mouth. She scrubbed at her tongue with the palm of her hand, tasted nothing instead of salt and skin. Only a memory—and it faded as quickly as the nightmares that had brought it to her tongue.

God. She opened her eyes, hoping to push away the images of blood and torn flesh that flashed behind her lids. The feather lay crumpled in her fist. Her clothes were damp with sweat. *Dear God.*

Her hands shaking, she carefully lifted the edge of the blanket. A faint strip of light ran along the bottom of the drapes, but it was too white to be sunlight. Probably the glow from the fluorescent fixtures outside, then.

The shower was running, and she could hear, *feel* Jane's heartbeat. Her book lay open and upside down on the table—Jane had managed to get through a quarter of it. Not much. Hopefully she'd slept the remainder of the time.

Charlie wasn't certain she had; her body felt tired and achy, as if she'd gone several rounds and hadn't cooled down. Hunger gnawed within her—not just her stomach, but from each cell, chewing every nerve on a path to her fangs.

She glanced in the mirror over the dresser as she slid off the bed—then froze, looked again. It was as if she'd lost fifteen pounds overnight: her cheekbones sharp, her eyes dark and sunken.

Strung out. Needy.

Almost frantically, she washed her face and hands in cold water, ran a comb through her hair. Unplugged the phone from the charger and grabbed a gun from the table. The weight of the weapon in the pouch pulled the sweatshirt tight across her shoulders.

She knocked on the bathroom door, then poked her head in. The wafting steam settled on her skin, made her jerk her face away from the opening. "Jane? I'm going outside for some air."

And some blood some blood some blood.

Her teeth clenched, and she was outside an instant after Jane made a noise indicating she'd heard.

And was assaulted. Exhaust. The flickering motel sign. The roar of a semi on the highway, the cry of a baby in a room on the first floor. Bleach in the storeroom. Dogs and conversations and televisions and—

Verdi. Panting, she covered her ears, backed up against the door. *La Traviata.* Maria Callas's intricate, emotional performance.

The rest fell away.

Slowly, she stuck her hands back in her sweatshirt pouch, opened her eyes. Still loud, still strong in her lungs and nose, but not overpowering.

Footsteps sounded on the stairs. Boots, judging by the heavy tread, but she couldn't see their owner yet—the stairwell split directions at a landing halfway up. Whoever it was would exit the stairwell almost directly in front of her—but she'd have half a flight to see who was coming.

Their room was at the end of the long balcony that ran along the front of the motel. An ice dispenser and vending machines hummed behind a door to her left. No one would be sneaking up behind her . . . and she'd have time to hide the pistol if someone came out of the rooms.

She held it in the pouch, her heart hammering as he walked into view.

Ethan. His dark brown hair and amber eyes were exactly what she wanted, *needed* to see.

But even as the relieved laugh passed her lips, she pulled the gun and took aim down the stairs. Her hands were steady, though none of the rest of her was.

He stopped. His gaze ran over her face before it settled on the weapon, and he nodded. "All right then."

"How do I know?"

He placed his foot on the first step, but not to climb. His arm rested on the banister as if he intended to wait awhile. "I reckon there might be something we've said in private—"

"Behind the spell," Charlie interrupted. "So no one could have overheard."

His smile rayed from the corners of his eyes. "I just visited a heavenly little city whose name starts with a 'C,' not a 'K.'"

She barely restrained herself from jumping into his arms. "And a backup," she whispered. "Because Sammael knows I do that, too."

He hooked his left thumb in his suspender, his coat falling behind his hip. "Well, Miss Charlie, if you insist on something personal—even though it makes me blush so powerfully to say it—I'll admit I still ain't wearing skivvies."

She closed her eyes against the surge of emotion that rose beneath her laughter, pushing it up though it didn't come out with it. *Love.* And it felt bright and clean and so wonderfully deep—though it was on the surface, too, as if it clung to her skin.

Then Ethan was taking the gun from her, sliding it into her pocket to lay heavy against her belly before cupping her face in his hands, driving her back to the wall. His body came up hard against hers.

His gaze skipped from her mouth to her hair to her eyes. "You all right?"

She nodded, too overwhelmed by the feel of him to speak. The thirst roared through her. Her nipples hardened; she fought the urge to rub herself against him, loosen the constricting need that coiled in her womb, on her tongue, her fangs.

His thumbs drew half circles beneath her eyes. "Bad dreams?"

Swallowing, she forced herself not to remember, to focus on the weight against her, the intensity of his stare. "Yes."

"Hungry?" His voice deepened.

He didn't let her turn her face away. "Yes," she said breathlessly.

His gaze dropped to her lips again. "Open your mouth."

"Ethan—"

"I aim to kiss you, Miss Charlie, but I'm not practiced at kissing vampires. I don't want your fangs cutting you, or me, and getting the bloodlust out of control before we can do something about it. So just open up a little, and then keep real still."

Still? She was trembling, on the verge of sliding to the balcony floor—or climbing up the length of him and sinking her fangs into his neck.

Her lips parted, and he guided her teeth farther open with gentle pressure of his thumb against her chin. Then he braced his hands on the wall, either side of her head. He stepped slightly away and angled down until his eyes were level with hers.

No part of him would touch her, she realized, but his mouth.

"I ought not to be taking this risk at all," he said. "But seeing you here has made me lose my sense."

She'd been wrong; his breath was touching her—heated, moist. "Me, too," she rasped.

"That's just fine," he murmured against her lips.

Carefully, slowly, he eased in, sliding his tongue between her fangs to curl lazily around hers. Longing shivered through her, tightening, tugging, shaking little bits of her free. Her nails dug into her palms, and she closed her teeth on him—oh, so softly—before letting him go.

He drew back an inch, his breathing harsh. "Yes. I reckon this was a damn fool idea."

A door opened farther down the balcony; Charlie's eyes widened with surprise and laughter. Ethan held her gaze as the other guests approached them, paused, and retreated in the opposite direction, leaving a psychic trail of discomfort in their wake.

When they got to the stairs, a slow smile curved Ethan's mouth. "We'd best get inside, Miss Charlie. You used your blood to put the spell up in there?"

She nodded, sliding out under his arm. Her knees were still weak. "I set it up last night. I should go in first, anyway, because Jane might be undressed."

The door didn't open. Charlie frowned, tried her keycard again. The handle turned, but she couldn't push it. She glanced over her shoulder. "Is it not unlocking?"

Ethan shook his head. "Let me feel it out."

A light percussion wave rolled through her; Charlie placed her hand against the door to steady herself. Though the keycard was in her hand, the indicator switched to green. "What was that?"

"My Gift. I pushed pretty hard, and you'll feel it more now that you're sensitive." It struck again, and he lifted his gaze to hers. "The lock is releasing, Charlie. The spell is what's keeping the door closed."

"But—" That meant that Jane had keyed it with her blood. "Why would she . . . ?"

Ethan's face was grim. "Did she leave during the day, and needed to be able to get back in?"

"I don't know. I was . . . Oh, Lord." Charlie yanked the phone out of her pouch, flipped it open. Looked at the recently dialed numbers. Her stomach cramped. "She called Sammael."

And talked to the demon without Ethan or Charlie there to counteract his arguments, to provide a balance. Could Charlie fix whatever damage he'd done? How long had Jane spoken with him?

Charlie pushed another button, and the pain in her stomach moved up through her chest, her throat. Almost two hours.

The door swung open. With only a towel wrapped around her, Jane took a quick step back, her hand flying to the tuck of the terrycloth between her breasts. She glanced up at Ethan with a startled expression. She said something, but Charlie couldn't hear it.

Jane's eyes and nose were red. Had she been crying all day, or just recently? She spoke again. Charlie spread her hands, lifted her shoulders—and Jane finally got it, wiped the blood from the symbols.

"—realized I hadn't told you that I changed the . . ." Jane's gaze fell to Charlie's phone.

"You called him?" Disbelief squeezed Charlie's question into a hoarse whisper.

Ethan laid his hand against her lower back. "Go on inside," he said softly. "You want me to come in with you?"

Yes. But that wouldn't be fair to Jane. "Do you mind waiting a minute?"

"I'd wait much longer than that for you, Miss Charlie." He turned, leaned back against the wall.

She closed the door, but didn't activate the spell. Whatever Sammael had told Jane, Ethan would know better than Charlie if it was a lie.

Jane sank down on the bed. The paleness of her skin made her nose and eyes all the brighter. "I called him. I hadn't intended to, but I was reading, and it was so quiet, and I realized . . ." Her mouth set; Charlie felt a chime of fear, faint as a memory. "I couldn't hear you breathing. And when I checked, not only had your respiration stopped, but your heart rate was at ten beats per minute, Charlie. It wasn't like that last night."

No. Jane had taken her pulse when Charlie had been describing everything that had happened to her, and had said Charlie's rate was on the low side of average—just as it had been when she'd been human.

"And then there was your face. You weren't moving, appeared dead—and you looked *petrified*, Charlie. Like you were scared, and in pain and skinny as hell . . . and so I freaked out. I didn't know if it was supposed to be like that—and I didn't know if, because you'd gone to bed hungry, you were starving or dying in your sleep."

"So you called him." Though she understood Jane's fear, Charlie couldn't seem to get her brain around that fact.

"Yes. Who else could I have called? Mom? 'Hey, Charlie's a vampire, what should I do?' " Jane shook her head. "Anyway, he said it was normal, told me not to worry, that you'd be fine by sunset."

Charlie walked to the table. Putting the gun away was a relief; she hadn't known how to use it, hadn't really felt any safer with it. "And that's all?"

"No." Jane half-turned on the bed, facing her. "I'm returning to Seattle. Now that I know what I'm working on, Dylan said that—"

"His name isn't Dylan," Charlie said tightly. "It's Sammael, and he's a demon."

"And what does that mean, Charlie? What does that mean,

exactly? That he's evil? Yet, unlike the guy you're with, he's never killed anyone." Jane's brows arched. "At least your standards are getting higher—on the bad boy scale, a druggie musician has absolutely nothing on a murderer."

Charlie sucked in a breath. "Low fucking blow, Jane. Did Sammael coach you on that?" she asked, and a flicker of Jane's eyelashes and a note of guilt told Charlie that had gotten through, at least. But, God, she wished she'd put up the spell so that Ethan wouldn't have heard her sister say that. He deserved a lot better. "Whatever Drifter did, it was over a hundred years ago. Last night, he was trying to save me, and Sammael was laughing while a vampire sucked my blood out. Guess who I'm going to trust?"

Jane closed her eyes. "All right. I'm sorry. But that still doesn't mean—"

Charlie wasn't done. "And the only goddamn reason Sammael hasn't killed anyone is because the Rules say he can't."

At that, Jane straightened up and shook her head. "He wouldn't. He said there are different factions of demons, and some are looking for ways to be forgiven. He's one of them."

Charlie leapt onto the bed and bared her fangs a foot from her sister's face. "Turning people into vampires against their will seems like a really shitty way to get on Heaven's good side, doesn't it?"

She felt the flare of Jane's temper, saw it in the blood that rushed under her skin. "Yes. And he admitted that he's been approaching it in the wrong way. That we could—"

"And you believed him? I *told* you what he said to me. That you'd 'come around.'" Her chest was heaving; the room was too warm. Jane was angry, but calm—in comparison, Charlie felt like a rabid bitch. She tried again. "He's playing you, Jane," she said as evenly as possible. "And you're letting him."

"I'm not blind. He fucked up, he admits it—but he's willing to change. And this is my work, Charlie. This is why he chose me in the first place. I can make a difference."

Charlie's control dropped away. "This was my life," she hissed. "His 'fuck-up' was my *life*."

"And you've already said that being a vampire isn't bad. That you are doing okay." With agitated movements, Jane stood and pulled on her underwear, her shirt. "This is something I can do . . . for you, for a lot of people like you."

"Like me?" Charlie echoed, sitting back on her heels.

Jane shot her a dirty look. "Don't take offense to that. You know I mean vampires. And you can't tell me you *like* the idea that you're dependent on someone supplying you blood. And what goes with it."

No, Charlie couldn't. "It doesn't have to be that way for me, though. Drifter can—"

"And what about the others? Are Guardians feeding them, too?" Jane sighed, dragged her fingers through her hair. "Then there are the healing aspects of it. The research needs to go on."

"Then do it somewhere else," Charlie said, desperate. How had she ended up on the defensive? She was too far behind, or not understanding. Why the hell would Jane ever go back to Sammael after what he'd done? What wasn't Charlie *getting*? "Why does it have to be with Legion? Why can't it be with . . . with—" Oh, fuck fuck, she couldn't think. It started with "R." From the hallway, she heard Ethan offer a name in a low voice, and she finished with "Ramsdell Pharmaceuticals? They're connected with the Guardians. I'm sure you could do the same work, but it wouldn't have to be with Sammael lying to you and using you."

Jane yanked on her jeans. "He's not going to lie to me anymore. I've told him that I want to know everything that's going on with the research, and that if anyone is there against their will, it has to stop or I'd leave. And I told him if I catch him in a lie, I'll leave. It's that simple, Charlie."

Charlie stared at her, and the boiling frustration and anxiety within her just seemed to vanish, leaving her cold, empty.

That was what Jane had told her, too: Stop, or I'll give up on you. And Charlie had quit, because the thought of not having Jane had hurt more than the pain of stopping had.

But did Jane really believe Sammael would be the same? "If it were 'that simple,' " Charlie said quietly, "you wouldn't be going back to him."

"Maybe not." With another sigh, Jane slid on the bed next to her, wrapped her arms around Charlie's shoulders. "You know I love you."

"Yes. And you love him." That was why she wasn't getting through to Jane. Charlie couldn't fight that if her sister wouldn't fight it, too.

"And I love him." Jane's arms tightened. "And I'm pissed, and I want to know what's going on, and I don't really have any idea what I'm doing. But I can't figure it out from here. It may be that once I get up there, I'll just kick him in the nuts and come back."

Charlie couldn't respond, couldn't make a joke.

Jane said, "I'm trying not to be stupid about this—"

"Well, you're failing. This is the fucking stupidest thing I've ever heard."

"Will you just listen to me? Jesus, Charlie." Jane bounced up off the bed, began pacing. "First, I want to hear from your Drifter or Ethan or whatever his name is what he knows about the blood, and vampires, and what he thinks Legion is doing. So that if Dylan does try to pull something over on me, I'll have a better idea of it."

Charlie banged her forehead repeatedly against the mattress. "You accept that he might try and you're *still going back*?"

Jane made a turn at the table and continued as if Charlie hadn't spoken. "Then I'll call you every night, and send an e-mail every day, letting you know what I'm finding. Because I don't want you to worry."

"No, I won't do that at all." Her sarcasm didn't carry well, so she added, "He can copy your voice, Jane. He can fake an e-mail."

"I'll put something in there he won't know. Something from when we were kids that I've never told him."

"And what if I don't hear from you one day? What do I do?"

Through the door, she heard Ethan softly tell her, "We come and rescue her, Charlie."

Charlie whirled in his direction, her fist clenching. "But you said you weren't a hero."

Jane frowned in confusion. Ethan didn't speak for a long moment, and when he finally answered, it was with laughter in his voice.

"Well, hell, Charlie—I sure wish I'd been a hero to you last night. And so the notion of being one must be growing on me."

Jane pointed at the entrance. "Is he listening?" At Charlie's nod, she pulled the door open, made a sweeping gesture to wave Ethan in. When he stepped into the room, she examined him with narrowed eyes and her hands on her hips. "So you're going to make sure my sister gets the blood she needs?"

Ethan's brows rose, and he darted a glance at Charlie before looking at Jane again. Amusement lurked at the corners of his eyes. "Yes'm."

"For how long?"

"I reckon as long as she needs me, I'll be happy to oblige her."

Charlie closed her eyes, hung her head, and hoped they thought she was laughing.

CHAPTER 18

Ethan couldn't figure Charlie at all.

During the two hours he'd spoken with Jane, explaining the Rules and answering the questions she'd thrown at him, Charlie had withdrawn into herself. Not numb, as she had been after the attack in the phone booth, just quiet. Her only strong reaction had come when he'd taken Jane's blood to have as an anchor, should Selah, Michael, or Jake ever need one. Unless Jane was behind the spell or shielding, they'd be able to teleport to her.

When the crimson drops had welled on Jane's finger, Charlie had risen from her seat on the bed. She'd closed the door to the bathroom behind her, her bloodlust licking tongues of fire over his skin.

She must have been feeling it bad, but she wasn't showing it—though her body was. She'd lost weight already; a hell of a lot more than he'd have expected in one day of not feeding.

But she'd returned to the room with a smile on her face—a smile that had remained through the good-byes and embraces that she and Jane exchanged in the parking lot. She waited until her sister had driven out of sight.

Then she turned, and he'd had barely a moment to brace himself for the quick series of punches she aimed at his chest. Not landing them hard—just working out whatever had been simmering in her. And then she was leaning on him, her cheek pressed over his heart and the heel of her left hand weakly thumping the other side of his chest.

He laid his lips against the top of her apple-scented hair, held her tight.

When she stopped beating on him, she asked in a tired voice, "What time is it?"

He'd given his cell phone to Jane, and had to look around and peer in through the window of the motel's office to see. "About ten thirty."

"Shit. Shit shit shit." She pulled away and was on her phone a second later, turning her back to him as she coughed and told Cole she might be in tomorrow, that some medication had put her to sleep so she was late calling.

She didn't face Ethan again when she finished, but stared down the road with a haunted expression deepening the hollows in her cheeks.

"Charlie," he began, but she shook her head.

She looked up at him before gazing down the road again. "I'll tell him tomorrow that I'm not coming back. I can't do it today." Her breath hitched, but her expression didn't change. "Hell, maybe tomorrow he'll just realize I've been lying and fire me. You still have my laptop, right?"

He frowned, but nodded. "Yes."

"I guess I can finish my classes, then." She rubbed her forehead. Her fingers were trembling. Ethan watched them shake, wished she'd lean on him or hit him again, and make him good for something while she was hurting. "I'm sorry about what she called you," she said quietly.

The bit about being a murderer? "It's true enough."

She whipped around to face him. "That's not the point—"

"Easy, Charlie." He held his hands up in surrender, grinning. "You already defended me real well. And Sammael must have put that particular concern into her—I ain't about to fret over a demon's opinion of my character."

She sighed. "He must have said a lot to her."

"I reckon. But it may be once she returns home, she'll start looking instead of just listening."

"I hope so." She paused, and her eyes searched his. "Was there anything different *I* could have said?"

He studied her for a long second. Was she feeling she'd done an inadequate job of convincing her sister? Even when she'd been angry, every point Charlie made had been sensible; Jane just hadn't been in the same place.

"I figure there was one thing you might have done," he said slowly. "And that was if you'd gone for her heart, and given her the same choice she gave Sammael: telling her that if she didn't come around, you'd be writing her off as lost."

Her dark brows drew together. "But I couldn't say that, let alone do it."

He'd known that; he thought Jane did, too. "Then there was nothing short of tying her down."

Charlie pursed her lips, tilted her head as if considering it, and cast a speculative glance down the road.

He felt the grin sliding over his mouth and turned to conceal it. She really was something. "You have anything in the room you want to take?" He'd already retrieved all of his weapons.

"No."

"You want to feed before we check out?" She'd spent the day sleeping; her scent would be all over the bed. She could crawl right up onto him and he'd be surrounded by her, the soft mattress beneath and Charlie firm and aroused all over the front of him.

He stopped walking, pulled his coat forward before looking around for her answer.

She had her hands tucked into her sweater pocket again. "I don't want to feed in there. Where are we going?"

"San Francisco."

He felt her hesitation before she said hoarsely, "How long will that take? I don't know if I can . . ." She trailed off, and her jaw firmed, her pink lips thinning to white.

She sure didn't like needing something so bad. He'd have to make certain it didn't get to this point again.

"A little over an hour and a half, if I fly quick."

She blinked. "Really? All the way down in an hour and half?"

"Yes," he replied, smiling when eagerness projected briefly from her psychic scent, cutting through the now-constant heat of her bloodlust. "And if you need to, you can drink a bit on the way."

Her gaze lowered to his neck. The hunger flaring in her brown eyes brought out the green as well as the sun had, and within an instant he was hardening again.

God Almighty. She'd have him falling out of the air, laid out moaning on the ground like a dying horse. And he suspected he'd just lay there grinning as she worked herself over him.

Her mouth softened into a tiny smile. "That doesn't sound like a good idea."

"No," he said, and took her hand, pulled her toward the office. "I reckon it's not."

Though the more he considered it, the more he thought it sounded just fine.

And when she was in his arms and the wind preventing easy conversation, her bloodlust eating through him like a thousand fire ants, there wasn't much to do but consider it. By the time he flew down low over the Golden Gate Bridge, giving her a view that made her sigh in pleasure, he'd imagined taking her in just about every way a man could take a woman, and in his mind she'd sucked the blood from his body a hundred times over.

He figured she'd imagined the latter, as well. She'd touched his throat twice, each time jerking her fingers away from his skin. And he didn't know if the physical scent of her need was caused by the bloodlust or by her wanting him—but if he slipped his hand low, he reckoned he'd find her wet enough that he wouldn't need to put his mouth on her in order to ease his way.

Wouldn't need to, but he'd still have taken real good care of her.

Her brows pulled together in a frown as they flew over Hunter's Point, banked toward SI, and dropped in quick.

"It ain't much to look at," he said as he set her feet on the ground. His nerves began jumping as her gaze lifted and ran over the building. It wasn't much at all; even her inexpensive little apartment had appeared better maintained, and had more space than her room in the warehouse did. "But it'll do until we can find a place for you. And it ain't so bad inside."

She nodded and turned in a slow circle, taking in the empty parking lot and the high fencing without expression. "Okay."

He figured if he'd been human, his palms would have been sweaty as he clasped her hand, led her up the stairs.

"You'll get a card to use here. Jake likely has already made it up." He pulled in his identification and swiped it. "And Jeeves up there, he'll be checking to make sure you are who you say."

"Okay." Her whisper was strained as they stepped into the blank white corridor.

Maybe he ought to have given Jake her things, so her room would be comforting, not just cleaned and ready. Or thought of setting her up in a hotel. He glanced at her; she looked away from Jeeves, her lips curving into a pretty smile, and some of his tension eased.

"You'll be safe, Charlie. The security is awful tight."

"So I see."

From behind his glass shield, Jeeves ran his gaze over Charlie with open curiosity—as open as Jeeves's sour face could manage, that was. "Good evening, Miss Newcomb. Mr. Drifter."

Charlie's brows lifted a little, and her smile deepened. "Good evening."

"You have her ID, Jeeves?"

"Indeed, sir. I have only to record her measurements first. Miss, if you will step up to—"

Ethan shook his head. "Just prints and retinal, Jeeves. The rest tomorrow." Charlie wouldn't be so thin, and it was best to get her features in when she looked as she normally would.

And he didn't want to have to tell her why she was being scanned for the same record twice. He figured calling her too skinny at this moment would be much worse than saying a woman was plump.

Jeeves frowned and opened his mouth; Ethan laid his hand on the narrow ledge in front of the window and leaned in.

"Tomorrow, Becca," he repeated softly, but the novice couldn't miss the edge in it.

"Very well, sir." The stiff tone told Ethan he'd soon have to be letting her win a poker hand or two, or she'd be sore at him for a week.

Ethan talked Charlie through the scans, then submitted his own before leading her past the door. Fortunately, Becca was upset enough that she didn't come out and introduce herself.

Most of the offices they passed were dark, though a few vampires and Guardians were working on computers or talking on phones. Past the hall and offices was a large room that opened to the practice areas and the metal staircase that led to the second floor. The clash of swords sounded from the gymnasium, but the majority of the noise in the warehouse was coming from upstairs.

He looked over at her; she was examining the ID card, a tiny line between her brows. "You all right?"

"Yes." She tucked the ID in her pouch, and he heard the slide of her fingers over the feather. "Just feeling a little processed." Her smile wasn't quite steady; she glanced away from him and added quickly, "But you're right, it's much nicer inside. And I like the . . . the . . . *that*."

She pointed at the zodiac painted on the ceiling, but Ethan continued to study her face, fighting the impulse to dig under her shields and discover what lay beneath the bloodlust.

Laughter rolled down from the second floor, and she eyed the stairs, her fingers practically sawing across the feather.

Ethan clenched his jaw as his name was added to the conversation above. "You stay here a minute, Miss Charlie."

He cleared the stairs in a single bound. Cards lay over the table in the common room, the game in full swing; the sofas were filled with novices chatting and reading and watching a film on the giant television. Eleven young Guardians and three vampires—and fourteen pairs of eyes swung toward Ethan, then searched the space behind him.

Ethan shook his head and gestured for them to pay attention. *She's feeling uneasy, and she's awful hungry. I don't want anyone rushing at her,* he signed. *No questioning, no staring. You just sit where you are now and say your greetings polite.*

He ignored the surprised glances that were exchanged, and turned back to the stairs. At the head, he paused.

And her privacy's real important to her. If I see one wink or one wrong smile, any little indication that you think you know what's going to happen in that room, then I'll be rolling a few novices over pretty damn hard.

Silence followed him back down, but he assumed they were furiously signing back and forth—likely making wagers about who would be the first to smirk and how many teeth they'd have to regrow.

Charlie was standing in the same place he'd left her, but no longer alone. Jake and Mackenzie had come in from the gymnasium, and Jake was turning his head to the side so Charlie could see how well he'd healed up. She rose up on her toes to look close.

Mackenzie frowned at them as he slid his sword into the scabbard on his back, then met Ethan's gaze. The vampire pushed his flop of dark hair from his forehead, then signed, *Drifter, would you like me to feed—*

Mackenzie's pale hand closed tight when Ethan narrowed his eyes.

Never mind, the vampire quickly gestured. *And I wouldn't have taken any from her—Becca is it for me. I was just offering because she's in bad shape.*

Ethan nodded sharply, then slid his thumbs beneath his suspenders and studied his boots until he was certain he wasn't going to say something he'd regret later. The thought of Charlie letting anyone else provide for her about tore him up and got jealousy roiling hot in his gut.

He reckoned that meant Charlie was it for him, too.

Jake was telling her about the tanker now, and her eyes were wide and bright when she glanced away from the novice to Ethan's face, as if she wanted to gauge his reaction to Jake's version of it.

Ethan hadn't been listening, but Jake must have been making him out to be a heroic warrior; she held his gaze, her bloodlust flaring. Jake blinked, and his words stumbled before he finished his story by falling to the floor with his arms and legs spread-eagled, projecting intense relief.

Ethan's jealousy receded, left his nerves jittering again. The feeding was just ahead, and she needed more than blood from him.

She needed his control, and at that moment it was in short supply.

He cleared his throat, forced himself not to think about her mouth or the heavy-lidded glance she cast at him each time the bloodlust turned her eyes more hazel than brown. "Which room, Jake? I ought to get Charlie settled in."

Jake raised his head. "It's the last one on the right." He rolled to his side, propped his elbow on the floor. "And Savi found a connection between Katya, Vladimir, and the Brandts, but it's not much. It can wait."

"All right then." He held out his hand to Charlie. "You ready?"

Her lips parted, and she nodded. Her breath was slow and shallow. "At the motel, you asked Jane if Mark Brandt had contacted her," she murmured as they climbed the stairs. "Why?"

"Mostly my gut," he said. "I wouldn't like to be hit from the side, particularly if it's regarding Legion, so I'm looking around to see what might be coming."

"Are the Brandts?"

"Don't know yet. It may be they're just feeling things out, too."

She was silent for a moment, as if she was thinking it over. "I can call Mark. He asked me to dinner—probably to talk about Jane—but I can feel *him* out."

They reached the top of the stairs. "Maybe you could do that, Charlie, but I don't reckon you'd enjoy dinner much."

She touched her lips. "Do you think he'd notice?"

Ethan thought any man who sat across a table from that mouth and didn't pay attention to it probably had little to offer for information or brains. "Yes." He raised his voice a little, and kept hold of her hand as they moved into the common area. "This here's the brood, Charlie."

He pointed and named, then hurried her on through moments afterward, not trusting that the novices would behave much longer than it took for Charlie to respond to their hellos.

"So, this is like a dorm?" she asked.

"That's as good a description as any."

"But you live on Caelum?" Wistfulness fluttered through the rasp in her voice.

He paused in front of her door. "I have a place in Caelum, but I don't reckon I live there," he said slowly. "Not in the sense that you mean. I don't stay in Caelum for any length of time. Just visit."

"And drift? Is that why you went today?"

"Yes." He didn't look away from her as they entered the room. Her expression didn't change, except for a quick blink when her gaze lit on the twin-sized bed. "It's not much," he said again.

"It's okay. Like I said, kind of a dorm. Were the flowers your idea?" She turned to face him again with a smile.

A huge burst of red roses sat atop the tiny desk. "That they were, though I'll admit I didn't select these. I'd have chosen something yellow." Daisies or daffodils, or even yellow roses—any flower that looked more like the sun than like blood.

He thought her smile dimmed, but he couldn't be certain: she dipped her chin and dragged her fingers through her hair, letting it fall across her cheek. "It was still a nice thought. And they smell great." She inhaled, and her eyes closed with pleasure. "I guess being a vampire does have benefits."

"Well, you won't want to breathe that deep when it ain't flowers," he drawled.

She laughed, but it faded when she met his gaze. Her lids lowered sleepily, and his entire being wound up tight, pulled his body with it.

He turned and cut his thumb, activated the spell.

"Ethan," she whispered. Her need slammed through him, and she moved in quick. Her fingers circled his wrist as he pivoted to face her. "God, Ethan. Let me . . . let me—"

Her lips closed over the tip of his thumb.

The pleasure ripped into him, like she'd closed her mouth over every inch of his flesh. His knees near gave out, and he staggered back against the door. Charlie moaned, her fingernails digging into his skin, holding his hand to her mouth.

The wound healed, and she released his thumb with a long lick.

"Charlie," he said hoarsely. That small taste hadn't begun to assuage her thirst—it had only made her need worse. And now that she'd had some, the bloodlust wouldn't be letting her stop. Her gaze rose to his throat, hungry and feral. "Miss Charlie. Let's do this slow and easy—"

She curled her fingers around his jacket collar and leapt astride his waist. Her knees banged against the door.

Her fangs sank deep in his neck.

She began sucking, and ecstasy replaced the pain. Her lips and tongue were cool against his skin, her bloodlust a raging fire through his veins.

God Almighty.

Ethan groaned, slid down the door until his ass hit the

hardwood floor, and turned his head to give her a better angle. She sat in the cradle of his thighs and stomach, straddling his erect length. Her fingers buried in the hair at his nape, then fisted. Her hips rocked, hard, fast.

Rough-woven cotton burned over his shaft. He panted her name, and within seconds she was matching her rhythm to his voice. He slowed, and she did, her tongue massaging the closing punctures on his throat, her hands sliding between them to flatten against his chest.

Then her fangs pierced him again. He bucked beneath her, stifling a shout. *Son of a bitch.* His teeth clenched. It'd be so easy to vanish his clothes and remove hers, and push himself deep. He could almost see it: her pink flesh parting, glistening as she slowly, slowly took him in . . .

He opened his eyes again to the sound of shredding fabric. Her blue sweatshirt lay torn on the floor.

She whimpered against his throat, and her thin camisole ripped beneath her frantic hands. The buttons on his shirt popped and scattered.

Her cool palms met the heated skin over his stomach, her thumbs sliding alongside his navel. His head swam. Her moans took on a needy, erotic note, as if they welled up from far beneath her throat and chest. Each harsh exhalation she made from her nose was an icy whisper over the back of his neck.

He caught her wrists when she traced a line to his waistband, dipped her fingers in. Their cool tips circled his cockhead, her touch a shot of electricity and pure bliss. Ethan reared up against her hands, seeking more.

He ought to have been drawing away.

Desperately, he tugged her wrists up. She pulled them free and bit him again.

A zipper rasped. Hers.

"Charlie," he gritted, and forced out the words he didn't want to say, but had to in order to remind himself. "Much as I want you, we decided we ain't doing this. Not until you adjust."

He clasped her hips to halt her rocking; the denim of her jeans was stiff beneath his hands. Stiff . . . but loose, and sliding against the silk of her red panties. Her scent mingled with the heavy perfume of the roses. She'd be so sweet, her aroused flesh slick against his tongue—

He squeezed his eyes closed again, resisting the image, his need, her need. He stopped breathing.

Her thighs flexed around his waist. Her weight eased from his aching length as if she meant to lift herself off him—though she didn't seem about to quit; the suction at his neck continued, her bloodlust was still hot.

And he heard it: the slippery glide of her hand between silk and skin. Her soft, muffled cry against his throat as her fingers penetrated deep.

"Miss Char— Ah, *sonofawhore*—" Ethan clenched his jaw, rapped his head hard against the door, and forced himself not to succumb as her heightening arousal spiked his blood.

She began moving. Her knuckles ground into his shaft on each downward stroke of her hips. Painful, but mostly because it wouldn't let him forget how badly he wanted to be inside her, to be the one fulfilling her need.

Her left hand searched out his chin, his mouth. Though desperate for any taste, he fought the temptation to suck her middle fingers in and stroke his tongue to the same tempo of her hand between her legs.

Her pace increased, and Ethan reckoned he was going to plumb lose his mind. She was sweating now, leaning in against his chest. Her nipples repeatedly kissed his skin in a cool, wet path that matched the rise and fall of her body. Beads of perspiration fell against the back of his neck, icy drops that trickled beneath his collar.

He nearly wept with relief when tremors ran through her. She tensed and arched, her hips coming off of him but her mouth still fastened to his throat, her palm slapping flat against the door beside his face.

His hands tightened on her waist, held her as she barreled through the orgasm, gritted his teeth against the amplified wave of pleasure that rushed into his body.

Two more icy drops fell and rolled down the back of his neck.

Horror gripped him. "Charlie?"

She made a panicked noise low in her throat.

The bloodlust still hadn't released her—hadn't released him. Ethan ran his hands up her spine, fighting the desire so that his touch wouldn't ask too much. He pitched his voice to soothe. "You'll be all right. It'll break soon. You're just newly transformed and hungry."

Her tears were a steady stream down his back in the following minute; then the bloodlust finally freed her. She lifted her head, gasping with sobbing little breaths, wiping at her mouth.

"Ethan." Her face was stricken when she pulled back. She cushioned his cheeks between her hands, her moist eyes frantically searching his. "Are you okay? I just—I couldn't stop—"

"I know, Miss Charlie." Concern melted through her psychic scent; his chest swelled, and he thought his heart actually skipped a beat. He smoothed his hand down the windblown tangle of her hair, from her crown to the middle of her back. Her features had lost the skinny, haunted look. "And I'm doing just fine."

"But . . ." Her gaze lowered, and he glanced down at her chest. Blood smeared her golden skin—and over his, darkening the edge of his shirt. "Oh, Jesus," she whispered.

"We got a little messy," he said easily, and repressed his grimace as he vanished it. He forced himself to look away from her perfect round titties, the tight rosy nipples. "But next time it won't hit you so bad, and you'll know better how the blood flows, how fast to drink."

"Next time?" Her hands shook against his jaw. "You're *sure* I didn't hurt you? You wouldn't just say that?"

He frowned. "Why are you so certain you did?"

"I heard it." Her eyes closed briefly. "It wasn't mine."

"Heard what?"

"Screaming." She swallowed hard. "Or—that shriek bending metal makes? Only louder."

"That doesn't sound like anything I was feeling." His frown deepened, and she brushed her thumbs along the sides of his mouth. "When did you hear it? When you first bit me?"

"No." Pink tinged her cheeks. "That was good. It was after that."

"At the end?" He lifted his hand to her cheek. Her tears had dried.

"I heard it then, yes," she rasped. "And during the rest of it."

He stiffened. "The whole time? From just after you bit me until you were done?"

Her lips pressed together and she nodded.

He'd thought the intensity of the bloodlust had spooked her. But what she'd described sounded more painful than frightening. "Was it *hurting* you?"

"Ethan—" She tried to avert her face but he ducked his head and followed. He looked up at her, holding her hair away from her forehead.

"Miss Charlie." It was gentle, but undeniably a command. "I can't help you if I don't know."

She slapped her palm against his chest, gained a couple of inches until her back came up against his thighs. "It hurt. But it wasn't me." Her jaw clenched. "It was separate from . . . and I couldn't control either one. *Obviously.*"

The last word carried embarrassment, bitterness, fear.

She meant the sexual response. Ethan sat up straight again, stared over her head. How could he not have recognized she was in pain? For certain, he'd never heard of anything like this—not when both parties were willing, leastwise—and hadn't thought to watch for it. He'd been focused on fighting his own response.

"Could it just be that I was so hungry?" she asked softly.

He met her eyes, saw the hope in them—and the uncertainty. "I don't rightly know. Next time, we'll see if it's the same, all right? And if it doesn't get better, we'll maybe ask someone."

He saw her struggle with that before she nodded. "Okay." She drew in a deep breath, her gaze holding his. Her fingers caressed his cheeks as she studied him. After what seemed a long while, she finally said, "I should probably get up."

He wasn't in a hurry to go anywhere. Her titties were naked, and she had the tightest, sexiest belly he'd ever seen. Her ass was seated firmly over his pelvis; he was no longer hard, and her weight felt just fine. "I'm all right holding you like this, Charlie, until you're steady."

She looked down; her face flushed, and her hands flew to her waist, buttoning and zipping. "This can't be fair. I drank your blood and came all over you, but you didn't even get off—"

"And it's a goddamn miracle I didn't, Miss Charlie." He waited for her to finish and glance back up at him. "Don't be thinking you need to do anything about it. You were just hurting, and though you're looking awful pretty and sweaty, I ain't feeling so lustful right now."

"Okay." She watched him for a second longer. "I'm probably keeping you from work."

"I ought to do some tonight. But if you need me to stay with you—"

"No." She picked up her sweatshirt, held it against her breasts. "I'll be fine."

The swiftness of her response stabbed at his chest, but he pushed it away. She likely just needed a private moment. "All right; then. But if you need anything, don't you fret about whether you should come downstairs and ask me for it."

"Ethan." Her brows drew together; she laid a soft, cool kiss against his lips before pulling away. "You've already given me everything I need."

She scooted off him a second later, headed for the bathroom. He stared after her, then rapped his head one more time against the door.

He hadn't given her a damn thing worth having.

CHAPTER 19

Charlie quickly bathed and dressed in the tiny bathroom—just a vanity sink, a shower, and a mirror—before making her way out to the common area. She didn't want to be alone in that cell of a room; it reminded her far too much of days she'd spent wallowing in self-pity, when she hadn't truly cared if she lived or died.

She cared now.

Only four female Guardians were chatting on the sofas—and no one was at the poker table. All four turned to look at her, and, as one, their brows rose in surprise and curiosity.

Charlie resisted the urge to touch her face, her hair. A glance in the mirror had told her that she looked better. She didn't *feel* better—only sore and tired.

"Is Ethan—" Charlie broke off when two Guardians exchanged a glance. "Is Drifter here?"

One shook her head, her dark bowl-cut hair gleaming beneath the lights. Charlie thought her name was Pim. Or maybe Pam. "He's in the tech room . . ." The Guardian tilted her head to the side, and she pointed at the stairs. "Actually, not anymore."

Charlie turned; Ethan strode toward her, his gaze searching her features.

"You all right?"

"Yes. I just . . ." Wanted to be with him. In the same room, talking with him, seeing him, hearing him. How needy would that sound? "I was just looking for something to do, so I thought I'd work on that class project. And you have my laptop."

It appeared instantly in his hands, but he didn't give it to her. He darted a glance over her head, then met her eyes again. "You want to come with me? It's a bit quieter."

She couldn't halt her relieved smile. "Yes."

His own smile was slightly crooked. "All right then." Her computer vanished again. "It ain't nothing exciting," he said as they walked downstairs. "Mostly, we're just taking a look at Brandt's financials."

"We" was Jake and the female vampire Charlie had met in Cole's. Savi's black hair was short and spiky now, instead of long and straight; she sat in front of a computer in jeans and a *Hello Kitty* T-shirt that Charlie thought must have been purchased in the kids' section.

Savi's dark eyes widened. "Charlotte Newcomb?" she asked, then studied her in a way that reminded Charlie of Jane at her microscope.

With a nod that Charlie hoped didn't appear as stiff and uncomfortable as she felt, she said, "Yes."

"You look good," Savi said, then narrowed her gaze on Ethan. "You didn't tell Colin or me that you brought her down from Seattle."

Ethan's mouth tightened. "She's just fine here."

"In a hole upstairs? Did you even tell her she could stay with us while we find her a suitable partner?"

"Miss Savi, I didn't much consider it." An edge of steel sharpened his drawl.

Savi caught her upper lip between her teeth, looked at Charlie again. "Okay. I didn't realize it was like that. Sorry." She stood and extended her hand; her palm was the same temperature as Charlie's—perhaps slightly warmer. "My partner and I look after the vampire community here in San Francisco. If you need anything, don't hesitate to come to us."

Charlie nodded again. "All right." Then, because an awkward

silence had fallen, she added, "Your house on the lake was incredible. Thanks for letting me stay."

Savi waved it off with a shrug that suggested she was accustomed to breathtaking views and beautiful houses. "I'm just glad it could be of some use," she said. "Colin and I picked it up because we thought we'd be spending more time in Seattle, but we haven't had as much success meeting with Manny as we did Vladimir and Katya."

"Katya and Vladimir were the heads of Seattle's vampire community," Ethan explained when Charlie glanced at him. "But they were killed about three months ago."

"And the new guy hasn't been very receptive," Savi added. "We've been looking at a few other ways to set up something similar to our club for the vampires in the Seattle community—actually, that theater across from Cole's is one of them." Smiling, she performed a little side-to-side headshake. "They were playing *Dracula* that night Hugh sent us to talk to you, so Colin couldn't resist going in. And then we realized it'd make a great live theater, something like what they've got in Ashland, so we made an offer for it."

Charlie narrowed her eyes, tried to think. "Why does that sound familiar?"

"Well, hell," Ethan said. "Brandt mentioned it when he spoke with you, Charlie. If he knows it's Colin and Savi who's interested in it, he might be trying to block the sale."

"With the historical marker thing?" Savi snorted. "It won't go through—they don't meet half the requirements."

Ethan nodded. "Throwing up red tape, maybe, so it's too much a hassle and you'd move on."

"He doesn't know Colin," Savi said. "Establishing a solid community in Seattle has become one of his new obsessions." She caught her tongue briefly between her teeth, her eyes widening with amusement. "And I think it's to spite Manny, too. The mustache offended him."

Charlie blinked and looked to Ethan, who said, "Her partner believes that no self-respecting vampire ought to have a varmint on his lip."

"Manny's just a weasel all around," Savi said as she walked back to her computer. "The community could do a lot better. But I guess it was easy for him to just move in and take over everything of Vladimir's . . . like his car renovation shop. Charlie, you knew Mark Brandt?"

"Yes, a little," she said, and because it seemed she was going to be included in this, she followed the other vampire to the desk.

"Did he strike you as the type to spend a substantial amount of time and money having a '65 Ford Mustang restored?"

"No," Charlie said immediately. "Not unless the restoration included exchanging the engine for something that ran on batteries instead of gas."

"Which would be a waste of a damn good car," Jake muttered from his desk. "I used to have one. She was the sweetest little machine. The chicks loved it."

Charlie lifted a brow at the back of his head, then glanced down to see Savi in the middle of an eye roll.

"I had myself a real fine mustang once," Ethan drawled. Charlie turned, found him watching her with amusement fanning from the corners of his eyes. "I took awful good care of her. Fed her, brushed her, and carried her across the desert after she threw a shoe."

"And, once again, Drifter wins the *I'm a Man, Not a Pig* contest," Savi said.

Jake grumbled, and a five-dollar bill appeared in Ethan's hand.

"Thank you kindly, Jake. And to you, Miss Savi, for judging so well." The money vanished. Ethan held Charlie's gaze, the amusement fading from his expression. "You sure about Mark Brandt and his car?"

Charlie nodded. "Pretty sure. He was very passionate about it—and convincing. He's one of the reasons Jane got a hybrid. Why?"

"Because Savi found out that young Brandt had some work done at Vladimir's shop—or rather, there was a transfer from his accounts to the shop. But we're wondering if this was money for something else, and what, because the numbers don't add up—and we ain't got a record of any flights from D.C. around the same time, though his father had plenty." Ethan shook his head. "I'll have to see what I can get out of Manny."

Jake swiveled in his chair. "Are you going up tonight?"

"You plan on teleporting me? How about you try to get over there first?" Ethan gestured to the opposite side of the room.

Jake set his jaw; a low, wavering thrum slipped through Charlie's body, similar to what she'd felt when Ethan had used his Gift, though not as strong or as steady.

Ethan grinned. "Should I ask Miss Savi to scare you real bad?"

Charlie might have thought that a joke if Jake hadn't begun eyeing the small woman warily.

"Boo," Savi said without glancing away from her computer. "Do you need me to set up a new identity for you, Charlie? Identification, education, background? Or do you plan to keep living as yourself?"

Charlie's brow furrowed. "You can do that?"

Savi nodded. "A clean slate, if you want one. About half of us do; after the transformation, some have to completely start over, because they can't keep their old lives."

Charlie's life *would* be different. Was there any reason not to make it as easy as possible to slip into a new one? Never having to check the "convicted" box when she applied for a job or an apartment; not killing herself working toward a degree she wanted.

But at least what she had was hers. It wasn't much, and it wasn't all flattering, but she'd earned it.

"I don't think so," she said finally. "Except maybe a driver's license."

"Done," Savi said. "Washington or California?"

"Washington," Charlie responded, then paused. She'd answered automatically—but was it an indication that she was clinging too hard to her life in Seattle, just because it was familiar? Or was some part of her hoping that she'd go back, return to what she'd been?

But she didn't change her answer; she was distracted by the stiffness in Ethan's shoulders as he moved away from her and set her laptop on a table in the middle of the room.

"You ought to be able to get something done here, Miss Charlie." He pulled up two chairs, swung one around and straddled it. Whatever tension had been in him seemed to disappear with that lazy posture. "And I'll sit a spell with you.

Otherwise, I'll just be hovering over them while they work. Computers and I ain't exactly bosom friends."

"Why?" Charlie opened the laptop, booted it up.

"Passwords," Ethan said in an intimate tone, leaning forward and resting his forearms on the table. His thigh brushed hers. "It seems such a hassle to type them out or remember them. So I use my Gift."

Charlie blinked. "Does it work?"

"Well, it works all right with locks and such, telling a security system that I'm feeding it the correct code. Computers aren't quite so accommodating. More often than not, they quit working altogether."

"Even through a security system is basically a computer program?"

Ethan dropped his chin in a slow nod, his gaze holding hers. "And then there's this." He lifted his hand, spread his fingers wide. "I just ain't made for them tiny keyboards."

Which immediately made her think of what those big hands could have been made for. Charlie squeezed her legs together, focused on her computer, and Ethan's soft chuckle filled the air beside her.

"I'm awful sorry, Miss Charlie."

"No, you're not."

"I'm awful sorry I ain't showing you what else they can do."

"Oh. Well, me, too." She bit her lip as soon as she said it, looked past his shoulder. They'd been speaking in low tones, and neither Jake nor Savi were giving any indication that they were listening, but they must have been able to hear.

Ethan shook his head, lowered his face into her line of sight. "We block, Charlie. You listen for certain things—a partner's voice, your name—but the rest is just background noise."

"Okay." She turned back to her computer. That explained how he'd gotten upstairs so fast—listening for his name. She thought if he was in her range, she'd always hear him, as well. And not just his voice; her body seemed attuned to his presence on every level.

She shifted in her seat. At least she could be certain that it wasn't just his blood in her; it had been this way before she was transformed.

"Are you uncomfortable here, Charlie?"

She quickly met his eyes again, was surprised by the troubled expression in them. "No. Not because of the people—everyone seems nice." And obviously like family to him; she hoped her discomfort hadn't suggested they were lacking in any way. "I'm just not sure of my place yet, or how everything works. It's a little unsettling."

"All right." His features relaxed into a smile. "Then I'll just sit and watch you settle. Ain't nothing in the world like watching a pretty woman study."

Her face felt hot. Even a vampire's cold cheeks could blush, apparently. "I've heard that before," she said, and opened her browser.

From the corner of her vision, she saw his grin, broad and white. "You got a story for me, Miss Charlie? Can you talk and work?"

"I do it all of the time—" She clicked her tongue when an error message popped up on her screen instead of the university login. "Okay, just a second. How do I connect to the wireless?"

Ethan sat up. "Savi?"

Almost instantly, the slim vampire was leaning between their shoulders, clicking and typing. "This is a great little system," Savi said. "I almost got one of these a year or so ago."

A wry smile curved Charlie's mouth. By the time Charlie could have saved up enough to buy it, it would have been beyond obsolete. "It was Jane's. She gave it to me when she upgraded—"

Savi's fingers froze above the keyboard. "Jane's? As in, your sister who is employed by Legion? Did she use this for work?"

Charlie hesitated until she met Ethan's eyes over Savi's arms. "Yes. Sometimes. It was her backup system for when she forgot her other computer at the lab."

"Oh my god." Savi's fangs were gleaming with her enormous, laughing smile. "Can I have it? I'll take off all of your files and settings and put them in a new one. A better one."

"But Jane deleted all of her . . ." Charlie trailed off when Savi shook her head.

"There's a chance I can recover some of it."

"Oh. Well, okay then, I guess—"

"Yes!" Savi grabbed Charlie's face and smashed their lips together in a quick, cool kiss. Stunned, Charlie watched the computer disappear from the table and the other woman practically dance back to her desk.

Jake looked from Charlie to Savi, who was already plugging wires into the laptop. "Can you do that again, please? I'm sure her contribution deserves more than one kiss."

Ethan took her hand, tugged her to her feet. "As Charlie apparently can't do her work tonight, I reckon I'll show her how grateful we are by familiarizing her with the warehouse," he said. "And maybe taking her for a ride over the city before I head back on up to Seattle."

"And Drifter wins again," Savi chuckled.

ᔥ

By the time Charlie had finished brushing the wind out of her hair, Ethan had switched the small bed for the one from her apartment, set up her stereo on the desk, and placed her shelves of CDs along the wall.

He was moving the roses to her nightstand as she came out of the bathroom, and he turned his head, his gaze running her length. It stopped her in her tracks, and she lost her voice yet again. Perhaps it was for the best, this time. There was only one thought in her head, and only one thing she might have said.

Good Lord, but she was hopelessly in love with him.

It didn't seem so light this time, but a weight held over her head, waiting to drop onto her shoulders. But it was still clean, still bright, and amid everything else, something good that she desperately wanted to hang on to.

Except she'd never been good at judging when hanging on became a chokehold—or a death grip. He was solid, and it was so easy to rely on him, especially when he seemed so determined to help her adjust.

But it would have been nice if he needed something, or if he'd asked for something in return.

And she was uncertain about expressing her gratitude; he hadn't wanted it before. But it was the only thing she had to offer.

"Ethan." It sounded rougher than normal, so she swallowed to ease the dryness in her mouth and throat.

He raised his brows in question, moving from beside the bed to tower over her. "Miss Charlie?"

"I just wanted to say that I know I've been resentful of . . ." The bloodlust. Having no control over her life. Losing so much with a couple of swallows of Henderson's blood. "Of parts of what happened to me, and angry, especially with Jane—and kind of self-absorbed with all of that."

His brows drew in; the corners of his mouth pulled down. "Charlie—"

She shook her head, dropped her gaze to his chest. "But I wanted to make sure that I said thank you for saving my life, and for doing all of this." She indicated the room with a sweep of her hand. "And also that I hope you don't feel any guilt about not being able to get to me until after Henderson had taken my blood. Because if you hadn't been around I'd still be a vampire by now, but dependent on Sammael—and he'd probably have me locked up somewhere, I guess."

"I reckon." Ethan tipped her chin up with a touch of his fingers. His eyes were solemn. "I wish it had gone differently, Charlie. But if you're resentful and angry, you've good reason to be—and if you think your reaction has been irrational or that you've put a burden on me, you unthink it."

She shifted her feet. "I just wish there was some way I could repay you. For saving me—and for the rest." She darted a glance at the door to the hallway. Her knees had cracked the wood when she'd jumped on him; further down, he'd splintered a plank by banging his head against it. "For feeding me, because it couldn't have been easy."

"It wasn't a hardship, either. You don't owe me for it, and I sure in blazes don't want anything from you in payment," Ethan said softly. His lips curved slightly. "Except maybe a story now and then."

That wasn't anything; it didn't take any effort. But she bit back the reply that leapt to her tongue: *I want you to need something from me, too.* It would have sounded too pleading, too pathetic.

"That's easy enough," she said instead, but she thought her smile was probably wan, so she dipped her head. He was close, and she desperately wanted to touch him. She settled for reaching out, sliding his left suspender between her thumb and fingers. "And when we sleep together—"

She broke off when his taut abdomen turned to steel beneath the backs of her fingers. She glanced up, but he wasn't looking at her. He was staring down at the floor, the muscles in his jaw bunched.

"Ethan?"

His response was as tight as his body. "Is that the kind of man you think I am?"

She blinked quickly, her eyes searching his face. "What kind?"

"Using the bed in trade for blood."

It took her another second. Then her fingers curled hard around the leather strap before she forced her hand open and stepped back. Not far; the room was too small, and her shoulders came up against the wall.

"No," she said evenly, though hurt and anger were singing within her. "But *you* must think I'm the kind of woman who'd trade sex for blood, or it wouldn't have occurred to you that I was insulting you like that."

His head jerked up, and he stared into her face for a long moment. "No," he said finally. "I don't think that. I didn't get that far into considering it. I reckon I just heard you jump from repaying me to sleeping with me, and made a jump of my own."

"Oh," she said, trying to decide what that meant. Except when he was joking, she'd only known Ethan to be particular in his replies, working everything through before he answered. But if he'd been so stung by the first conclusion he'd drawn that he hadn't tried to go deeper ... well, she didn't know *exactly* what it meant, but it felt pretty damn good. She couldn't stop the smile that lifted the corners of her mouth. "Okay."

Ethan's brow was furrowed, as if he had thought about his reaction and come away just as surprised as she had. "All right. Suppose then you tell me what you were jumping to?"

"The opposite, actually. That even though you say I don't owe you anything, I still feel ... like a leech."

His jaw tightened at that, but he didn't respond except to nod.

"So I want them to be separate, so that it doesn't seem—*to me*—like I'm trading sex for blood. Because if that's the only thing I'm giving you back ..." She spread her hands and dropped them to her sides again. "I just don't know how they wouldn't get mixed up."

"That would be just fine, Charlie, save for one thing." Ethan stepped forward, cupping her cheeks. He tipped her head back and held her gaze as he said, "You're a vampire now. They *are* mixed up and they always will be. When you're feeding, I can prevent us having sex, but not the bloodlust that makes us want it so bad. And when I bed you, you won't be able to finish without blood. You can use yours instead of mine, and control when you'll let yourself go, but it'll always be there with us."

She searched his eyes. He was laying it out straight for her, but she wasn't certain she understood the last part. It seemed unbelievable. "Are you saying that I can't have an orgasm without it?"

He leaned in, his voice lowering. "I'm saying that I could work at you for hours, and it won't matter how much you beg or moan, how fast or slow we go, whether I use my fingers or my mouth, or if you take me as deep as you can. Without blood, you'd just stay riled up."

She was suddenly breathless. "But I can control it?"

"Yes."

At least it was *something* she could choose, then. Her gaze dropped to his mouth. She reached up and brushed her thumb over the scar on his lip. "Ethan," she said huskily, and watched as desire flared in his eyes. "I think I'm in too close."

"That's a damn shame." He slid his hands back to palm the wall beside her head. "I reckon you ain't got no choice but to kiss me, then."

"No choice," she agreed. "You probably shouldn't move, because I don't have much practice."

He closed his eyes, his lips curving beneath her thumb. "I'll stand real still."

She eyed the six inches between her and those lips; Ethan was already leaning in a little—just not far enough. But his arms were braced on either side of her . . . and she was incredibly strong now.

Her hands curved over his shoulders. Lifting her own weight was nothing, and he didn't seem to feel it either. She wrapped her legs high on his waist so that her feet weren't dangling above the floor.

Ethan was solid and hot between her thighs, the wall hard against her back.

His breathing quickened. She held her mouth close to his, let his exhalations brush her skin. His lashes cast short spiked shadows below his eyes, and she thought it would be so easy to lose herself in the play of light and dark across his face. Until her gaze fell to his mouth, and looking wasn't enough.

She trailed her tongue across the width of his bottom lip, then lifted her head and waited.

Ethan squinted one eye open. "That was just plain mean—"

Her mouth caught his. He tensed, his hands fisting in her hair, holding her in place. The pressure increased between her legs and against her back as he leaned into the kiss.

Then he offered her the lead, his lips softening.

Practice. But it didn't feel like it; her mouth learned his too easily, as if she'd been doing it this way forever—or as if she had been made to kiss him with fangs. His tongue teased their sharp tips, and she felt the echo of that caress in her nipples and her sex, in the sensitive bud pressed tight against his abdomen.

And losing herself in this came easily, too. The inside of his mouth was slick and hot. Her fingers tightened on his shoulders as she licked deep. Her fangs clicked against his teeth, and she shivered with pleasure.

Ethan released her hair, and it tumbled heavy over her shoulder. His big palm curved down her waist, then burned a line of fire beneath her shirt hem to her breast.

Her lips left his, and she let her head fall back when his heated fingers circled the taut flesh.

His voice was harsh. "Do we stop, Charlie?"

The choice was hers. But she couldn't focus long enough to work it over, to think; he was dropping openmouthed kisses into the hollow of her throat, his thumb dragging roughly across her nipple. Just the gentle flexing of his stomach muscles threatened to make her lose control, and he was all around her, surrounding her. So much texture, so much heat.

"I don't know," she gasped.

Ethan stilled. Then his mouth captured hers with scorching need before he released her and stepped away. She sagged against the wall, her senses on fire, her knees weak.

Ethan half-turned, ran his hand over his face. "All right

then." His chest heaved. "All right. I'd best go, Miss Charlie, because I shouldn't make this decision for you."

She swallowed past the sudden knot in her throat and straightened up. "I wasn't relying on you to make the decision. I'm just being slow."

"Hell and damnation, Charlie, that's not what I—" His eyes closed. "I'm just tempted to make you want me so bad you *can't* say no."

She thought a weak, needy part of her wanted that, too— but of course he wouldn't take her choice that way.

And she was too grateful and frustrated and mixed up to respond.

Ethan released a long sigh, met her eyes again. "I ought to get up to Seattle before dawn, anyway. You need anything before I head out?"

You. But that wasn't fair. He had work to do and she had . . . to sleep. Eventually.

"No," she said. "I'll be okay."

CHAPTER 20

Fuzzy, in less than a day. There were a million other mysteries that ought to have been pressing on his mind harder than Charlie's face when he'd walked out her door. But instead of puzzling over the nephilim, instead of planning how he'd approach Manny, Ethan spent most of the flight back to Seattle remembering how good she'd felt against him, and wondering how a woman could want anything so much and still not take what he'd been offering.

She didn't like to need something so bad; but she wouldn't be needing it if she had it. And God knew he'd have done anything to give it to her, make certain she'd want for nothing, if she'd just let him provide it.

Hell. One hundred and fifty years old, and he still couldn't comprehend some women. And it just figured he'd go and fall for a difficult one.

Difficult . . . but she sure was a comfortable fit. She'd gotten under his skin and itched something terrible, but he didn't reckon he'd ever been so easy with someone, so eager to spend time in her company, so anxious to please her.

He shook his head as he flew in over Manny's building. Fuzzy *and* smitten. He was like to get himself killed soon.

Vladimir and Katya had lived on the second floor, and their rich furnishings had been a better indication of their long life and history than the stark garage below. A glance through the garage windows confirmed that it had been cleaned out. Manny had likely sold the equipment, which would account for all the new sparklies the vampire had been sporting the last time they'd met up.

A woman's screech split the predawn quiet. Ethan palmed his sword, but he wasn't expecting trouble. That had been more pissed off than afraid, and Manny's girls were . . . something else.

There were difficult women, and then there was Cora and Angie.

Cora opened the door at his knock, cocked her hip. "Hiya, Drifter."

"Miss Cora," he returned, thankful that she'd dressed her lips with a smile. It gave him something safe to look at, considering that she wasn't wearing anything else. "I don't suppose—"

Two bare-assed figures dashed through the foyer, then out through another room. Well, hell—that wasn't something Ethan saw every day. Angie was after Manny with a butcher's knife.

Cora turned to look, twisting a lock of black hair around her finger, a gleam of pleasure in her eyes. "He called her a whore while he was feeding from her."

Ethan took a moment to debate whether he should let Angie have at the vampire. Manny had been their pimp before he'd transformed them, and Ethan reckoned the only reason they were with Manny was to make his life hell.

Ethan was inclined to let them—but if Angie cut out Manny's heart, that wouldn't help Ethan discover why Brandt might have visited Vladimir and Katya.

Reluctantly, Ethan headed in after the screeching woman. Angie didn't fight once he got ahold of her in the parlor, just turned around and snuggled in close.

Damnation. That likely wasn't going to get Manny to open up any, either.

But Manny didn't look jealous as much as he did relieved. "Thanks, Drifter. The crazy-ass bitch doesn't know her place."

Ethan let her go.

Angie took one step and burst into laughter when Manny cringed back, his hands over his genitals. She turned, her auburn hair falling like a curtain across her shoulder. "You smell like a vampire, Drifter. Anyone we know?"

"I don't imagine so, Miss Angie. She's just been turned."

Cora slipped into a silk robe, but didn't bother to tie it before sinking onto one of the elegant sofas and resting her right foot up on the cushions. "Word is you slew a handful of rogue vampires a few evenings back. That have anything to do with it?"

Ethan had no idea how word spread when there hadn't been anyone but him, Sammael, and the nephil as witnesses— but it always seemed to spread, right quick. "Yes'm."

Angie slid onto the sofa alongside Cora, pillowed her cheek on the other woman's ample belly. "You see, Manny, that's what you should be doing. I could get excited if I was with someone who acts like a leader instead of just calling himself one."

Ethan suppressed his grin; these women could work Manny over better than his fists could, but it wouldn't do Ethan good if it clammed Manny up. "I ain't much of one, Miss Angie. I'm just doing my job," Ethan said before he turned to Manny. "I got a few questions about Vladimir and Katya, and you'll need to be warning your community about a new kind of demon in town. He wears black feathered wings, and he's targeting vampires."

Manny's brow creased. "Why?"

"Don't rightly know—except that he killed one of those rogues, turning her upside down and slashing her throat open to drain her. And he'd have gone after another last night." Ethan frowned; Manny's thumb had begun working the ring around his middle finger, and the vampire was darting uneasy glances at the two women. "That sound familiar to you, Manny?"

Manny clenched his teeth, his brows shooting skyward as he gestured with his head to a door leading out of the room. Cora and Angie didn't take his hint to leave, and a moment later, Ethan was fighting back impatience and following the vampire into the kitchen.

If the bastard hadn't been naked, Ethan might have already been laying into him, but he sure as hell didn't feel like starting off his day by touching anything Manny had on display. Instead, he just stopped in the middle of the room and breathed slow and long. The counters weren't needed for food preparation, and either Cora or Angie had filled them with long rows of flower beds. The room smelled of sweet perfume and rich potting soil.

Manny put the spell up at the door, then sucked the blood from his finger, his mouth in a sullen frown. "Drifter, man, why you gotta do that? Coming here asking about Vladimir and Katya, then letting Cora and Angie know it wasn't me that killed them."

Ethan didn't let his surprise show. He'd suspected Manny hadn't slain the couple, but he hadn't thought it was connected to the nephilim. Letting his instincts guide him, Ethan hardened his voice and said, "So you wasn't ever going to tell me that's how you found them—tortured and bled out?"

His mouth twisting, Manny walked over to a flower bed and snapped off the head of a tulip. "For ten years I was their enforcer, always doing what they asked, and coming home to, 'You're the strongest, Manny, why don't we live in a place like that?' You know what that does to a man, Drifter?"

Apparently, it made him whine a whole lot. "You found them here?"

Manny pointed to the corner of the kitchen. "Right over there."

"Anything out of place? Broken?"

"This table knocked over. If I hadn't smelled the blood, I wouldn't have realized anything was wrong until I was on them."

It must have killed them quickly, then. No time to fight. And the kitchen was situated in the center of the house. Had the nephil shape-shifted to be let in, and come after them then? "But you never saw it."

"No." Manny hesitated. "You gonna tell the girls?"

Ethan figured they'd always known. Not what had killed Katya and Vladimir, just that it hadn't been Manny—and the brief conversation they'd had outside the kitchen likely clued them in on the *what*, too. "No. But you tell them if they encounter something they ain't sure about, they should get off the streets and behind the spell as quick as they can."

"All right." Manny nodded. "That all?"

"No." Ethan pulled a picture of Mark Brandt in from his cache. "You seen this one anytime in the last year?"

Manny studied it, shook his head. "No."

Ethan replaced the photo with the senator's. "What about him?"

Nervousness spilled from Manny's psyche before he began blocking hard. "Yeah. A few times, talking to Vladimir."

"When?"

"About six months ago. Then he stopped coming around."

Ethan's eyes narrowed. "You listen in on any of those conversations, Manny?"

"Yeah," the vampire said, and though Manny wasn't moving, everything about him seemed twitchy as hell. "Mostly they talked about letting people know about us. And whether Katya and Vladimir would be willing to be the proof humans might need if the senator went public. He kept saying people deserved to know the truth."

Maybe so, but it'd likely unleash a commotion unlike people had ever seen. "Did they agree with him?"

Manny hesitated. "No. And he stopped coming around after that."

Something wasn't sitting right here. Ethan didn't think Manny was lying—but he wasn't telling the whole truth, either.

"You know if money changed hands, Manny?"

"I don't know anything about that."

Ethan would have wagered *that* was a flat-out lie. "If it did, maybe as an incentive for Vladimir to help the senator out, you know of any reason he wouldn't have given it back?"

"Jesus, man—maybe Vladimir sold the guy some blood or something."

Maybe, but that didn't sit right, either. If Vladimir hadn't agreed exposure would be good for the vampire community, then he wouldn't have been giving the senator evidence.

Manny edged toward the door. "Drifter, man—I can feel the sun coming."

Ethan clenched his jaw in frustration, then nodded. "Go on then."

He watched the vampire scamper away. He'd take a few seconds to look around, but three months of living would have erased most of the evidence of the encounter with the nephil. He eyed the phone on the wall, then shook his head, frowning.

San Francisco was just far enough south that the sun rose a couple of minutes later than in Seattle, but there wasn't enough time to call Charlie and make sure she'd settled in before the daysleep hit.

In any case, the one thing that'd settle Charlie more than any other was if he tracked down Jane, saw how she was getting on. There'd likely be a record of a hotel stay under her or Sammael's name, as she wouldn't be returning to the burned out house.

Then he'd best be on to Caelum, for another long drift and searching through the Scrolls before he headed back to San Francisco.

He frowned up at the sky as he left Manny's house. The sun was just coming up, and he was already looking forward to sunset. He sure couldn't go long without thinking of her, without wanting to hear her. Already, he was planning his day around when he'd be seeing her again.

And that sounded awful similar to something Charlie wouldn't want, something that might have her chewing her arm off to escape.

He'd best be careful not to spook her; God knew, he'd rather chew off his own arm than send her running.

❧

The Gate to Caelum lay pretty much in a direct line between Seattle and San Francisco. Though Ethan usually kept over the ocean when making the long flight between the two cities—the better to keep from being seen—he veered inland to a forest clearing just outside of Ashland, Oregon.

Though invisible, the Gate was a hum in his blood, and he could clearly sense its shape and position with a psychic probe. He dove through the shadows, and moved instantly from air rich with moisture, the scent of pine and dark soil, into Caelum's bright and dry atmosphere.

The sun shone against white marble, dazzling his eyes until he blinked and adjusted. Ethan swooped back up, above the tiled courtyards, skimming over a brilliant smooth dome. Caelum's library was housed in an enormous temple near the center of the city.

Scarce few Guardians walked below, and Ethan was the

only one in the sky. Just fifteen years before, Caelum had been teeming with life; not so since the Ascension, when thousands of Guardians had chosen to move on to their afterlife.

Most of those that remained in service—particularly the novices—had drawn in close to one another. And as they'd suddenly been without mentors, many Guardians had taken on one or two of the novices for training, knitting the groups even more tightly.

Now that Castleford had taken over a good chunk of their training, it had loosened up. But not much—and Ethan reckoned not one Guardian who'd been in Caelum after the Ascension would ever forget the sudden, terrible silence that had fallen over the city.

It made the hairs on the back of his neck prickle, his gut twist, just thinking of it.

And there were some it had hit worse than others.

He found Alice standing motionless in a long aisle of gleaming marble shelves, her arms crossed and her head tilted back as if she was looking for something on one of the higher rows. There wasn't a bit about the archivist that wasn't sharp—not her brown hair in its severe braid or the tall, thin figure that she'd wreathed in black. Her appearance hadn't changed any since the Ascension, but her manner had. Whereas once Alice had moved with the elegance of a dancer, now she reminded Ethan of a many-jointed spider—and he could easily imagine her creeping around inside the Archives. And he didn't know if she was aware that the novices had taken to calling her the Black Widow, but he figured she was—and that she didn't care much.

He was just glad to find her there; she disappeared from Caelum for irregular stretches of time. But excepting those absences, he didn't figure she'd stepped out of the temple since the Ascension, with only the Scrolls, books, and the occasional visitor for company.

Though she must have heard him coming, Ethan opened his shields and projected a warm greeting. He and Alice had been transformed around the same time, trained by the same Guardians—and she was one of the few who hadn't ever taken to calling him Drifter.

"Ethan." Her eyes thawed slightly at his approach. "You

look well. Considering what I've heard of your brother, I hope your appearance is not deceptive."

"It ain't." He grinned when her mouth turned down with her disapproval. She'd never been a schoolmarm, but he figured if she had been, she'd have used the ruler well and often. "Is yours?"

Her frown disappeared, smoothing into a tiny smile. "No. Is this your usual social call, or are you looking for something?"

"Looking for something. You got anything on the nephilim? The offspring of humans and demons—it may have been recorded as a myth."

She tilted her head, almost birdlike. "I seem to recall coming across a mention of them about thirty or forty years ago. I believe I can locate it, if you have some time to wait."

"I do. I'll be in my quarters three, maybe four hours. If you find anything, it'll need to be transcribed."

Only Michael could vanish the Scrolls, or carry them through a Gate. Nor could they be photocopied or scanned; if a copy was to be made, it had to be written out by hand.

"Would you like me to translate it, as well?" Alice asked with a teasing lift of her brow.

Ethan shook his head. "I'll be taking it to Hugh." Castleford could easily read the Latin; Ethan still stumbled over his.

Alice nodded. "Very well."

"I'm much obliged."

She gave his arm a poke with her bony elbow. "Are you so obliged that when you pick these up, you'll tell me a little about this vampire I've been hearing about?"

Ethan figured he might just talk her ear off; but for now, he dropped a kiss to her cheek and walked away to a sound that was eerily like a cackle.

❧

Ethan's quarters were halfway up a large spire at the edge of the city. There weren't any doors; just an arch that opened to a view of the silent, waveless sea surrounding Caelum. Looking out, it was near impossible to tell where sky and water met at the horizon—the sea reflected an image of pure, dizzying blue.

Inside, it was just dizzying white. Ethan had broken it up

some with items he'd collected—from other Guardians before he'd gone active duty, and in his own travels after he'd returned to Earth.

Still, it wasn't much to look at. He'd never had much of a hand at decorating, and most everything he needed he kept with him in his cache. It was certainly nothing like Charlie's brightly colored and cozy space.

Thinking of her room, he reckoned maybe he'd take his bed with him this time. He didn't much relish the idea of having his loving interrupted every time his feet became caught between the slats in her footboard.

He vanished his clothes, laid faceup on the mattress. No breeze to tickle his skin. No sound or smell. He closed his eyes, got rid of the white, and let himself drift into the emptiness.

It was vast, and more than capable of taking everything he had to throw into it . . . until he brushed up against something that was Charlie's. Then she tugged at him, pulled him back in.

Less than ten minutes after he'd lain down, Ethan sat up, frowning out into the blue.

He was missing her—and didn't want to rid himself of the effect of her touch, her smell. Not when he didn't have something to fill him right back up again.

Instinct led him to searching through his cache, looking for something to use. He'd left most of her things with her, but there were towels from her laundry that likely held her scent.

He dropped one onto the bed beside him, tried again.

Not perfect, but better; she was still there, and he could get rid of the fuzz without fearing so much that he was losing something of her.

But everything else . . . everything else, it could go.

$

When he got back to SI, Ethan paused only long enough to drop off the transcribed Scrolls at Castleford's office before running up the stairs. Sunset was five minutes away, and Charlie would be more comfortable waking up to a familiar face than a strange room.

He frowned walking through the common area; he was still getting those grave looks, and everyone was speaking real quiet-like when he entered a room. They all needed a talking-to, or a solid beating at the poker table. Losing a bundle of money would make them a bit less sympathetic.

Charlie's door was sealed with the spell. Ethan blinked and tried again, fighting the disappointment . . . and failing.

Well, son of a bitch. He hadn't even considered that she'd lock everyone out while she slept, but she must have been worried about her privacy.

"Drifter."

Ethan swung around, suddenly uneasy. He couldn't mistake the concern in Jake's psychic scent.

"Is Charlie all right?"

"Yes," Jake said. "And, no. I had to put up the spell about thirty minutes after sunrise because she was projecting so hard that we couldn't block it out. I went back inside around noon, but there's been no change."

Jake swung the door open.

Everything looked just fine. Two new throws lay over the foot of the bed; she must have knitted both after he'd left. She'd taken the time to dress in her pajama bottoms and a—

Jake lowered the spell, and the psychic wave hit Ethan hard, left him struggling for breath. *God Almighty.* Fear, despair, and loss were pouring from her, choking him under their weight.

He went in; Charlie was sleeping curled up on her side. She clutched the ragged feather beneath her chin, and her grip on it didn't loosen when he pulled her up into his arms.

But there was nothing to do but hold her. A vampire's daysleep—and the dreams that came with them—was solid, unbreakable.

"Jake." His voice was rough. "Get the spell up."

Jake drew in a sharp breath. "She's skinny again."

Ethan couldn't answer for a long minute. "Yes," he finally said hoarsely, and brushed her hair back from her cheek. Almost as bad as the previous night, but she'd fed enough she shouldn't have lost any weight. A healthy vampire might go two, three days without looking so emaciated, even if the bloodlust was tearing at them. "You go on out now."

Jake hesitated. "Milliken didn't feed much, but when he did, he still woke up looking starved like that—"

"*Go on out, Jake.*"

Ethan waited for the click of the door before rolling onto the bed and tucking Charlie against him. She wasn't breathing, didn't react, couldn't respond.

And a vampire's daysleep had never seemed so much like death to him.

CHAPTER 21

Charlie gasped herself awake, clawing her way out of darkness and frigid blood—into Ethan's strong embrace and the warmth of his voice murmuring her name over and over.

The lights in the room were off, but she clearly saw his face, his cheek against the pillow and only inches from hers. And she saw the worry in his eyes, even before he said, "Bad dreams again?"

Charlie nodded, pressing her lips tight. Did every vampire go through this?

His gaze was direct. "What are they about?"

"Jane," she rasped. "Blood."

He trailed his fingers along her jaw. "I saw her this morning. They're staying at the Marriott, downtown. Separate rooms."

She couldn't halt her smile. "She'll make him pay, at least a little. Although I guess for a demon, it wouldn't be punishment."

"I reckon it is. It may be he began sharing her bed to strengthen his hold on her, so as she wouldn't leave him—but he loves her, so it's likely it also gives him some measure of satisfaction when he pleases her. Denying him that opportunity would be punishment." The corner of Ethan's mouth tilted up, but the lines beside his eyes didn't echo his smile. "He sure did look awful sorry. And I didn't speak with her, but she seemed all right, Charlie."

"That's good." She couldn't come up with a better response; he was so close, and she was so, so tired. She cleared her throat. "Did I sleep the whole day?"

"Yes. It's half past eight."

She blinked. Sunset was at seven thirty, and she'd woken just after it the night before. "That late?"

"Yes." His eyes closed for a long second before he met hers again. "You hungry?"

"No. A little, maybe—but not like last time." She sighed, rose up onto her elbow. "I should probably call Old Matthew before it gets too—"

"It can wait a spell, Charlie." Ethan's palm smoothed over her shoulder, brought her closer to him. "And if you feed now, when you're not too hungry, we can see if that's why it was hurting last night."

"Oh." Her gaze fell to his neck, and her thirst swelled, a mild ache in her fangs.

Mild . . . *not* uncontrollable. She scooted toward him; he was on his side, but she was leaning so far over she was almost on her stomach, her thigh against the front of his trousers.

Sexual excitement was threading through her veins now, almost indistinguishable from the thirst—but Ethan wasn't hard.

She touched his throat, his skin like rough satin beneath her fingers. "Just feeding again?"

He nodded. "Yes."

There was an odd, hollow note in his voice. She studied his face, looking for evidence of whatever was causing it, but didn't see anything except an expressionless mask.

"Ethan . . . is everything okay?"

His only response was to cup the back of her head, draw her gently down to his neck. Her fingers rose to unbutton his shirt.

"Are you sure?" She smoothed his collar back until it folded over his suspender, and she had to stifle her soft moan of anticipation when she revealed the muscle bunched atop his shoulder. Almost of their own volition, her hips rolled against the mattress. "Because I could probably find a rat or something. That was how I earned my extra spending money when I was in New York. I used to steal my roommate's flute, and head on down to the subway—"

Her lips touched his throat. Ethan tensed beside her. Something was wrong. Something was wrong, but his scent, so masculine, almost undetectable, was filling her head. She hadn't known it was there, but now that she'd inhaled it, she didn't think she'd ever get enough.

She eased into him, his skin parting beneath her fangs with the faintest pressure. His hands clenched on her hips, his pleasured groan an echo of hers, a hum against her tongue. And then there was *Ethan*, heated and liquid, a symphony of strings and reeds, all rising together in a strong, steady beat.

So incredible. She memorized the sound, tried to tease out the notes. The agonizing scream was there, but she barely heard it beneath the luscious tones that made up his lifeblood, beneath Ethan's harsh breathing in her ear. She pushed him onto his back and slung her leg over his stomach.

And because she *could* stop, she did, licking across the already-healing punctures.

Ethan's hands settled on her waist. "Was it hurting you, Charlie?"

"No." She kissed his jaw, his chin. "I could feel it, but it's not so painful this time."

"It shouldn't be painful at all."

She lifted her head, met his eyes. "Maybe not, but it's not *so* bad." She paused, studied him. His features were still unreadable. "And you're okay?"

A smile broke the flat line of his mouth. "Even though I don't mean to, Charlie, you take just one little bite and I'm stretching out my britches and feeling mighty fine." His hands caught her cheeks, prevented her from sitting up. "Now, don't you go looking or touching, or this won't be just a feeding."

She nodded breathlessly. "What about later tonight?"

"I'd like that, Miss Charlie." His gaze fell to her lips, and his throat worked before he repeated softly, "I'd like that an awful lot."

"Me, too." She smiled, dropped a kiss to his mouth before

trailing her tongue down to his throat. "I'm going to bite you again, Ethan."

"All right. I reckon I'll just lay here and moan."

She was laughing when her fangs pierced him. Could he feel her emotions when she fed from him? The erotic pleasure of it, obviously—but did she send anything else, or did he have to deliberately look into her? And could she get into him?

But even if she could, it wouldn't be right to go in without asking; and if he'd wanted her to know, he'd have projected as he had before.

And the blood told her some: grief, arousal, and determination sang louder than anything else, and all of them ran deep.

As deep as her own. Lust and love and thirst . . .

Thirst. It struck quick, hard, disguised and gathering below her sexual need, then tearing its way through. She'd been feeding softly, leisurely, but now she was sucking down great drafts, her fingers digging into Ethan's shoulders, and she had to have him in her *in her*—

"Charlie." Ethan panted her name. "You're all right. I swear I won't—"

But the rest was lost beneath the shriek that ripped into her mind.

She couldn't scream. Tears slipped from her eyes, and she tried to brush them away before Ethan felt them, but her hands were tugging her pajamas, tearing them, her fingers fanning and flaming the cold fire burning inside her.

Until she came apart, ecstasy splintering and flinging her wide—and agony followed every sharp piece.

When she pulled herself together, she was soft and dull, with Ethan ebbing into her. His palms ran gently over her hair, down the damp skin of her lower back. Her shirt was gone again. She slid her fingers from the wetness between her legs, her fangs from his throat, and licked the puncture wounds as they closed. Only a few crimson drops marred the pillowcase.

"Ethan." She couldn't look at him. "Are you all right?"

His hands found hers, clasped them tight. A now-familiar harmony vanished from her mind; she hadn't noticed his psychic presence until he slipped away.

"No, Miss Charlie." His voice was ragged around the edges. "I don't reckon I am."

§

Ethan waited until he heard the spray of the shower before slipping out of the room. He didn't like leaving her alone, but he couldn't put this off—and he wasn't going to feed her again until he had some answers.

Charlie had called whatever she'd been hearing painful.

Ethan hadn't *heard* it, but he'd felt it when he'd pushed his way into her head—and it hadn't been anything like what he'd expected. "Painful" was the stab of a knife, a gunshot wound.

Not his skin slowly being flayed from his flesh; that was more like torture.

And it had worsened—not when the bloodlust had grabbed hold of her, as he'd half-expected, but when he'd begun actively resisting the need tearing through him.

The previous night, she'd said it wasn't hers—and now he figured she was correct.

It was his.

Had it been hindering her transformation? She'd been adjusting in every other way, but feeding was central to a vampire's existence. And there hadn't been much good to come out of living as one yet—only loss and pain.

He stepped into one of the soundproofed communications rooms adjacent to the main offices to make the call, and he'd spoken just a few words when Selah was suddenly in the room with him, her cell phone against her ear.

"This is so much easier," she said as she lowered the phone. "What's the problem?"

This was about as uncomfortable a topic as he could imagine, but there wasn't anyone who knew more about being with a vampire than Selah. "Feeding," he said quietly. "It's hurting Charlie."

A line formed between Selah's brows. "Are you forcing yourself to submit to her?"

"No. I'm more than willing." He drew a deep breath, and he focused on a point over her head. "I've heard that when you first fed Marsden, you kept him from . . . well, from—"

"Yes," Selah said, and he felt her studying him. "You're giving her time."

Ethan nodded. "Was it painful for Marsden—you resisting him?"

"I didn't resist him," Selah said. "I kept us from having sex."

Ethan frowned and leaned back against a desk, crossing his arms. Most times, he had no trouble understanding Selah. But when feelings and the bed came into a conversation, he figured some women just started speaking a different language. "You want to explain the difference to me? Because I sure ain't following."

"If you resist what the bloodlust is doing to you, you're going to hurt her."

"And if I don't resist, I'll hurt her another way." If not physically, then by destroying the trust between them, breaking the promise he'd made. He couldn't determine if that would be worse than what his resistance was already doing to her.

Selah's eyebrows winged upward. "You already want her. The bloodlust only increases the intensity of it."

"That it does. Makes it near impossible not to—"

"*Near* impossible. But if your reaction to her is anything like mine to Lucas, I'd bet that even without the bloodlust, it's near impossible, too," Selah said.

He scrubbed his hand over his hair, feeling damned awkward as he admitted, "That's true enough."

"Yet you're able to stop, no matter how badly you want to keep going." A small smile touched the corners of her mouth. "Have a bit of faith in yourself, Drifter. The bloodlust takes their choice, not yours—and you won't hurt someone you mean to protect. You aren't an Enthralled novice anymore."

And he wasn't—but he sure hadn't trusted himself any more than if he still had been one.

Well, hell. He closed his eyes, pinched the bridge of his nose. "In the past twenty-four hours, I've said something similar to Jake about faith, and told Charlie the same thing about not being a novice."

"Funny how that happens. I find myself quoting Hugh about once a day," she said, then added wryly, "And, depending on the situation I find myself in, I change the wording about ten times a day."

Adapting, adjusting. Selah vanished, and Ethan walked

back to Charlie's room. He'd be doing his own adjusting now. Maybe it wouldn't make a difference, but he wouldn't be re-sisting Charlie again.

And if it *didn't* make a difference . . . he simply didn't know what he'd do.

❧

Ethan was quiet when he returned, and he stood watching her as she finished getting ready—but Charlie couldn't find much to say, either. And her attempts to reassure him, tell him that she was okay only seemed to deepen his silence.

It continued as she walked with him to the tech room and endured a searching glance from Jake. Even seeing the e-mail from Jane did little to lighten her mood. And though Jane had included a personal reference to let Charlie know it truly was her sister, the bulk of the message wasn't for her.

After she'd read halfway through, she turned in her chair. Ethan was frowning down at the new cell phone Jake had placed in his hand.

"Drifter," she said, and he looked up. "Jane says that Sam-mael let the vampires go, and gave each of her colleagues the option to stay or leave—although those who left couldn't take any of their research with them. Five of the scientists—and all of the vampires—stayed."

Jake frowned. "All of them? How'd Legion manage that?"

"Because a demon could likely convince a wolf to shed its fur in the middle of a blizzard," Ethan said dryly, then re-leased a heavy breath. "Or he's lying. I ought to contact those who left, then, and see if they want any help from us."

"Or a job at Ramsdell Pharmaceuticals," Jake said.

"When Michael shows up, I'll put that in front of him," Ethan said. "I can't see as it would hurt to study the blood, but I don't know if he'll be wanting to follow in a demon's footsteps."

Charlie read a little more. "Also, she's making Sammael give her samples of demon blood. She wants to know if she should send some down, so you have another link to her if you need one."

"I reckon we can just keep it stored here. Ain't no one go-ing to want to carry it around in their cache." Ethan glanced at Jake as the younger Guardian shuddered. "And how is it that you know what demon blood feels like?"

"I don't," Jake said. "I've just heard."

Charlie's brows rose in question, and Ethan explained, "It creeps, Charlie. Nosferatu blood, too—but just when it's in our cache. I've heard a few vampires mention that it tastes better—more powerful—than vampire or Guardian blood." He straddled the chair next to her. "Not that there's many vampires who've fed from demons or nosferatu—leastwise, not many who've lived to talk about it."

Charlie angled the monitor so that he could more easily read Jane's message. "What's a nosferatu? Was that what you were fighting at Jane's house?"

"No, that was supposedly one of the nephilim," he said, scanning the e-mail. "But the nosferatu ain't any more partial to vampires than the nephil was, Charlie. So if you ever encounter one of them, you take off running and get behind the spell." He glanced over her head. "Jake? You want to show her what they look like?"

Charlie blinked and turned. Instinctively, she kicked at the floor, but Ethan caught her before her chair skidded across the room, away from the huge hulking monster Jake had become: pale and hairless, with membranous wings, pointed ears, and fangs twice as long as hers.

Then he was Jake again.

Ethan's hands smoothed over her arms. "Easy, Charlie. Hell, I should have prepared you for that." His apology was almost lost below the choking noises he made, keeping his amusement in check.

She couldn't stop hers; now that the scare had passed, fear bubbled into laughter, and she said, "I saw that movie a couple of years ago. He wasn't that big, and his fangs were—" She held two fingers below her front teeth.

"All of that stuff is bullshit. The movies, the stories. They're just bits of the truth that humans have picked up over the years." Ethan held her gaze, and his palms ran the length of her arms again, warming her skin. "You ready to make a few calls?"

To Jane, and then Old Matthew. Her stomach ached, but she nodded. "Yes."

"We've got soundproofed rooms if you don't want to be overheard," he said. "But if it's all right with you, I'd like to listen in."

"You might as well." She glanced at the computer, and offered him a shaky smile. "It'll probably be for you, anyway."

❧

Charlie hadn't been far off; Jane never asked for him, but the call wasn't much about Charlie, either.

Ethan watched her sit at a desk and smile her way through the conversation. She barely got a word in edgewise, but her fingers were busy. She fiddled through a small box of paper clips, straightening them out and lining them up in front of her, then using her ID card like a plow and pushing the pile around the desktop.

Sammael had done a damn good job of latching onto Jane where she was most vulnerable—and most ambitious. And wrapping both the research and Charlie's vampirism up into one goal meant that Jane was more excited about what her work might do for her sister than concerned about finding out how her sister was doing now.

Ethan reckoned Jane asked all the right questions—how was Charlie doing, did she have a place to stay, was she feeding—but Jane didn't listen to the answers all that well. Instead, she went on about everything she'd learned . . . and everything Sammael had told her.

Some of the information she relayed might have been new to Charlie, but not most of it—and there was nothing that Ethan hadn't already known or already figured.

Yes, Sammael was playing Jane real well.

And no matter how often Charlie called herself slow, she surely wasn't about this. Her face wasn't giving much away when she finally disconnected, but he could hear the hurt and frustration in her voice when she said, "It doesn't even matter what Sammael did to me, to all of those others. Or rather, it *matters*—but she just rationalizes it so that she doesn't feel like shit that she's still there, and so that she doesn't hate herself for it. Because she just can't cut herself off from him, can she?"

"No."

She met his gaze and flushed, as if struck by guilt that she'd been critical of her sister. "I know she's doing what she thinks is best, but—"

"You also reckon she ain't thinking with her head."

She struggled with that before admitting, "No. She's

probably not." She closed her eyes, and the tired smile curving her lips tugged at his chest. "Okay. Old Matthew now."

A call that would force her to take another emotional beating. The dread was already dripping heavy from her psyche, and he saw the way she bolstered herself, staring at the phone as if it was an opponent to be defeated.

"Charlie." He dropped into the chair beside hers, swiveled her to face him, and scooted forward until his knees bumped up against the front of her seat. "Just wait another day."

He couldn't fight this for her. But maybe he could find some way to lessen the blow.

She firmed her lips and shook her head. But she held on to his hand when the old man answered, her fingers closing on Ethan's with crushing strength when a long pause followed her rough greeting.

"Well, Charlie—since you're calling, I'll assume it means you aren't coming in again."

"I'm not." She couldn't seem to get any more out.

There was another silence, until Old Matthew asked, "Are you sick, or are you just saying you are?"

She gritted her teeth and leaned forward, her shoulders hunching, and Ethan pulled her onto his lap. Resisting the need to take the phone and finish this for her was about the hardest thing he'd ever done.

"I'm just saying it." She buried her face in the curve of his neck, the phone pressed tight to her ear. Her voice was thick. "I'm so sorry."

"So am I, Charlie. But I'll tell you: I thought it was odd that the healthiest white girl I've ever seen, and who never missed a day of work in two years, suddenly came down with something so bad. But now I think what's even stranger is that she lied to me for a couple of days, all the while sounding like she's miserable—even though I've never known her to spin a lie that wasn't a hell of a good time, and that didn't have a laugh underneath of it. So I'm wondering, Charlie girl: Are you in some kind of trouble?"

She curled in on herself. "Yes."

That had been more a sob than a word. A sharp pain cut through Ethan's chest, and he tried to pull back to look at her face, but she followed the movement, kept her cheek against his throat. Her free hand lifted and made a swiping motion.

"Where are you at, Charlie girl? Do you need me to come get you?"

"California." She drew in a shuddering breath; resolve suddenly strengthened her psychic scent. Her fingers wrapped around Ethan's suspender strap, and she began rubbing at the leather. "But I'm okay. I'm with someone, and he's helping me. I just don't think I'll be back anytime soon."

Doubt filled Old Matthew's voice. "Charlie, if it's keeping you away, what kind of trouble is it? Now, it's been a while, but I know a few lawyers. And if it's worse than that, there are a couple of guys from inside that owe me favors—"

"It's nothing like that." She tipped her face back, and Ethan was finally able to meet her eyes. Her dark lashes were moist, but a smile tilted the corners of them. "I was turned into a vampire."

Despite the ache in his chest, Ethan grinned and shook his head. But there was no humor in Old Matthew's reply.

"Charlie girl, that's what I expect from you. And if I hadn't thrown some clown out of here yesterday after he came in looking for you, asking about your sister, saying that your apartment had been cleaned out and that you were in danger from bloodsuckers and demons, I might have been laughing now."

CHAPTER 22

"So it was Mark Brandt," Lilith said.

Though the woman's voice was slightly muffled over the phone, this time Charlie was close enough to hear her responses. Ethan was standing now, and had set her up on the desk in front of him—but hadn't quite relinquished his hold on her. His large hand rested on her hip, his body a mountain of heat in front of her.

"By Cole's description, I reckon it must have been," Ethan said, and Charlie nodded her agreement when he met her eyes. "And Charlie had the same impression."

Lilith made a growling noise before she said, "I hate this unexpected shit. Rael didn't know much about the son—just the father. And he had the same impression that you got from the bloodsucker up in Seattle: he was looking to expose all of us, but not wanting to venture further without proof."

"It may be why he's trying to contact Jane, then—hoping she'll provide scientific evidence that can be presented to the media. And as she's already inside, has access to vampire blood, she'd be the right person to approach."

"Through the son? That's a good possibility—that's what

I would do." Lilith sighed. "All right, Drifter. Hugh and I are looking over those Scrolls tonight. You'll be in Seattle tomorrow, and then back in the evening?"

"Yes'm."

"We'll meet up at ten. It'd be real fucking nice if the goddamn golden boy Michael would get his ass back here."

Ethan's expression turned grave as his gaze roamed Charlie's face. "I've got an awful pressing reason to speak with him, as well."

His phone vanished a moment later, but he was still looking down at her, his eyes the color of honey caught in the sunlight. Slowly, he flattened his palms on the desk beside her thighs and lowered his head until his mouth was even with hers.

"You got anything else you need to do tonight, Miss Charlie?"

Her heart pounded. "No."

"Then I'm about to hand you a whole lot of choices, and maybe we'll come up with something to fill the time." His lips brushed a feather-light kiss across hers. "Do you like the desert?"

"I don't know," she whispered, and added quickly when his head lifted, "I've never been."

His mouth crooked into a smile. "A damn shame, Charlie. We'll have to rectify that." The warmth of his fingers settled on her waist. "You want to take a trip? Because this warehouse has a few too many folk living in it, and I've got a big bed that'll fit nicely out in the middle of nowhere."

She had to swallow to moisten her tongue. "That sounds really, really good."

He lifted her against his chest, strode immediately for the door. "It sure as hell does. And I reckon we can play poker on it or I can teach you to hog-tie a calf—"

Her laugh almost choked her; he was moving so quickly the hallway was passing in a blur. "Fuck you, Drifter."

"You just keep calling me that until we're on that bed, and don't lay your hands on me, or else we'll be falling out of the sky."

Her head swam as he launched them into the air, and she held on tight, her fingers linking together around his neck. The wind burned past her cheeks, whipped her hair. "Have you ever . . . while flying?"

"Sure I have, Charlie. And damn near broke in half when we hit a tower." His heated gaze dropped to hers for an instant before he looked ahead again. "Any man who attends to air currents more than he attends to his woman ought to just tuck it in and fly on home."

She smiled and nipped softly at his throat. "I'll attend to you, too. And I should probably practice, so that my fangs won't poke anything sensitive."

"My sensitive bits wouldn't last long enough for you to get any learning in. So you can do that after I've been inside you ten, maybe fifty times."

He was going too fast to keep chatting, and she watched the landscape beneath them change as the minutes rolled by: the houses farther apart, then only sparse vegetation, scrub, and flat, jutting stones.

His voice was as rough as the terrain. "Will you give me your clothes, Charlie? I'd sure hate to rip anything while getting you out of them."

A tremor shook through her. This apparently wasn't going to be a gentle undressing, a leisurely exploration. "Yes."

Her clothing vanished. He wasn't flying so quickly now, and they were losing altitude; the wind caressed her skin, brushing and teasing.

And despite his arms beneath her legs and back, her body against his chest, Ethan still wasn't touching her.

The bed appeared below them, huge and white. Her stomach dropped as Ethan swooped, then pulled up to land beside it. He set her on the edge, and his jacket disappeared.

"Wait!" She scrambled up to her knees, her hands moving to his collar. He froze. "I want to take them off."

Except for his slow nod, Ethan was absolutely still. "I'll be happy to oblige."

She pushed the suspenders over his shoulders, let them fall alongside his thighs. After another second, his shirt fluttered to the ground, and she paused, sat back to look.

"Jesus, Ethan," she breathed. "You should just walk around like this all the time."

Ethan cleared his throat. "I was thinking something along the same lines about you, Miss Charlie."

She glanced up in disbelief, but his face confirmed what his voice had suggested: a light flush stained his cheekbones.

"I'm awful modest," he said softly. "But I sure am grateful that the look of me pleases you so much."

"Pleases me?" She shook her head. "I've imagined you naked a million times since I saw you in the kitchen without your shirt. But you still knock me loopy." A tug on his suspenders had his hips swaying toward her. "And I've never thought these looked good on anyone, but on you, they are the sexiest things I have *ever* seen."

"Then I reckon I'll keep them on a bit longer." He placed his hands on the bed, his gaze holding hers. She slid back, and he followed her, stalking slowly across the mattress on his hands and knees—his suspenders dangling and his trousers on, but his feet bare now. "And I'd be mighty appreciative if you wouldn't put your hands on me until I'm in you deep, and you just can't stand me working at you anymore. Because once you touch me, I figure it'll be over."

Desire licked beneath her womb, heavy and moist. "Okay," she whispered.

"Now, you've got another choice to make, Charlie."

"What choice?" She'd stopped in the middle of the bed, but Ethan kept coming.

"Whether it'll be my hands first, or my mouth," he said.

Oh, Lord. She dropped back on her elbows as he moved over her and planted his hands beside her shoulders, his knees outside hers.

But Ethan didn't lower his weight; he just held himself braced above her. The desert air was cold, arid; she drew it in hard and fast, her excitement closing her throat, leaving her unable to speak.

His head bent toward hers. "My mouth," he repeated softly and caught her lips in a fiery kiss. Her fingers clenched in the soft mattress padding, and her feet slid across its smooth surface. "Or my hands?"

He pushed his thumb past her lips, ran the rough pad beneath the tip of her left fang.

It might as well have been a brush over her clitoris, a lick to her nipples. Her hips lifted; a needy moan rasped from her throat.

But any sound louder than that was beyond her. Frustration only made it worse. She lifted her hands to cup his face, her brows drawing together with her anxiety. "Both," she forced out, and it wasn't much more than a husky vibration of air.

He studied her for a long second, and his thumb traced a warm, wet trail over her scar. "Why don't you show me what you want, Miss Charlie? I'll give it to you, slow and easy. But you've got to think it hard."

What she wanted . . . ? *Oh, Jesus.* Familiar images flipped through her mind: her legs wrapping around his big body. His gentle touch on her skin. Her panties ripping. Her soft sighs of pleasure. Her hands bound with leather, with metal. Her nipples abraded by his teeth, the rough hair of his chest. Her nails digging into his back. A nightgown pushed up over her hip, her sex exposed. Panting and crying as he took his time, took too much time. Against a wall. A table. Tied to a bed. Bent over on her apartment balcony. His tongue on her clit, his fingers sliding—

"Charlie," he groaned, his eyes closing. "Slow and easy."

Ethan kissing her.

His need flared between them, and he lowered his head again to murmur against her lips, "Just like that, Miss Charlie."

And it was hotter, wetter than she'd imagined, and she matched each erotic stroke of his tongue.

His hands on her breasts.

But the pale image shattered against the reality of his palms cupping their soft weight. Her nipples puckered beneath his fingers. Tight and aching—not from cold, but heat.

She wanted his mouth.

Ethan leisurely made his way down, tasting and licking her chin, her throat. Her hands smoothed over his shoulders.

He caught her wrists, pushed them over her head at the same moment his lips captured her nipple. His tongue seared her flesh. She cried out, a thin, ragged exhalation. His teeth scraped gently, and he began suckling the taut peak.

She needed more.

Needed Ethan, finding her slick and ready with his fingers, his mouth.

His groan rumbled across her skin, and he raised his head, shifted up until his face was just above hers again. "All right, Miss Charlie," he said hoarsely. His fingers tightened around her wrists; his opposite palm slid down the sensitive curve of her belly. "I figure you'll want to come once or twice before I'm done. You can do that with a couple drops of your blood. It'll be when you choose, and how you choose it."

She nodded and squirmed, tried to lift her hips, to force his touch where she wanted it to go. Desire held her tight, but his easy heat had softened her frustration . . . and her throat.

Not much, but enough to whisper his name.

"That's awful good to hear," he said, and dropped a rough kiss to her lips. Then another, deeper, before tearing his mouth from hers. "I'm on the edge, about to ride you hard, and that's from barely touching you. So if I'm going to keep my britches on a bit longer, we got to do something about you forgetting your hands."

His mention made her realize her fingers were rubbing against each other; she stilled them, but they immediately itched to be moving again. "They like to be busy."

And they liked touching him even more.

"I know it, Charlie. I reckon you just need a little reminder, and after those images you sent me, I have one in mind." His amber gaze searched hers. Metal clinked beside her. "But not if the reality of it spooks you. I want to make this real good for you."

She turned her head, saw the slim cuffs beyond the spread of her hair. Her heart raced. Fear and pain had always threatened this fantasy—the memory of real cuffs, and the devastation of losing her voice. But the arousal had always been sharper in contrast, as if heightened by that threat and the triumph of not succumbing to it.

And this time, it would be with Ethan.

She met his eyes again. "There's nothing to tie them to." No headboard, no posts—just an endless sea of a mattress.

"I ain't thinking of tying you down," Ethan said, then grinned. "Not today, leastwise. I figure if you associate that jangling sound with not touching me, use it as a reminder, we'll be all right. And when you're ready to get rid of them, you tell me and I'll unlock them right quick."

"Okay." Excitement was tightening her voice again. The metal was cold, cooler even than her skin. Ethan lingered over it, watching her face as the bracelets clicked home.

His thumb ran along her wrist. "I aim to be attending to

you a good while. If you need anything, or you get lonely up here, you just let me know."

She grabbed as much of the soft mattress top as she could and held on. "I think I'll be okay."

Pushing Ethan onto his back, running her hands over his shoulders, kissing her way down the muscular ridges of his abdomen. Unbuttoning his trousers, lowering her mouth . . .

She let the image fade.

With a groan, Ethan said, "That was awful mean, Miss Charlie."

"So is not letting me touch you." She panted as his palm slid low on her belly, his fingers spreading wide. She lay between his knees, his body so big above her, his breath so warm on her lips.

His gaze never moved from her face as he lightly dipped in.

She shuddered; her thighs trapped his hand.

Ethan stilled. "You closed up real quick there. You all right?"

"Yes." She moved against his palm, gasping. "It's just too good."

His lids lowered fractionally. "Are you thinking of denying yourself this, then?"

Deny herself Ethan like she would fried foods, alcohol? Those things, when she had too much or couldn't control her need for them, might hurt her.

Ethan never would.

"No." Her reply trembled from her, and she forced herself to relax. Hard to do, when the shape of his fingers felt like a brand against her flesh. "It was just habit. And it's so *hot*," she said breathlessly.

"And you're awful wet, Charlie." His voice was gruff. His long middle finger gently cajoled her soft folds apart, circling her entrance before drawing a path of fire up to her clitoris.

The handcuffs clinked; she grabbed the mattress again. She turned her cheek to the side, tried to keep her hips still.

"You want to move, you want to moan or kick, you go right on ahead. Ain't no one to hear you but me." Ethan's teeth tugged at her earlobe before he licked the side of her jaw. "And I'd sure like to hear you sing for me, Charlie."

Was that what she was doing? His lips covered hers as his

thumb repeatedly strummed her clit, as she arched and cried into his mouth. As he took up a slow rhythm with his fingers, teasing from her each rattling breath, the uncontrollable roll of her hips.

It almost felt like it, the swell of emotion in her throat and lungs, releasing it to Ethan's murmurs of appreciation—and his gaze, urging her on.

And it came easy, too—the soft bite against her tongue. She didn't taste the blood, but it roared through her, a crescendo throwing her body high. Ethan caught her with his mouth and his hands, holding her up against him until she sagged to the bed.

He dragged his lips from hers, his chest heaving. His palms smoothed up over her trembling stomach, her skin glistening from his heat. Her fingers were buried in the hair at the nape of his neck, and metal jingled as he slipped from under the loop of her arms, moved down.

His thumbs parted her, and his throat worked as he looked. "Oh, Miss Charlie. What you showed me ain't half as pretty as you really are."

No. And she couldn't have imagined how his pleasure could feed hers. He closed his mouth over her sensitive flesh, but it was his gratified moan that ripped an echo from her throat.

Her teeth locked together, but a part of her screamed. Silently cried for him to continue tasting her as if he'd die without it. To keep looking at her as if she was a necessity. To touch and lick and thrust as if she was the key to gaining something he wanted, needed.

If he needed her for this, it might be enough.

It was almost more than she could stand. Her body was singing again, rising and falling with the leisurely pace of his feast, the drumming of her blood. She kicked and moaned, and he held her, his tongue swirling, flicking, and it was hurting now, strung too tight, pitched too high.

"Ethan." She was twisting, panting. "I need to . . . but not without you."

Ethan fucking her.

It didn't matter how, only that he was inside her. But though he stiffened when she hit him with image after image, he didn't relent, but pushed her higher, licking, sucking, his fingers sinking into her, big and hot.

Desperate, she tugged on his hair. Metal clinked. Again, as she pulled harder. "Ah, God, Ethan—*please*. Please, *please*."

She almost sobbed when his mouth released her. He kissed her nipples as he rose over her, then her throat.

"You ready then?"

Never more. And his fingers were still slick and full inside her, so he must have known. "Yes. Yes, yes—"

Ethan swallowed the last yes. His hands left a moist trail from her sex to her inner thighs; he pushed them wide. Cold air teased her exposed flesh, then heat as he settled against her, the thickness of his cock nestled between her folds.

Her fingers scrabbled on the mattress over her head. His left hand smelled of her when he brought it up, bunching it in her hair.

He rocked forward, not entering her; his hard length gathered moisture, glided over her clit. Again.

Again.

She went mad with it, frantically jerking her hips toward him, whimpering with need.

Until, finally, he closed his eyes and breached her entrance with burning pressure. "Easy, Charlie," he whispered, but his voice was as tormented as the sounds she was making. She tried to pull him in hard and fast, but he went slow. So slow.

But not easy. She was adjusting to him, so wet he slid as if she were oiled, but tension clamped her muscles tight around him. Soothing noises came from his throat, but they roughened when she lifted her knees, tilting her hips to take him at a new angle.

He dropped his forehead to hers with a heavy groan. "God Almighty, Charlie. Just stay real still so I don't hurt you."

"I can't. You aren't. *Please*." She couldn't control her body, her tongue. "I need it, need you—"

He shoved deep, muffling his shout behind clenched teeth. Her back bowed. Her eyes opened wide; her body stretched to envelop and caress every inch.

Hard, thick—and so hot. Her awareness narrowed down to the heat of his hand on her thigh, the heat of his mouth against her temple, the heat of his cock buried within her.

Ethan gathered himself, rose up to look at her. He untangled his hand from her hair, drew her cuffed wrists over her head. "I'm plumb losing my mind. You all right?"

She nodded, not trusting her voice.

"All right then." His skin was taut over his cheekbones, his amber eyes glowing. "Now, Charlie, you got a choice. If you're like this—" He pushed her knees down. "I'll be able to work you just right."

He withdrew and then drove back in with short strokes, stopping only when he was seated firmly, grinding against the aching bud of her clitoris.

Her mind was going. She turned her cheek against the mattress; harsh, whistling noises broke from her throat—and she didn't care, only wanted him to do it again.

His body shook. He let go of her hands, caught her behind her knees. "Or like this, Charlie." He pushed her legs up toward her chest, then braced his hands against the bed, her knees over his elbows. Immediately he sank farther into her, tighter, hotter. The pressure was almost unbearable; she closed her eyes, shut out everything but the feel of him. "I'll be deeper, but you won't be able to move much, and I won't be able to rub up against your sweet little—"

"Deep," she cried. "Deep deep deep."

"All right. So we've got it just how you like it, then." His breathing was ragged. "Open your mouth, Charlie. I aim to kiss you all the way through this."

She met his eyes, parted her lips, and he thrust with his body, his tongue. Her scream locked in her throat, and Ethan inhaled the air that escaped as he pushed into her again. Her toes curled, her fingers gripping his hair as hard as she could, hanging on to him.

But she was losing herself. Losing her mind, her control, to the frantic burn inside her. She had no way to move, to give— only to take. And she took him again and again, until she was full, overflowing with the frenzied pleasure of his possession, but she couldn't release it.

Blood—she needed blood. But she couldn't bite herself, couldn't turn away from the penetration of his tongue.

Ethan increased his pace, a rondo rush toward the finish. Her nails dug into his nape, and he ate each moan, each pleading cry.

Until he stopped. He lifted his mouth from hers but the intensity of his gaze held her frozen, prevented her from closing her teeth on her tongue.

"You have a choice." His voice was low, and he slid into her again. "But I want you to choose me. Take the blood from me."

Excitement and fear gripped her, the memory of shattering pain and exquisite flavor, and she trembled against him. She searched his face, but couldn't halt her strained reply. "I don't want to ruin this."

Ethan's eyes closed. "All right, Charlie." The fierce need smoothed from his expression, and after a short nod, he hunched his shoulders, dropping his jaw beside her temple. His hips pistoned with even strokes.

It felt incredible . . . but she'd managed to ruin it, anyway. The craving, the connection between them was gone, replaced with mechanical coupling.

Her eyes stung, and she blinked quickly, until the brilliant stars above were sharp points. She'd wanted Ethan to ask her for something.

And he had.

Maybe the pain wouldn't be so bad. Maybe it would stay beneath the pleasure, as it had before her bloodlust had brought it shrieking to the surface.

Her hands flattened against the back of his neck, and she lifted her face to his throat. His skin was smoldering satin under her mouth.

At the touch of her lips, Ethan missed a beat, drove into her with a quick lunge. His voice strangled her name. Her fangs sank deep.

It blazed over her tongue—each note rich with sensation, passion.

And no pain.

Relief pushed a staccato sob from her chest, but it was swept away in the wake of the blood. Ethan wrapped her legs high around his waist. His fingers speared into her hair, and he held her against him as if afraid she'd pull away.

"Just like this, Charlie."

Like this. She moaned her agreement.

He moved inside her, his thick groans anchoring the soaring tones of his lifeblood. Mixed, impossible to separate her pleasure from his, the arousal of her body from the ecstasy of drinking.

The cuffs jingled and pulled at her wrists. She needed to touch but telling him meant breaking away; she formed an image of the metal, falling away from her skin. An image of her fingers, tracing the line of his body.

A pure, perfect harmony pulsed through her veins; Charlie stiffened against the cold force of it, then let it sing through her. The sound of his Gift was unmistakably *Ethan*, but distilled, as if the abrasive and conflicting emotional notes had been boiled away, leaving the essence of him.

Unbelievably, inhumanly beautiful. Without flaw.

Without passion.

Then her hands were free and the notes were warm again, heating as his heartbeat quickened. Her heels dug in, urging him faster; his hand fisted in her hair as he surged, and she was hot now, wet, from the inner clasp of her sex to her skin, all absorbing the volcano of his body and blood, all so tight and the pressure too high. And then releasing, rolling through her flesh in great quaking waves, and she clutched Ethan as he broke, his breath jagged, his blood molten.

She didn't want to let him go. Ethan turned, taking her with him, and she still drank. Arousal lay beneath the sweet pleasure of it, soft and buoyant—but it only lay, without grabbing and piercing her.

And she thought she wouldn't mind if it did eventually sharpen, so long as it remained painless.

But she couldn't drink forever. She had to come up. To face him, and find something to say that wasn't the *I love you* welling through her.

Would he even want it? Though it lifted her from inside, she felt heavy, grasping; and if she placed it on him, would it just become another weight for him to carry?

She still held him within her . . . and she was taking blood from his throat like an addict who couldn't cut herself off.

The puncture wounds had almost closed. It had been easier to stop than she'd thought it would be, but she carefully wiped his skin clean with her fingers rather than with her tongue. Slowly, she began to inch off of him. Ethan guided her with his hands on her hips, and her breath caught as he gingerly slid from inside her.

Say *something*, she told herself. Something that wasn't about her emotions, or her need, or how very much she loved him. She settled in next to his side, and Ethan half-turned to face her, looking her over with a soft, searching gaze.

Could he see what she was feeling? Did he already know? She hadn't sensed him inside her mind, but he could have slipped in, and she just hadn't recognized his mental touch over the sound of his blood—or his Gift.

She grabbed at that, and cleared her throat. "When you unlocked the handcuffs, it sounded . . ." She couldn't come up with the right word to describe it, but she forced her way through. "Different. Beautiful, but strange. And not as it did when I felt it before, when I wasn't drinking your blood. Though it was still *you*, and a lot like the way you taste."

He continued studying her for a long moment, his brows lowering as if he was trying to work through a puzzle. "And how do I taste?" he finally asked.

"Good." She needed to touch him; she lifted her hand to his jaw, smoothed her fingers down the strong line to his chin. "Really, really good."

His smile crooked his lips. "Now, that's more like what I expected to hear from you when you rolled on over, Miss Charlie."

So much for his modesty. She turned her cheek against the mattress to laugh, and he drew her in close against his length. Her legs met the fabric of his pants, but he didn't replace his shirt as quickly.

Ethan pushed her hair back from her face. "You stiffened up a bit with my Gift; it didn't hurt you?" When she shook her head, he pressed, "And the rest went all right, too?"

"Yes," she said, and he looked at her again so seriously that suddenly she was laughing. "Stop that. I'm okay."

But it struck her now that something in the way he had asked was expectant, as if he'd anticipated that there would be a change.

Her amusement faded, and curiosity had her rising up on her elbow. "Did you do something differently?"

"Well, I didn't resist it at all, Charlie—what you make me feel when you're drinking from me." He rolled onto his back, cocked his arm up behind his head to prop it up. "But don't you worry that you still can't have the feeding separate, if you want it. I figure I can control myself well enough."

"That doesn't sound like a very good plan." She leaned down to swirl his flat nipple with her tongue, to scrape her fangs over the small nub. "I think I could get used to feeding this way." She glanced up with a wry smile. "Probably *too* used to it."

"That's fine by me." He shuddered beneath her mouth, and an instant later his unbuttoned shirt was covering his torso, and she was teasing cotton.

She lifted her head, narrowed her eyes. "That's cheating."

"I'm just awful scared of being naked with all these snakes and scorpions crawling about." His gaze dropped to her breasts, and their peaks tightened when his lips widened in an appreciative grin. "But I'll protect you real well, so you ain't got to worry none."

But he must have been concerned that she was uncomfortable; an instant later, a big shirt landed in her lap. She pulled it on, smiling. The hem almost reached her knees. "Would I have to worry if I was bitten?"

"No. You could shoot bleach into your veins and it wouldn't do much but burn a little." He sat up, caught her mouth in a hard kiss before pulling back. "Unless I'm drifting, I ain't much for lying around. You feel like taking a walk?"

CHAPTER 23

She did, and it was odd—marvelous—to stroll barefoot across the desert sand under the moonlight as easily as she might have a beach and the sun.

And there was little need to block. There were only the sounds they made—and the occasional scurrying of feet, the beat of tiny hearts. When she stopped, tried to locate the source of a strange, whirring chirp, Ethan pointed out the bat hunting insects.

Charlie watched its flight over a distant mound of flat, stacked stones, every motion of its small body clear to her in the darkness—and she was suddenly, stupidly overwhelmed.

She didn't turn away fast enough. Ethan cupped her face, frowning down at the tears that spilled over her cheeks. Yet it was a laugh that broke from her, and she didn't think she could relate the absurdity of it. But she managed to say, "It's so ugly. But *not*. It's not at all."

He smiled, and she smoothed her thumbs over the wrinkles at the corners of his eyes. "Oh, it's an ugly little thing," he drawled. "But they have their charms. And I reckon that one sings '*Nessun dorma*' on his way back to his cave and his belly full of mosquitoes."

She couldn't help but picture that, and fell against him, laughing. He was still smiling when she finally got ahold of herself, and her gaze fell to his scar. Her amusement faded.

"You going to kiss me now, Miss Charlie?"

"No." Her fingers traced the line of his upper lip. "I was just thinking—Caleb gave you this?"

He stood motionless beneath her touch. "That he did."

"When you were in the desert."

"Yes."

She hesitated for a moment. "What happened between the two of you and Sammael?"

He brushed her hair behind her ear. "You're wondering how it is that I like it out here, if I also died out here."

"No. I can see why you enjoy it. But because there is a connection, it made me think of what Jake told me about you . . . and what he didn't tell me. But maybe I shouldn't have brought your brother up."

Ethan shook his head. "It's no problem, Miss Charlie. And I'll give you the choice between the long version and the short one. Just remember I ain't much of a storyteller—"

"Long," she said.

"Well, hell," he said, but she didn't hear any real displeasure behind it. He turned, began walking again, and she fell into step beside him. "All right, then. So you know my ma and da bought a place outside Leadville?"

"Yes." She watched him pick up a small stone, skip it across the sand as if it were water. "After your dad got out of a P.O.W. camp."

Ethan's brows rose, and he glanced over at her. "Jake dug that up?" At her nod, he chuckled a little and continued, "Hell. Well, yes. And it changed my da, so as he couldn't tolerate being hemmed in or the crush of people in the city. So we headed on out west."

"That must have been hard on your mom."

"I reckon so. But you'd never have known it." Ethan shook his head, smiling. "You saw my da at Cole's, Charlie. So it won't come as a surprise to you when I tell you she was an Amazon of a woman. Both Caleb and I favored her—though Caleb, he wasn't quite so tall."

Charlie pulled at his dangling suspender. "She must have been a handsome, sexy woman."

"You hush." He grinned at her. "And she sure as hell was. My da, he loved her more than any woman had ever been loved, and she did him more than any man. I figure that's what got them through some of those early days. We had a big spread of land, and didn't do much with it—we had money, so we didn't need to work it to live off of—but still, them first years were hard, with a lot of adjusting. And then Ma took on our schooling after Caleb and I ran into some trouble in town."

"What kind?"

"Just the kind that boys get into when they talk in a way that sets them apart from the other boys," Ethan said. "We weren't so big then, and we got into one fight after another. Usually lost, too, due to numbers. So Caleb and I both figured if we couldn't beat 'em, we'd just fit in—but the first time she heard us talking like that, my ma took us out of the school." He slanted a glance at her, then skipped another rock across the sand. "Of course, Caleb and I still practiced, and it came in right handy when I was working later. I couldn't disguise my height, but I could cultivate the image of a dude with all of the newsletters and stories that were spread about me—and so when I rode into a town looking for someone, dressed like this and talking real simple-like, folks often caught on too late as to whom they was speaking to, and I got the information I needed before they clammed up."

Charlie stopped, and sized him up. "I'm trying to imagine you on a horse. I just can't. But the wings look right."

"The wings suit me fine." He sent another rock skipping, and looked back at her, the humor slipping away from his expression. "In those years, most everyone near us was invested in mining somehow—either working the mines, or depending on the money from it for their businesses. One company owned by a man named Billings approached my ma and da, and there was some prospecting done on the property. They found one hell of a lode running up our side of the mountain. Billings made an offer, even talked partnerships—but my da, once he realized it'd mean people coming and going, the mountain getting torn up, he just backed away from it. And nothing much happened for eight or nine years, except Caleb and I both went east to study, and then came back west to work."

"And Caleb started practicing law?"

Ethan nodded. "I didn't want to be cooped up in an office, but he thought it was all right. And after Caleb and I had gone, my da and ma had begun taking on more help, using the land a bit more, making it a working concern. So they were supporting a few families—and my da had grown real attached to the property. But the mines in the area, they were hitting some hard times, and my da was getting pressure from Billings to sell the rights to that lode."

"But he didn't?"

"No. And both Caleb and I had to step in a couple of times when the hassling got bad. Billings was sending in thugs to spook the women, poisoning some of the livestock. But there wasn't much proof. And we weren't getting much sympathy from the town, because so many of them wanted the mountainside opened so as they could keep working. Caleb and I went in and warned Billings several times, telling him to back away—but there wasn't much else to do. And for a while, it died down."

Ethan picked up another rock but didn't toss it. He looked at it lying in his palm before he closed his hand. "And then I got word that my ma had been hurt. A couple of Billings's men had come upon her when she was alone, and—" Dust was falling from between his fingers, and his voice was strained when he continued, "And they hurt her real bad. But she hung on . . . as long as she could."

His throat worked, and he shook out the handful of dust. Her chest aching, Charlie watched him struggle for his next words. He finally met her eyes.

"You look awful torn up, Charlie," he said hoarsely. "You want to come over here so I can comfort you a bit?"

She was in his arms less than a second later, and he was holding on to her tight, burying his face in her hair. He spoke through clenched teeth. "Son of a bitch. A hundred and twenty years, and it still rips my guts."

Her fingers curled in his shirt. "Ethan, I'm so sorry," she whispered against his throat. "I shouldn't have asked—"

She broke off as he pulled back, shaking his head.

"No." His thumbs smoothed across her cheeks, wiped away the wet from her skin. "She ought to be remembered. And she ought to be cried over." He drew a long, shuddering breath. "We did, Charlie, but then we got to work. She'd told us not to go off half-cocked—told us to do right by her. And so we did. All by the book. And when Caleb and I were done, we had a right solid case. Not just against those that was hired, but Billings, too. But Billings had real deep pockets, and he bought himself a jury. And my da . . ." His brow furrowed. "After my ma passed, I can't call what my da was doing 'living.' And on the day Billings and his men were acquitted, my da took a walk out to where she was buried, and he didn't come back in." Another breath shook from his chest. "My da sure taught me a real good lesson about what it means to love a woman so powerfully, Charlie."

That to let himself feel so much was inevitably self-destructive? What was safe then—friendships and fuck buddies?

But contemplating it would only hurt, and this was about Ethan, not her. She laid her cheek over his heart again, held on. "What did you and Caleb do?"

"We went off half-cocked. Made certain each one of those men wouldn't be hurting a woman again. But we let them live, because that was worse than dying. Then we tried to go after Billings."

"Tried?"

She felt his nod, and looked up at him as he said, "He knew we were coming, and we weren't just coming to hurt him. Because he may not have been one of those who'd murdered my ma, but he ordered it, and we had every intention of stringing him up. So he got out of there, and under a whole lot of protection. When we realized we wouldn't be able to reach him, we targeted what would hurt him the most, and what he'd killed my ma over: his money. For a long while, we didn't take anything but what was his—and we took a lot of it."

She smiled a little at the note of satisfaction in his voice. "When did you realize he was a demon?"

Ethan's brows shot up. "A demon? No, Charlie—Billings was human."

"Oh." She blinked a few times. "Did you eventually get a chance to kill him?"

"No." A deep sigh moved through him. "No. What happened instead was that Caleb and I became something just as bad. We shot back at Billings's men, because we figured it was us or them. Then the lawmen started coming after us—men who weren't much different than Caleb and I had been. We didn't put up a fuss when we saw it was them, but went along. And they knew what kind of man Billings was, knew the truth of some of it—so the first couple of times we were brought on in, they still treated us like we was one of them, and our busting out a bit of a joke. But then one day, it wasn't one of Billings's men we had to shoot back at, and we knew they weren't going to bother bringing us in any longer."

His lips compressed, and he stepped back, running his hands up and down her arms before turning and picking up another rock, tossing it across the sand. His gaze followed its bouncing path, his profile set in a hard line.

"At night, Caleb and I would be hiding out in places not much different than this, wondering how we'd come to such a state. I'd sit there thinking that I'd overturned every one of my principles—and I still couldn't figure if what we'd done was wrong, because when we went the right way, there wasn't any justice in it. But before long it wasn't about justice at all, but just doing everything we could to stay alive. Because you've got to keep living. If you give up, you're swinging at the end of a rope, and that seems just as much a betrayal of your principles as killing the lawmen coming after your head." He turned back toward her. "And I'll tell you that I still don't feel a bit of remorse for what I did to Billings's men—but I'd give anything in the world not to have the blood of good men on my hands."

"But you can't."

"No. So I got a lot to atone for—but I also reckon that I'll be doing it on my terms, and relative to how bad I figure what I did was. Which means I'll be a Guardian for an awful long time." A faint smile curved his mouth, and he looked down at his feet before slanting a glance at her. "And the only reason I can atone at all is because Caleb and I rode into the wrong town."

She remembered that he'd mentioned it before. "Eden?"

"Eden," he echoed softly. "It had a reputation for being real clean, full of upstanding citizens. Particularly the sheriff, Samuel Danvers, who'd gotten rid of the bad elements in the town—men like Billings—and renamed it Eden about two or three years before we arrived."

Charlie's eyes widened. "He was the *sheriff*?"

"With a passel of human deputies who'd do just about anything for him," Ethan said, nodding. "And on the surface, everything looked just fine. But we found out real quick it wasn't."

"What happened?"

"Well, he was waiting for us at the saloon, Charlie. He was awful polite, and I was tired of shooting my way out of a town. So we walked right into that cell, figuring I'd let us out just as soon as I could. Only Danvers, he never slept, or went to drink or eat, or even take a piss. He just watched us from his big rosewood desk."

Charlie's flesh was crawling. She knew that feeling too well—of being under constant observation, of never having a moment alone.

"And then someone in the town found a girl who'd been hurt and left to die out in the desert. She named one of the deputies as the one who did it."

Charlie hugged herself and shivered. "Sammael wouldn't have liked that." When Ethan glanced at her, surprised, she said, "In his car, with Henderson—Sammael couldn't tolerate the idea of him touching me, and he thought anything sexual was dirty unless there was love involved." She swallowed the sickness that rose in her throat. "I guess he's probably the reason I wasn't raped."

Ethan's face was like stone. "Sammael used Henderson to take a choice from you, Charlie, and it was a violation just the same."

"No, I don't mean that one is worse or—" She shook her head, fidgeted. "I'm not *grateful* to him. But I am glad I don't have to deal with both. And remembering how Henderson . . . it's bad enough."

Ethan closed his eyes. "I ought to have staked him out and left him to burn."

"I'm glad you didn't," Charlie said quietly. "Because although he was fast and strong, he wasn't very good at blocking when I hit him. But now I'm fast and strong, too—and maybe I'll run into him someday."

Ethan's gaze was hard and assessing, and he nodded. "All right. I'll see that you get some training in, so that your weapons include more than your fists. And I'll hold him down, if you like."

"That wouldn't be fair," she said, smiling.

"You don't worry about fighting fair with vampires and demons, Charlie. If something ever comes up, you hit as low and as mean as you can."

His tone was serious; her smile faded, and she nodded. "Okay." She absently pushed a rock aside with her bare toe, and startled when a huge spider scurried out from beneath. After a few running steps, she looked up to find Ethan grinning at her.

"We'll be training a long time, Charlie, toughening you up."

"Fuck you. It was *hairy*."

Laughing, Ethan took her hand, and they walked toward the mound of rocks she'd seen the bat flying over. Hard, bare earth appeared in patches, as if the wind had swept the sand from it.

She took a deep breath; the air was still now, and crisp—but not uncomfortable. "What happened when the deputy was accused?"

"Danvers wouldn't believe it, and he had us to lay the blame on—although the times didn't add up, and the townspeople knew it. So I reckon his lie just broke them."

"Broke them? How?"

"Well, it seems he'd been running the town real tight for several years. Dictating behavior and morals, using his deputies to scare those who didn't fall in line or who disagreed with anything he did. And I don't think he saw anything wrong in the way he went about it, because, to all appearances, it was working. But I figure the townspeople were just seething—and when they boiled over, his little piece of Heaven started falling apart. A few deputies killed, the whores wearing their unmentionables on the stoop, people drinking in the saloon when it wasn't the appointed times, not showing up for church services. Are you laughing, Charlie?"

He tugged her against his chest, turned around and stepped backward in time with her. His grin was broad.

"Yes." It shook from her. "Sorry. It was the last part."

"Ah, well—his deputies kept on bringing reports to him, and he'd rant on and on about disorder being the downfall of man. Caleb and I thought it was plenty ridiculous. Even more so, that he was certain we'd been some corruptive force that brought this all down on him. But we weren't laughing by then."

Neither was Charlie. Ethan continued moving backward, his hands low on her back. Walking, but their only scenery was each other, and Ethan's face was slowly becoming overcast.

"He'd closed up the shutters, and during the day we just baked in there. Sweating, and then after a while nothing left to sweat. And once the girl was found, the sheriff didn't bring us any water—because a demon can't kill a man, but his deputies were the ones who physically locked us in, so letting us slowly die wasn't actively killing us. And though we had no inkling of what he truly was, we figured by then that he wasn't . . . wasn't *normal*." His fingers moved against her waist, drawing small circles over the cotton shirt. "Of course, now I know that Caleb and I might have gotten out at any time."

Charlie blinked. "What?"

"He couldn't deny our free will. If I had gotten up, picked that lock open, he couldn't have prevented me. Or prevented either of us from walking on out of there. But I didn't know that, and he was always watching us, so I didn't even attempt it until the end. We were going to die anyway, so I reckoned I might as well get up and try it."

"What'd he do?" she whispered.

"He took out his gun, but its threat wasn't going to stop me, Charlie. So he crushed it in his hand."

"And that stopped you?"

"Scared the piss out of me. Then he pulled out the key, and he said that we looked awful thirsty. And all we had to do was drink what he had in two special cups, and he'd give us that key instead of crushing the lock."

Charlie was trembling, and her steps felt as heavy as a zombie's. "He had *two* cups?"

Ethan nodded. "But he just said that they both had to be drunk, not that we each had to drink one, and I held him to that. Then I beat the hell out of Caleb until he agreed to give me his cup, and made the best bargain with Danvers as I knew how—because Danvers had said he'd keep a bargain. I didn't believe him, but we had nothing to lose by negotiating the terms of it." He took a long breath. "And that was that. I drank the poison, and pushed Caleb the hell out of there. It killed me sure enough—but next thing, Michael's there, giving me another choice. I figure Sammael must have run to the next town as soon as Michael showed."

Charlie's gaze dropped to his chest, and she tried to process it all. She wasn't sure she could. "Sammael still thinks it was your fault, doesn't he? He said something at the bridge—about you having to pay for Eden."

"I reckon he does. Which suits me just fine, as I got a few things to settle with him."

She blinked up at him; he'd said that as easily as if he'd announced he was paying a tab. "You don't seem angry, though."

He sidestepped, swinging her with him until they were walking side by side again. "I figure I'm like those townspeople. Just simmering." He slanted a glance at her. "I want Sammael's head for plenty of reasons. I'm feeling mighty vengeful, Charlie, but if I rush on in and get myself killed, there's other things that won't be provided for. Atoning is more important than revenge. Being a Guardian and protecting the living is—and so is making certain you don't need for anything."

That he'd placed providing for her on the same level as atoning and being a Guardian filled her, warmed her, left her struggling for something to say; but she couldn't respond except to nod. And although she didn't want to be one of his obligations—and wanted to assure him that she intended to support herself as quickly as she could—to protest that she didn't need anything would be silly and ungrateful and trivialize everything that he *had* given her.

She'd have done anything just to give him a little in return. She managed to offer in a thick rasp, "I'll hold him down."

Ethan's laugh rumbled through her, and he dropped a hard, closed-mouth kiss against her lips. "I'll let you take the first stab, if you like."

"Okay. Or sucking on him might be a good payback—but don't let Jane see me do it." She blinked, grimaced. "Never mind. That sounded weird and just *wrong*."

Ethan's laughter deepened, though he was shaking his head and apparently trying not to imagine that, as well. When it faded, he glanced down at her, a perplexed expression lurking in his gaze.

She drew back to see him better. "What is it?"

He hesitated only a second. "I just can't figure you, Charlie. You're joking now, even though Jane laid a terrible blow on you today, staying with Sammael even after seeing the truth for herself. And I also can't figure how it was Old Matthew had you crawling over to my lap, when you made it through Jane's call just fine. Do you want him to come for you?"

"No." Wherever Ethan was, that was where she wanted to be. But she looked away from him, unsure she could explain.

A small shelf jutted out from the mounded pile of rocks; she carefully tucked the tails of the shirt under her bare bottom before sitting on its flat surface. The stone was still warm, like a lingering touch of sun.

She took a deep breath. "It was just that Jane, she didn't seem to notice . . ." Her throat closed.

"How much you were hurting," Ethan said, coming to sit beside her.

"Yes." She tilted her head back; the stars were blurry again, and she blinked them into focus before looking at Ethan. "But Old Matthew heard it, somehow. Or he was listening for it, even though he has no real reason to. Aside from, you know, caring about me. Even though he has no real reason to do that, either."

Ethan's brows drew together. "That's the most damn fool thing I've ever heard," he said softly.

"Thanks." A short laugh slipped from her, and she drew up her legs, wrapped her arms around them. "I was about to wallow in a lot of really old self-pity, and I don't mean to."

"I know you don't, Charlie—but you'd best explain what you do mean."

She nodded, and gathered up the story. Unlike most, it didn't come easily, but more like an engine that had to be choked to start. "Old Matthew said when he hired me that, because he took on so many ex-cons, he had to be careful. And that his employees could keep their private lives private—but if he found out that any of his employees was lying to him about something that affected Cole's, and if anyone couldn't stay straight and clean, they could take a walk."

"So you reckoned that when you said you had been lying to him, that was it."

"Yes." But instead, Old Matthew had ended their conversation by telling her that she'd have a place if she ever made her way back. "And I still don't know why he took me on in the first place. You know what I did to his restaurant, right? Running that car through it?"

Ethan's nod was slow. "That I do."

"There was insurance to cover the damage . . . but Cole's was his *baby*. The one thing that was really his. And he told me that the night I went in—and that it made him crazy to think that a spoiled rich white girl could be so stupid, and so careless." She offered Ethan a wry smile. "We weren't rich, but the rest of it was correct."

He returned her smile before adjusting his seat, bringing her in close against his side. "So I take it you hadn't ever thought of yourself in those terms before."

She shook her head with a self-deprecatory laugh. "I was too busy feeling sorry for myself, actually—and I was numb. Jane had just given me her ultimatum, and I was doing what she'd asked, but I was still reeling from it. And whenever I'd thought of the accident, it was always about me losing my voice. And whenever Jane talked about that night—which wasn't often—it was to remind me that our dad had just flown me out to Seattle so that he could tell us he was dying. Like she thought it excused what I'd done . . . and in those years after I got out of Mission Creek and before I began working for Old Matthew, I was happy to rationalize everything, take any excuse. When the truth is, I would have been drunk that night anyway."

She stopped. The story had begun coming out smoothly— pouring out of her—but now Ethan was silent. She didn't want to look up at him, see his reaction, but she forced herself.

Her stomach knotted tight when she met his heavy frown. She tried to smile, wasn't sure that she managed it. "It's not a pretty picture, is it?"

"No, it ain't," he said. "But it's also an old one, and I've done worse, so it don't matter much to me. But I'm afraid you lost me, Charlie. Why'd you go see Old Matthew, and what's this about an ultimatum?"

"Oh." She reordered her thoughts, brought in the dangling threads. "Well, after Mission Creek, I moved in with Jane— and was pretty much leeching off of her. I had jobs, but they never lasted long, and a few boyfriends, but I didn't really care if they stayed or went. Because Jane was there, and she was so easy to lean on." She looked down at her hands. "And it wasn't all bad; Jane and I have always gotten along great. And after so many years apart—and after what she'd gone through taking care of Dad while I was in Mission Creek—I think we really needed each other. But she pulled herself together . . . and there I was, taking a lot more than I was giving. Not just money, but needing her to tell me I was worth something, because I was having a hard time finding it myself."

She paused, wondering if Ethan would say anything. But he only smoothed his hand over her hair, and she took it as a signal to continue.

"And it was around that time that Jane finished up her research at UW and published her paper, and then didn't get any of the credit for it. But although I knew she was struggling with something, because she talked about it a lot, I also wasn't really listening to her. But I think now that was part of it— why she just gave up on me. Or snapped, rather. And the stuff she found in my room was what pushed her over."

"What'd she find?"

Charlie laid her cheek against his chest, stared out into the desert. "Cocaine. And the funny thing is, it wasn't mine. Well, not *funny*, but . . . but . . . it starts with an 'I.' "

Ethan began shaking with laughter, though he didn't make a sound.

"Anyway," she said, "maybe not funny, just stupid. I wasn't into anything that hard, but in another year or two, the way I was going, I might have been. And although I didn't bring it in, the guy I was with did, so it was the same thing." She turned her head to look up at him, and was thankful that he didn't seem upset at the mention of another man. "He was actually kind of a nice guy. And he wrote the worst lyrics I've ever read, all about dark, deep emotions, though he didn't seem too upset when I told him not to come back. So he was probably doing the same thing I was; getting by, trying to feel *something*. But really only faking it, because—except with Jane—the feeling always went away when the buzz did."

She searched Ethan's face, remembering how she'd almost always been numb; she couldn't comprehend returning to that now. And she'd been different before he'd moved in next to her—she'd gone a long way by herself, had been slowly coming out of that sleep.

And she didn't know if the shock of the past few days had brought her truly awake, or just forced her to recognize that she already was. She only knew that she was sitting there, the bloodlust had passed, her body was satiated in every conceivable way . . . and she still felt wonderfully alive.

His brows rose in question when she continued to look at him, and she shook her head with a smile.

"All right," he said. His arms tightened around her, and he drew her against him for a gentle kiss, then leaned back to study her face. "So Jane tossed you out then."

"No. She gave me a choice: either I'd sober up and settle down, or she'd cut herself completely out of my life."

Ethan was nodding. "Like she did Sammael."

"Yes." She rolled his soft collar between her fingers. "A lot of it was fear that I'd lose her, but there was also a lot of guilt. I thought that there couldn't possibly be anything worse than waking up in the hospital and finding out I wouldn't sing again. But walking into the apartment, seeing her face, realizing how much I'd been hurting her . . . *that* was the worst moment of my life."

She glanced up at his face. Lord, this all sounded depressing—and, after the horror of his experience with Sammael, pathetic. She rolled her eyes, laughed at herself before continuing, "And it was the *best* moment, because it got me into rehab again, and looking for another job. But I was still just going through the motions until I got to the part in my therapy where I had to make amends, and I went to see Old Matthew. And . . . I don't know. Maybe he meant to teach me a lesson or scare me off by offering me the job. Maybe I took it because I felt so guilty, and I wanted to repay him somehow. But it worked out, and as soon as I could, I got my own apartment and began taking classes. Everything just fell into place. And I thought I was going to lose all that tonight—not the job, really, but whatever respect I'd earned from Old Matthew, whatever it was that made him willing to put a part of his baby in my hands. Because he's . . . my hero, or something."

Her cheeks heated, and she buried her face against Ethan's chest again. She'd made it sound so simplistic and stupid, and couldn't possibly encompass the entirety of what she'd been feeling when Ethan had been holding her, and Old Matthew had offered to get her out of trouble. The overwhelming sense of disbelief that two men whom she admired and loved would stand by her, though she hadn't given them much in return— and the overwhelming gratitude that she had them.

"Anyway," she finished in a small voice, "that's why it hit me harder than Jane's phone call did. Because I was expecting some rationalization from her. I wasn't expecting Old Matthew." Ethan didn't immediately respond, and she added, "Although maybe I should have. I underestimated him."

"Yes. And yourself."

Her skin flushed again. "Yes. I'm not suggesting that I don't think I'm worth it. I do."

"I ain't talking about your worth." He caught her face, forced her to look at him. His brows were lowered, his eyes shadowed. "And I ain't blowing sunshine up your ass. My ma was about the strongest woman I've ever seen. Then there's Lilith, and Selah, and a thousand other women I could name who've taken their knocks, but still got back up, doing whatever it was they had to do to get on their feet. It's like they were born strong, and that the core of them is so tough it's impossible to break. And I admire the hell out of women like that."

"Me, too," she said softly.

"But you're not one of them, Charlie." His fingers tightened when she bent over against the pain that ripped through her, and white edged his lips. "I ain't trying to put a hurt on you," he said fiercely, quickly. "I'm trying to tell you that some women, being strong seems to come easy to them. Now, I know it probably ain't easy, but that's the way it seems. And then there's you, Charlie. I've never seen anyone fight so hard against what was weak and needy and natural to her; never seen anyone fight so hard to be where you're at. Never seen anyone get shoved into becoming a vampire, and immediately try to make the best of it, even though it scared you so bad to become one. And what you do fight, you ain't stubborn or stupid about—you don't fight just for the sake of fighting."

He eased back, his fingers caressing her cheeks as if to soothe, but her throat was so tight with emotion that she couldn't speak. And his words had been coming in a rush, but now he slowed them.

"So you ain't one of those strong women, Charlie; you're something else. If I looked into your head—without knowing what you've made of yourself—I'd have thought your chances of surviving were slim to nothing. I'd have figured you'd just give up, because with no chance, that's what I would do, and maybe hope for a miracle. But you didn't wait for someone to offer a miracle; you kept playing the shit hand you dealt yourself, and you pulled a good life out of it. So I'm awful glad you needed me to protect you, and it brought me over that wall—because I reckon I'm a better man just for having known a woman like you."

She stared at him, but still couldn't get her throat to cooperate. Her gaze fell to his lips. What would she say? She didn't know.

Concern drew a line between his brows. "You all right, Charlie?"

She pushed against his chest in frustration. No, she wasn't *all right*. There was a lot wrong, a lot she couldn't control— but she was wonderful, and she didn't know if it could possibly get any better than this.

He swayed back when she pushed again. Not enough; it wouldn't be enough until he was on his back and she was showing him exactly how wonderful everything was. He caught her hand, frowning. She formed an image of a kiss.

His smile rayed from the corners of his eyes. "Well, hell, Charlie—then why are you beating on me? I just can't figure you—"

She leapt at him. His mouth was firm and warm; she closed her eyes and fell into him. She couldn't see why he had such a difficult time figuring her out.

Loving him was the easiest thing she'd ever done.

CHAPTER 24

San Francisco was shining across the bay when Charlie asked, "Do you have to go to work right away?"

Ethan banked to the south, slowed the beat of his wings. "No. I ought to check in, make sure nothing's come up—but I'll stay with you through sunrise."

She turned her face toward the city, but her hair was blowing back, allowing him to see the corner of her smile. Well, hell. If such a little thing would please her, he'd try to stay through sunrise every morning. It was a damn shame he'd had to go talk to Manny the night before; now that he'd had time to ponder the send-away Charlie had given him, he'd wager anything that she'd wanted him to stay then, too.

At least she'd know now to ask if she wanted it; he'd told her straight-out he'd provide anything she needed.

Hell, he wished that she'd ask him for more just so he could give it to her. But if it made her uncomfortable, threw her back to feeling like a leech, he could be content with the little she did allow him to provide.

Content. He drew in the scent of her hair: apples and desert stone. *Content* was a damned pale word for how powerfully he felt toward her. More likely, it only applied to a life without Charlie, and only in the sense that he'd never be content again. Never settled again—and always aching.

And that made her sound an awful lot like a salve, which would probably spook her right quick.

Colin and Savi were pulling out of the lot as they swooped down; Savi's slim arm stuck out of the window in a wave before the car sped onto the street.

Ethan cleared his throat. "I ought to take you downtown to their club soon, let you get a feel for the community."

"Do you dance?" Charlie's grin exposed her fangs, and he realized with a tug to his chest that they were slightly crooked.

"Not much," he said, and set her down near the entrance steps. "But I'd be willing to stand up for a few slow ones with you."

"Then I'll definitely be interested in going." She paused. "Not that I'm not interested otherwise, because I'm curious about other vampires. But big crowds and lots of strangers . . ." She trailed off and shook her head; her hands patted her pockets.

"I never took you for shy, Miss Charlie. You talk real easy with strangers," he said.

"Yeah, but clubs, there's lots of shouting and no real conversation, because you can't hear anything." She glanced up at him, then stuck out her bottom lip and blew her hair out of her face. "In New York, we'd hit the clubs . . . but my favorite part was going for fresh air and a cigarette. Because all of the other smokers were out there, and you got a chance to talk to someone. You ask for a light, and then you end up finding out half their life story."

He'd wager it wasn't as simple as someone spilling their story; never had he known Easterners to be that friendly. More likely, she'd put them at ease by giving them her full attention and listening well. It was as comfortable talking to her as it had always been to Caleb.

Hell, maybe more so.

"And even now, when I see someone smoking outside a restaurant or on their break, I want to stop and chat. I think I miss that instant connection more than I do the cigarettes." She stopped digging in her pockets and sighed. "I've lost my ID card."

"I reckon it's still in the communications room, since we left in such an all-fired rush," he said in his slowest drawl, mostly so he could see her crooked fangs again. "I've got mine, but it'll be more entertaining to piss off Jeeves."

He saw her brace herself when he used his Gift, and remembering the nervous comment she'd made after rolling off of him, he gave the locks another push before he asked, "That's different than when you're feeding from me, then?"

She nodded as they moved into the corridor. "Like standing next to a speaker with the bass pounding. No noise, but that thump through your chest. With the blood, though, it sounded like you. Only cold, like the . . ." She glanced at Jeeves, and her cheeks flushed. "Like the metal."

Ethan suppressed his grin. Like the handcuffs.

She said under her breath, "And it wasn't *hot*. You know."

Ethan frowned into the retinal scanner. If she meant what he was thinking she did, and it hadn't felt sexual, that was downright peculiar. He'd been damn near crazy with wanting her.

"Hold on a minute, Jeeves," he said when Charlie finished her scans. She looked up at him, her brows lifting. "You fed real well, Charlie, so I figure this won't trigger your bloodlust—and I'm curious to see how opening this door feels to you. It's an electromagnetic lock, not metal."

She blinked several times. "You mean you want me to . . ." Her gaze settled on his neck. "Here?"

He pushed up his left jacket sleeve, exposing his wrist. "I was thinking more like hereabouts."

She shook her head, smiling. "I meant *here*, in front of—"

"I know it, Charlie," he said softly. "I'll hold on to you; I wouldn't ask you if I thought it meant you'd be embarrassing yourself."

She darted a glance at Jeeves, but the novice had the sense to be staring straight ahead with one hell of a poker face on. "All right."

He drew her in, turned her around so they were both facing the door, and wrapped his right arm around her waist. Anticipation tingled over his skin as she brought his wrist to her mouth, but he pushed the pleasure away, concentrated on the lock.

"Now, you get a good sip, Charlie, and as soon as you're in, I'll slide it on open."

"Okay." Her response was a puff of cold air against his wrist; a sting followed it, then the soft euphoria of a sated vampire drinking hummed into his veins.

Ethan closed his eyes before they rolled back in his head. Sweet Jesus. Maybe he'd just ask her to do this all the time.

When they weren't out in the corridor.

He felt the locks with his Gift, taking his time. Charlie stiffened up at the first touch, then relaxed back against him.

She released him as soon as the door opened, tilting her head to the side and looking up to meet his eyes. "It was different. Still *you* underscoring it all, but more like . . . Have you ever touched a nine-volt battery to your tongue?"

Ethan shook his head. "If we got one lying around, I will."

"No, no." A laugh tripped from her. "It hurts, but it was like that without hurting. But it makes your tongue—" She demonstrated with her hand, straightening her fingers then bowing them, holding them so tight they shook. "Just, zapped."

"The electric current running through your cells."

"I guess. Only, with your Gift, make the current a sound that goes through all of you, and not contracting anything— but just *feeling* like it."

He couldn't quite figure that, so he asked, "And . . . hot?"

"No. Not after you used your Gift."

"Well, damn." He reckoned his grin was about a mile wide. "Don't move out in front of me just yet, Charlie, because I want to try a few more of these. But first we'll dance on out of here."

She let her face fall forward, out of his line of sight. Laughter choked her reply. "Okay."

He twirled her through the security door; the hall was empty, so he pushed her up against the wall and kissed the hell out of her. When she was flushed and panting, he stepped back, took her hand. "All right then. Now we're both addlebrained, and there's a deadbolt on a closet not far from here."

A moment later, she announced, "It's like the cuffs. Just cold." Her voice was considering, and her gaze held his. "You're working up to something."

"That I am. Because what you're telling me, Charlie, is that the sound you're hearing is an awful lot like the lock itself. Metal, electromagnetic."

"Yes." She drew it out, slow.

"I want to know what the shielding spell's made out of. It's the one lock I can feel, but can't get around—I just don't know what its components are or how to fiddle with them. But maybe you can give me an inkling of that, a place to start, and I can go from there."

She looked at him for a long moment. "Okay."

A bit of fear was projecting from her psychic scent; Ethan had to admit he was a mite jumpy, too. And, hell, it'd be foolish to lock themselves in a room and then try to mess with magic. If Charlie gave him something to work with, and it didn't go right, they could be trapped.

"All right," he said. "We'd best get Jake, then."

❧

Charlie thought Jake didn't look too certain when Ethan told him to stand in the center of the communications room. A second later, Ethan had pricked his thumb, set the spell and joined her outside in the hall. He didn't bother to close the door.

"You ready?"

She nodded, and his Gift hit her almost at the same instant she bit him. It sang through her, stronger than before . . . but it was just Ethan.

He sighed when she shook her head, and she reluctantly lifted her mouth from his wrist. "It wasn't cold, though," she said. "I don't know if that helps, but it was just you—I couldn't feel anything else beneath it. And you must have been pushing harder?"

"That I was." He scrubbed his hand through his hair. "Well, shit. I was hoping for *something*."

The low thrum of his heart seemed to echo his disappointment, then it disappeared when he strode into the room. She could hear its beat again when he wiped his blood from the symbols.

His blood. "Ethan," she said, then hesitated. She wasn't sure why, but the thought of his blood had caught at her memory. He approached her, his brows raised in question, but she shook her head, looked at her hands, tried to make the connection. She'd only felt *him* when he'd used his Gift, and it tasted like his blood did.

"What are you thinking, Charlie?"

"Nothing, maybe. Just that—your blood cast the spell, and you're the only one who can go in and out." That was nothing new, and she could see him trying to follow her, but of course he couldn't. It was nothing but a vague concept in her own head. She spread her hands. "Like you're a key. So you already match."

That made him frown and turn to look at the symbols. "You're thinking you don't pick up anything but me because it was my blood? My flavor was already there, so you wouldn't detect more of the same."

She nodded, feeling it come together as the memory congealed. "Right. Like how I couldn't taste my own when I bit myself."

"That's a right interesting notion." His speculative look deepened. "But we're talking two different things, Charlie: the way I feel it, and the way you do. And I pushed at the spell around Sammael's SUV until my head about exploded, but I didn't sense any difference between the lock in his shield and the one we just had here."

"But we're also talking blood, Drifter," Jake said. He was leaning against the wall, a wooden toothpick in the corner of his mouth.

Ethan glanced at him and nodded. "And she's a vampire. We sure don't taste it the same way they do. So I reckon it's worth another shot, at any rate."

"With my blood this time?" Charlie asked.

Ethan shook his head. "If there was nothing, we might have the same questions, wondering if you just didn't feel it because it's your own. Jake?"

"Mine," Jake agreed.

"All right, Charlie," Ethan said as soon as the spell was up again. "You let me know."

She leaned back against the solid warmth of him, and almost choked the instant his Gift thrummed into her. She pulled her mouth away.

"It's different," she gasped. "You're there, but it's not just you."

She thought shock held him motionless for a second before he dropped his head low to look at her. "What is it, then?"

"It must be Jake, right? It's . . . it's . . . all over the place.

The force of it is solid and steady, like yours, but the register much wider. But also broken, like it has missing notes."

Ethan's brows lowered, and he shook his head. "I can't . . . I have no idea what you're hearing, Charlie. I'm not getting anything like that. Can you try to project it?"

She automatically took a huge breath, expanding her lungs and tightening her diaphragm before she realized what she was doing. She couldn't have sung something like this, anyway—she couldn't have hit most of the notes.

She filled her head with the sound instead, and thought it as hard as she could.

Ethan blinked. "Well, damn. That *feels* like Jake—though a hell of a lot less juvenile than he usually lets on. But I ain't getting a noise, Charlie." He met her eyes, and she could almost see him puzzling it out before he said slowly, "Maybe it's psychic then. You get that as sound; I get it as scent or touch."

"Can you use that with your Gift? Project it somehow?"

He looked away from her, toward the open door. "Let's see."

The percussion wave hit her, and she gripped his hand to steady herself. A discordant, jagged noise accompanied it; Ethan, projecting—though she could barely hear him beneath the sharp sound.

He lifted her and walked them forward, reached out. His fingers stopped on a plane even with the line of the door, curling as they hit the shield. He shook his head, and the noise faded.

"It wasn't the same as Jake's," Charlie said. "It was too forced, and had too much interference."

Ethan's chest heaved with his sigh, and he turned to lean his shoulder against the invisible shield, as if trying to stare down the symbols scratched into the door frame. Finally, she felt the press of his lips against the top of her hair. "All right then," he said. "I can't sing, but you can, so we'll try that. Only project it as hard as you can directly into my blood, Charlie, so I don't interfere with it so much."

His Gift pushed at her again, and she grinned against his wrist. "You're a stubborn man, Drifter."

"Only because it feels so damn good when you're biting me like this—*Holyfuckingwhoreson*—"

He bent as if he'd been kicked in the stomach, his arm around her waist nearly crushing her, forcing her to curl with him.

Crimson ran over his skin as she tore her mouth away. "Ethan? Eth—"

"Harder, Charlie." His voice was ragged against her ear. "Bite me, and send it to me harder and louder."

Blood dripped to the floor beside her feet. Not from his wrist; that was forming a different puddle. Panic and fear rattled her teeth. "Ethan—"

"Miss Charlie." He straightened them up, settled heavily against the shield again. "Now, goddammit."

Anger replaced the fear. She bit, and filled herself with the sound before imagining it exploding past her lips.

And then they were falling, Ethan's weight smashing her into the floor. His harsh swearing rent the air as he rolled, pulled her over him.

Stunned, Charlie looked up. They were inside the communications room. A tiny click caught her attention; Jake's toothpick, bouncing against the floor. His mouth was hanging open.

"Holy shit," she whispered, and glanced down at Ethan.

Her heart stopped. She scrambled off him, kneeled next to his head. Blood trailed from his ears; a smear under his nose told her he'd already wiped some away.

"Oh, my God." Her hands shook. "Ethan?"

He smiled, squinted his eyes open. The whites were shot through with red, but the blotches of crimson were shrinking as the broken vessels healed. "You've got one hell of a voice, Miss Charlie. I'm pretty sure you busted my eardrums from inside."

"And you had an audience," Jake said, and pointed at the door.

Charlie looked. Outside the room, a group of Guardians and vampires had gathered, their faces reflecting the shock that she felt.

Ethan lifted his head. "I can't hear them."

"The spell's still up," Jake said. "But it wasn't just you that came through. How did Charlie get in here?"

With a groan, Ethan propped himself up on his elbows, and didn't seem in a hurry to move out of his reclining position. His gaze roamed her face. "You all right?"

She nodded. "You?"

"Mighty fine." His eyebrows pulled in tight. "I reckon the blood maybe tied us together. That's the only way I can figure the both of us matching, becoming that key. My Gift going into you, the noise you was making going into me."

"What kind of noise?" Jake asked.

Ethan sat the rest of the way up, climbed to his feet. "It was your psychic scent. Which says to me that the psychic energy in the blood powers the symbols somehow or another—like a current through an electromagnetic lock. And it also occurs to me that's maybe why we have to cut our fingers open each time we set the spell. When the blood ain't from a living source, nothing much happens."

He moved in front of the door, his head tilting as he examined the symbols.

Charlie ran what he'd just said over in her head, waiting for it to make sense. "You mean, you think that the blood on those symbols is still living—carrying that psychic energy? Even though it's not in a body anymore?"

Ethan slowly nodded. "That's what I'm wondering, and I reckon we can discover whether it is awful easy."

Yet there was no way to measure it; if there was, the possibility of Legion replicating a food source might not be so far-fetched.

Charlie shook her head. "But how can you . . . oh. Oh. Well, licking a door is kind of perverted, but okay."

Ethan stepped aside as she approached the door frame. She had to stand on her toes. The scent of the blood was incredible; the door frame was flavorless—except for the three drops that sang across her tongue.

The excited voices of the Guardians swept inside the room. Charlie turned, and nodded. "Just like Jake."

❦

Only thirty minutes remained before sunrise when Charlie finally got back to her room. She headed straight for the restroom, running through her nightly routine as quickly as she could.

She was yanking on her shortest nightgown when Ethan stepped through the door. He hurriedly closed it, activated the spell, and Charlie grinned as she finished shimmying into the wisp of lace. "Did it work?"

Ethan shook his head, his amber gaze sweeping her from hair to toes. "Mackenzie felt my Gift well enough, and the difference when we ran it over the spell, but he couldn't give me anything to open it with." He stalked across the room, his jacket and boots vanishing. "And he said I tasted like the dust that lies in the coffin of dying dreams. But I imagine that was only because Becca was watching, and his dream was of sexing me."

Charlie edged toward the bed. "So it was . . . hot?"

His uneven smile had her heart racing. He began unbuttoning his shirt. "You jealous, Charlie?"

"No." *Yes.* She and Ethan had practiced several times after that first success; each attempt had been easier. But when the inevitable suggestion that Ethan try it with another vampire had come, Charlie had used the first excuse she could think of to escape. "But like I said downstairs, it's almost dawn. So I'm in a hurry, and I was hoping he warmed you up for me."

His amusement rumbled through the small room. Her eyes followed the trail of dark hair that led from his chest to his stomach, and lower. He was very obviously warmed up, and she decided that there nothing sexier in the world than a half-dressed, fully aroused, and laughing Ethan.

When she felt the mattress against the back of her thighs, she turned, bent over the bed, and lifted up on her tiptoes.

His laughter stopped. "God Almighty, Charlie."

"I warmed myself up before you got here," she said huskily. "So you don't have to waste time getting me ready."

"That's a damn fool thing to say." His fingers traced fire up the insides of her thighs. Her eyes closed, and she swayed forward, her hands clenching in her sheets. "Every moment *not* touching you is what's a waste."

And she was already wet, but he still used his mouth, until she was grinding and twisting against his tongue. He braced his hands on the bed as he slowly pushed into her, not touching her except for that heated, stretching penetration.

But that was all he took slowly. His harsh groans were punctuated by raw, erotic descriptions of her sex, his cock, her breasts and lips. Her legs shook. The pulse in his wrist beat a rapid pace.

His tanned skin was smooth, unmarked.

"Where did he bite you?" It ripped from her before she

knew it had risen, but once it did she couldn't stop its refrain. "*Where*, Ethan?"

His right hand slid toward her mouth, and she lunged toward it, gripping his forearm as she sank her fangs into his wrist. Ethan made a low noise behind her, a moan, a growl, and then he was lifting her left knee onto the bed and reaching around her hip, his fingers delving, stroking. She came apart, and Ethan turned her, his eyes never leaving hers as he filled her again, slowly, slowly until he shuddered over, into her.

She still drank, and he carefully pulled her with him to the center of the bed, watching her face.

His voice was soft as he pushed her hair back. "Will you try to send me something now?"

She'd been trying. A song, a note. But he apparently hadn't gotten them, so she ventured what she'd wanted to tell him. *I love you.*

His expression didn't change. A lick cleaned the puncture wounds, and she shifted around, spooned against him. "You didn't hear me?"

"No. Some nosferatu-born vampires can hear thoughts when they're feeding, but so far as I know, no Guardian receives thoughts or sounds—only images." He pushed his knee between her thighs; his opposite foot thumped against wood. "It may be it's only with the focus of the Gift."

"Will your bed fit in here? You have permission to take anything of mine, if you need space—" She suddenly fell about an inch before sinking into his mattress. His deep sigh of relief had her rolling forward onto her stomach, laughing into the pillow that had landed with her. She turned her head, met his eyes.

"I was jealous," she admitted.

He looked as if he was trying not to appear pleased with himself. "Hell, Charlie—it'd sure put me out if you went to someone else, so I reckon it's only fair."

She was suddenly feeling pleased with herself, as well. Her smile pressed against her fangs, and she arched a brow. "Fair? I hit mean and low."

"That you did. It was awful dirty."

"Yeah, well, speaking of dirty, you apparently really like words that start with 'P.' Pretty, plump, pink, pus—"

"You hush, Miss Charlie."

"And 'F.' I must say, you fraternize really well, Ethan." She wriggled back against him to the sound of his laughter, let her hearing fill with the metronome beat of his heart. After picking up the rhythm, she let it fade, and wondered quietly, "What will it mean—what we did tonight?"

"I don't rightly know. Breaking through the spell will be real handy, but unless I can figure a way to hear sound and blood like you do, it won't be practical except in the most critical situations."

"Because you'll have to take me along?" she asked, and he made a sound of assent.

"You fight pretty well, Charlie, but 'critical' would probably mean demons and nosferatu. And I'd sure hate to see you hurt."

"I'd like to help as much as I can, though." She glanced at the clock. Only five minutes until sunrise. How frustrating—and frightening—that no matter what she did, she'd be asleep as soon as the sun came up. "But I guess I couldn't even go during the day."

"Maybe not. Though if we teleported you halfway around the world, you'd wake up fast enough."

"I should wear more than this to bed, then." She watched a minute tick by. "Do you think they'll be able to use the symbols to provide vampires with living blood?"

His long silence was only broken by his movement. He pulled her in tight; his arm was a heavy, wonderful heat around her waist.

Finally, he said against her temple, "I'm not certain of that either, Charlie. The way I see it, it's a matter of practicality again. Even if they figure a way to use the symbols and keep the blood living in a container, there's still got to be a blood source, and artificial blood won't have that energy. Guardians and vampires could donate their blood, but it wouldn't add up to much; leastwise, not much relative to how many vampires there are. So maybe it could be used when a vampire has no other choice or the animal blood has run them down; but there just wouldn't be enough blood to support everyone."

Her throat felt thick, but she turned around, smiled down at him before resting her head against his shoulder. "Thank you for donating yours."

"Hell, Charlie. If we're being all grateful with each other, I ought to thank you for blowing my ears out. That goddamn spell has been troubling me for a year now."

The tightness in her chest eased. "I've got about two minutes until I fall asleep," she said. "I intend to spend them kissing you." Anything else would be a waste of time.

"Well," Ethan said. "All right then."

CHAPTER 25

Charlie was facing the clock when she woke. Seven fifty-five—less than half an hour after sunset.

And not as tired as she'd been the previous night, or as sore. Ethan's big body was behind her, and the heat of him warmed her through his clothes.

She turned, searched out his solemn gaze. "Have you been waiting long?"

He shook his head. "Just a few minutes before sunset. Good dreams this time?"

"Yes." Erotic, full of music, blood, screams of ecstasy. And Ethan.

The tips of his fingers traced over her cheek; his eyes and voice were soft. "You hungry?"

"No. I think I had enough for a week last night," she said.

He didn't return her smile, and seemed to hesitate for a moment before he said, "All right. We don't have to feed right away, Miss Charlie. But you dropped a little weight—just a bit—while you slept."

A trickle of dread burned like molten lead into her belly.

She studied his face, tried to figure out what he wasn't saying. She couldn't—but she remembered his reaction the night before . . . his insistence that she feed right away.

She swallowed hard. "How bad was it yesterday?"

"You were skinny." He held her gaze. "This is better; it's six, maybe seven pounds."

Better. Like she was recovering? "Am I sick?"

"I don't rightly know. It's something similar to what happens with vampires who were forced into the change. The sleeping late, the weight loss. You feeling weak?"

"A little tired, maybe. But I don't know what I'm supposed to feel like." She sat up, holding the sheet to her chest. Her breaths came hard. "What happens to them?"

Ethan's jacket sleeves were coarse against her skin as he slid his arms around her. "Some of them decide they want to live, and get better; some of them don't."

"I want to live. Oh, God, how I want to." The sheet tore beneath her fingers. "I chose to drink the blood because I wanted to. So why do I need to get better, and how am I already doing it?"

So she could do it faster.

"I ain't certain." His arms tightened. "I don't mean to scare you—but I thought I ought to lay it out."

"Why didn't you tell me last night?" It came out harshly, and he took a long moment before answering.

"Well, I reckon my head wasn't on all that straight. If it had been, I'd have been thinking about how you'd do everything you could to put yourself together. And I figured I was to blame, resisting you like I was; your feedings ought not to have hurt so much."

She forced her fingers to still, held them clenched between her breasts. Deliberately slowed her breathing until the panic slipped away. "The feeding *is* a lot better. And that makes it . . . easier to be like this."

"Like this—?" He stiffened briefly, then shook his head and said, "A vampire."

"Yes. But if that was the only way I could live, Ethan, I'd have taken feedings like that forever." She let out a long sigh, allowed herself to relax against his chest. "Okay. I'm better than I was?"

"Yes." ·

She smoothed her palm over his forearm. "I don't . . . I don't think I want to feed right away, though."

"Well, this conversation ain't exactly how I'd choose to warm you up for sexing," he said, and she smiled, shaking her head in agreement. His chest lifted behind her as he drew in a deep breath. "And I've taken a real powerful liking to you, Miss Charlie. So knowing that you're feeling poorly ain't inspiring lustful urges in me, neither."

She pressed her lips together, watched her fingers stroke his sleeve's rough weave. A real powerful liking. It wasn't the all-consuming love she wished he felt, but it was *something*. And maybe, with time, he would let it become more.

They had time. She knew Ethan would stay as long as she needed him, and she'd always need to feed. They already had a strong connection in and out of bed; surely that would deepen, until he wasn't staying because of *her* need, and it wasn't just liking and lust.

And coming from Ethan, liking and lust were more than just something; they meant more than she could possibly say.

Still, the ache in her chest didn't immediately go away, and she only trusted herself to lower her head and press a kiss against his hand, before patting his forearm and making a move toward the edge of the bed.

She desperately needed to talk to Jane.

Awkwardly, she stood, tugging the tiny nightgown into place. Ethan was frowning down at his hand, braced with his fingers spread against the mattress, his jaw set.

"Do you mind if I call Jane by myself tonight?"

He didn't look up. "That's just fine, Miss Charlie."

"I won't mention anything about the spell or the blood—"

She blinked; Ethan was standing now. He'd gotten off the bed so swiftly, she hadn't seen his movement.

"I didn't figure you would." He slid his thumbs into his suspenders, cocked his head toward the door. "We've got a game set up, and I'll be there until Castleford and Lilith come back around ten. So if you need anything—" He broke off, and his gaze searched her face before he said slowly, "But you won't, will you?"

She held her hands still at her sides, tried not to fidget as she studied him. His voice had that hollow note she'd heard once before, but his expression was firm, his eyes were as intense as ever. Everything about him looked just as strong.

And she couldn't shake the feeling that she was being slow, not *getting* something—but she had no idea what. "I should be okay. Are you?"

He nodded as he turned toward the door. "I'm right dandy, Miss Charlie."

❧

She *was* okay, but Charlie thought she was on the shitty side of it as she walked though the common area, heading for the stairs and the communications room.

Her gaze searched out Ethan at the poker table; his face was as blank as it had been in her room, but an uneven smile flashed across his lips when he glanced up, met her eyes.

Then his brows lowered in a severe frown, and he tossed his cards to the table, shaking his head. Across the table from him, Jake leaned forward and scraped a huge pile of poker chips back to his side, laughing hard and in a tone that suggested his humor was at Ethan's expense.

"You distracted me, Miss Charlie," Ethan called out as cards whizzed across the table, Pim dealing them almost faster than Charlie could follow. "I had them going until you showed up looking so damn pretty."

That pulled a smile from her, but she had no idea what to say in response. And though she'd intended to go straight downstairs, she found herself walking to his side instead.

He rose to his feet. "You planning to stay a minute?"

"A few seconds, maybe," she said, her eyes widening as she took in the action around the table. This wasn't anything like the slow play he'd taught her in his truck. Cards were flying from Pim's hands, the players were turning them over against the felt, the pile of chips in the center of the table was growing, all at an incredible rate—and no one was speaking a word.

But it wasn't silent. A heavy psychic hum surrounded the table; now and then Charlie heard a note flutter up. And their hands were constantly moving—on their cards, but also what must have been a sign language.

A chair appeared behind Charlie's legs, and she sank into it.

"I'm out this one," Ethan said before turning to her. "Now, you're throwing everyone off, wondering so hard what in blazes we're doing." He shook his head when she began to apologize. "Far as I'm concerned, it's good for them. They need a psychic distraction now and then."

She watched for another second, feeling dizzy. "I can barely keep up."

"Mackenzie and Savi said the same thing, first day. You'll get it, eventually." He caught her gaze. "You're all vampires—Savi's faster, but even she ain't as fast as a Guardian."

Jake snorted. "That's why she cheats."

"The aim of this game is cheating." Ethan glanced over at Jake, then back at Charlie. "He's sore she took him for a bundle by counting cards. When we're playing blackjack, we deal from ten decks to stop some of that, but Savi's brain is something else."

Charlie's brain was still stuck on the first part. "You're *supposed* to cheat?"

Ethan nodded. "Cheat, bluff, steal cards from the deck, pull an ace in from your cache—if you can get it past five of us without being caught, it means you've done something right. When you came in, I was holding just about nothing, but was doing real well until I saw you and my shields fell a bit."

"Oh. Sorry."

"That's a lie, Miss Charlie."

She grinned. "Sorry you didn't call me pretty until *after* you'd won."

"Well, so am I, then."

Her smile slipped when his focus shifted to her mouth, his eyes like sun-warmed honey, and she felt the slow lick of bloodlust.

She cleared her throat and turned back to the table. "So you're trying to block, and feel out the other players' hands at the same time," she said as she attempted to track the movement of cards. And it wasn't just the psychic awareness, she thought; they were obviously forced to think quickly, to constantly adjust, to look for any way to gain an advantage. Her brow furrowed. "Is it a training exercise?"

Play stopped dead. Five Guardians looked at her as if she'd

said a baby was ugly, and Charlie sat back, eyeing each of them warily.

"Whoa boy, Charlie," Jake said. "We're trying very hard to pretend we aren't *always* in Guardian boot camp."

There was just enough humor in his reply that her discomfort faded. Ethan leaned in toward her, tilting his head as if he intended to share a secret.

"They're feeling a bit cooped up," he whispered. The lines beside his eyes were etched deep with his silent laughter.

The game started again, but this time with a thread of conversation that Charlie could follow taking place above the nonverbal one they were still signing with their hands.

"I should have become a vampire," Pim said. "At least they can leave."

Jake threw a chip into the center of the table. "You might be getting out earlier than you think. I've just been given parole."

"I reckon it's more like probation," Ethan said. "You'll still be here a good part of it."

Jake folded his cards. "I'm going to eat a hamburger next week," he announced.

"No, you ain't," Ethan said, but no one seemed to hear him above the sounds of jealousy running around the table.

"Freedom," Pim sighed. "No tiny rooms."

"No scheduled workouts," another said.

Ethan shook his head, and made a gesture with his hand. He was dealt in a second later. "No crybaby novices."

"You don't get to eat?" Charlie asked. "I know you don't *have* to, but you aren't allowed to?"

The corner of Ethan's mouth quirked. "Each one of these novices has slunk out for something in the past week." He added over the denials that rose, "They're just whining."

"It's prison, Charlie," Pim said. "We don't get to fly out to the desert and—" There was a thump under the table, and she winced, glaring at Jake. "—learn to hog-tie cows."

A muscle was flexing in Ethan's jaw. "Pim, you'd best—"

"No, it's okay," Charlie quickly said. Pim's tone was too good-natured to cause her any real embarrassment, but judging by the hard stare Ethan was leveling at the other Guardian, he was ready to go across the table. "I understand the frustration.

And I'm kind of relieved it's not just me, because it was my first thought when we got here, too."

"That you'd like to learn to rope cattle?" Jake asked, and his smile seemed to urge her into a story.

But this wasn't a tale that Charlie wanted to spend any time on, so she simply said, "No, the feeling of it—the fence outside, the processing through security. The little rooms and the common area." She shrugged when the psychic hum disappeared, and play slowed to a crawl. "You know."

But something was wrong. Pim looked at her, and hesitated before she said, "I wasn't really—" She bit her lip. "We don't *really* think that, Charlie. Drifter's right that we're just whining for the sake—"

"Shut it, novice." Ethan's voice had the crack of a whip, and Charlie flinched back from it, got to her feet. Ethan slowly stood, his skin pale, the edges of his mouth white.

Oh, God. Sick mortification balled in her stomach. The words came in a desperate rush. "I don't think that now—and I *never* thought you were bringing me in to a prison. It was just the appearance that reminded me of it, that first impression," Charlie said, but his expression remained taut, and she had to close her eyes against the burning in them. She'd insulted him, soiled the help that he'd given her—and she didn't know how to fix it. "I need to go call Jane."

Before she said something even worse.

"What do you think now?" he asked before she'd taken a step.

Her throat was so tight she could barely get it out. "That it doesn't matter, anyway." She heard his harsh inhalation, realized that by saying only half of it she'd just managed to make it worse, and forced herself to lift her gaze to his face and finish. "Because when we're in the same room I don't notice anything but you."

The tightness melted away, the color coming back to his features, warming his eyes. "Well, Miss Charlie, that's because I'm so almighty tall."

Relief tore through her, weakened her knees. "Actually, I think it's the suspenders," she rasped.

One long stride carried him close, his hands in her hair, but although she lifted her face to his, he only lowered his mouth to her ear and said softly, "You go make your call, because if I kiss you now there won't be another chance for you to talk to Jane tonight—and I'll lose the pile of money that's just waiting for me on that table. I'm feeling so lucky I could probably cheat the devil himself."

"I've done that," a familiar feminine voice broke in. Charlie turned her head at the same time Ethan did, saw the woman who must have been Lilith. Dark hair, dark eyes, and with a smile that Charlie could only call wicked. "And luck didn't have a thing to do with it."

Ethan glanced down at Charlie, and she saw the flicker of frustration in his eyes before he said, "Don't believe her."

Charlie blinked. Lilith was already turning around, gesturing for them to follow her. "She didn't cheat the devil?"

"She did," Ethan said, taking her hand. "But luck rode real tight on her ass that day."

§

Ethan needed five minutes alone with Charlie, but Lilith and Castleford showing up early told him he wasn't likely to get it just yet.

He'd thought for certain he'd spooked Charlie in the bedroom by giving her an indication of how powerfully he felt, and that she'd grabbed at a quick excuse to run. But he'd jumped to conclusions about her before, and now he was thinking he had again, because her response at the poker table had been the same: needing to speak with Jane. He'd sensed her spinning uncertainty then, the desperation and fear; maybe she hadn't been running to Jane as an escape, but for comfort.

And it hadn't taken much of a push for the rest to come out, to discover her emotions were running deep. So it might be she was just all around spooked, and feeling anything she laid on him was a burden. Might be that she'd been tiptoeing as carefully as he'd been, and he would have to ease her into looking to him when she was uncomfortable or hurting—particularly as she sure in blazes didn't like accepting anything else he had to give her.

Ease her into it . . . but he figured he'd have to push a bit more, first—and he'd be doing it just as soon as he finished up here.

Jake settled into the chair in front of Lilith's desk, but Charlie remained standing beside Ethan, her hands buried in her pockets. She didn't waver beneath Lilith's penetrating stare.

"So you can get Drifter through the spell?" Lilith said as she sat on the edge of her desk next to Castleford.

Sir Pup lay on the floor at her feet, and Charlie only blinked once when he lifted his three heads to study her before lowering them back to his forepaws.

"Yes," Charlie said slowly, raising her gaze to Lilith's again.

"Can you do it now?"

Charlie was shaking her head before Ethan could respond. Castleford and Lilith had already seen recordings of them busting through the shield; they didn't need a demonstration, particularly one that might trigger her bloodlust.

"I haven't fed yet," Charlie said. "And Drifter hemorrhages every time, so I'd prefer not to unless we're practicing, or it's critical."

Lilith nodded, a smile curving her lips. "That last part sounds like something Drifter might say. I assume he's told you how much this will benefit us."

"Yes." Charlie's response had a wry note beneath it. "I'm well aware of what can happen when someone is locked inside the spell with a demon or a vampire, and a Guardian can't get to her."

Lilith slanted a glance at Castleford, as if to see his reaction. She probably couldn't read Charlie's face much better than Ethan did.

"No, Miss Charlie," Ethan said. "Agent Milton's wondering what you want out of it."

"Oh." Charlie blinked. "Am I supposed to bluff and hold out for a million dollars? No one's going to believe it. The second someone needed the help, I'd be doing it anyway."

Ethan looked down at his boots, fighting his laugh. No, he reckoned Charlie couldn't offer an ultimatum to save her life. "We ain't talking trading, Charlie, because we ain't much for bargains when they matter. We're talking payment. Putting you on retainer, so to speak."

When she shook her head, he fully expected her to refuse and to declare that she didn't need anything. But her brows knitted, and a moment later she said, "I'm sure there's something I could use. Let me think about it for a while."

"You probably won't want to wait too long," Lilith said. "Savi called us just after sunset, saying that Sammael checked out of the hotel. So she looked, and you didn't yet have an e-mail from Jane. Then Savi tried the phone Drifter gave to Jane, but she hasn't gotten any response but voice mail."

Charlie paled, turned to look up at Ethan. "I'm going to see if anything's come in since then. Or try her number at Legion. Maybe she just forgot, is still at work."

Ethan nodded, had to unclench his jaw before he said, "Jake? You give her any help she needs." He waited until the door closed behind them. "I can't see as anything called for how abruptly you laid that on her."

Lilith frowned. "And here I thought that you had a brain to go with those pretty eyes, Drifter. Two minutes with her told me that's how she'd prefer it; if I thought she'd wanted coddling, I'd have let Hugh tell her."

"I'd have been as blunt," Castleford said.

"All right." Ethan took a deep breath. "You ain't wrong about her. I'm just feeling awful protective."

"Half a second told me that," Lilith said. "Now, do you want to know what the Scrolls told us about your nephilim friend in Seattle? Or do you want to wait?"

Even if Charlie managed to connect with Jane, Ethan figured he wouldn't be long in San Francisco, and he'd rather be as prepared as possible to face it again.

"Let's hear it now," Ethan said.

"First," Castleford said, "there's no mention of a prophecy, or the grigori. Neither does it explain how the nephilim were created."

"Don't matter much to me, anyway. I ain't looking to make more, but to kill one."

Lilith pulled her heel up onto the edge of the desk. "That'll be the difficult part, because there's no mention of any weaknesses, like sunlight or hellhound venom. They must have been incredibly powerful if it took both Lucifer's and Belial's demons to imprison them."

"Considering I'm only alive because Jake teleported me out, that don't surprise me a bit. If I do happen to encounter it again, I'll be calling Selah for backup."

Selah could teleport in—and, given a few extra seconds, bring other Guardians with her.

Castleford nodded. "We'll alert everyone active, let them know what she might be carrying them into."

"All right," Ethan said. "Do the Scrolls say what sets it off?"

"Lucifer used the nephilim to enforce the Rules," Lilith said, frowning slightly when Sir Pup lifted his heads and a growl rumbled from his chest. She leaned forward to scratch at his neck. "How isn't exactly clear. But when a demon obstructed free will or harmed a human, a nephil was called, teleporting out of Hell to slay him."

That fit what Ethan had seen; once Jane had set her mind on going to Charlie and the demon had held her back, the air had been humming with that odd psychic energy. "But it didn't stink as if it had just come in from Hell."

Castleford hesitated, then shook his head. "The Scrolls suggest that the nephil possessed a human, and used that body when it was on Earth—just long enough that the nephil could kill the demon. Then it was called back to Hell."

"Which doesn't make sense," Lilith said, turning to Castleford. Her tone suggested they'd already discussed this detail at length, and couldn't come up with an explanation that satisfied either of them. "Assuming that a nephil could just take over a human's body like that, possession would deny the human's free will. That's too big a contradiction, even for Lucifer."

She frowned again as Sir Pup got to his feet, his noses scenting the air.

The odor of sulfur and rot hit Ethan just before he heard Michael's melodic voice. "The humans whose bodies they possessed were dead."

Ethan only had a second to meet the Doyen's gaze, note the black wings and bronzed skin, his white toga stained gray with soot and dirt. Then Charlie slipped through the door and wordlessly shook her head; she hadn't been able to reach Jane.

Her eyes widened when she saw Michael, and her nose wrinkled.

Lilith didn't hide her revulsion. "I guess that answers where you've been, Michael. You stink. And the smell is disturbing my puppy; he doesn't have fond memories of Hell."

Michael sighed. "Tell me, Lilith—who does?" He looked at Charlie as she moved to Ethan's side, his obsidian eyes narrowing. The familiar touch of his healing Gift slid gently through the room. "Were you forced into the transformation?"

"No," she rasped. Her cool hand found Ethan's, and he squeezed it reassuringly. With his opposite hand, he quickly signed the details of her transformation, the feeding, and weight loss to Michael before she added, "I wanted—*want*—to live."

Michael shook his head, and his toga disappeared, immediately replaced by a linen tunic and long pants. His wings vanished.

"It is not enough to simply want to live. Even those forced want to live," he said, and Charlie's breath caught, her fingers tightening painfully on Ethan's. "You must want to live *as a vampire*. It is a small difference, but one that your body and your will recognizes when the change tries to take hold."

"It's getting easier to be one." Her hands, her voice were trembling.

"Then you will continue getting better," Michael said. "But because of your initial reluctance, it will be some time before the transformation completely sets."

· "I've always been slow," Charlie said with a rough laugh, and tears clung to her lashes before spilling to her cheeks.

Well, hell. Ethan stared down at her, trying to figure the source of her tears—her expression didn't show the fear or relief he'd have expected. She stared at Michael, her face open and seeking as if she wanted to reach out to him, her psychic scent projecting shimmering fingers of heat and light.

Awe and wonder.

She added in a whisper, "Do you sing?"

"I have not in a very long time." A smile softened the line of the Doyen's mouth, and now that her question made Ethan listen for it, he heard the distinct tones running through the complicated harmony of Michael's voice. "And if we are very fortunate, you will never hear me do so."

CHAPTER 26

Charlie eventually had to block out some of Michael's incredible voice, force herself not to pay attention to the intricate, shifting melody that made up his words, as if each sound contained a song. And once she listened to what he was saying rather than just his voice, she had to rush to catch up.

That the nephilim had been created by Lucifer was clear, but Michael didn't explain how it was done. Charlie thought his evasion of their questions left Castleford and Lilith frustrated, although it was difficult to tell—and Charlie only received the impression because Lilith was stroking her dog's heads a little more than she had been. Some of that frustration eased when Michael confirmed that the nephilim had attempted to take Lucifer's throne, but that the creatures were imprisoned—and that he'd teleported throughout Hell for the last few days, searching for the nephilim's prison.

"For what purpose?" Castleford asked.

"To see how many had been released." Michael stood with his arms crossed over his chest, a huge painting of Caelum forming a backdrop behind him. Charlie didn't know how he stood so straight and still without appearing uncomfortable, but he managed it. "The nephilim are methodical and powerful—and I began to suspect them responsible for slaughtering the vampires after we visited Washington, D.C. I did not wish it to be true. And yet, given what Ethan has told us, it must be."

Michael glanced over at Ethan, and Charlie fought not to shudder. Like Sammael's eyes had been, Michael's were all one color, but obsidian—and the only way to judge the direction of his gaze was by the turn of his head. "When I do find their prison," Michael said, "I will likely need your assistance."

Because it would be locked, Charlie realized. But although Ethan agreed, he was frowning. "Why is it that you need to return, if we've evidence that they have been released?"

"There were just over a hundred imprisoned," Michael said. "And apparently he has allowed more than one to return to Earth. We must know what we are facing."

"A hundred?" Lilith shook her head, as if she couldn't believe it. "A *hundred* of them brought Lucifer and his armies to their knees? How is it that he dares to release even one?"

"The Rules *must* be enforced," Michael stated. "And I anticipated that Lucifer would release one, so that it could be called to Earth if a demon should break them. It would not need to use a Gate."

Ethan's hand tightened on Charlie's. "You expected it, but you didn't warn us?"

"To be truthful, it was of little importance and—I thought—no danger to us. The nephilim are called, they destroy the demon, and they are called back to Hell. They cannot teleport at will, and they have a purpose that did not interfere with our own."

"But that ain't what happened," Ethan said. "It didn't return to Hell after slaying the demon."

"No. Lilith is correct—with Lucifer embroiled in his war with Belial, he must have feared the consequences of having the nephilim free in Hell. Which is the second reason I only expected the one."

Castleford pushed his hand through his short dark hair. "So they are free on Earth instead? A force that powerful?"

"Not as powerful," Michael said. "Not when they are in human form—and they must bind themselves to a human form. Even if he does not call them back to Hell, Lucifer cannot alter that aspect of their nature." He turned to Ethan again. "And that is where you will find a weakness in them."

"Slaying it when it looks human?"

"Yes. It does not have a nephilim's strength or speed—it is hardly more powerful than a vampire would be."

Ethan's brows lowered, as if he was working that through. "The human's dead—for certain?"

"Yes."

"It won't be difficult to find out who it is, then," Lilith said dryly. "We just have to compile a list of everyone on Earth who's died in the past year—all fifty million of them—then go knocking at their doors."

The corners of Michael's mouth lifted slightly. "Unfortunately, possession takes place almost immediately after death, so there might be no more indication than a mild heart attack, or an injury from which the person seems to have miraculously escaped."

"Do I have to concern myself that as soon as I kill it, it'll jump into another dead body?" Ethan asked.

"No." Michael looked at each of them, then drew in a short breath. "Being called is nothing more than Lucifer allowing the nephilim to take possession of a human's essence—the psychic energy—as it crosses the realms, from Earth to Hell. The nephilim sheds its physical form, forces the human essence back through at the point of entry, then returns it to the body."

"And the nephilim piggybacks its way in," Ethan guessed, and when Michael nodded, he asked, "Why isn't every demon trying to get out that way? Seems to me I've heard that angels were spirits of light—beings of energy, who took on a solid form only when they wished."

"I have no definite knowledge regarding the angels' construction—and even if Lucifer allowed demons to possess a human's essence, they cannot shed their forms in the same way as the nephilim," Michael said. After a brief hesitation, he added, "I can only speculate that, when demons were cursed and transformed, their psychic energy was bound to flesh. As was the nosferatu's, although they were bound much closer—and so they cannot shift their shape except to form their wings, and they feel the urges of the flesh: sleep, hunger, and arousal."

Bloodlust, Charlie thought. And vampires weren't much different.

"But you aren't certain?" Lilith asked.

"No. I assume it is so, because when I transform human to Guardian," Michael explained, "one task I must perform is to bind the psychic energy to flesh with the symbols—but I do not bind it so tightly as it once was. Some of those human physical urges are relieved, some are not—and the will has greater control over form."

"Well, hell," Ethan muttered, laughing softly, and Charlie glanced up at him. "Considering that my will can't control my form for nothing, I reckon that means I'm spineless."

"Stubbornness is as great an impediment to shifting as a weak will," Michael said with the first real smile Charlie had seen from him. It didn't last long. "In almost every manner, a Guardian's strength and powers are similar to a demon's—but I can find no evidence of symbols within demons or the nosferatu, or any indication of what they've been changed *from*. And that is why I can only speculate; however their transformation was done, it was with an invisible hand."

The thought of that made Charlie slightly uneasy, and she was grateful when Ethan said, "Will the nephilim be changing its human shape, then?"

"No. It will be enough of a struggle to remain in the body it chooses. A nephilim cannot simply animate the flesh; there must be a bond, and it is specific to an individual. And by mimicking the human's psychic energy—"

"Like the damn spell," Ethan said, and when Michael frowned, Ethan must have signed an explanation: his fingers were a blur, and Michael's smile appeared again.

"That is well done, both of you," he murmured, and he looked to Lilith and Castleford. "The symbols' power is not so easily breached. What did Ethan not mention?"

"There's hemorrhaging unlike anything I've seen with a Gift—only in novices who've lost control of their form," Castleford said.

Lilith must have caught Charlie's confused expression. "Their brains turn to mush," Lilith explained. "It's likely that Drifter's Gift is literally trying to wrap his mind around the power within the symbols—shifting his brain's makeup so that he can understand it, and get through the lock."

Oh, dear God. Charlie thought for a moment that she'd be sick.

Castleford glanced at Charlie and quickly added, "It heals at a normal rate, however. Charlie seems to suffer no ill effects."

"If she did, I wouldn't be doing it."

Michael was nodding, but at that he turned to look at Ethan—or at her, but Charlie couldn't be certain. But although his face hardened slightly, he only said, "It is the same principle when the nephilim matches the psychic energy to gain entrance into the body. And just as destructive, for when the nephil asserts his own form, it loosens the bonds on the flesh—essentially, the body begins dying again. And as the body dies, the human's psychic energy attempts to break away from the nephil's possession. The body heals when the nephil reverts to the human form—but that moment is when the nephil is at its very weakest, for it also must strengthen its hold on the human's essence again."

"I can't imagine it'll take its own form often, then," Ethan said. "Is there any tell that will let us know a body's housing something else inside it?"

"No," Michael said. "Temperature, psychic scent—everything will appear human. And as it must use the human's body—including the brain—it will have that person's memory, adopt the same mannerisms, and many of the same thought patterns. There would be differences, but you would have to know the human well to see them."

"So I pretty much got to wait until it ain't hiding in the body, and figure who it turns back to when it's done."

"Yes."

Ethan whistled low between his teeth, shaking his head in frustration. "All right, then. I'll be heading up to Seattle, soon as possible—maybe hope that someone sees it."

Seattle. Charlie squeezed Ethan's hand, lifted her gaze to his. "Do you have the blood that Jane gave you? You said Michael can teleport."

"He sure can," Ethan said, and a small drinking glass from the motel appeared in his opposite hand. He held it out for Michael. "We're looking for Charlie's sister."

Michael frowned at the glass, and after a moment, looked at Ethan again. "I cannot anchor to her."

Which only meant that Jane was probably behind the shield, Charlie told herself. And probably with Sammael. "What about the demon blood she was going to send? Did it arrive today?"

"I've got it," Jake said, and a small white box appeared in his hand. A wry smile passed over his lips. "I was wondering what it felt like. Drifter was right; it creeps."

Lilith gave an exaggerated shudder, and Castleford nodded. "Yes."

Charlie took the box from him, tore off the sealing tape. Cold steam curled from inside—a coolant in the packaging, Charlie realized, and then a startled laugh escaped her. Nestled atop the gray cushioning foam was a tiny porcelain unicorn.

"Definitely from Jane," she said, and lifted out the first vial. Jane had even labeled it: *Samuels, Dylan. Demon.*

"Don't expect too much, Charlie," Ethan said softly. "Even if he's not behind the shield, Sammael has good psychic blocks."

He was correct; a moment later, Michael shook his head.

"I will continue trying, however," he said. "If you will give me one of those vials."

Charlie nodded, then quickly lifted out another to check the label. A yellow sticky was wrapped around it. The packaging pulled it loose, and Ethan picked it up from the floor.

His lips twitched before he read, " 'Yippee kai yay, motherfucker' ?"

"Oh." Charlie's cheeks flared as she held out the vial to Michael. "It's just a thing from a movie. From when we were kids. For Jane, it's kind of like—I don't know—a victory dance or something."

The vial vanished from her fingers, and Michael said, "Then you are certain this is Sammael's blood?"

"Probably, but"—she removed the stopper from another vial—"I should recognize the smell. I was stuck in a car with it for hours."

Oh, God. The scent struck her, incredible, irresistible. She drew it closer, breathed in deep, and she suddenly couldn't think.

"Charlie?" Ethan said softly.

The thirst roared through her. She heard Ethan swear, and

Jake's quick intake of breath. A drop gathered on the bottom of the stopper. She could see her reflection in it, distorted, bulbous. Closer now . . . too close.

She brought it to her lips, sucked it off—and dropped the vial in shock.

"Son of a bitch." Ethan caught it before it smashed against the floor, then turned to her. "You all right?"

She stared at him. Swallowed the extra saliva in her mouth—and the lingering flavor of the blood. "I tasted it."

His brows snapped together. "You what?"

A victory dance. "I tasted it," Charlie repeated, more strongly this time. And Jane had known when she'd sent it; she must have gotten it out of Sammael. "It's living, just like licking Jake's blood from the door. No wonder they got those vampires to stay at Legion—they offered them *this*."

"No," Lilith said, shaking her head. "We've tested this before, looking for alternative food sources. The vampires said the demon blood had no flavor."

"I have attempted it, as well," Michael said. "Vampires could not feed from it any longer than they could animal blood."

Charlie frowned, then tried another drop, and had to catch her breath against the torrent of sensation and sound. Deep, rich. "It's there," she gasped. "And it's so beautiful . . . but *not*. Frightening and dark."

She projected it, and Michael's brows lifted. "That *is* demon," he said.

"Jake," Ethan said slowly. "You take a vial to Mackenzie, see if he tastes it."

Jake grabbed one and ran out; Lilith watched him go, then looked at Michael. "Why would it be different?"

Castleford had been quiet, frowning thoughtfully as he cleaned his eyeglasses on his shirt. Now, he put them on, and said, "They were dead. All of the demon blood we used, we could only get by first slaying the demon. Sammael still lives."

Jake returned, his eyes wide, the vial empty. "I couldn't keep him from drinking all of it."

Lilith sat back a little, her lips parted. She blinked, then looked down at her hellhound, and blinked again. "Well, fuck me," she said. "Lucifer's demons don't know about this. How long have Belial's known?"

No one could answer that—and Charlie was thinking of

Sammael, and his long-winded explanation in the SUV. "They're still researching the vampire blood, though," she said, trying to work her way through it. "They're promising the vampires a food source like this, but they already have it. Why worry about the rest?"

Ethan sighed, scrubbed his hand through his hair. "I sure don't know. Maybe it's the same concern we talked about last night—not enough of it. But that doesn't sound right, does it?"

Charlie had no idea; as far as she could tell, nothing about demons seemed right.

⟡

Uncertainty followed Charlie back upstairs. Ethan walked quietly beside her, and his silence gave her time to formulate all of the reasons she should return to Seattle. When it came time to convince him, hopefully she wouldn't stumble over her words.

A few steps away from her door she finally felt as if she'd rehearsed them enough. "Drifter," she said, "I was just thinking that because you've had to keep coming to San Francisco and feeding me, and spending the evenings here—"

"Just spit it out," he said softly.

She stumbled, tried to pick it up again. "Well, with the nephilim threatening the vampires, obviously you need to be in Seattle more—"

He stopped, turned to her. She couldn't read his expression. "Spit it out, Charlie."

"I want to go back to Seattle with you."

"All right," he said, and pushed through her door.

She blinked, then headed in after him. Her room was already cleared by the time she shut the door behind her, and she watched him walk into the bathroom to finish it.

When he returned, his gaze settled on her. "Before we go, we've got to get a few things straight."

His voice was hard and soft at the same moment; she didn't know how to interpret it, only knew that it started a trembling low in her belly. "Okay," she said.

"Firstly, you ain't going anywhere alone once we get up there. Not until I kill the nephil—and Sammael, too. But if you need privacy, you feel free to take it. Just tell me you're heading behind the shielding spell, so I know where you are."

She nodded, tilting her head back as he approached her. "All right."

"Secondly, we're going to make ourselves real obvious to everyone in the community, so they know where to come if trouble hits. It won't do me any good to fly around, hoping I run into the nephil. But if someone sees him, and everyone knows how to find me right quick, I might be able to track him down."

"Okay. Can we also mention Jane?"

His smile made her stomach perform a long, lazy roll. "That was the next part. We'll keep searching for her, and we won't be quiet about it. Word travels quick, Charlie. If Sammael has hidden her away somewhere, eventually someone will hear, and they'll know where to find us."

She sagged back against the door. "Thank you."

"Which brings me to the last thing," he said, bracing his hand beside her head. "You've got gratitude down real well, but you had best start complaining more. If something is making you uncomfortable, I can't do nothing about it unless you tell me what's bothering you."

"But I don't mind being uncomfort—"

He leaned in close, his eyes blazing. "I *never* had such trouble as I do with you, Charlie. I sure as hell mind if you're uncomfortable—and it ain't leeching or ungrateful to say you need something different than what I think to give you, especially if it's something you normally provide yourself. And I can't figure you half the time, so I reckon half the time I won't be right. But I won't know to change it unless you tell me I've got it wrong."

Her fingers curled on his suspenders so he couldn't pull away. "But you didn't get anything wrong. I was the one who brought that impression of prison into it."

"Charlie, goddammit—" His lips tightened. His chest rose and fell on a long breath before he said softly, "Knowing what you do of my history, would you ever give me a noose—even if it was made out of gold?"

"Oh." She closed her eyes. God, she really was slow sometimes. He hadn't been insulted, just feeling as ashamed as she had been for unintentionally hurting him. "I don't know what to say."

"Just tell me when I've lain something on you that I didn't mean to give."

She nodded, pressing her lips together to keep them from wavering. If he asked it of her, she would. "And you will, too?"

He shook his head. "It ain't becoming for a man to admit he's hurting; I'll just moan a bit, and wait for you to figure out that I'm weak and in need of consoling. And considering I don't eat or sleep, I reckon the solution to soothing all of my ills will be real simple."

Her laugh was soft and breathless. No, he didn't have many needs—and he was *so* strong. She slid her hands up to his shoulders and lifted herself up to his mouth, and he was steady.

But only for a moment.

With a low groan, he released her. "You want to feed here, or at the lake house?"

The bloodlust was rising. It'd probably be torture to spend the entire flight quiet in his arms, but she immediately said, "The lake."

"That sounds mighty fine." His smile was crooked. "All right, Miss Charlie. Let's bust you out of this joint."

CHAPTER 27

They didn't as much bust out as just walk past Jeeves, and Charlie's steps were lighter than she'd have thought, her heart thumping with a wild mixture of hope and fear.

She carried the same combination into Cole's the next evening.

Ethan walked beside her each time, and his presence made the crazy roll of her emotions easier to bear—and let her open herself up to them, knowing that he'd tell her if she veered too far one way or another.

Old Matthew stood behind the counter, studying her as she slid into one of the stools. "Are you coming in to work or to drink?"

She fought to keep her fingers still. "I guess that depends on whether the idea of my drinking freaks you out."

"I ate dinner with the Emerald City Slasher every night for four years without freaking once." He laid his meaty forearms on the bar and leaned in. "Show me what you've got."

Charlie bared her teeth.

He stared, slack surprise smoothing his wrinkles before he

shook his head. "Damn. A part of me still thought you were funning, Charlie girl." He glanced at Ethan. "And him?"

"This is Drifter." She fought to breathe. "He's got wings. No halo, though."

Old Matthew straightened up, his hands huge and dark in the folds of his white towel. Finally, he said, "You'll be mostly in the office now, and when you're up front I think we'll be all right if you don't smile too much. Will we have to adjust your schedule?"

Her chest swelled, leaving her throat tight. Charlie nodded, but couldn't get anything out.

"She'll need a later shift and fewer hours when daylight runs long in the summer," Ethan said. "And if it's acceptable to you, I'll be sitting here most evenings."

Charlie found her voice. "He drinks the Balvenie. And he tips well."

Old Matthew turned and selected the bottle from the top shelf. "If you've got someone to watch over you, does that mean you're still in trouble?"

"A little," she said. "But Jane might be worse off. We haven't heard from her for two days now."

"Anything from that boyfriend of hers?"

Charlie shook her head. They hadn't told Old Matthew about Sammael, but demon or man, it was equally frightening to say, "No, but we think he's got her with him. And if she could, Jane would make sure that I knew she was okay. So we don't think he's letting her talk to anyone."

"That's bad news, Charlie girl." Old Matthew heaved a deep sigh before setting the whiskey in front of Ethan. "If you're going to be sitting, son, it must mean you're waiting for information to come to you. Will you be bringing trouble in?"

"I aim to avoid it. But if I can't, I'll take it outside right quick."

"*Very* quickly," Charlie said. "If people see anything, it'll probably just be his coattails when he goes out the door."

Ethan smiled slightly. "And it may be that folk like Charlie will be coming in for no other reason but curiosity. They won't eat much, though most know to buy a drink for appearance sake."

Old Matthew nodded. "As long as their money's good."

"It will be," Ethan said. "And Charlie tells me you've been trying to set up a mutually beneficial arrangement with the Heritage Theater, but mostly getting a cold shoulder due to the sort of people you employ. But in a few months, I reckon changes will be taking place at the Heritage. Most of the employees won't eat, but it can be made real clear to those folks who'll attend the performances that Cole's is open across the street."

Old Matthew's face wrinkled into a grin. "Well, then. Charlie girl, you and I had better head on back to that office, make room for all that Bobo cash."

❧

Old Matthew didn't stay with her long, but pointed out the various piles of paperwork, described their contents, and left her to familiarize herself with and organize it all to her liking. Ethan produced the new laptop that Savi had shipped to the house, and Charlie had a moment of astonishment when she realized all of her settings were intact, her setup exactly the same—only faster.

And so was she. Charlie listened with half an ear to the easy conversation between Ethan and Old Matthew, and had to stop herself from looking through the one-way mirror every time her name was mentioned in passing.

Until she realized where Ethan had steered the conversation. He'd offered Old Matthew an abbreviated version of his human history, and Old Matthew had seemed pleased by it, observing that Cole's was the right place for an outlaw.

"And for Charlie, too," Ethan said quietly, and when she looked through the mirror she almost believed he could see her, his gaze was so direct.

"Yes," Old Matthew said. "And no. Eight years ago, you couldn't have paid me to take her on, and it wasn't just what she'd done to the place."

"What was it, then?"

Old Matthew stopped for a minute, braced his hands on the bar. "I saw her at the sentencing. If you'd asked me then, I'd have said she wasn't going to make it a year, and it wouldn't have mattered if she was locked up or free. Even if they're still walking, there are some people who aren't living—and you could tell she was one of them."

"Like a zombie, I imagine." Ethan's voice was rough, and he took a sip of his whiskey. "Like her whole world's been turned upside down, and just looking at her, you wouldn't think she'd ever pull herself upright again."

Old Matthew made a sound of agreement, but Charlie couldn't see his expression. "And so you could have knocked me over when she came in two years ago. She wasn't looking as good as she does now, but there was more fight in her than I'd ever have guessed—though I don't think she had any idea of where to start, and a part of her just wanted to slide back to where she'd been. But while we were sitting here talking—she was on the same stool you are now—she was looking at all the bottles, looking at herself in the mirror, and I swear to sweet baby Jesus that I *saw* the second she decided not to buy a drink. A moment later, she told me that I was wrong, and she wasn't a rich girl, and went on with a story about playing a pipe to rats in the subway." Old Matthew began chuckling, pulled off his kufi to rub his head. "It was one of the most ridiculous things I'd ever heard, but she told it like she meant it, and had me right there with her. So I offered her a position, thinking either that fight would keep on coming, or that one day I'd find her passed out on the floor with a bottle in her hand. It was about six months before I realized the second wasn't going to happen."

"It took me a good while, too," Ethan said softly.

Old Matthew's head tilted forward in a nod. "And now, I just like having her around. Never knowing what's going to come out of her makes life more interesting—and I'll tell you, this latest will keep me going for at least another two years."

"At least," Ethan agreed, then glanced at the mirror. "I don't reckon you'd best tell her any of this, though, even if she did happen to wonder why you took her on. She'd like to start crying and carrying on about how grateful she was, and how she doesn't deserve any of it."

Charlie swallowed a laugh, wiped her cheeks. "Fuck you, Drifter," she whispered.

❧

Charlie took five more minutes to compose herself before joining Old Matthew behind the bar, briefly laying her cheek against his shoulder before tying on her apron.

Her fingers fumbled when he said, "I hope you've got great hearing to go along with those teeth and that cold skin, Charlie girl."

She pulled the strings tight. "I do."

"Good. Because I'd hate to think I told all of that to a man I don't know for nothing." He smiled as she laughed and shook her head; then he added, "Did you get bored back there already?"

"No," Charlie said, trying not to grin as she glanced from Ethan to Old Matthew. "I'm done. With the final project for my class, too."

Old Matthew stared at her a minute before walking through the door to the back. Charlie leaned against the bar in front of Ethan, but had to present him with the top of her head, keeping her face down to hide her fangs when she couldn't hold back her smile.

She looked over at Old Matthew when he came back through.

"I haven't unburied that beige file cabinet in ten years; I forgot how ugly it was. Do you want to tell me where I can get a set of those teeth, Charlie girl?" He laughed when her eyes widened. "Well, not today. Today, I'm just going to sit back there and do nothing but look at how nice and clean everything is."

"Okay." She waited until he'd gone again, then met Ethan's steady gaze. "It was easier."

"You think faster now, Miss Charlie. Things that gave you trouble still will, but you're quicker all around."

She nodded, pressing her lips together. "I still can't spell."

Ethan studied her, smiling slightly. "Are you figuring to cry or to laugh?"

"Maybe both. This is a really, really good thing. Better than getting a hit in on Jake now and then."

"You say that after you've known him a bit longer."

Her laugh finally escaped, and she touched his hand, squeezed his fingers lightly. "I know I'm not supposed to do this unless we're alone, Ethan, but I can't help myself."

He held on when she'd have kept it brief and pulled away. "We ain't surrounded by demons right now, so the distraction's all right."

"But doesn't it—" What had he called it? "Fuzz you up?"

"It ain't one touch that fuzzes me, Charlie. It's the buildup I get rid of; if I go too long or take in too much, then a touch like this would hit me so powerfully that I'd be hard pressed not to throw you on your back." He grinned when her breath caught. "I ain't there yet. And I have to get rid of it more often now, but I sure ain't complaining. I'll just drift a little longer tomorrow."

She knew he hadn't gone to Caelum that day. And with no one to tell him if trouble came, she didn't think he'd have sealed himself in another room while she was sleeping.

She searched his face, looking for any sign of the fuzziness—but he appeared as alert and focused as usual. "How are you going to drift if you don't leave me alone?"

"Well, Jake will be coming up most days, heading back during the evenings. So I suppose I could lock myself behind the spell while he's here. But the past two mornings I've been drifting while I've been in bed with you, and it's been just fine."

Her mouth fell open. "When I've been in my daysleep?" At his nod, she shook her head. "I don't understand. If this fuzzes you up faster"—she moved her fingers against his—"then how can you drift with me there?"

"It don't make a lick of sense," Ethan agreed. "But that's how it is. I can't seem to settle without you there, without knowing you're all right."

"Oh." That familiar emotion swelled in her chest, her throat, trying to push itself out. But she only said, "Sorry."

"Miss Charlie," he said, chuckling softly.

Her laugh was equally low. "Okay, I'm not." It was impossible to be. She held his gaze, desire sparking through her. Not from bloodlust—just Ethan. "I get a break in a couple of hours."

His focus shifted to her mouth. "And no one yet knows we're here, so I figure this is the one night we can sit on that swing for a spell."

"You should have sat with me the first night you came to my rescue," she said, grinning. "I was feeling really grateful."

He seemed transfixed by her teeth for a breathless moment; then he closed his eyes and said, "By the time your break comes around, Miss Charlie, I'm certain I can think of a few other reasons you ought to be thanking me."

She broke into laughter, certain she'd never looked forward

to fifteen minutes more in her life. And certain that even if she was *just* sitting with Ethan, it would pass much too quickly. Always before, it had been such a struggle to fill that time, and she'd relied so heavily on her calls to Jane . . .

Her smile faded slowly, and she sighed. "It doesn't seem right that I'm laughing when Jane's missing. Like I should be crying all the time, even though it wouldn't help anything."

Ethan traced her jaw with his thumb, lifting her chin. His expression was as tender as his touch. "I know it, Miss Charlie. And if you do feel like crying, you go on ahead. My shoulder cleans up real easy." His hand rose to push her hair behind her ear. "And with luck, we'll hear about her soon."

❧

Luck didn't accompany Charlie over the next week, and Jane's absence continued to wail its note in the background, only completely fading when she was holding Ethan close.

Their days and nights had fallen into an easy rhythm. Charlie awoke to the soft murmur of Ethan's voice, his touch, his blood. Each night, a little earlier—and though they never talked about her weight loss, as if discussing her recovery might jinx its progress, the worry on Ethan's face seemed to lighten as the days passed.

Then they left for Cole's, where Ethan's predictions held true; each evening brought in new vampires. Some only sat and listened, but others came up to the bar for a brief word or a long conversation. And after a few days, Charlie noted, they'd already picked up regulars.

Closing time found them flying to various locations in the city, visiting with as many vampires as they could, alerting them to the nephilim and seeking information about Jane. By the second week, Charlie knew by sight almost every vampire in the community, except for Manny and his girls. Ethan's first destination each evening was Manny's house, claiming he had questions for the vampire, but Manny had never been home. And Ethan had shaken his head, smiling, when Charlie suggested visiting him wherever he worked.

And every night, she and Ethan returned home with no word about Jane—every night, the tension of not knowing wound tighter and tighter.

Charlie thought it must be like getting fuzzy. It was never

overwhelming at the beginning of the evening, but by the time Ethan set her feet on the deck at home, she was ready to scream from it, ready to go off at the slightest provocation. Ethan must have felt it building in her—and perhaps the frustration was rising in him, as well. After the second night, he'd cut the time they remained in the city by an hour, returning home to engage her in an exhausting training session. The sweat and contact inevitably led them to bed, always hot and rough—and where she finally found release, laughter that didn't have an edge of guilt, and the impenetrable bliss of falling asleep within Ethan's embrace.

But Ethan never stopped working. They'd reported Jane missing, and every night over his whiskey at Cole's, Ethan updated her on the progress of the—equally slow—police investigation. Jake remained at the house when Ethan had to leave, but kept in constant contact from the tech room, researching locations and names whenever Ethan required the information.

So far, they'd only been asked to break through the spell once. Charlie had recognized the blond Guardian who walked into Cole's, and she'd tapped on the one-way mirror. Less than a second after Old Matthew relieved her at the bar and Ethan rushed Charlie through the back door, they'd been standing in front of a burning house.

Two minutes later, she and Ethan were back at Cole's—and to her surprise, Ethan had truthfully answered one vampire's question of why they both suddenly reeked of smoke.

And Selah hadn't been the only Guardian visitor; a few others had dropped by. If not for Ethan's introductions, Charlie wouldn't have realized they weren't human: a hard-edged female who sculpted a tiny metal piano with keys that Charlie could play with a toothpick; a brooding male whose unblinking stare gave Charlie the creeps, but who managed to crack a smile while speaking with Ethan; another woman who reminded Charlie of a crow, who seemed to surprise Ethan simply by coming in, and who talked music with Charlie for almost two hours.

Nothing about the Guardians was similar, except that they all sized Charlie up, and they all appeared to relax in Ethan's presence.

Before she and Ethan had returned to Seattle, she'd mostly

seen him fighting, or with the novices; she hadn't realized how good he was at putting people at ease—even when they had no reason to be so. A few days into the second week, he convinced the two scientists who'd left Legion to join Ramsdell Pharmaceuticals—though, he told her later, not on his own. Savi's partner had flown up from San Francisco, then had left for the airport once they'd finished their negotiations.

Charlie hadn't met Colin Ames-Beaumont since her encounter two months before, but she could easily imagine what had taken place when Ethan recounted the meeting over the bar that evening.

"We offered them a real nice position, and what with Ramsdell investing in a lab here in Seattle, didn't even have to ask them to relocate—but I reckon all of our sweet-talking didn't matter much," Ethan said, his gaze holding hers. "They took one look at his pretty face and that was it."

Charlie had to hide her grin, and let the sound of his soft laughter roll over her. She didn't know how Ethan created such an intimate atmosphere between them with just a low tone and that intense focus, but when he spoke to her like this it was as if they were alone.

And similar to those moments before dawn and after waking from her daysleep, it pushed the helpless anxiety away, just for a while.

But her stomach tightened when Ethan paused and said slowly, "And as tomorrow's your day off, I set Jake up for a date with Mark Brandt."

Charlie blinked, but it still didn't come together. That he intended for Jake to copy Charlie's form and meet with Mark was clear, but not why.

Special Investigations had been treading carefully with the Brandts due to the senator's status. Ethan had called it pussyfooting when Lilith had told him to stand by—but he had agreed that a strong response would give the Brandts reason to think themselves more of a threat than they were.

Charlie knew SI was tracking Mark's purchases, and that he'd been spending most of his vacation at his father's house in Bellevue. But Ethan hadn't yet approached him, except to fly over the property and get a feel for the location.

Charlie's gaze fell to the counter when a short stack of papers appeared beside her hands.

"Colin brought these up," Ethan said. "Savi got onto Legion's e-mail server last night, and downloaded quite a bit before they caught her and booted her off. SI's still sorting through the messages, but before she went into her daysleep, Savi wrote up a list on the front page detailing what she's found so far."

"But why is Jake—?"

She broke off as Vin slid in front of her with an order, and as soon as she'd placed the foaming mug on his tray, Ethan continued.

"Brandt's name showed up, and after reading what he tried to send to Jane, we thought we ought to talk to him."

"*Tried* to send?" She glanced up from the bulleted list on top of the printout.

"Sammael screened all of her incoming mail; these never got to her."

"The asshole," Charlie muttered, but she didn't rush ahead to the e-mails; she made herself read all of the first page. "What's this about IP addresses and mailing lists? What does that mean?"

Ethan's smile was broad. "It means we have a real good idea of the aliases several of Belial's demons are using, and their locations around the country. And there appears to be a demon-only list within Legion, which doesn't include near as many demons as we'd been led to believe. Here in Seattle, there's only Sammael and three subordinates . . . although one of those, I'd wager, was the demon that the nephil killed."

That all sounded like great news, until she read a little more. "The messages they send one another are encrypted?"

"Yes," Ethan said, and tapped the papers. "But Brandt's aren't."

The messages dated a month previous began simply—and were exactly what Charlie would have expected to read from an old acquaintance looking to renew a friendship.

But after two weeks, the tone changed, and they weren't directed to Jane anymore. Halfway through the fourth, Charlie glanced up at Ethan. "Did he figure out that she wasn't getting the messages? He doesn't open with a name, and just says 'You' . . . like here: 'You can't hide behind your mask forever.' And all of these 'I know what you are' and 'Humans deserve the truth' statements. I can't see him saying that to Jane."

Ethan was wearing a slight frown, and he absently swirled his whiskey. "Neither can I, Miss Charlie."

"Actually, I can't imagine anyone saying that," she said, looking at the e-mail again. "It's kind of movie-of-the-week. But I guess since he's a politician-type, maybe he reduced it to sound bites."

"Yes."

Charlie blinked; Ethan's reply had been terse, and his jaw was like steel. He let out a long breath, turned in his seat.

She hadn't been listening. But all of the other vampires in the lounge must have been—everyone's attention was on Joel. He didn't have his laptop that evening, and he wasn't drinking a screwdriver—and the man with the thick neck who was crowding in on Joel's space apparently didn't like having his expectations blown to hell.

More emotions hit her, now that she was focusing on the two men. Anger that bordered on violence, arousal, a need to dominate. Joel pulled away, said no—and was crowded a little more.

Ethan stood, but Charlie was already over the bar, striding across the lounge. She leaned her hip against the table, crossed her arms. Joel wouldn't meet her eyes, so she settled her gaze on his date. The guy was completely 'roided out: acne, overdeveloped muscles, and she could practically smell the testosterone.

"Leave," she said quietly. "Right now."

The musclehead barely spared her a glance. "Fuck—"

She had his arm up tight behind his back before he could finish, forcing him to stand. "That's the second word that starts with 'F' that I've heard you say tonight, and I've only been listening for a few seconds," she said, not caring that his veins were throbbing at his temples, his teeth were grinding, and pain was screeching from his psychic scent. She shoved him toward the exit without releasing his wrist. "This hurts, doesn't it? I haven't even broken or torn anything. Next time you walk in here, I will."

She passed Melody, whose eyes widened before she rushed past the hostess podium and pushed the front door open, then held it wide.

Charlie considered planting her foot in the musclehead's ass, but wasn't certain if she'd misjudge the force—and injury might bring her more attention than this guy warranted. She marched him across the street instead, through drizzling rain, and left him groaning and holding his arm in front of the Heritage.

Ethan stood at the door with Melody, a deep smile creasing the corners of his eyes. "I aimed to be all menacing and formidable until he ran away."

"He'd have tried to get a few punches in first," Charlie said with a shrug. "My way was faster and easier."

She slid her arm through Melody's as they walked back into Cole's, then left her at the podium with a brief squeeze and a thanks.

"That it was, Miss Charlie. And I reckon it answered a question for most everyone here."

"Everyone" must have been the vampires; as she walked through the lounge she couldn't miss the tension and unease pouring from them.

"What answered what?" she asked after she'd checked in with Joel and returned to the bar, wiping the last of the rain from her arms.

"Well, Miss Charlie," Ethan said as he took his seat, "I haven't slain you."

"Oh, my God." Her stomach lurched, gooseflesh rose on her skin. "I broke the Rules."

"That you did. And I figure if you made a habit of twisting a man's arm up behind his back, hurting him for no good reason, we'd be having some real strong words between us. But you had a good reason, so I ain't all that riled up about it."

Her heartbeat regained its normal pace. Ethan was sitting in his easy sprawl, facing her across the bar, yet his words were obviously for everyone.

But he was going about it indirectly. Charlie shook her head, and said, "I thought we had to follow the Rules."

Ethan watched her face for a long second; then he sat up a little straighter and nodded.

"All right. For vampires, they're more like real important guidelines, and the 'not killing' part the most critical one. You're stronger than humans, quicker—most times, no matter what he's threatening, you can get around a human without resorting to killing him. And so long as you don't abuse your strength, we'll be all right. I sure ain't going to slay a vampire for defending someone, or for doing her job." His lips curled slightly. "Though maybe next time, you might jump over that counter a little more human-like."

She smiled, pulling the stack of e-mails back in front of her. "If they're just guidelines, why does it matter so much if demons and Guardians break them?"

"They ain't *just* guidelines for us; for a demon or a Guardian, they're absolute. If I'd done what you did, Michael would soon be showing up to give me a choice to Ascend or Fall." He was silent until she met his eyes, and his tone became intimate. "I'd be Falling—which only means that I'd be transformed back into a human to live out the remainder of my life. I've got too much to atone for to visit an afterlife just yet. But you ain't got to worry if it ever happens; once I became a human again, you could turn me, so as I could continue providing for you."

She dropped her gaze to the printout again. Ethan, a vampire? She couldn't even imagine it. And though it would mean he would need her to feed him, too . . . she wouldn't want equality to come that way.

"I like the wings," she said finally. "So if you run across a human you want to hurt, maybe you should bring me, and I'll beat him up for you."

"Well, Charlie, that's about the sweetest offer I've had in years."

She glanced up; although there was humor in his reply, he was staring down into his glass, his jaw tight.

She swallowed, trying to think of any reason for his response. "Although I guess that would make me like Henderson, and you like Sammael."

He blinked in surprise. "I reckon it would."

It must not have been that, then. She might as well be blunt. "Are you moaning, Drifter?"

"Maybe." His jaw clenched again, but his frustration seemed to shift, encompassing the others in the room. "Maybe when we're in a private moment, we'll discuss why it is that whenever I talk about providing, you look away from me."

She did? Her throat suddenly ached; she wanted to look away *now*. But she wouldn't allow herself to avoid his gaze. "I didn't realize," she said quietly.

His eyes narrowed. "You only didn't realize that you were giving yourself away, Charlie. You know damn well that you squirm every time I say I'll give you anything you need."

She tried not to fidget. Tried to hold herself still. But something seemed to be rupturing in her, tearing and hurting as it opened. Something needy and desperate that wanted to dig its claws into him and beg and plead. Something that wasn't strong, but dependent and revolting. Her fingers curled around paper, and she clung to it.

Clung and backed away from the bar. "I'm going back to the office to finish reading these," she said hoarsely. "And I'm going to put the spell up."

He shook his head; a hat appeared in his hand, and he got to his feet. "That ain't necessary, Miss Charlie," he said in a soft, hollow voice. "I'll return at closing."

No. If she could have screamed, she might have as she watched him walk through the lounge. His name, or simply "Please." But it might not stop there, and become more. *Please don't leave. Please don't give up on me so easily.*

Please need me.

❧

Her fingers didn't stop shaking while he was gone. Even after she heard the footsteps on the roof and realized that he hadn't gone far, the papers fluttered wildly as she turned them, and she rattled bottles against rims with every pour.

Why couldn't she be content with what he'd already given her? How many times had she reminded herself that more might come—that his emotions might deepen? She couldn't know unless she waited. But everything in her was grasping and pulling and she wasn't sure she could contain it.

Had she ever wanted anything so much? Needed it so much?

And he'd give her anything she asked for—but she couldn't ask for this. Asking meant that she'd never know if it was his need, or just his need to provide her with what she wanted. Just as his blood, if it didn't have life flowing through it, would taste the same as hers; she'd never know the difference.

She craved *his* need, *his* love.

But even as she slowly accepted that this particular need wouldn't go away, her nerves wouldn't settle. She read through several e-mails without seeing the words, had to go through them again.

And read them yet again, before she realized what had caught Ethan's interest; Charlie had been searching for references to Jane. But it was the description of a demon's form that Mark had written as evidence that he "knew" the truth: crimson skin and black feathered wings.

"Drifter," she said softly. He'd listen for his name. "You think he's seen the nephilim?"

She heard him faintly over the distance and music. "Yes. Mostly, I'm wondering under what circumstances—and if he saw one here, or in D.C."

Trying not to imagine the Seattle community wiped out like D.C.'s had been, she simply said, "Oh," then took a deep breath. "I didn't mean to make you moan."

There was a sigh in his reply. "I know, Charlie. But we'd best wait to discuss it. Right now, I'm feeling like pushing—but I ain't so eager to see you running."

She wouldn't run. But even as she began to make the promise, she saw the careful non-interest of the vampires in the lounge.

"Everyone's listening anyway," she said, and watched several of them startle and blush.

Ethan's deep laugh carried better than his voice, and some of her shaking eased. "That was just mean."

Whatever it was, acknowledging the eavesdroppers so explicitly seemed to break the reticence of a couple who had only sat and watched for several days. They joined her at the bar, and though Charlie's anxiety never quieted, the familiar roll of conversation made the weight of his absence easier to bear.

She was in the office and the lounge was empty when Ethan finally returned, his coat dark with rain. The one-way mirror didn't give her an advantage; she couldn't read his expression, and her stomach was still heavy as she prepared the night deposit, her feet dragging when she finished and pushed through the door to the lounge.

And she had no idea what to say, so she only said, "You're wet."

Ethan's gaze was steady on hers. "It's coming down pretty hard, and I'm pretty fuzzed up," he said quietly. "Maybe we'd best hold off on the visiting tonight and go on home."

The heaviness lifted a little, and she didn't let guilt take its place. They wouldn't be out there looking for Jane—but neither she nor Ethan would be very useful going out like this, anyway.

She nodded and turned toward the employees' door again, listened to his footsteps as he followed her through the kitchen to the alley. Just inside the exit, she paused to slide on her coat. Ethan caught her hand, pulled her against him.

He circled her waist with his arm. His gaze lit on her hair, and he smiled slightly. His hat was damp and heavy; he covered her head with it, then slid his fingers along the flat brim, tipping it up so she could see him again. "You might need to hold on to it when we're in the air."

She flattened her hand over the crown, and he swept her into the familiar cradle of his arms.

It was pouring, raindrops beating against the pavement, splashing and dancing like thousands of tiny sparkling fountains. Each one clear to her vision, each one separate and part of a glorious whole.

Her arm tightened around his neck. "Ethan," she whispered, wonder swelling her throat. "Look at that."

"It gets better, Miss Charlie."

She glanced up as his wings unfolded and cut a swath through the silver curtain of falling rain. Her breath caught. For an instant, the diamond drops clung to his feathers before their downward sweep flung them in glittering arcs.

"Oh, my God," she laughed, and met his eyes. A line formed between his brows, and she smoothed it away with her thumb. "You couldn't see it," she said. "But you were amazing."

He stared at her before clearing his throat, but his voice still sounded rough to her ears. "I aim to please."

"You do." She laid her cheek against his shoulder and held on to the hat as he launched them into the air. It was always with speed, straight and high; but once he gained enough altitude, he usually slowed his flight. This time, he hovered.

"Now look at this," he said quietly. "It only lasts as long as it's raining this hard."

She turned in his arms, and suddenly couldn't breathe. The city was blanketed in shimmering silver, with colors shooting through like the facets of a jewel: the garnets and emeralds of traffic signals, the diamond-bright streetlights, the soft topaz from square-cut windows.

But even as she watched, the downpour eased. Ethan sighed and leveled out, heading east. His hair was plastered against his head; they were both soaked to the skin, her clothes uncomfortable and clinging, her coat sodden. She'd only worn it to keep off the rain, but now it was just an extra weight.

"Will you take this?" She tugged at her collar, and her fingertips met when the drenched fabric between them vanished. The lake slid by below them, dark and flat. She lifted her gaze to Ethan's face, but he was looking down.

She recognized his expression. Hunger, arousal. It pulled at her own, and his lids lowered as if he felt it.

No, she realized. He'd seen it beneath the thin, pale pink cotton of her wet shirt. Her nipples had tightened under that intense focus—and now she was thinking of his hands, his lips.

"Son of a bitch," he said on a soft growl. His mouth closed over her breast with shocking heat. She arched toward him, and her stomach dropped as they swooped.

He immediately straightened out their flight, but didn't halt the movement of his tongue, his teeth. Her fingers clenched on his shoulder, his hat. Her head fell back, the rain misting over her face, her eyes, and the lights at the shore wavering as they flew in closer. She could see the house, and she knew they wouldn't get inside, but it would be hard and slick in the rain, on the deck, where even now a light was flashing in quick bursts . . .

She blinked. "Ethan?" And then gasped as he went rigid, his teeth digging painfully into her flesh before he ripped his mouth away. She scented blood—but not hers. Feathers exploded in all directions.

The arch of his left wing collapsed.

The world tilted as they flipped, dropped through the air. Ethan was swearing, adjusting her position until she was full-length against him and he was holding her tight with his legs. She wrapped her arms around his waist so he could use both hands to fire his guns; each shot flared bright, the sound muffled by the silencer and the racing of his heart against her ear.

And his voice. "We're going to land hard, Charlie, and it ain't going to be water. Fast as you can, you get in the house and put up the spell."

A pistol appeared in her hand; after a week of training, it was comfortable. "Okay."

She didn't know if he heard it; he was twisting again, until she was on top of him, the ground rushing up at a terrible speed. Items were spilling onto it. Pillows, blankets, clothes. The mattress from her bed. Everything soft from his cache, she realized almost hysterically.

He met her eyes. "You hit mean and low."

She nodded and tried to hold his gaze but he forced her head down against his chest, turning her on her side and pulling her knees up, her gun clutched against her belly.

She didn't hear them land, only the tearing and breaking from deep inside him. Pain ripped through her in a sharp, blinding wave, digging into her shoulder, her hip, her right ankle. She couldn't turn her head for an endless moment, couldn't move, couldn't see.

Ethan wasn't moving, either. She whispered his name, and was surprised that her voice worked at all.

The urge to run filled her like the rising tumult of a fiddle.

She must have been already crying, because the sob that tore from her was only louder than the others. He'd projected that urgency; there was too much broken within him to speak. His heartbeat was too slow, sounded too wet.

"I'm going," she assured him, though she wasn't certain she could get up. But she'd promised, and now footsteps were approaching over wooden stairs, then over gravel.

She lifted her head, looked down at Ethan, and everything inside her stilled.

His wings had crumpled. Something was wrong with the shape of his head, and blood soaked the mattress beneath his body, as if he'd split open.

"Charlotte," a familiar voice said.

Sammael. And he was close.

Ethan couldn't defend himself like this.

Hit mean and low.

She crouched over Ethan's quiet form. Her right shoulder hurt too much; she palmed the gun in her left hand and slid the barrel under her bent right knee, hiding it between her thigh and upper calf. And she let her sobs tear free again, asking for Jane, she needed Jane, would do anything to see Jane.

"I truly hope so, Charlotte," Sammael said. From the corner of her vision, she saw his shoes appear on the ground beside the pile of fabric and the mattress. She turned her head and met his eyes when he sank to his heels. "Because I plan to ask a lot in return for sparing him."

She fired, felt the flash of heat through her pants at the same instant the small hole appeared in his black shirt. Another, and this time she heard a sizzle of the barrel against wet cotton.

Sammael fell back, his eyes wide with shock, flaring crimson.

Ethan's wings vanished under her feet. She didn't dare take her eyes from Sammael.

"Go, Charlie." Ethan's command was barely audible, and he wasn't getting up.

She only needed another shot, just to give him time to heal. One to the head. She adjusted her aim, watched the furrow plow through Sammael's cheek.

He slapped his hand against the wound, his eyes narrowing.

She leapt to the side, but her ankle didn't hold her weight. Sammael's wings formed and snapped around. Her leg went numb as the talons at the tips razed the length of her thigh. He'd knocked the gun from her an instant later, had his arm around her throat.

"Charlotte," Sammael crooned in her ear. "I'm disappointed."

She closed her eyes. Three bullets with hellhound venom. He'd be slower; she'd have a fighting chance.

Apparently, he realized it at the same time. A dagger gleamed in his hand, and he buried it deep in her thigh, cutting through an artery before bringing the blade to her throat.

She clenched her teeth against her scream. Sammael was weak, but the loss of blood was sapping her strength, too.

"*Very* disappointed," Sammael said.

Charlie wasn't listening. Ethan's head looked almost normal, and his hands were fisting.

The demon sighed. "I suppose this means a change of

plan." His voice lifted. "We'll see you in the house, McCabe. If I hear you call other Guardians for help, I'll take her head."

Sammael was still fast. He dragged her up the steps to the rear entrance, kicked open the door, and stopped in front of the security panel.

"Tell me the code, Charlotte."

She shook her head. "I don't know it," she rasped. And if it set off the alarm, it might alert someone at SI.

"Don't be a fool. Tell me." The dagger cut into her skin.

Sweat and blood itched a trail down the front of her throat. Ethan had written the numbers for her, but they were in her bag; she hadn't memorized them. "I don't know it."

Ethan's voice was stronger now—hopefully closer. "Give him the code, Charlie."

She stared at the panel. Why couldn't she remember it? Did Ethan really think she did? No . . .

No. He wouldn't.

A list of numbers ran from her mouth. Ten of them seemed like a good place to stop. Sammael held her in front of him, turning her toward the door as if to use her as a shield. The tip of his wing tapped out the series of numbers on the panel.

A whirring click sounded from the wall. Charlie's eyes widened; Sammael's grip loosened slightly as he turned his head.

The landscape painting beside the security panel shifted to the side. Barbed darts shot out, trailing wires. She heard them sink into Sammael's flesh.

But he was holding on to her, and she was wet.

Zapped. Sparks flew behind her eyes and from the wall. And she was bending, convulsing, the current blowing her from Sammael's grip, burning a white-hot hole through consciousness.

Darkness filled it.

CHAPTER 28

"Charlie."

Ethan's voice cut through the black—and came from in front of her. But someone was sitting behind her, his arms around her, his body warm . . .

Feverishly warm. And the pressure against her throat told her Sammael still had his knife. He must have reached her before Ethan returned to the house, but Ethan must have been the one to put the spell up. The silence from outside was deep.

She drew a breath, and wished she hadn't. The stink of singed meat hung in the air. Hopefully, that wasn't her.

"We burned the duck," she rasped, and blinked her eyes open. She was sitting on the floor between Sammael's legs. His knees were drawn up; his shoes were gone. She hadn't thought his bare feet would look so human.

Two yards away, Ethan crouched with his crossbow aimed at her head.

No—just slightly to the left of her head, on Sammael's face.

Neither he nor Sammael spoke.

Charlie said, "We didn't follow his directions. Jane was the one who suggested turning up the oven. I think she completely disorganized one of his utensil drawers, too."

Ethan's lips twitched a little. "That's a shame, Charlie. They sure ain't suited for one another, are they?"

"No. He should really let her go, let her come back to us." She had to swallow, bring up saliva to her mouth when Sammael's arm tightened. "What's going to happen now?"

"Well," Ethan said slowly, "we got ourselves a real interesting situation. Between the hellhound venom and the shock therapy, Sammael's feeling awful poorly—but not so much that he can't pull back on that knife."

And take off her head. Charlie stared at Ethan's face, forced herself not to shake. He didn't meet her gaze; it remained steady on Sammael.

"I guess if he killed me and tried to get away, he wouldn't get far."

"That's a fact, Miss Charlie. Even if I missed—and I won't—the security system would have alerted SI. And as Sammael insisted the spell go up as soon as I walked on in, he likely knows this. So it may be he's waiting to heal, thinking he'd have a better chance at full speed." Ethan's eyes narrowed. "But I figure it's something else."

What else could there be? Hoping to run and take Charlie with him as a hostage? Sammael must have wanted her for something; he'd been ready to make a bargain of some sort, even offering to spare Ethan . . .

"He wants you alive," she realized. Sammael could have forced her into almost anything just by overpowering her. He wouldn't have needed a bargain.

"I reckon. It's peculiar that a demon who suffered such a terrible insult in Eden would be willing to forgo the easy opportunity to kill me—particularly as he doesn't gain anything by letting me live. Unless I have something he wants. And as he was preparing to bargain with you, Charlie, it must have been something he thought you'd be able to get him."

Her fingers twisted together on her lap. "Breaking through the spell?"

"Word travels awful fast," Ethan said softly. "But I'm wondering why he wants through it so bad—though I can figure one reason right quick."

A strange hope lifted through her. "Jane?"

Ethan's left elbow lay easily on his thigh, and his hand had been relaxed and open beside his knee. A gun appeared in his grip, and he added its threat to the crossbow's.

Oh, Lord. If Ethan was only now using it, had he not been able to before? How badly was he still injured?

However badly, he didn't show any sign of it. His voice was low and speculative, with no suggestion of pain. "I reckon so, Charlie. Jane's locked herself away from him—or maybe one of his demons or vampires double-crossed him. Either way, he needs us to get to her. Which puts us in a mighty fine position."

She felt a slight movement behind her. The pressure at her throat increased, forcing her to tilt her head back against Sammael's shoulder. The skin around Ethan's mouth paled.

The demon's breath was hot against her neck. "My life for hers, Guardian. If I won't live to see Jane, then it hardly matters to me if Charlotte lives to free her."

Charlie closed her eyes, her heart pounding sickeningly in her chest. Sammael was going to force him into a bargain.

Ethan was silent for a long moment. "Your life for hers ain't good enough," he finally said. "You'd best sweeten the deal, demon."

"Not good enough?" Sammael stiffened, and disbelief added a sharp note to his reply. Then his laughter, hard and contemptuous. "No, perhaps her life isn't worth much. What else do you have in mind, McCabe?"

That couldn't have been what Ethan meant, but her nerves were stretching thin. Air whistled from her throat; Charlie made herself stop breathing, concentrated on the non-rise of her chest.

"That it ain't enough for you not to kill her *now*. I reckon that ought to be permanent."

Sammael didn't hesitate. "As long as it is equal: I will never kill her, if you never do the same to me."

"That's acceptable," Ethan said, and Charlie squeezed her eyes more tightly together. He'd agreed so easily, but it must be tearing at him to give up any chance to avenge his brother. "But it still ain't enough. You demons are right sneaky bastards, and your promise not to kill her wouldn't prevent you from asking any of your subordinates to carry out the same. So what we need here is a promise that, for as long as you live, you'll protect Charlie from all harm, and that you'll do everything within your power to prevent any hurt from coming to her. And, should an occasion arise where she needs something from you, you'll provide it to her."

"And you'll do the same for me?" Sammael's voice still held laughter, but triumph threaded through the tones now. "You'll protect me from other Guardians?"

"No," Ethan said flatly. "You ain't just asking for your life; this bargain is assuming we'll retrieve Jane. And what you're hoping to get is a lifetime of living with Jane, protecting and providing for her. So if we give you that, then it's equal that you're giving Charlie the same."

Charlie swallowed. "What if Jane dumps him?" she rasped.

Sammael hissed in her ear; the sting of his blade was followed by the cool slide of blood down the front of her throat. She stopped breathing again.

"Bargain or not, that's the last hurting you'll ever get in on her." Ethan's statement was delivered softly, but with an edge as sharp and dangerous as the blade. Gooseflesh rose over her skin. "And if Jane leaves you, that'll be of her free will—but you'll always be bound to protect Charlie from any threat, except for those threats that are from humans. In that way, human free will is honored on both sides of the bargain, and you won't be required to break the Rules."

Sammael's hand lay still and burning against her neck for what seemed an endless time. Charlie opened her eyes, stared up at the beams striping the ceiling. The silence was filled by the quick pounding of Sammael's heart, and she wondered if it was anger or fear or hope that sent it racing. What did a demon feel at such a time?

But there was no evidence of emotion in Sammael's reply. "It is done, then."

Charlie lowered her chin, met Ethan's gaze. His response was rough, his eyes glowing amber. "It is done."

No, she wanted to say. But it couldn't be undone. Ethan had bound himself to this demon . . . for her.

But goddamn if she wouldn't give just a little back to him. Sammael's hand fell away from her throat. Charlie braced her feet, snapped her head back. She heard the crunch, then added an elbow to his stomach before flipping upright.

Sammael scooted away from the kick that would have

liquefied whatever a demon carried between his legs. He stood, his eyes crimson, and moved like a shadow to the French doors.

Ethan vanished his gun, but kept the crossbow leveled on Sammael, and his grin was wide. "Ain't it just fine that you'll be having to watch yourself around Charlie?"

Sammael's lips curled mockingly, but he didn't insult her as she'd expected. "As you will with me, Guardian, once Jane is free." He looked out the window. "How many of them are outside?"

"I reckon three or four," Ethan said.

Sammael's eyes narrowed. "We won't go for Jane tonight. She's not in danger, and I've no intention of endangering myself, either. So I'll come to you when you do not have so many others around who might kill me as soon as I've given you the location."

Ethan nodded once. "You do that." His finger flexed; an instant later, the bolt embedded in the door frame near Sammael's head, the feathers quivering.

Noise rushed in from outside; the arrow had destroyed one of the symbols.

Ethan raised his voice, called out, "The demon's fleeing—you all just let him fly." His touch was light against Charlie's waist. "You stay here while I walk him out."

She did, trembling as she watched Ethan follow Sammael onto the deck. Behind the demon's back, he signed something with his free hand, and a psychic wave of dismay sounded faintly from the Guardians outside.

He must have told them of the bargain.

Ethan remained on the deck, talking silently with the other Guardians until Sammael was nothing but a speck against the ink-dark sky.

His face was taut and unreadable when he returned, scratching new symbols beside the door, and her stomach rolled as she searched for anything to say. *Thank you* and *I'm sorry* and *I love you* were all about what she was feeling, and whatever came from her should be only for him.

She clasped her hands together in front of her breastbone, so tight the ache in her fingers matched the one in her chest and throat. Quiet descended around the house. He turned to her, his crossbow hanging from his hand by his thigh.

"Ethan." She wished she had something better than "Are you all right?"

His eyes closed, and his knuckles whitened before he abruptly flung the crossbow across the room. Charlie flinched, and was left hunched in anticipation of the crash that never came.

He'd vanished the weapon. Angry enough that it showed, but too controlled to let it damage anything.

And she'd seen him in many moods now, but never like this. What would he need from her? He'd been wound up even before they'd been attacked. Would he want her to talk to or touch him? To leave him alone?

Her legs felt soft with her uncertainty, but her step was firm. Until Ethan told her to go, she'd stay.

She didn't stop until her palms met the solid wall of his chest. It rose and fell heavily beneath her hands, and she searched his downturned face for any sign of rejection or withdrawal.

Lifting her fingers, she traced his jaw, so like iron. Her breath caught when he opened his eyes, caught her hand.

His voice was low, with a gravelly undertone as if his throat had been scraped raw. "Don't tiptoe, Charlie."

So she'd already fucked this up. She dug within herself for a smile, but knew it came out weak. "I just didn't want to do anything wrong, or make this worse for you." Her tone was supposed to be light, but seemed frightened to her ears. She sought to modulate it as she said, "After all, if you wanted to, you could get rid of me now—and forcing Sammael to provide me with blood would be one hell of a punishment for him."

The scar over his lip paled, and she told herself to stop talking, nothing was coming out as she meant it to. That hadn't been amusing, but instead sounded so needy, practically asking for confirmation that he wouldn't use the terms of the bargain as a way out of his promise.

Ethan would never do that; she'd have wagered her own soul on it.

His fingers slid into her hair and clenched. "Don't look away from me, Charlie," he said quietly, and that dangerous edge was there again.

She steadily held his gaze. "I won't."

"All right." His face and his grip didn't soften. "Now

suppose you tell me what the hell is going on in your head, and what you are meaning to say to me."

Her hands fell to his chest again, and she felt the thud of his heart beneath her palm. Racing, though his voice was flat, and she couldn't read the emotion at the source of it any more than she had Sammael's.

Her throat thickened. "I'm just trying to figure out what *you* need right now."

A shudder tore through him. His gaze lifted from her face, and he stared over her head for a long moment.

"My needs are real simple, Charlie," he finally said, and swept her up against his chest.

No, they weren't. If they were simple, he'd kiss her as he walked toward the stairs, rather than approaching them with the measured tread of a man heading into a fight he feared he might lose.

Charlie smoothed her fingers over his collar; if Ethan thought she would put up any resistance, surely the press of her lips against his throat, the lay of her head against his shoulder would reassure him.

As soon as he set her on her feet beside the bed, he gripped the hem of her shirt, drew it over her head. He'd never removed her clothes with his hands before; he'd always vanished them. Not because he was in a rush, but so he wouldn't ruin them.

But there was no saving these. Even if her blood hadn't stained them, her pant leg was torn the length of her thigh, her shirt singed at the collar.

Swelling emotion squeezed at her heart as he slid the pants over her hips and followed their fall with his palms, lowering himself and examining the unmarked skin above her knee. She touched his hair and he rose, but he only came part of the way, tipping her chin back to expose her throat. His thumb traced a line above the scar; the cut Sammael had made must have still shown faintly pink.

"Ethan." The muscles in his shoulders were steel beneath her hands. "You were hurt worse than I was. And I'm all right."

Another shudder wracked his large frame. "You need blood," he said hoarsely.

Yes. She'd lost too much, and the hunger had been

smoldering deep. She'd been inhaling as little as possible and always through her mouth, so the bloodlust wouldn't flare with the odor, but his words were a breath across tinder.

"*My* blood." He spoke fiercely against her neck, and for a wild second Charlie thought he would bite her, take whatever it was he needed in the most basic way.

"Yours," she whispered, and stiffened in surprise when his clothing vanished. He always waited until the last moment to remove them, to feel his skin against hers.

And now his body burned the length of her, but she had no time to revel in the sensation: he was lifting her to his neck, where a crimson stream already flowed. *What on earth had he—?*

His hand cupped the back of her head and guided her with relentless strength to his throat. At the first taste, she was lost, wrapping her arms around his shoulders and drinking deep.

The bloodlust whipped through her. His forearm across her lower back held her trapped, and she rubbed herself against his stomach, seeking release. It didn't come. Dimly, she realized that she was clinging to him, her legs around his waist, and he wasn't moving toward the bed but simply standing as she fed. Each hard pull from his veins made him shake; she wanted him overcome and senseless and as helpless to his need as she was to hers.

But Ethan weathered the storm of her bloodlust as solidly as a mountain, and was still upright when it broke.

Charlie lifted her head and closed her eyes, thirst slaked but her body an inferno. She hadn't come; now she didn't know if she wanted to. Didn't know if she wanted to be alone in this.

And when he carried her to the bed, she was still separate. Those were not her hands braced in the middle of the mattress, her knees sinking deep. Not her back arching in anticipation of his fingers and mouth when Ethan kneeled behind her.

But it was her cry of surprise when he buried his cock inside her with a single, hard stroke. She snapped into herself, panting his name, her hands fisting.

Never before had he come into her without readying his way. Even when they'd been frantic with desire, even though she'd begged and assured him he didn't need to give her so much attention—he'd always taken his time.

Now he was just taking *her*.

But there was nothing frantic about it. Slowly, ever so slowly, he withdrew and slid back in. An erotic wave undulated through her, concentrated in her slick inner flesh, where sensation began and ended. Charlie muffled her tortured moan, biting folds of white cotton.

Fire slipped over her skin as his palms traveled up the length of her body, journeyed down her arms. His hands covered hers, his chest hot against her back. He pushed forward.

Colors danced in front of her eyes, settled into the swirling lightning-bright rapture of his possession. He was touching every possible inch of her skin. *Never* before. They'd been like this so many times, but always it was the thrusting of his hips, raw and powerful. His hands pinning hers or sweeping her to new heights. But the rest of him he'd held away, as if afraid with too much contact he'd lose control.

And she'd gloried in everything he'd given—but this was heaven. He stroked into her with the whole of his body, his chest rough over the slickness of her back. His mouth and his breath heated a path from her neck to her temple with each deliberate thrust.

Taking, touching, silent. All giving the appearance of control.

But he'd lost it.

He'd lost it. The realization tore through her, her nerves screaming with excitement. She couldn't keep still, couldn't be quiet. His name spilled from her, rising and falling.

He released her hand; she reached back, cupped the nape of his neck. She tried to twist, searching for his lips. His fingers found her nipple instead, taut and aching.

And he continued sliding into her, thick and hard, ceaselessly.

Mindless with the ecstasy of it, she let her head fall forward and looked down the length of her body. Watched his big hand flatten over her belly. She bowed her back, angling her hips to see him slowly sink into her, to see his fingers begin their virtuoso play over her clitoris.

His name locked in her throat. Her arms trembled. She couldn't withstand this. Her eyes closed, and she heard the wetness of her body, the pounding of Ethan's heart. Her labored breathing. Tension held her tight, though Ethan was warming and loosening everything inside her.

But she didn't want to break apart yet. Not without his blood. He always wanted her to use his; it was the only thing he asked for himself.

"Ethan." It was barely a whisper. "*Let me.*"

His voice was rough, his lips against her ear. "Tell me what you need, Charlie."

He held himself there, as if waiting for her answer; she couldn't give him one. He'd stopped his long, slow movements, but ground against her, tiny circular digs that left her gasping with small, sobbing breaths. He caught her engorged clit between two fingers, began sliding them around it, mimicking the motion his cock wasn't performing.

She couldn't scream. Charlie reared back and Ethan pulled her upright, her nails cutting into his nape, her knees spread wide on the mattress, her back arched in front of him. It was impossible to control her hips, and they swung in tiny erratic jerks from side to side when his hand prevented her from moving them forward.

"Tell me, Charlie."

How could she think? What did she want? "You," she gasped. "I need you."

"You've fed with my blood." He cupped her jaw, held her seeking mouth away from his. "You can come with your own. Why do you need me?"

It was welling, but she held it in. Her eyes filled. His control was gone—yet it was still about her needs, not his. *Don't make me ask you to love me.*

His thumb brushed over her cheekbone. His body hardened into stone behind her. "Damn you, Charlie."

His mouth covered hers an instant later. Her lips opened, and he pushed in—but not to kiss. His tongue stabbed her fangs. The sound of him overwhelmed her senses; his fingers stroked furiously as he withdrew and slammed himself into her.

Oh, God. Nothing had ever been like this. Charlie sucked

desperately at his tongue. Ethan's need was there, like a deep, grating cry; his arousal, a separate harsh note.

Her body shook, tightened around his, but she fought to keep her mind from falling into that sweet numbing bliss, to ride through the crash of her orgasm. He'd pushed that onto her, too, taken her choice—another loss of control he'd never allowed himself before. What did he want so badly? What could she give him?

Why do you need me?

She cried out into his mouth. So slow. Always so slow. That question wasn't about her need, but his. And she could only hope that the answer he was seeking was the one she had to give.

She dragged her lips away to the sound of his despairing groan.

It swelled up and burst through. "I love you," she rasped, but it wasn't enough, she'd held it in too long, and she chanted it to the slowing tempo of his body, projected it, throwing it wide. His hold on her slackened.

His voice was sharp with disbelief. "Charlie?"

She couldn't stop. "Love you." He wasn't moving; she did, turning and pushing him over, taking him inside her again. "Love you." She kissed his chest, his neck. "Love you." She had to lift herself off of him to reach his mouth. Her tongue touched his, softly. He moaned against her lips before she slid back down.

She closed her eyes against the exquisite heat and pressure, her flesh so sensitive she thought she might explode, even without blood. Felt all of her might explode with the sweeping joy and release of simply telling him. "Love you," she said again.

And when she looked at him, her heart skipped its beat; her breath lost its rhythm. His gaze was on her, but his eyes were glazed and unfocused. And his need was there for her to see in the tight angle of his jaw, set yet tilted to expose his throat. In the hard curve of his mouth, taut but open for her kiss. In the way he strained toward her and held himself back, all at once.

Ethan was utterly, completely naked.

And so amazing. She rocked forward, watched him clench

and lift toward her. Hiding so much, and she hadn't even known he'd been concealing it.

Did he realize he was revealing it now? Or was he completely lost to this? Heat surrounded her fingers as he pulled them into his mouth and began sucking; a groan rumbled from him as she rippled her inner muscles.

She was heading there, too. His heart thundered under her palm when she braced herself, took him hard and fast, afraid a controlled pace would give him a chance to hide again. Her gaze never left his face, not until he arched up beneath her, pulling her down to his neck. Until his breath caught on a guttural moan.

She lay against him as he settled back to the bed, her hands smoothing his heated skin. Aftershocks trembled through him, and she absorbed each one with her mouth, her flesh.

And when he quieted, she remained still, unwilling to disrupt the silence that fell. She didn't know if it was cowardly; if so, Ethan proved himself braver than she was.

He lifted the sweaty tangle of her hair from her cheek, then rolled her beneath him. His brows were drawn, his expression closed once again; but she thought some of his need lurked in the movement of his gaze over her face, in the softness at the corners of his mouth.

In his voice, still rough and seeking. "I don't—" He swallowed, glancing away from her for an instant before trying again. "I don't have words, Charlie. I wasn't expecting that you'd give me so much."

No words, but he wasn't projecting anything, either. And she'd told herself not to expect a declaration in return, but she must have been hoping for one. It was a struggle not to let her disappointment and anxiety show.

Her smile felt lopsided. "What were you expecting?"

"Maybe something about my irresistible scars, or my manly form, or how tasty I am." He touched her lips, and her smile leveled beneath his hand. His matched hers, before it fell away and he buried his face in her hair. "God Almighty, Charlie. I've never been so scared as lying there and hearing Sammael coming toward you."

The words were ragged, and she wound her arms tight around his neck. Forcing away the memory of his broken body wasn't as easy. "It was close, but we're all right," she said fiercely. "And I'll slay him for you. Jane can just get over it."

She heard him draw in a deep breath through his nose; the humor in his tone sounded forced. "I suppose that nothing says I can't shoot him full of venom every month and then use my fists. Maybe that'd be more satisfying than just killing him once."

Oh, Ethan. Her chest ached. Of course he knew it wouldn't be; but did he know his simmering frustration had slipped through his shields? She wanted to pull him in even tighter.

After a second's hesitation, she did. "I'll still hold him down."

Ethan's grin was a deep curve when he raised his head. "That'd be just fine. We'll make good partners, Miss Charlie." His grin faded, and the intensity of his gaze sharpened. "And I ain't just saying that for fun, now that we're relaxed and easy. We fit real well, you and me. Even though I'm like to go crazy at times trying to figure you out—but there's no one I'd rather go crazy over."

Warmth stole through her. "It's not difficult, Ethan." His focus shifted to her teeth when her smile widened. "Just imagine me needy, and then imagine me afraid of it."

"If it were that simple, I'd have had you figured months ago." His thumb brushed the tip of her left fang, and she shivered. "And if I'd have known that getting busted up and striking bargains would send you toppling over in love with me, I might have broken myself up a bit earlier than this."

"Oh, Jesus. That wouldn't have been a good plan—and, anyway, I'm not *that* slow," she said, trying to control her breathing as he cupped her breast. "I've loved you for a while now. I just didn't know if you'd want it."

Ethan paused. "How's that?"

She couldn't think of anything beyond his fingers against her nipple. "Until tonight, I didn't know you needed anything from me so much that you'd lose control and take it."

He paled, and she caught his face between her hands. "That came out wrong," she said. "I loved every second of it. Loved that you used me to get what you needed. I was with you the whole way; it just took me a while to realize what you were looking for. And even then, I was hoping it really was something you wanted, not a burden."

"It ain't." His voice was thick. "I want it, Miss Charlie. And you already know I'll provide you anything you need, give you everything you want."

She didn't let her gaze move from his. Anything above a whisper was impossible, and she pulled his face to hers, said against his lips, "I know."

CHAPTER 29

Ethan gave up trying to drift half an hour after sunrise. Charlie lay unmoving in his arms, her heart barely beating. He'd hoped that their hours together in bed would prevent the terror of the previous night from touching her dreams—and judging by the soft yearning in her psychic scent, the faint arousal, she'd escaped it.

But he thought the yearning might tear him apart faster than terror would. Even the fierce pleasure of having her love didn't cut the agony that she was still needing something—and that she was still not asking him for it.

With a sigh, he forced himself out of bed, scrubbed his hands over his face and hair. He wasn't overly fuzzy; having his brain smashed had gotten rid of most of it. Then he'd steeled himself against his rage and fear, focusing on Sammael, and not much else had gotten in.

Leastwise, not until Charlie had said something about letting Sammael provide her blood.

He hadn't done right by her. He'd known she'd been trying to put him at ease, but the thought had provoked such a cold dread, he hadn't seen much beyond making certain she admitted her need for *him*.

And she hadn't spooked, though he'd pushed her awful hard. Harder than he ought to have. He couldn't regret it, not when it had drawn such a sweet declaration from her—but he also couldn't shake the feeling that as far as she'd gone, he'd somehow ended up in the same place he'd started, and now he was flying to catch up.

He sure as hell wished he knew what she needed—and if pushing again would just shove her farther away.

Dressing took longer than normal; there was plenty of blood to vanish into his cache, all of it his. Forming his wings so as they could heal was going to hurt like a son of a bitch.

But he did, and then groaned his way downstairs. No one was in the house to hear him, and when he saw Jake waiting on the deck outside, he was tempted to just turn around and lay next to Charlie until the novice went away.

He sucked up his groans and lowered the shield instead. "Her eyes are more hazel-like," he drawled. "Her teeth ain't so straight, and her bosom's not inflated like one of your video girls. She wouldn't ever wear a skirt that short. You forgot the scar on her throat, and her natural hair color is darkish brown."

Jake tore his wide-eyed gaze from Ethan's wings, opened his mouth.

Ethan shook his head, silently cursing Lilith and Castleford, Mark Brandt, the nephilim, Sammael, and the damn sun. Charlie would like to have enjoyed taking a few hits at Jake right then. "Before you say some fool thing that'll have me setting those teeth crooked for you, I'm talking about the hair at her scalp."

A wry smile curved Jake's pretty lips. The novice's expressions were his own; there was no mistaking him for Charlie if someone knew her well. Mark Brandt didn't, so Ethan figured that'd be all right. Sending Jake in wasn't altogether a bad plan, just mostly one.

"I think this is the first time I've seen you pissy, Drifter."

"I ain't pissy," Ethan bit out. "Just a mite disturbed."

Jake's gaze rose to his wings again. "That looks like it hurts."

"Shucks, no." Ethan turned away. His left wingtip dragged

on the floor, and the arch still showed raw flesh; his right had been mangled pretty bad when he'd landed on it, and bent a couple of ways that it shouldn't be bending. "This ain't nothing but an itty bitty scratch. Hurting is what'll happen to you if you decide to take a look-see around that body while you're in this house."

"I wouldn't."

Ethan looked at him.

". . . anywhere that you can hear me." Jake's grin showed fangs.

"You ought to get rid of those, too," Ethan said. "You ain't a vampire tonight. You'll play her a little scared—knowing about us, but not being one of us."

Jake's fangs shortened into human teeth. "What if he knows she's been turned?"

"Even if he's heard rumors, Brandt hasn't seen her close up. Maybe it'll unsettle him a bit, make him realize he doesn't know as much as he thinks." And if Brandt hadn't heard—if he thought that Charlie was still human—then there wouldn't be any fangs to frighten him. It wouldn't do for the boy to bolt before he'd talked.

Ethan carefully maneuvered through the door to the tech room. Hopefully Savi would have come up with something more on the Brandts or Legion; his instincts were still saying he was missing something big, and he sure didn't like going in without finding what it was. With luck, they'd get it from young Brandt.

"Should I let him mention the demons first?"

"Yes." Ethan glanced over at Jake, wished he hadn't yet again. "Charlie ain't the type to flutter her lashes like that. You plan on being in that form all day?"

Jake's eyes widened, all innocent-like. "It's good practice for later."

Ethan couldn't rightly argue with that, but he wasn't going to stay around and watch. "Then you'd best practice being *her*. You go online, check if we've got anything from SI. I'll be scoping out that restaurant, seeing where our best vantage point is. Most likely, you'll have to listen for Charlie to give you answers to personal questions."

"You're leaving with your wings like that?"

"I reckon I'll swim."

"I must look hot in this skirt."

Ethan shook his head and kept on walking. The worst part of this whole plan, he reckoned, was that Jake wore a shape Ethan just didn't feel comfortable hitting.

❧

Mark had remembered that she liked sushi; he'd chosen a small, trendy restaurant in Madison Park.

Sitting on the roof of the real estate office across the street, Charlie watched Jake contain his grimace as he looked over the menu, and tried to decide if the food or the prices had produced that expression—then decided she didn't want to think about it too much. The sight of someone else filling out her skin held the same surreal disbelief as watching a home video. *That's how I move, how I sound?*

Jake looked up as Mark spoke to him, and coyly pushed his hair back behind his ear. Good Lord. Did she do that as much as Jake apparently thought she did?

Judging by Ethan's deep sigh, probably not. She glanced over at his face; his focus on the scene before them was intent, but she read impatience there, too. From the little Charlie could hear and the questions Ethan had relayed to her, Mark hadn't moved beyond small talk, asking about her job and classes.

And from the little of Mark's psyche that she could sense, he hadn't been surprised when Jake had smiled the first time.

Ethan squinted his eyes and turned his head as a diesel truck rolled by, trying to hear over the rumbling engine. His gaze met hers for a moment, softened.

She couldn't suppress her smile, or the heavy thump of her heart. Jesus. In the middle of a stakeout—or whatever this was—and one look had her chest swelling, leaving her speechless with love and wonder.

She'd woken just after sunset, and Ethan's expression had been soft then, too—and it had been the first time she'd seen him drifting. He'd lain motionless except for the rapid movement of his eyes behind his lids, and when they'd slowed, when each of his breaths hadn't been so deep and even, she'd slipped down his body to find the only other soft part of him.

She hadn't had many opportunities to love him with her mouth, and she'd watched his face, her nails digging into his hips, silently asking his straining form to remain still beneath her tongue—until her burgeoning excitement and an accidental scrape of her fangs had stolen her control. But she'd seen what she'd been looking for: his need, the tension between holding back and reaching out.

Had it always been there, and she was just now recognizing it? Perhaps feeding had prevented her from witnessing such a vulnerable moment; once the bloodlust gripped her, she rarely saw Ethan's face. Or maybe he'd been hiding it, and like her, simply couldn't hold it in anymore.

Whatever the answer, she thought it must be love, or a step away from it—and desperately hoped she wasn't just projecting her need onto him, mistaking the desire and affection she knew he felt for something more.

Everything he did seemed to say it *was* much more, but she wished she could trust herself, and be certain of it.

With a sigh, Charlie focused on the scene in front of her again, and wanted to whack her head against the rooftop when Ethan told her Mark and Jake had begun discussing the menu. She'd already briefed Jake on her preferences; there was nothing to do but sit and watch them chat.

This was the most boring dinner date she'd ever had. Ethan must have been thinking the same; he slid a deck of cards her way, and caught each of her attempts to cheat without ever appearing to glance away from the restaurant.

After he'd won her small pile of chips, Ethan finally said, "All right, Jake—give him a little nudge. Let's mention Jane and Legion. Play it modest; just say what you've been doing doesn't compare to the goings-on in Washington, or Jane's research."

Jake did, and Charlie practiced feeling out Mark's psychic response. A stuttering note of uncertainty combined with the sweet tones of affection, and Mark hesitated before he replied.

Poor guy. He really had it bad for her sister.

But Ethan was shaking his head, his lips tight. "He's too damn good at blocking," he muttered.

A vibration in her sweatshirt pocket kept her from answering him. She glanced at the incoming number, whispered, "Old Matthew," and scrambled across the roof so her voice wouldn't interfere with Ethan's hearing.

It was her first night off since she'd reorganized the office;

Old Matthew was likely just wondering where she'd put one of the files.

But a few moments later, fear was crawling in her belly. Ethan was on his feet before she'd returned to his side.

"He says Cora and Angie are in his office, asking for you," Charlie said, her eyes wide. "The nephil murdered Manny."

Ethan's lips tightened, and he half-turned. "We've got trouble, Jake. You all right to keep this up?"

Jake gave no indication that he'd heard except for the movement of his hand against the table, signing his assent.

Ethan looked back at Charlie. "Tell Cole we'll be there directly."

She'd barely relayed the message when Ethan lifted her, ran to the rear of the building, and jumped into the air.

❧

As leaky as Angie and Cora were, Ethan would have thought they'd just seen Manny killed—but it had happened almost a week previously.

Hearing that they'd holed up all that time had him staring down at his boots, containing his frustration. Theirs was the only sighting of the nephil since Ethan's return to Seattle, and the trail would be damn cold by now.

And he sure as hell couldn't summon much grief for Manny, no matter how many tears Angie and Cora were shedding.

He looked up as Charlie offered the ladies a box of tissues she'd retrieved from the office's supply cabinet. Her eyes met his before she asked softly, "Angie, you're sure he had black *feathered* wings? Not just black, like a bat's?"

Angie wiped her eyes, nodding. "We were over at the Seattle Center, out in front of that ugly-ass museum, waiting for Manny to come pick us up. And it was crouching up on the monorail, and the feathers were resting against the track. I saw them, told Cora we had to run."

"Because Drifter warned us about it," Cora said, blowing her nose—though Ethan hadn't ever known of a vampire getting leaky there.

Charlie slanted a glance at him, but if she was amused by their antics or disgusted, he couldn't read it in her face.

Angie lowered her tissue, and her eyes hardened. "Then Manny drove up, but we didn't think we'd make it to the car."

"It was right behind us," Cora put in. She'd dropped the pretense, too. "And Manny could have driven away, but he got out."

Angie cupped her hands together, like she was holding a weapon. "And he had that sword he'd used when he was enforcing—"

Cora muttered, "Goddamn Katya and Vladimir."

"—and he ran past us, and that demon just caught him up. Started cutting," Angie said. This time Ethan thought the moisture shining in her eyes was real. "We heard him scream once, but then we got in the trunk."

"Manny always said it was big enough for both of us to hide in. So we put up the spell for as long as we could stand being cooped up in there, because we didn't know if it would be waiting for us."

"He wasn't," Angie said with a shrug and a bit of embarrassment. "We'd been towed sometime during the week. Scared the shit out of the lot attendant, too, when we kicked open the trunk."

"Then we went back to the museum, where we saw Manny last." Cora's full lips flattened and paled. "And we finally found his clothes, stuck way back on top of the monorail station. I guess the ash must have washed away in the rain. There were streaks, but nothing else."

"He deserved it," Angie said as she wiped her eyes again.

Charlie frowned, and her brows drew together. "If he deserved it, why were you faking it before, and why is it real now?"

Angie and Cora exchanged a glance before Cora said, "He was a prick, but he saved our asses. It doesn't hurt anything if the others remember that we were crying when we came in; it gives something back to Manny." She gestured toward the one-way and the vampires in the lounge. The shield was up, so they wouldn't be hearing anything now.

Angie added, "And we talked a lot in that trunk—about making some changes, getting a new line of work. We'd heard Drifter was opening up a theater, and would be hiring vampires."

The waterworks had been an audition? Charlie appeared too confounded by their response to tell them the Heritage would be owned by Colin and Savi, and Ethan just studied his boots again.

"And we wanted to get Drifter here as fast as possible, so we laid it on thick—but your boss was so sweet, trying to help us out, we didn't stop," Cora said.

"Now *that's* a man," Angie said, and looked through the one-way again as if she'd like to eat Old Matthew up.

Though Charlie's eyes widened, Ethan relaxed a little. Taken all together, the foolishness they were spouting was finally starting to make sense. "You're aiming to take Manny's place."

"Yes," they said in unison. Angie added, "And we want your approval."

Ethan shook his head. "That ain't my decision—it's for your community to determine."

Cora smiled as she said, "Do you know what we've heard from every vampire since coming out of that trunk? 'Drifter and Charlie, Drifter and Charlie.' Your support will go a long way for us."

The truth was, Ethan could easily see Cora and Angie heading the community, but he sure in blazes wasn't going to get pulled into a discussion of vampire politicking now. "You ladies stay in Vladimir and Katya's house, keep your fingers in everyone's business like they've always been, get some legitimate income, and you'll be in a fine position to take over. You won't be needing me." He held out his hand for Charlie's; a moment after her cool fingers clasped on his, another thought occurred to him, and he pinned a stare on Cora. "I sure hope you ain't figuring to use me as an enforcer."

"No," Angie said, and coolly examined one of her long red fingernails. "I can handle that part of it."

"Unlike Katya and Vladimir, we'll own our responsibilities." Cora's smile became thin and sharp. "And we definitely won't be killing any humans. Now, didn't *that* come back to bite them on the ass?" Cora let out a hard laugh.

Ethan paused at the door; Charlie's grip tightened. He met her gaze, saw the same unease that flashed through him, then turned back to Cora. "How's that?"

Eyes narrowing, Angie glanced between them. "Manny told you about how Vladimir and Katya died."

"That he did—and that it was the same method the nephil used. How's that relate to them killing humans?"

Cora leaned forward. "Manny put up the spell just after

you mentioned how the nephil killed the rogue in that alley. And Manny told *us* that he told you about the guy who did it—are you saying he didn't tell you?"

"He didn't," Ethan said. Reining in his impatience wasn't easy. "How about you tell us now?"

With a laugh, Angie said, "The weasel chickened out. Probably thought you'd slay him for his part in it."

That was just about enough of that. "How about you tell us what goddamn part you're speaking of?"

Cora lifted her brows. "Do you have time for a long story?"

At his side, Charlie shook her head. "No. Give us the condensed version."

"Okay." Cora hooked a strand of black hair back from her forehead. "You know what's-his-face, the senator, was trying to get Vladimir and Katya to go public about six months ago?"

"That we do," Ethan said. Just the mention of Brandt was giving him a bad feeling.

"Well, he paid Vladimir as compensation for coming out and for submitting to whatever testing needed to be done to prove vampires existed."

Charlie said slowly, "We've seen something like a payment from the Brandts."

"It was supposed to be the first payment of many," Angie said. "Except once Manny told us what Vladimir and Katya were planning, Cora and I went and talked some sense into them. Coming out wouldn't do anyone any good—human or not."

"That's a fact," Ethan agreed. "So I take it Vladimir and Katya tried to pull out—and weren't going to return the money. From what little I've seen of the senator, I reckon he didn't take kindly to that, threatening to expose them anyway."

And if Vladimir and Katya had killed someone, obviously whomever Brandt had sent to collect them hadn't been properly warned of what he was facing.

"Yes. Broke his neck, and then they asked Manny to dump him—"

"Him?" Charlie was blinking, and Ethan thought he probably looked as confused as she was. "They killed Senator Brandt when he threatened them? But—"

"Yes. And no." Cora grimaced, lifted her shoulders. "Manny said that he'd just driven the body to the highway when he heard thumping in the trunk. The old guy was still alive, even though Manny said he could have sworn he was dead. So he dropped him on the side of the road, still wrapped up in sheets, and took off."

Christ Jesus. *A dead man walking.* And the senator wasn't a vampire—though apparently he'd developed one hell of a grudge against their kind.

"Maybe we should go talk to Mark," Charlie said quietly. Her face was telling him she'd just come to the same conclusion he had.

He nodded. No more pussyfooting around.

CHAPTER 30

Ethan began cursing as they flew over Madison Park. Charlie turned in his arms. Far below them, she made out the passing cars, the pedestrians . . . and Mark and Jake, leaving the restaurant.

The trip to Cole's had only taken twenty-five minutes; they couldn't have finished dinner in that time.

"You'd best have a good reason for this, novice," Ethan said.

A few seconds later, Jake pretended to play with his hair, and replied with a gesture over his head. Ethan drew in a sharp breath.

"Well, I'll be damned," he said quietly, and met Charlie's eyes. "He's got Jane."

"*Mark* does?" Startled, Charlie glanced down at the two as Mark opened the passenger door of his car, and Jake slid in.

"Yes." Ethan raised his voice. "All right, Jake—we'll follow you. Be certain you don't do anything to obstruct his free will; if he tries to keep us from taking Jane, Charlie can handle him." He hesitated before adding, "And if you see his father, you run. We've got reason to think the nephil has possessed him."

Charlie watched the car pull away from the curb, then looked back up at Ethan. "This will change things."

Ethan hadn't wanted her anywhere near the nephil; they'd intended to speak with Mark here, then Jake would return with Charlie to the lake house and Ethan would locate the senator. But if Jane was locked behind the spell, Charlie needed to be there.

"Not all that much," Ethan said. "If the senator's at home, you ain't going in. We'll get Jane after I slay him."

Charlie hesitated for just an instant, but it needed to be asked. "Are you going to do it when he's in his human form?"

"I'd prefer it."

"Can you be sure, though? What if Manny was mistaken? What if the senator's neck wasn't really broken, and he was never dead? And there are all those stories about people doing impossible things, coming back to life . . ." She trailed off as she realized, "Oh. Those are you. *Us.*"

Guardians, vampires, and demons, performing miraculous feats.

"Yes." His chuckle was warm, and his arms tightened briefly. "All right, Charlie. It looks as if Brandt is heading on home, and we're flying slow enough you should be able to use the phone. I need you to tell Selah to be ready, and then let Lilith know she's going to have a senator's death to cover up."

His cell appeared in her hand, and she began scrolling through the address book. "How do you think she'll do it?"

"Most likely, a Guardian will take his form for a week or two, then he'll have a heart attack in public or some such thing."

"That's scary," she said softly. "That the truth can be twisted so easily."

"It's necessary."

"I'm not arguing that." She smiled a little, shook her head. "But it's still scary. I'm glad you're the good guys."

"I don't rightly know about that. Mostly, we've just got better intentions than the demons."

Her eyes narrowed. "You'll never convince me you aren't a hero, Drifter."

"Well, hell," he said, and a hint of color appeared on his cheeks. "Then I sure hope I never do anything to disabuse you of that notion."

Satisfied, she placed the two calls. By the time she'd finished the second, they were almost across the lake, headed
toward Bellevue.

Ethan flew lower, said loudly, "Jake, you have any idea
whether his father's at home?"

Jake projected a carefree, relieved note.

"All right, then. It may be that Sammael's lurking about, so
watch your back and stick close to Brandt. Charlie and I will
fly on ahead, see if we can get Jane out before you arrive."

❧

The Brandt property was practically a mini-estate. A tall, dec-
orative fence surrounded extensive landscaping and was lined
with trees and shrubs for privacy. The residence had been built
in a similar style to the house on the lake, but from the glimpses
of the interior that Charlie caught as they circled above, it
looked as if the Brandts had taken "lodge" much deeper to
heart. The furniture was heavy and masculine, the colors dark.
She wouldn't have been surprised to find animal heads hanging
from a wall.

The house was eerily silent.

"The shield's up. Someone's got to be inside," Ethan said,
and the thrust of his Gift reverberated through her chest. "The
symbols are on the front door, but let's fly around a bit, see
if we can figure where Jane is before we go in."

A few seconds later, Charlie pointed at a window on the
third floor, overlooking the backyard. Yellow light peeked
through the curtains. "There."

Ethan nodded. "Those iron bars ain't exactly a match for
the rest of the house, are they?"

Charlie swallowed her anger. "No."

They landed on the front porch, and Ethan caught her arm
before she could move toward the door. He unbuckled his gun
belt and cinched it around her hips, replacing his revolvers
with her automatic pistols.

"They don't fit in the holsters quite right," he said quietly,
adjusting the length of their straps so the weapons lay against
her upper thighs instead of her knees. "But they'll be there if
you need them." He raised his gaze to hers. "If you need them,
don't you hesitate to use them."

She practiced drawing them a few times, then pulled in a deep breath. "Okay."

Ethan palmed his own guns, stepped in front of the door, and peered through the panes of glass forming a semicircle at the top. His jaw was tight when he glanced at her. "I sure hate going in blind—"

His eyes narrowed; he spun around and fell to one knee, aiming out into the yard. "Show yourself, demon."

Charlie turned, her hands resting on the holsters. A movement on the lower limbs of a tree caught her attention an instant before Sammael dropped to the lawn.

Oh, this was bad. Very, very bad. Charlie darted a glance at Ethan. He wasn't giving anything away, but he must be thinking that as soon as they got Jane, Sammael might try to kill him.

Ethan would be blind coming *out* of the house, too—and he'd be watching his back, watching for Jake and Mark, and watching for the senator all at once.

Slowly, Ethan got to his feet again. "I figured you might be around."

"But I did not think *you* would. At least, not until I told you of her location." Sammael's smile had a sharp edge of displeasure. He stepped in front of the tree trunk, and his shirt and pants changed from black to the color of the bark. "How is it that you discovered where she is?"

"Charlie had dinner with young Brandt," Ethan said, turning back to the front door.

Sammael's gaze lit on her. "Charlotte's been a busy girl. I tried that, too, but he caught on to me when he touched my skin."

Luckily, Jake's was the same temperature as a human's. "How long have you known she was here?" Charlie asked.

A yellow square of paper appeared in Sammael's hand. Even from across the yard, Charlie could read Jane's messy handwriting. *Mark, 1:00.*

"She didn't come back from lunch," Sammael said. His gaze lifted to the third floor, and his expression softened. "I've been here almost every moment since then."

"Every moment, except those when you're shooting Jane's sister out of the sky." Ethan held out his hand, pulled Charlie in front of him, and folded the sleeve of his jacket back over his wrist. "If the senator arrives before we return with Jane, it'd sure benefit us if you provide him with a distraction. Maybe go on up and give him a hug."

His Gift thrummed through her and she bit, sucked in his blood and the sound of the lock. Steady, strong, soft—absolutely lovely, if a bit frayed around the edges. She held on to it for a long moment before projecting it back to Ethan.

He convulsed and pushed his way through; the door slammed open, the glass shattering.

Ethan didn't let them fall, but kicked the door shut behind him. His guns were out, and he made a quick sweep of the room before returning to her side, wiping the blood from his ears and nose.

He met her eyes, his gaze clear and focused despite the bleeding around his irises, the blotches of crimson. "Let's go find her, then, before Jake arrives and is an easy target for Sammael."

She nodded and followed him toward the stairs. He wasn't moving as fast as he could—or even she could—and she felt his psychic touch probing the spaces around them.

They passed a library, and Ethan quickly ducked in. He was out an instant later, shutting and locking the door behind him. A game room was on the other side of the hallway, and she caught a glimpse of an elk head before he closed that door, as well.

"I knew it," she said quietly. They'd reached the stairs, and Ethan was gazing upward.

"What's that?"

"The hunting thing. Although I can't really see Mark liking it—or even liking this house. It doesn't seem to fit him at all."

"That it doesn't," Ethan agreed, and she copied his stance as he moved up the stairs, keeping her back against the wall and her guns drawn.

"Did you feel what I sent you? That was him." There had been strength, but no hardness. Nothing that would have made her think Mark could kill an animal—or kidnap a woman.

"Yes. A good man." Ethan darted a glance at her. "Making some real bad decisions."

"Those ragged portions?"

"I reckon. He's breaking up; it likely ain't a stretch to say that learning about demons and vampires has caused a lot of it."

"And his dad. God knows what he's been getting from that end."

Ethan nodded, then moved around the second-floor landing and started up the next flight. "It may be he'll pull himself together—but there's no telling which way he'll go before he does."

Charlie sighed, and joined him at the top of the stairs. A window overlooked the front of the house. No headlights, and she could see the barest outline of Sammael's form against the tree.

"Ethan," she said. "When we go back out, let me go in front of you."

A smile flashed over his mouth, and he turned down the hallway taking them to the rear of the house. "No chance in hell, Charlie."

"Just listen," she said, her heart beating wildly. "You made sure I was protected by striking that bargain. Let me use it to protect you a little. If he has to go around me—"

"Then I have to worry about hurting you as I defend myself. It's best that you're behind me." He stopped in front of a a heavy wood door. Both the dead bolt and the knob locked from the hallway; they had been supplemented with a chain and a padlock that popped open with a touch of Ethan's Gift.

Charlie frowned. "Why can't I hear her inside?"

"Spell's up. So either they've got her tied down so as she can't disturb the symbols, or she's determining when they visit her."

"Probably the second," Charlie said, holstering her guns. Ethan brought his wrist to her lips again, and yes, there was Jane, hard and bright and sweet, the chime of glass against steel.

This time, they fell—but Ethan controlled it, rolling imme. diately to the side, using his body to cover hers.

A moment later, his heavy weight lifted, and Charlie opened her eyes to Jane's stunned expression. She was sitting at an equipment-crowded desk, her computer open, with a rack of blood-filled vials beside it.

Charlie blinked. "You're using a microscope in your *underwear*? You are such a nerd."

"Jesus. Charlie? How did you—" Jane stood, grabbed the robe hanging from the back of her chair. "How—?" She tore her fingers through her hair. "You're really here?"

Charlie accepted Ethan's hand, got to her feet. "Really. But we've got to go right away. Get dressed."

Jane quickly began gathering up items from the desk, and Charlie went to her side, stopped her. "We've got to go *now*," she said, meeting Jane's eyes. "Ethan can take all of this, if you give him permission."

Jane looked over Charlie's shoulder, nodded. "Yes. Okay. All of the samples in the little refrigerator, too." She pulled Charlie in for a quick hug, then ran off to the other side of the room.

Charlie frowned down at the now-empty desk. "What were you working on?"

Jane came out of the closet with a shirt and jeans. "Same thing I was at Legion, only the senator wanted proof vampire blood wasn't human."

"Did you find any?" Ethan asked quietly.

"No. Wouldn't have with this equipment—and I told them it's a match down to the DNA level, anyway. The only difference is the healing behavior." Jane zipped her jeans, then shoved her feet into a pair of already-tied tennis shoes. "They were talking about getting more lab equipment—"

"More lab equipment?" Charlie shook her head with a short laugh of disbelief. "So Mark brought you here as, what? His personal scientist?"

"Oh, no. Well, partially. Maybe that's just his dad." Jane straightened up, and rolled her eyes. "Mark brought me here to *save* me. Because I'm sleeping with the devil."

"I knew Mark was a good guy," Charlie muttered under her breath, and caught Ethan's grin before he turned toward the door.

"We ready, then?" he said as he swiped the blood from the symbols and glanced out into the hallway.

"Yes." Jane ran her hands down the sides of her jeans. "Is Dylan still here?"

"Yes." Charlie took Jane's hand, held her gun ready in the other, and started out after Ethan. "What do you mean, 'still'? How did you know he was outside?"

"He spent the last two weeks outside my window, keeping

me company." Jane almost tripped on the first stair, and Charlie slowed her pace. "*Trying* to keep me company, at least, since we couldn't say anything."

Charlie checked her immediate response. Any negative comment about Sammael would probably spark Jane's temper, so she simply laid out the facts. "Last night, he shot Drifter and almost killed him. So I shot Sammael. He stabbed me, then threatened my life. It was all so that he could get you out of here—although he knew he could have just given us an anonymous tip and we'd come to your rescue. And now that you're out, he'll probably try to kill Drifter as soon as he can."

They reached the main floor, and Jane's expression was tense when she disentangled their hands. "I don't know what you want me to say, Charlie."

Charlie averted her face. Her chest felt heavy. Nothing was going to change. She looked up as Ethan strode by on his sweep of the ground-level doors, and his warm fingers brushed her cheek.

Encouraged by that brief caress, Charlie swallowed and said, "How about you give Sammael an ultimatum—that if he kills Drifter, you won't see him again? Because it would kill *me*."

Jane's gaze was steady on hers. "I'll say something."

Charlie closed her eyes and nodded, though the sinking sensation slipping through her told her it wouldn't matter. Sammael knew her sister too well; even if Jane left him, he could just take on another identity and find her again.

And Jane would let it happen, rationalizing away every clue that told her the truth, convincing herself that he really was a different man. And if not completely different, then at least a *changed* man.

But Charlie only said, "Thank you," then went to stand beside Ethan as he drew back the curtains from the large picture window and studied the front lawn. Sammael wasn't by the tree.

"Be easy, Charlie," he said, quietly enough that Jane couldn't have heard. "He likely won't make the attempt when she's here to see."

"But isn't that exactly why he would?" she said, equally low. "You wouldn't expect it. And he could twist the truth to Jane later."

"Maybe so." He nodded slowly, then slanted a narrowed, amused look at her. "But don't be thinking I'm so easy to kill, either."

She had to smile a little. "I don't. But you said before that all it takes is one distraction. You've got quite a few right now."

"That's true enough—and, hell." He sighed as the gates at the end of the short drive began to open. "Here comes Jake. Let's get out there, Charlie. I'll be mostly concentrating on Sammael; you keep young Brandt from taking hold of your sister again. Once Sammael leaves with Jane, I'll fly you home—then return with backup, wait for the senator."

She caught Jane's hand again, and put her finger against her lips when Ethan wiped the blood from the symbols. He cracked the door open an inch and cocked his head. Charlie strained to listen, as well—but she only heard their heartbeats, the quiet whine of Mark's electric car, the sounds of the house.

Ethan nudged the door open wide, then slid around the frame, crouching low. After another second, he said quietly, "All right, Charlie. Take her to the edge of the lawn. If he wants her, he'll have to come out in the open."

Jane did a double-take as they passed Ethan; Charlie's heart skipped. He'd formed his wings, and they angled from his shoulders and pressed into the side of the house, creating the elegant shape of a harp, with feathers for strings. And as soon as they left the porch, Charlie heard the familiar heavy beat, felt the rush of air. She glanced back, up; Ethan perched on the edge of the roof, his crossbow and sword in his hands.

Jane blew out a soft, shaky breath. "Wow."

"Yeah," Charlie agreed, squeezing her fingers, and she looked toward the approaching car. Mark was leaning forward in the driver's seat, his eyes narrowing, then widening, as if he couldn't quite believe what he was seeing. An instant later, the car stopped, and his door opened.

"Watch yourself, Jake." Though Ethan spoke quietly, Charlie easily heard the command. "Sammael's about."

"That isn't our only problem," Jake said as he stepped out of the car, shifting back into his own shape. Mark issued a deep sound of surprise and staggered back onto the lawn. "Apparently, there's a coffee shop in the neighborhood where they wait when the other has locked the house up. So Papa just got a call, and he's not far behind us."

"Son of a bitch." Ethan stood and replaced his sword with his cell phone. "Sammael, we ain't got time to play. You take Jane out of here now—or I'll be taking her."

"What the hell is going on?" Mark's hoarse yell scraped Charlie's ears, and she had to shut out his wildly projected confusion. He scrambled toward her and Jane, but seemed to give up halfway, falling to his knees in the grass. The tumble of his emotions quieted.

Ethan cursed. Startled, Charlie glanced back at him. He was shaking out his hand, and bits of plastic rained to the roof.

It was another second before she realized what had happened: Sammael had shot the phone. A moment later Jake was swearing and yanking out the arrow that had embedded in his palm—and pierced the guts of his cell.

Charlie doubted Jane had seen any of it. Her sister's face was tilted up, her lips parted, and her eyes shining.

From above them, Sammael said to Ethan, "I will not have you contact your Guardians so that they may destroy me—"

Ethan wasn't listening. He dropped off the roof, letting his wings catch air and settling lightly on the ground beside Charlie. His weapons weren't aimed over her head, at Sammael, but beyond her . . . and now she heard the footsteps approaching.

She turned her head. The senator hadn't bothered to drive in, but was walking with measured strides through the open gate, his hands in the pockets of his dark slacks. His eyes met hers across the expanse of lawn, and gooseflesh prickled over her skin. Her fingers tightened on Jane's.

"Go into the house, Miss Charlie," Ethan said softly. "Slow and easy, and put the spell up."

She nodded, and tugged on Jane's hand. Her sister frowned, glanced away from Sammael. "We've got to get back inside," Charlie said, and raised her voice. "Mark?"

A thump against the ground warned her that Sammael had landed. His black membranous wings were outspread, blocking their way, and Jane rushed into his arms. Sammael caught her in a tight embrace and spoke over her head. "I may have to protect you, Charlotte, but I will not allow you to return Jane to that pris—"

"It ain't a human coming this way, but one of the nephilim," Ethan said in low tones, and backed up a step. His gaze never left the senator. "And maybe now you're thinking of running with Jane, demon—but leaving Charlie with only a Guardian and a novice to protect her would hardly be 'doing everything within your power to prevent any hurt from coming to her,' would it?"

Sammael's jaw flexed, and he set Jane away from him, looked down at her before pressing a kiss to her lips. "Go inside with your sister," he murmured.

Charlie took her hand again, began pulling her toward Mark. Ethan and Sammael kept pace with them, positioning themselves between Charlie and the senator. He'd crossed half the distance from the gate.

Ethan had his swords in both hands now. "Jake, we've got two humans and a vampire who need protecting. You go in the house with them."

She almost expected Jake to argue and insist on being part of the fight, but the novice nodded and crouched in front of Mark. "Listen, kid. We've got two women to save, so you pull yourself up to your feet." When Mark only responded by looking up blearily, Jake leaned in, his voice hardening and changing. "Pull yourself up to your feet, son."

Charlie blinked; Jake had mimicked the senator's voice, and Mark shook himself out of his stupor. "What the—"

Jane let go of Charlie and reached down, tugged on his arm. "I don't know either, Mark, but I think it's bad. Come on."

Relief swept through Charlie when Mark got to his feet and walked with Jane toward the house. Following Jake's cue, Charlie moved backward, her guns drawn, watching the senator's approach. Jake let her go up the porch steps first, but she had to stop when Mark paused in the doorway, looking out over the lawn.

"Hold on, hold on." Mark's eyes narrowed, and he shook his head. "That's my dad. You don't have to—"

"That's *not* your dad," Charlie said, impatience and fear tightening her throat.

Ethan and Sammael had been backing up with them, but they halted on the pavement as if drawing an invisible line for the senator to cross. Ethan had vanished his wings; he'd told her once that they slowed him down.

So would a distraction, and his worry that she wasn't yet protected.

Charlie turned to Mark and bared her teeth. "Get inside, or I'll throw you in."

Mark paled and opened his mouth, but whatever argument he'd been about to make died. His mouth just remained open. Charlie glanced back at the lawn. The senator held two swords now, and his eyes were glowing red.

"Go in, Charlie," Jake said quietly, and she realized that Mark had finally stumbled past the threshold.

Charlie followed him, then ran to the large window and tore the drapes down. The curtain rod clattered to the floor, then everything went quiet, and she hated it, hated that she couldn't hear Ethan's heart beating—that she had to rely on what she could see.

Jake joined her, and she looked up at him. "Can we help him from in here?"

Jake nodded. "If you've got a good shot, you can take it. Just make certain it won't hit either of them."

"Okay." She drew in a long breath. "Mark, do you have any guns? Rifles or anything?" Anything that would do more damage than her pistols.

"Yes." His strained response came from directly behind her. She glanced back; he was staring out at the lawn, his expression bleak. "What is that thing, and where's my father?"

The "thing" was growing, his clothes vanishing. Crimson skin stretched over his muscles, and his wings were so incredibly beautiful . . . but *not*.

Charlie swallowed hard. Ethan and Sammael were circling it now, each taking a different side and splitting its attention.

"It's kind of a demon," she said quietly. She'd have taken Mark's hand before she said the next part, but she thought her skin might frighten more than it would comfort him. "It took possession of your father's body after he died."

So fast. She blinked, and suddenly Ethan's and the nephil's swords flashed. Then Sammael's, coming in from behind.

"Goddammit," Jake muttered, dropping to his knee and aiming through the window. Their positions changed too quickly for a gun to be useful. Jake was trying to follow them, but he hadn't yet fired a shot—and Charlie was even slower. She stared, feeling helpless.

"What do you mean, died? It murdered him?"

It took her a second to remember what Mark was asking, but she couldn't take her eyes from Ethan. A stain had begun spreading down his pant leg.

"No," she finally said. "Vladimir and Katya did after they withdrew from their agreement with him."

"The vampires?" A harsh note slammed into her—hate, anger, grief. "Animals. They shouldn't be exposed, but slaughtered."

"They were. The thing out there went back and killed them."

"Good," Mark said. A moment later, she heard his footsteps retreating from the room.

Jane made a soft sound as Sammael took a slice across the tip of his wing from the nephil's blade. Charlie squeezed her eyes shut. She hadn't handled any of that very well, but she couldn't bring herself to care. Ethan's blood was dripping over the lawn, the drive, and he was weakening; so was Sammael. And they couldn't contact anyone for help—

Her eyes flew open. "Jane, do you still have Drifter's old phone?"

"It's upstairs," her sister whispered. Her hands were clenched tightly in front of her. "But the battery's dead."

Jake didn't look from the window. "Where's yours, Charlie?"

"In Drifter's cache. Maybe Mark—"

Jake was shaking his head. "It's still in his car. Drifter knew he had yours?"

"Yes."

"Check your holsters, then. He'd have hidden it, so Sammael couldn't destroy it like he did ours."

Charlie blinked, then gave Jane one of her pistols to hold and reached into her right holster. Her eyes widened, and she drew her cell phone out. "No service," she said, and met Jake's gaze. "Are you going, or am I?"

Jake stood and took the phone. "I am. I'll be in again as soon as I've contacted Selah."

White feathers and Ethan's back suddenly blocked their

view outside. Exposing himself, slowing himself down. "Go, Jake," Charlie rasped. "He's keeping them from seeing what you're doing."

Jake vanished the phone and ran out of the room, toward the rear of the house. She heard more footsteps, but they were Mark's, coming from the game room. With the rifle, hopefully—Ethan ducked away from the window, his wings vanishing again, and the nephil was there on the porch, just beyond the pane of glass.

Jane gasped and stumbled back, but Charlie focused on the nephil's form, took careful aim. It was moving from side to side, easily parrying every thrust of Ethan's and Sammael's swords, but maybe unloading a clip into its head would make that just a little more difficult—

The glass in front of her shattered, and her ears rang painfully. Charlie blinked and staggered forward, stared at the cracks radiating from the neat hole in the center of the window. Blood beaded on the glass like scarlet dew on a spider's web.

Her chest hurt. She couldn't breathe or see. Then the window collapsed, a shining waterfall of broken glass, and everything was clear again.

Directly in front of her, the nephil had a bullet hole in its side. Pale, human-looking skin surrounded the wound, but it was already healing and turning crimson.

She looked past it, toward Ethan. His face reflected his horror. Why was she sensing it through the spell?

She shook her head in confusion. Lowering her gun to her side, she looked down at her chest, and wanted to throw up.

Oh, God. Her ears were still ringing because Mark's rifle hadn't had a silencer.

The horror she sensed was Jane's.

Charlie slowly turned. Mark's eyes and cheeks were wet. The rifle lay on the floor by his feet. His arm was around Jane's waist, and he held Charlie's pistol against Jane's neck.

A scream climbed in her throat. She couldn't breathe, couldn't speak.

"Slaughter all of you," Mark said, his voice shaking as hard as the madness and fear in his psychic scent. Shrieking, tumultuous. "And your whores."

She tried to respond, but it only brought flavorless blood to her mouth.

"Charlie," Jane whispered, pleading, crying, and Charlie's hand steadied on her gun. She looked at Mark's forehead. Imagined the hole there.

Saving Jane from *this* was going to be so easy.

CHAPTER 31

The nephil slowed.

For only a few seconds, but if it hadn't, Ethan figured he'd have been dead. Seeing Charlie shot had just about torn him into pieces, and for an instant, his brain had shut down.

But now it was Sammael who was going to be dead if the demon didn't stop trying to see what was happening inside the house.

Ethan didn't—couldn't—let himself look. A bullet would hurt Charlie something terrible, but she wouldn't die. And getting himself killed would hurt her worse.

The nephil turned his head, and Ethan's blood ran cold. It had heard Jake. The kid's voice was coming from somewhere behind the house, and even slowed, the nephil would take him out as easy as—

Slowed.

God Almighty. *Something had slowed it down.* And maybe the nephil tortured vampires because Vladimir and Katya had killed the human it had been . . . but then again, maybe it had more reason to bleed out vampires than a grudge.

Ethan backed away, ignoring the ache in his thigh where

he'd been cut deep, and switched his swords for his pistols. This was taking one hell of a risk. Guns would leave him pretty much defenseless, and he already knew bullets alone wouldn't damage the creature all that much.

The nephil took a step toward him. The vials filled with vampire blood sat in Ethan's cache; quick as thought, he pulled them in.

He dropped the vials in the air halfway between himself and the nephil, and fired. Glass shattered, spraying blood.

The bullets embedded in the nephil's chest, and Ethan saw the ripple of pale skin that spread out from the wounds before he had to trade in his guns for his swords.

And once again, Ethan should have been dead—but he had just enough time to block the nephil's swing.

"Sammael," Ethan said, but the nephil caught his stomach with its taloned foot and he spoke his next words while holding his gut together, pain flaring white-hot through his innards. "You got any vampire blood?"

Sammael frowned; but a second later, his eyes widened. "And the blood that heals will bring glory, release the dead unto judgment, and the judged unto Grace," he said, laughing, and Ethan thought the demon was heading for crazy until a crimson tide poured over the nephil. Sammael spun his pistols in his hands once, then started firing.

Ethan used his sword. The nephil became smaller, and it turned to run, the senator's form breaking through the red skin. Blood coated Ethan's blade, and he buried it in the creature's chest, but it was still moving, still running.

"How the blazes did you demons imprison the nephilim before?" Ethan yelled.

"I have no idea!" Sammael called, still laughing and shooting.

A bullet dug into Ethan's back, and he gritted his teeth. His sword skewered the nephil's torso, and Ethan swung it around, using its body as a shield. He'd cut the goddamn heart in two, but it was struggling.

Son of a bitch. Ethan's second sword took its head, and it finally fell limp.

Sammael's next bullet caught Ethan in the throat.

His vision darkened around the edges, and he sank to his

knees, let the nephil drop to the ground in front of him. Sammael's smile sharpened, and he exchanged his guns for a sword.

A growl sounded behind Ethan. *Three* growls, as familiar to his ears as Hugh Castleford's voice, as Selah's softly spoken commands, the beat of feathered wings. Ethan's chest hollowed in sheer relief. Help had arrived. Too late for the nephil, but not too late for him.

Sammael froze—but he wasn't looking at Ethan, the Guardians, or at the hellhound whose massive jaws dripped foam and flecks of blood onto the lawn. The demon launched himself onto the porch instead, threw himself at the empty window, calling Jane's name. The shield stopped him. He whipped around, his eyes glowing. "Get me through it."

Ethan held up his hand for the others to stop, then signed, *Watch my back*, before staggering to his feet. His throat, his gut were on fire.

How much time had passed since Charlie had been shot? It felt like minutes, hours . . . but must have only been seconds. Thirty or forty. He looked through the window and his chest turned to ice.

A gun against Jane's throat. Madness in young Brandt's eyes. Charlie's choice would be simple, but it was the kind that wouldn't let her rest easy for a hundred years. Maybe never.

And he'd rather Fall than see her forced to make it.

Ethan signed, *Someone yell for Jake to come up here*. The kid hadn't returned inside the shield yet—Ethan couldn't see him, leastwise. He glanced down. His clothes were soaked with blood, riddled with tears and holes; if Charlie smelled it, saw the evidence of his injuries, it could very well push her over the edge before he took her place.

He signed a request for new clothes from Selah, then turned his attention to the demon. Sammael might try to get in the house when the shield went down; no way in hell was Ethan going to allow Sammael's tongue to influence anything that Charlie did.

Fortunately, Sammael was awful distracted by the scene inside. Ethan shot a dart of hellhound venom into him, saw the demon's surprise, watched him slide to the porch.

"This ain't killing you, or even contributing to killing you,"

Ethan said, the words sounding torn and wet. "They'll leave you alive if you just lay."

He looked away from the demon, met Selah's gaze, then Hugh's. Dismay filled Selah's psychic scent as if she realized the choice Ethan was about to make, and she stepped forward, but Hugh caught her hand. She closed her eyes, shielded her sudden grief.

Jake came up onto the porch, his brows lifted high.

"Just reach in through the door and wipe the blood from the symbols," Ethan said. "I'll walk in alone."

❧

Easy, but it needed to be precise. She couldn't make a mistake. Death had to be instantaneous, her aim perfect.

Ethan had taught her how: focus, exhale, then gently squeeze the trigger.

It was hard to focus. Jane's face was pale and terrified. But Charlie forced her gaze away from it, and everything narrowed down to Mark's forehead.

Now she had to breathe out and empty her lungs. It wouldn't be air, but blood. And Mark probably wouldn't even see the movement of her hand.

Her exhalation rattled from her chest, her forefinger caressed the trigger. So easy.

But she didn't lift the gun.

It hadn't been blood. She'd breathed air, and that meant she had another choice.

Oh, God, she thought, because when it mattered she always fucked up, nothing came out of her mouth like it should; she had a better chance of getting Jane out of this by shooting him than talking. But the words began bubbling up anyway, raw and wet, forcing their way out.

"Jane," she rasped, but had to stop and wipe her mouth with her free hand, and ignore the streak of red. Jane's eyes opened, but Charlie hadn't been asking for her; it was just where this story began. "Jane was nine when she fell in love with . . . with . . . his name starts with a 'B,' and he was in that movie where the terrorists take over the skyscraper, and he was just a lone cop against all of the bad guys. And we weren't supposed to watch it because there was too much violence in it, but we sneaked downstairs in the middle of the night anyway, and then for months Jane's response to everything was 'Yippee kai yay, motherfucker.' Because that's what the hero said to the bad guy when he killed him."

The chaotic, ragged noise that Mark's psyche had been making didn't vanish—but it lowered in volume. A steady note of confusion joined the madness, as if Mark was wondering what the hell she was saying . . . and if she was on her own way to insanity.

Good, Charlie thought, but she didn't holster her gun.

"She never said it in front of my mom and dad—only behind their backs. I did, except I sang it, drawing it out so that they couldn't tell what it was. I'll unfortunately never sing 'motherfucker' like that again, but let me tell you: It was amazing when I did. Jane could probably give you a demonstration, if she wasn't laughing so hard—but her contralto is reedy, so it'd sound like crap anyway."

Charlie paused for a quick breath. Jane's lips were pressed tightly together; she was trembling, and there was color in her face. And Mark was looking and his psychic scent sounded a little saner now—if completely bewildered—but his gun was still against Jane's neck, so it was time to tell him what she'd do if he didn't lower it soon.

"I didn't like the same what's-his-name actor, though—"

"Bruce," Jane said.

Charlie grinned. "Bruce, yes—because I liked the bad guy better. Until about a year or so ago, I was alone at home watching movies, and I see Bruce in another film, and he's looking up at this gigantic blue alien, and she's got this synthesized coloratura soprano, and he's about to cry because it's so beautiful. Then the singer gets killed—which isn't a surprise, because singers always get killed—but then Bruce suddenly turns into this big damn hero and goes after all of the bad guys. And at one point, a bad guy is holding a gun to a good guy's head. But Bruce just walks into the room, and before the bad guy can react there's a bullet through his forehead."

Mark blinked, and his gaze shifted to Jane, then to Charlie's pistol. Uncertainty chased away the rest of the madness.

Charlie wasn't smiling now. "I'm really, really fast. But I like to think you're a good man, Mark—and I've recently been told that it's hard to wash a good man's blood off your hands." The gun wasn't so tight against Jane's neck now, but it still wasn't enough. "For Jane, I'm willing to scrub. And if you do anything to her, not only will I shoot you like a bad guy, it won't even matter. Because I'll heal her with my blood, and if I can't do that I'll turn her into a vampire to save her. She won't like it as much as I do, because her boyfriend probably won't respect her free will—but she'll be alive. You won't be."

Mark swallowed hard. Charlie stood motionless, and didn't look away from him when she heard the front door easing open . . . and the sudden noise from outside. The tread of boots was unmistakable. Ethan. Oh, God, please please *please* don't let his appearance frighten Mark and undo everything she'd just done.

Mark's eyes widened, fear erupted from his psyche—and he tossed his pistol to the side. He touched his free hand to his forehead before holding it up in surrender.

Charlie bent forward a little, her relief so profound it hit her like a fist. She turned her head; Ethan was blinking, his gun aimed at Mark's head, his brow furrowed. Relief projected sudden and heavy from him, too.

"Well, hell," he drawled. "I was all set to be a bad guy. I sure am glad I didn't have to be."

Charlie laughed, but Mark still had a hold on her sister's arm, and he'd scared the shit out of all of them.

She moved quickly, then pulled her punch at the last second so she didn't take off his head. Unconscious was good enough. His head snapped back, his eyes rolled up, and he dropped.

"Holy shit, Charlie," Jane said, and collapsed to the floor, her laughter turning to loud, wrenching sobs.

Charlie sank down with her, shoving Mark's crumpled form to the side, and wrapped her arms around Jane's shoulders. She looked back at Ethan. His clothes had been cleaned, and there was a large healing splotch on his throat that she didn't want to think about.

"The nephil's dead?"

Ethan nodded, and he glanced at Jane before meeting Charlie's eyes again. "Seems that vampire blood does something to it. Heals the human flesh so the possession doesn't take and it can't maintain its form." His smile was crooked. "Leastwise, I figure that's what happened."

She held his gaze; she wanted to hold on to *him*, and she thought he probably wanted the same, but even this small, intimate connection of sight and speech felt wonderful, perfect. "So I guess it was a good thing Mark shot me."

"I reckon it was." But he didn't manage the easy tone she had, and he looked away from her for just a second. His voice roughened. "You all right?"

"Yes. Although it's also a good thing I don't have to pee anymore, or I'd probably have embarrassed myself when the senator showed up."

His face softened. "I'd have pissed myself about a hundred times over when that bullet busted through the window." His gaze searched her features for another moment. "I got to head outside, clean up, talk to Hugh. You all right to stay here a few minutes?"

Charlie nodded, watched him walk through the door, her heart pounding wildly. *A bad guy.* He would have killed a human, would have Fallen, would have had that blood on his hands—so that she wouldn't have to.

That man was crazy in love with her. She'd have bet anything on it.

Bet anything and everything—and she was going to. She was certain, but it wasn't enough. Because along with the love and the certainty was that same terrible need, and pretending it didn't exist wasn't going to make it go away, and denying it wouldn't mean she was stronger.

Getting what she needed was probably going to hurt, though. Hurt her . . . and hurt him.

She lifted her cheek from Jane's head. "Drifter? Where's Sammael?"

His voice carried across the lawn. "On the porch."

Frowning, Charlie looked out the empty window frame. If the demon was on the porch, then he wasn't standing. "Alive?"

Jane's breath hitched.

"Yes," Ethan said, and Charlie repeated his answer for her sister, but held on to Jane's wrist when she attempted to get up.

Jane sat down again.

"You're going to stay with Sammael," Charlie said, and it wasn't a question.

Jane's throat worked, and she averted her face. Her eyes filled. "I know you don't understand, but—"

"I understand better than you think. I know exactly how hard it is to give up something you love, but that isn't any good for you." And thank God Ethan couldn't qualify as bad for her, because she'd never give him up.

"He's good *to* me." Jane still wouldn't meet Charlie's eyes.

"I've seen that," Charlie said, and looked down at her hands. "I've actually got it easy now that I'm a vampire. I haven't had to fight myself at Cole's since I've been transformed because I don't crave anything except blood. And that's not bad for me—it's just food. Tasty food. It doesn't even matter if I eat too much; psychic energy doesn't have any calories."

Jane's lips curved into a smile, and her slim form began shaking. "You're nuts, you know?"

"Yeah," Charlie said softly, and waited for Jane to look at her. "I can't come around to your place anymore. Not if you're living with Sammael." She watched the shattered expression fall over Jane's face, felt her sister's sudden hesitancy and pained indecision—and for an instant, Charlie almost left it at that. Almost pushed Jane into making a choice. But she simply couldn't. "But I'll always be available whenever you need me— or for whatever reason. Available after sunset, anyway. At Cole's, mostly, or I can be a cheap dinner date, and a movie is always good, too. Because I'll need to see you; I'd just prefer that it isn't with Sammael. Maybe I'll change my mind in twenty or thirty years. But right now?" She shook her head. "I can't."

Jane pulled up her legs, dropped her face against her knees. After a long second, she said, "Okay."

"Fuck you," Charlie said, grinning with relief. "I can't believe it took you that long to agree."

"You scared me to death, made me think I was going to lose you. So fuck you." Jane lifted her head. "*And* you told Mark about my crush on Bruce Willis. Total breach of trust."

"Look on the bright side. Maybe Sammael will shapeshift, and you can be all 'Yippee kai yay—'"

"Oh, *Jesus*. Shut up." Jane dropped her head to her knees again, turned her face so Charlie could still see her. Her brows scrunched together. "Speaking of, did you get my note, with the unicorn?"

"Yes."

"So you know there's another option for feeding."

"Yes," Charlie said quietly, and her chest began to ache. Even the bullet hadn't hurt this much. "And Sammael's bound to give me anything I need if I ask for it. So if you could arrange to send a pint of his blood to my house every day, I'd appreciate it."

Jane's expression became confused and pleased, all at once. "But I thought you'd be with—"

Charlie cut her off before she said Ethan's name. "I am." And she didn't want Sammael to know the reason behind her request, so she added, "But he's like a cop, or a doctor—out saving people. I don't want him to worry if sunset comes around and he can't get home to feed me before I go to Cole's."

Jane nodded, but her gaze narrowed on Charlie's face. "And is that the only reason?"

So *now* Jane started paying attention to how she was feeling. Charlie couldn't halt her wry smile, and hoped Jane would attribute it to her response. "No. It's also because I know Sammael will hate doing it."

Jane's lashes fell, a mixture of pain and humor running through her scent, and Charlie almost took it back—but she couldn't. And there was still one other matter that needed to be settled with the demon. She touched Jane's hand.

"Let's go see him," Charlie said, and for Jane's sake, she held in her laughter when she spotted Sammael laid out on the porch—and the giant hellhound stretched out beside him, eyeing the demon's leg with the same hungry speculation that a dog would a meaty bone . . . only tripled.

Jane gasped in horror, but Charlie pulled her closer. After a second glance at Sammael, she realized the venom had at least partially worn off. Fear kept him still now.

Jane went to his head, and Charlie helped him sit up so that he was leaning back against her sister's chest.

"Charlie," Ethan said, and she looked over her shoulder, saw him crouching over the senator's headless form with Castleford and Selah. Ethan's brows drew together; he slowly rose to his feet, and she turned back to Sammael.

Jane was making murmuring, soothing noises, but the rasp of Charlie's voice scraped over them, and her eyes locked with the demon's.

"Jane was going to give you an ultimatum about not killing Drifter," Charlie said. "But I don't think she has to—you simply aren't going to do it."

Sammael's jaw clenched, and Charlie thought it was only so that he wouldn't declare his intention to do exactly that while Jane was listening. But the crimson sparking through his eyes said it well enough.

She continued, "Because the bargain stated that you'd prevent any hurt from coming to me—but if he dies because of something you've done, it's the same as ripping my heart out."

Sammael turned his head to look up at Jane. Her hand shook when she touched his cheek. His eyes closed for a moment, and he nodded. "Very well."

"She's also real good friends with Jake," Ethan said from behind Charlie.

She hadn't heard his approach, but she couldn't mistake his amusement. She glanced around; Castleford was there, too, impassively studying the demon, his hand absently stroking the hellhound's muzzle.

"And she's been getting to know a few other Guardians and vampires, too," Ethan added. "So I reckon before you slay any, you ought to stop and ask them if Charlie would cry over their graves."

Sammael's lips twisted. "Bargain or no, bothering myself with the likes of you would only waste my time. You are insignificant in comparison to the glorious path that awaits—"

"Jesus." Charlie stood, rolling her eyes. Even Jane's lips were twitching, though her expression remained fond . . . as if she thought Sammael's bluster was a joke.

Ethan smiled, but his gaze was curious as he looked over the demon. "That path to glory, the blood that heals—that foolishness you were spouting wouldn't be part of a prophecy, would it?"

"Yes." The gravity of the demon's reply was echoed in the stony set of his face. "I'll admit I did not wholly believe it myself until I saw the blood's effect."

"Yet Legion was trying to duplicate that effect," Ethan said.

"Yes, but we did not know how to use it, or what purpose it would serve. Or if we were fools for attempting it, based solely on the vague promise of an incomplete prophecy. Even a demon can begin to lose faith." Sammael rose unsteadily to his feet, and Jane tucked herself beneath his arm. He eyed the hellhound. "You are letting me leave—alive?"

Ethan's smile turned hard. "Only because of the woman who's with you."

Charlie stood beside him as Jane's car appeared in the drive, and Jane helped Sammael into the passenger seat. She looked over the top of the car at Charlie before she got inside.

"Was he speaking the truth?" Ethan asked quietly when the car drove past the gates. "The bit about not bothering with killing us, and the prophecy?"

Castleford answered him. "Yes. The only lie in all of that was yours."

Charlie blinked, then glanced up at Ethan's face. He didn't seem at all upset that he'd just been called a liar. "What?"

Ethan grinned. "Jane ain't the only reason he's alive. Truth is, every single one of us got a real powerful thrill when you neutered that bastard, turning the bargain around on him. And now that he's not a threat, he might prove more useful living."

Charlie looked back at the gates. She'd have said more pussy-whipped than neutered; unfortunately, it went both ways. Jane was just as controlled and blinded by her need for him. "I'm just glad I could help," she said quietly.

🪶

She was sitting on the porch steps, looking up at the stars when Mark woke up. He stumbled out and plopped down beside her, watching blearily as Ethan, Selah, and Castleford continued their examination of the senator's body. They were taking pictures now, and Ethan glanced over at Charlie a few times, but he apparently decided that Mark was harmless.

Charlie had just begun to wish that both she and Mark smoked when he finally said, "I think I turned into my dad back there. I know the stuff I said sounded exactly like he did in the last couple of months."

Charlie nodded. "I thought it might be something like that when you called Jane a whore."

"Yes." He blushed. "I'm sorry for shooting you."

"I'd have been sorry if I'd had to shoot you." She paused. "A little sorry."

The strobe of the flash highlighted Ethan's sudden smile,

pulled at the ache in her chest. He was monitoring the conversation, and it didn't feel like cold surveillance, but safety and warmth.

Mark sighed and propped his chin on his fist, then winced and jerked his head up again. "A part of me knew it wasn't him. I saw that thing in D.C. a couple of times. Told myself it was just around our house because Dad had been trying to talk to so many vampires, demons, whatever. And he'd become *such* an asshole lately—even more than usual. I just didn't let myself believe it."

"Well, not every asshole is a demon, so don't use that as a litmus test," Charlie said.

"Especially in D.C.," Mark replied, then turned to look at her blankly. "Where are the cops? Am I going back to D.C. or to jail?"

Charlie shrugged, but Ethan raised his voice and said, "It's not worth the effort of prosecuting you. And you'll have enough to deal with in a week or two." Ethan's camera vanished, and he said to Castleford and Selah, "You want to take him to SI? I'll come on down in the morning, after I get Charlie settled, and we'll talk to him then."

Beside her, Mark said with quiet unease, "Take me where?"

Although Ethan and Selah probably heard them, Charlie answered just as softly. "San Francisco. They'll ask you about the nephil, what he's been doing the last couple of months—and working out how they'll cover up all of this." She bumped his hip with hers when he still looked uncertain. "They're the good guys. And you fucked up pretty bad, but your reasons weren't so terrible. So grow a pair and go."

She felt the bruise that left on his ego, but he didn't respond except to straighten his back and shoulders. A few minutes later, she watched Selah teleport Mark, Castleford, and the hellhound from the lawn, and turned to see Ethan grinning at her.

She couldn't help but smile. "What is it?"

"You cut off a demon's balls, and hand them to a boy to make a man of him." He shook his head, chuckling. "I'd do well to be careful around you, Miss Charlie, or I might find myself talking at a higher pitch, and Jake with hair on his chest all of a sudden."

Good Lord, how she loved this man. Her heart lurched

painfully, and Ethan's amusement faded. He stepped toward her.

"You going to tell me what I just laid on you?"

Ethan was close now, but Charlie didn't tilt her head to look up at him, because then she'd be kissing him—or rising up on her toes, hoping he wouldn't make her lift herself all the way up to his mouth. She was strong enough to do that, always—and there were times she wanted to. But she wanted him to meet her in the middle, too. Because if he didn't, she would just be left poised on her toes, waiting.

"You didn't put anything on me," she said, and her voice sounded too weak—he didn't believe her. She tried again. "It's knowing that you might start being careful around me . . . and that I'll deserve it."

He drew in a long breath before letting it ease out. "And how's that, Miss Charlie?"

But she didn't get an opportunity to explain. Ethan stiffened and his focus shifted beyond her. Frustration sounded a sharp note through his psychic scent.

"They've already gone," Ethan said. "The nephil's dead."

Charlie turned, and a shiver of dread traveled the length of her spine. She recognized the Guardian standing on the lawn behind her: Michael, the Doyen with the incredible voice and strange obsidian eyes. They appeared human now, the irises almost the same color as Ethan's—but they were hard, and tired, as if he hadn't looked upon anything good in too long a time.

"I have need of you both," Michael said softly, and Charlie had to fight the weakness in her knees, the urge to sink to the grass and let that sound wash over her.

Ethan glanced at her in concern, and she shook her head. "I'm all right," she said. "I just wasn't ready for that."

Michael's response was heavy with apology. "You will need to prepare yourself for more, and you must do it quickly. I have cleared the way for us, but if we delay too long, we risk the demons discovering those I have slain."

Sudden tension paled the scar on Ethan's lip. "Where are you planning on taking us?"

"I have found the nephilim's prison." Obsidian swirled around Michael's golden irises. "But I cannot break through the shield surrounding it."

"Oh, God," Charlie whispered in numb realization.

Hell.

Ethan took her hand, held her steady. She clung to him, fighting the brain-deadening fear that washed through her, dimly aware that Ethan was signing a blazingly fast exchange with the Doyen. Ethan's fingers curled into a fist at the end of it, and he looked down at her.

"It'll be quick, all right?" He glanced at the Doyen. "Michael will make you up some heavier clothes, a jacket to ward you against the heat. You close your eyes, try not to look. And it'll smell something terrible, so try not to breathe."

"And not to listen," Michael added quietly.

Ethan's hand shook, and a look at his face confirmed that it wasn't in fear, but in fury. But he didn't round on the Doyen, and simply held her gaze as he said, "You just hang on to me real tight."

She did, but still the heat ripped the breath from her lungs, seemed to scorch her cheeks. She buried her face against his chest as quickly as she could, but the glimpse she saw was enough: they stood in an enormous cave, and directly in front of her a large black building carved with symbols was set into a foundation of rippling, moving flesh. People or things surrounded them, on the floor and the walls of the cavern, crawling, screaming, and everything was red and the stench of burning blood sank into her even though she hadn't drawn air.

"Charlie," Ethan said, and she wasn't sure if she heard his voice over the horrifying cacophony or if she just felt her name from his lips. His Gift slammed into her, and she bit the bare skin at his neck.

No no no, she screamed, because it was huge and beautiful and the most terrifying sound she'd ever heard, and she couldn't hold on to it, couldn't get her head around it.

Ethan fell to his knees on the soft wet floor, his grip slackening, his blood warm against her cheek. She fell with him, and then Michael's voice was there, lifting her, helping her fight the overwhelming need to sink into the dark miasma of that sound, to just let go, to give up.

Michael's hands were against her back. She felt the punch of a different Gift as it healed Ethan, and his arms tightened around her again.

"It's Lucifer's blood, Charlie," Michael said. "Don't attempt to hold it or replicate it. Let it run through you, then let me into your mind, and I'll sing it."

She felt the touch of him like a bright golden light, followed by Ethan's amazement.

And then nothing except the soaring voice that sang the dark and terrible sound that had been filling her, hitting each note, all of them at once, an impossible chorus from a single tongue. A hush fell around them in expanding waves, as if all of Hell stopped to listen to that voice, and it continued on, swelling far longer than any human could have sung it, longer than any lungs could have held air.

And he altered it, singing the same notes but transforming them somehow, so that she didn't want to cringe away from it and give up, but reach out and hold it to her.

She began crying when it faded, and when she found the courage to look, the carved doors were open. Michael strode through them into the yawning darkness, his wings as black as the stone. Ethan wiped her cheeks and she wiped his, and then the screaming started again.

Michael returned, his steps heavy, his sword stained with blood. "All of them," he said. "He let all but one go."

Ethan abruptly stood, hauled her up against him. His crossbow appeared in his free hand. He squinted, and when Charlie turned, she had only a glimpse of a brilliant, blindingly beautiful form before Ethan covered her eyes. "Don't look, Miss Charlie."

Michael's footsteps did not halt, even when an unfamiliar voice spoke, similar in resonance to the Doyen's. "You should have foreseen this, Michael. I taught you to think as Lucifer does."

"If I think as he does, Belial, then all will be lost." The Doyen's response held a dry note of humor. "Demons may even begin speaking in English."

"They ought to know of the prophecy. The nephilim's release—"

"Predestination precludes free will," Michael said, his tone sharp. "You may take your prophecy, and let it determine your way; I choose another path—and I will not have it chosen for me."

Charlie felt Michael's hand against hers, and then the nauseating spin of teleportation. Ethan held her as her feet touched solid ground again, as she shuddered and heaved.

"Will this location do?"

"It's as good as any," Ethan said, and Charlie lifted her head. Cool clean air washed her face, the familiar rush of city traffic hummed in her ears. Her old apartment—the balcony. The stench of Hell clung to them, so she breathed in through her mouth as deep as she could.

Michael looked out over the railing before facing them again. His gaze narrowed on Charlie. "Thank you for your assistance. And I am sorry for the pain it caused you."

"It was kind of a trade-off," she said thickly. She couldn't hold on to the song he'd created, but she would always remember·its effect, the profound experience of it. That was almost enough.

Michael smiled, and he lifted his gaze. "I shall speak with you soon, Ethan."

Ethan nodded shortly. "We'll have words."

As soon as Michael disappeared, Ethan began stripping her stinking clothes away, tossing them into a pile in the corner of the balcony. Charlie helped him with slow, trembling fingers.

He met her eyes, but couldn't seem to hold the smile that kicked up at the corners of his mouth. She touched the wan curve with her fingertips.

"I've got this for you," he said, slipping a clean shirt around her shoulders, then backing away to unbutton his own. "Too big, but it'll do until we get home. I can't figure why he brought us here, but it ain't no—"

"It was probably me."

His gaze skipped quickly over her face, as if searching for any indication of the emotions hidden behind it. "How's that?"

She swallowed, forcing the muscles in her throat to work. "I need something."

His mouth softened. "You know you only have to ask, Miss Charlie."

That was the problem. She couldn't ask—she needed it too much, and knew herself too well. And so she simply continued, trying to explain, praying it would come out right. "When Michael showed up earlier, I was thinking of asking you to bring me back here. I still have a week or two left before my rental notice runs out."

She saw his hands curl into fists at his thighs, and she closed her eyes. "Charlie," he said, and his voice was rough. "What are you saying? If you feel like you're leeching off Savi and Colin by staying at the lake—"

"That's not it. But your assignment's over, you don't need to protect me now, and there's no reason to be there."

"You can stay at the lake until I find us another place. Something similar, as I know how you've taken to that house."

She had, but this was going in a direction she didn't want it to, and this wasn't about where she slept. She looked up at him, felt her stomach clench. His face was a bleak mask.

She blinked back the burning behind her eyes. "Why do you want to do that?"

Please say you love me, you need me.

"You need me, Charlie. And I'll do anything to provide—" He cut himself off, his jaw clamping shut. After a second, he added hoarsely, "You love me."

"Desperately." Her head suddenly seemed too heavy for her neck muscles to support it, everything in her weak and tired, but she didn't let her gaze waver from his. "I made arrangements with Jane. She's going to send me some of Sammael's blood every day."

He paled. "And I heard the reasons you gave to her. Are you telling me now it's something different?"

"Yes—"

His eyes began glowing, and anger pushed color beneath his skin. *"You don't need his blood."*

"I know," she whispered, and almost couldn't get the rest out. "I don't need it. That's why I'm going to use it. With your blood, everything's mixed up. I need to un-mix it."

He stared at her, his throat working before he closed his eyes. "Why?"

"Because everything you've given me has been wonderful, amazing—but you haven't given me the one thing I need more than anything else. And I think that providing for me has gotten in the way of it."

Ethan flinched, his entire body flexing as if she'd hit him, and she had to cover her mouth to hold in everything she wanted to scream, to beg from him.

He glanced up in that moment, and the stark pain on his features was frozen in place as he looked at her. She watched him study her wet cheeks, the hand she'd slapped over her lips.

Slowly, his brows drew together. He clasped her fingers in his warm grip, pulled them away from her mouth, and asked softly, "What do you need, Miss Charlie?"

She hadn't known how to say it without *asking* for it. She hadn't known until he'd looked at her as he would a puzzle. But now it was easy. She threaded her fingers through his, and said, "I need you to figure me out."

CHAPTER 32

He'd thought for certain she was chewing her arm off to escape, ripping out her heart—and his—in the process. But that apparently wasn't it at all.

It sure as hell didn't bode well that he'd started out by jumping to the wrong conclusion, and Ethan was quiet as he followed her into the apartment, working it through.

Whatever she needed had swelled up in her so hard that she'd had to physically force herself to hold it in. And whatever it was, she wasn't going to name it or ask for it.

She'd said once she was real easy to figure out. *Just imagine me needy, then imagine me afraid of it.*

Ethan pondered that, but it didn't help him for shit. He couldn't imagine her needy, as he once had. Couldn't imagine her clinging and begging for affection, so emotionally dependent that she couldn't function without constant reassurance, asking him to coddle and soothe her every fear, until nothing existed between them but her need.

That wasn't Charlie. She'd likely still be standing on her feet long after the sun shriveled and the Earth stopped turning.

Well, all right then. He'd known this wouldn't be easy—and

he'd take it slow, so as not to misstep. And if that didn't work, he'd start throwing everything in the world at her feet until he stumbled on the correct thing.

Or do both at once. Because he had his own powerful need, to simply be with her, and the sooner they each had what they wanted, the better off they'd both be.

And Charlie didn't appear too steady. Clutching his big shirt tightly around her body, she stood in her dining room, blinking as she looked around her. Her cheeks were still pink from Hell's heat, but her disorientation didn't seem to be left over from their trip. Her eyes were bright, but not glassy. Surprised, then, as if she'd forgotten the apartment was empty.

Now, that was interesting. When she'd laid this on him out on the balcony, it had seemed as if she'd thought all of this through. But her decision to return to the apartment must have been an impulsive one, and made not long before Michael had shown up at the Brandts'—she hadn't arranged for her return or brought any of her things over.

"When exactly was it that you decided to un-mix?"

Charlie glanced at him, and pushed her tangled hair back from her forehead. Her gaze slid down, landed somewhere beyond his feet. "When you said you'd piss yourself, and asked if I was all right."

And she'd been holding on to Jane. "How was that different from any other time I've done the same?"

"Well," she said, sweeping past him to pick up the potted cactus from the floor, then moving into the small kitchen to water it. Keeping her hands busy, he realized, so she wouldn't give in to whatever other need was pulling at her. "Just before that, I went from 'kind of sure' about something to 'ninety-nine percent sure.' It gave me a little more courage—because otherwise, I'd never take this risk."

Courage, but her fingers were trembling. The ceramic pot rattled when she set it on the counter. His chest tightened. "But you're afraid you might lose."

She looked at him, her eyes dark, haunted. "There's that one percent."

❧

He left Charlie soon after pulling in all of her belongings that he still carried in his cache, and insisting she take his big bed.

Ethan wouldn't be using it, and hers had been smashed and bloodied when they'd fallen out of the sky.

He stopped in Caelum for a couple of hours, but it wasn't any use trying to drift. He'd best be figuring her out soon, or there wouldn't be many thoughts in his head that weren't fuzzed up.

And he couldn't risk losing, either.

Halfway to San Francisco, he determined that there wasn't any reason he couldn't start throwing things at her feet right away, and the first ought to be the house. He was certain that wasn't what she was after, but maybe it'd bring her a smile.

It wasn't yet dawn when he arrived in the city, so he went directly to the big, fussy Victorian mansion crowded in among the rows of other fussy houses. Colin Ames-Beaumont arched a brow when he opened the door, but politely invited Ethan inside. There just wasn't something quite right about any man who looked a picture of elegance at five thirty in the morning, and Ethan wished he'd dirtied himself up a little before knocking, just so it all balanced out a bit more.

"I have heard that congratulations are in order," Colin said as he led Ethan into a room that wasn't much different from parlors he'd known in Boston as a young boy. "And that vampire blood has suddenly become a valuable commodity."

"You've heard correctly," Ethan said, but declined a seat on one of the spindly little chairs. "But that ain't what I'm here for."

"I hope not," Colin said. "To hear it all again would make for a frightfully boring conversation."

"I think it sounds exciting," Savi said as she entered the room, and when she stopped beside him Ethan obediently bent for her kiss to his cheek. Her cool lips brushed his skin, then she sat next to Colin, curling her legs up beneath her. "Sword fights, stray bullets, a humiliated demon. All good fun."

"A regular shindig," Ethan said dryly. Dawn wasn't far off, and Savi looked to be in her pajamas, so he went straight to the point. "I'd be much obliged if you'd consider selling your place up in Seattle."

He'd surprised them, but they both were nothing if not quick. They glanced at each other, and Savi bit her lip as if she was about to put something delicately.

It was likely about the money. Ethan said, "I'd need a price. I've got cash—"

"Twenty thousand?" Colin said, but his teasing grin was for Savi.

"Yes. I can turn it into something more right quick. A lot more, if that's what it takes, but I'd like to have an idea of what you'd be asking, and if you'd be willing to part with it."

Colin stood and tucked his hands in his trouser pockets. "I'm afraid we cannot, McCabe. Just this evening, we've entered into another agreement regarding that property."

Disappointment might have hit Ethan harder if Savi's eyes hadn't been shining so brightly, and she wasn't biting her tongue to hold in her laughter.

"A one-hundred-year lease," she said. "With a newbie vamp who has already given notice at her current residence, and who we've decided would be a fantastic manager for the Heritage theater."

Ethan looked down at his boots, and his grin just about busted his cheeks. By God, Charlie sure was something.

But she sure as hell wasn't slow.

❧

By ten thirty, Charlie stopped glancing at the door every time it opened, hoping it would be Ethan. She was just going to make herself crazy, so she went through the motions of pouring drinks and conversation.

A few minutes before closing, when she looked up from the cash register and met a pair of amber eyes in the mirror, her heart let her know that it was still alive by thumping a furious beat.

Her smile showed her fangs, but his body would block most people from seeing them—and it was difficult to care, anyway.

"You came," she said, and leaned her forearms on the bar. His face was the most wonderful thing she'd ever seen.

"That I did. And if it's agreeable to you, I'll stay a spell."

She nodded. "It is."

Ethan relaxed into his seat, his gaze slipping over her features. "Word is, you've been busy."

"A little." She poured his whiskey, slid it across the counter. "I didn't have much to do last night after you left, so I walked here and got my computer."

"And chatted with Savi a bit."

"Well," she said, "I had been thinking about what you'd said about keeping me on retainer, and compensation for that. The only thing I really want but can't afford is that house."

"You want it," he said softly.

"Yes."

"But you don't need it."

She touched his hand, squeezed lightly. "No."

He took a long breath, and a longer drink—but only, she thought, so he had time to think that over. "And the theater?" he asked after a moment.

She shrugged. "I'm already familiar with the stage, and they'll be paying for the remaining business classes and training I need before it opens. I'll miss Cole's, but it's right across the street—and I'll keep helping Old Matthew with the office stuff until he kicks me out of the nest."

He smiled at that. "You're doing all right, then."

"Mostly." Her voice was rough.

His gaze dropped to his drink. "You wake up early again?"

"Right after sunset."

"That's real good." He fell silent for a long second. "And did Sammael provide you—" He bit it off, and a muscle in his jaw flexed. "Did you get fed?"

"Yes. Jane brought it—"

Ethan's mouth was on hers before she could finish, his lips gentle and warm despite the frustration she felt boiling through him. His tongue slipped over her teeth, pausing at the tips of her fangs. She shook. The bloodlust rose up fast. He just had to push, and bleed, and she'd be lost—but he groaned low in his throat and pulled away.

Charlie blinked; the span of the kiss had been almost the same. A blink, and then over—she didn't think anyone had even noticed.

And she was trembling with need, excitement. There was no doubt he'd been tempted to push; he hadn't forced it on her, but he'd wanted to, badly.

"All right, then," he said. His fist was clenched on the bar. "You don't need me for feeding. But you could have it from me. I'd make certain nothing got mixed up."

"Yes, it would." She covered his hand with her palm, lightly massaged his tight knuckles with her thumb. "I don't need your blood, Ethan, but I need *you*. So if I fed from you it would get completely mixed up."

His eyes closed. When he opened them again, a wry smile touched his mouth, and his hand turned to hold hers. "I ain't sorry for stealing that kiss."

She dipped her head to hide her grin. "I'm not, either."

"There's that, at least." He sipped at his drink, watching her. "Will you be needing a ride home?"

She nodded and held his gaze. "I made arrangements with Old Matthew, but I'd rather go with you."

His smile widened. "And you're all right to get back here for work tomorrow?"

This time, regret deepened her reply. "Jane will be picking me up, since she'll be bringing over the . . ." She trailed off, not wanting to mention the blood again.

But if it stung him, Ethan didn't show it. "All right."

She had to move away to fill an order, and when she returned she said, "Jane also told me that Legion might be forming something similar to SI here in Seattle. Not the investigations, but training demons and vampires so they are prepared to fight the nephilim."

"Vampires against the nephilim?" Ethan whistled softly between his teeth. "Demon blood would be a powerful incentive though, wouldn't it? That'd be sure to cause some problems in the community here. Few other communities, too."

"It seems easier just to drain us dry and store the blood. Or have us donate, rather than train."

"It sure does. Maybe it's something to do with that prophecy. Not knowing whether they need the vampires alive." He shook his head, met her gaze. "I sure don't know about that prophecy myself—but knowing what Legion is planning is useful."

"Unless they're feeding Jane bad information."

He nodded, smiling slightly. "There is that," he said, but then his humor faded, his gaze sharpened. "Until we see which way Legion is headed, you make sure you sleep with the spell up. Sammael can't hurt you, but there may be others looking to shake things up here."

"I can't. If I put it up, you can't come for me if we're needed to break through the shield."

He frowned. "Jake will likely be teleporting soon, so it

won't be any trouble for me to go back and forth to San Francisco. If my being in the house is acceptable to you, I can use my blood to cast it after you've fallen into your sleep."

"It's more than acceptable," she said, and it suddenly struck her why he'd come in so late. By minimizing their time together, he wouldn't fuzz up as quickly. She hesitated only an instant before adding, "And there's no reason you can't continue using the house for training, or as your base if you happen to be working in Seattle—or, I guess, anywhere in the Northwest. It's convenient for you, and I'll be sleeping. And then you can drift, too."

His eyebrows twitched, but the rest of his face was still. "In with you?"

"Yes."

"Before I figure you out?"

"Yes. It might take you longer if you're fuzzy, and you said you need me to drift."

"I do." Ethan sat back in his chair, staring at her. "All right then."

♦

Sure enough, Charlie had un-mixed them—but after a couple of hours holding her sleeping form, it became abundantly clear that she was also putting them back together. And the configuration wasn't all that different; the only things she left out were what created the most powerful need in both of them: the blood and the bed.

That was, the most powerful need aside from simply being with her—that one, which was the most critical, she'd never denied him or herself. And he'd get the others back as soon as he figured her out.

Ethan had to force himself to leave mid-morning. She smelled of apples and cocoa butter, and nothing looked as bright or felt so good as when she was close.

But he hadn't been able to drift. Her longing poured from her so hard he thought he could almost hear it, and his own need to provide whatever she was missing had been roaring deep within him.

It tempted him to push again, but that longing had appeared just after the first time he'd pushed her. He didn't know if he could withstand her need becoming worse.

And he didn't know what he feared more: her need becoming worse or him becoming too fuzzy to figure it out.

The ache in him didn't ease as the day wore on; he was only thinking of returning to Seattle. Wasn't thinking much at all, until Lilith tracked him down in the gymnasium, where he was overseeing the lack of progress Jake made attempting to use his Gift.

"Would you like Sir Pup to chase him, give him a good scare?" Lilith said, coming to stand beside Ethan.

"Maybe in thirty minutes," he replied. *Or five,* he signed when Jake wasn't looking. Lilith grinned, and Ethan added, "You got that info on Legion setting up a training facility in Seattle?"

"Yes."

He hooked his thumbs in his suspenders. "It might all be lies, but I figure it wouldn't harm nothing if I were relocated to Seattle semipermanently. Particularly during the evening hours. I'm familiar with the city, and I don't have to worry much about Sammael—who, at least for now, is still the high-ranked demon at Legion. Add to that, there's a vampire who's valuable to us, but who hasn't much by way of protection."

Lilith's brows arched. "You should have just skipped to the last reason."

"I reckoned I ought to lay out as many as possible."

"Unfortunately, I've got one to add," she said. "We've heard from a vampire community in New York, and another in Paris. We were too specific, trying to find a match to Brandt's method of killing them. He was angry; the others were just methodical."

Ethan studied her face, couldn't read much in it. "So there were vampires being murdered, just not turned upside down and bled out?"

"Yes. The community leaders in Rome, Berlin, and D.C. were all killed several months prior to the city-wide slaughter. And those who took their place were soon dead as well."

Just like Katya and Vladimir—and Manny. And because they hadn't known to look for the nephilim, they'd just assumed it was the usual vampire politics. "Seattle was next then."

Lilith nodded. "Perhaps that will change, now that Brandt has been killed."

"But we've no way of knowing if another of the nephilim won't just take up where he left off."

"Yes," she said. "And so we're alerting all of the communities, and we'll be assigning a Guardian to any city where the heads have been slain. Do you want Seattle?"

There was no way in hell he'd let anyone else take it. "That I do."

"Then it's yours. When Michael returns—again—I'll clear it with him, but I can't imagine he'll disagree." She crossed her arms, a tiny line appearing between her brows as she watched Jake concentrate, as the thrum of his Gift pushed through the room, and he still didn't get anywhere. She made a signal, and Sir Pup took off running. "Does everything have to be dragged out of you?"

Ethan nodded in satisfaction when Jake disappeared an instant before Sir Pup chomped down on his ass, then he turned to Lilith. "By that, I take it you've heard about my jaunt to Hell, and you're wondering what happened there."

"I know what happened: You opened the nephilim's prison, and Michael killed the only one left inside. What interests me is the little twitch at the side of your neck when I say Michael's name."

Ethan stared down at her, trying to figure if she was lying about the tell and just fishing, or if he really had given something away. When she bent to rub her hellhound's heads, telling him what a good boy he was for scaring the puppy, Ethan decided that it didn't matter.

"I may have heard something regarding Michael that gives me concern," he said finally. "But I'm thinking it over, wondering if that ain't exactly what the one who said it intended."

Lilith's expression was suddenly serious. "A demon?"

"Yes. But if what he said is true, I reckon it only means that I jumped to conclusions about Michael." When her mouth turned down in confusion, Ethan explained, "I always figured he possessed some innate goodness and some natural ability to forgive. After all, he chose a man with my history to become a Guardian—"

"And never killed me," Lilith murmured.

Ethan nodded. "But now I'm thinking that goodness might be something he picked up along the way."

"So he wasn't born with that stick up his ass, but deliberately shoved it up there. That's wonderfully twisted," Lilith said. She then added over Ethan's laughter, "Colin tells me you offered to transform several thousand dollars into several million. How was a man of your history planning to do that?"

"Vegas," Ethan said. "Lots of poker tables, very few demons." There was far too much wagering going on for their comfort.

Her eyes brightened with interest. "Would you have cheated?"

He considered that. It would have been so Charlie would have a home she loved, and there wasn't much he wouldn't do to provide for her.

Not much he wouldn't do, except push her so hard it frightened her away. But maybe a little push wouldn't hurt—and if it didn't work, he could come up with another way.

"Only if I started losing," he finally said.

❧

Ethan came in late again, and the knot in Charlie's stomach slowly began to relax. He'd left almost immediately after dropping her off at the lake house the night before. And although she knew by the faint scent in the sheets and the impression on the pillow next to her that he'd spent part of the morning in bed, she had no memory of his presence there.

A few minutes a day with him just wasn't enough. But this was what she'd dealt herself and forced on him, so she'd suck it up until they worked through it.

He sat, but waved away the bottle before she could pour his whiskey, and clasped each of her hands in his.

"Is it marriage?" he asked quietly. "I'll stand up with you."

Charlie's heart swelled, huge and full in her chest. "No. You called us partners once; that was enough for me."

"Hell and damnation." He blew out a long breath. "I thought for sure that'd be it." His head tilted as he studied her, the lines at the corners of his eyes deepening. "Is it something kinky? We've done everything you showed me that once, but maybe there's something you hid. Something real dirty."

"No," she tried to say, but she was choking on her laughter.

His voice roughened. "Maybe you have a fantasy, climbing up here on this bar, sitting right in front of me with all these people about. And maybe I'd push up your skirt, and I'd just lean forward and drink from you, long and deep, until you was crying for me to feed you in turn—"

"Oh, Jesus." Her grip tightened on his. He couldn't send her images, but the picture he'd created in her mind was just as clear. "You're cheating."

"No," he said, his tone suddenly grim. "I just ain't playing fair. Because being with you like this is real good, Miss Charlie, but I miss being *with* you something fierce."

"I do, too. But, Ethan, I know myself too well. If I ask, I won't stop needing it." Just the thought brought the knot back to her stomach, heavy and taut.

"All right, then." He withdrew his hands, and she closed her eyes, fighting back the need to grab hold of him. The familiar click of plastic against the counter had her opening them again, and she stared down at a tiny picture of herself. "Savi sent this up with me," Ethan said. "Your driver's license, as requested."

She said something that might have been a thanks, and slid the ID into her apron pocket.

Ethan seemed to hesitate for a brief moment before he added, "And I've got something for you as well, but it's a mite too big to give you here."

She wanted to laugh, to make a joke—so that he'd blush; so that he'd tell her to hush—but that tiny hesitation had her trying to read his inscrutable expression, instead. "What is it?" she asked warily.

An envelope appeared on the counter, and she opened it, her brow creasing. "A title for a car?"

He gave a slow nod. "So as you won't have to rely on anyone to get around." His fingers clenched slightly. "Particularly me. Until I have you figured, leastwise."

"Oh." She stared at the papers, her chest aching. The few minutes per day suddenly seemed to shrink into nothing. *Suck it up.* "Okay. Thank you."

His mouth thinned. "You'll have to arrange for insurance before you can drive it, however—so I'll still be taking you home tonight."

Relief swept through her. God, she should just end this. Should just live with him, even if it meant continually fighting the need to ask him, no matter how powerful it grew. But she'd never had a need this great; she didn't know if she could be that strong.

She was still debating when he set her down in front of the

lake house, and the car appeared in her drive. She barely looked at it, but studied his face. She'd seen the expression that flitted across his features once before—that of a man telling himself he shouldn't be doing something, but not quite convincing himself of it yet.

And she felt just as uncertain, but not of one thing: She wasn't ready for him to go. "Do you feel like coming in for a while?"

He met her eyes. "If I'm that close for that long, it might lead to kissing you."

"I'm willing to take that risk." She tried on a smile, but it faded when he turned away from her. "Ethan?"

"I ain't willing to take that risk, Charlie," he said, striding toward the front entrance. "Because kissing would lead to the bed, and then I'd push at you until you were biting me, and we'd be all mixed up again."

"No." She followed him through, shut the door behind her, then had to catch up with him. He was making a beeline toward the deck. "If that happened, it wouldn't be about feeding, or providing. Only how much I need you and love you."

And that's what he'd bring to it, too. It would be mutual, equal—giving and taking, and nothing that would be for one more than the other.

He halted at the edge of the sunken living room, swung around to face her. The moonlight through the French doors shone on the stone clench of his jaw. "Well, you've got me completely confounded, Charlie. Because that's what you told me when we were all mixed up."

Yes. She'd told him that she needed him, loved him.

"And you told me that you'd provide for me."

"You think I ain't trying? If you'd just ask for what it is you're needing so bad, I could give it to you, but you just . . . you just . . ." He raked his fingers through his hair. "Even if I took you to bed, I'd lay down money that you wouldn't ask me to stay until dawn."

"No," she whispered. Her heart was beating a sick, painful thud, and her chest felt as fragile as blown glass. "But I wouldn't ask you to leave, either."

Ethan closed his eyes. "I just wouldn't be man enough to stay. Going now will hurt something terrible. But it won't be anything like being with you through the night, as close as two people could possibly get, then watching you choose someone else's blood tomorrow—even though I'd crawl across Hell to give mine to you."

Oh, God. She hadn't even considered . . . "I wasn't thinking of tomorrow." Only that she wanted him with her so badly now, for any amount of time, any way she could get him. Her voice was raw, thick. "And I don't mean to make this worse. I'm sorry."

She was just going to have to drop this. Just wait for him, and keep fighting the need inside her, as she should have from the start—

"Are you sorry? Because every day I have to walk away from you, it'll get worse, and I ain't getting any closer to figuring you. So I'm thinking this hurting will only stop one of two ways." His chest rose and fell heavily. "You ask me for what it is you're needing, Charlie, and we'll head on up to that bed together. You keep quiet, and I'll go—and when I fly off that deck I won't be coming back, so as I won't be having to walk away again."

A tremor shook through her. Charlie clutched at her belly, her chest, curling in against the darkness unfurling within them. She couldn't have heard that right. Couldn't have. But no matter how she played it through her mind, it came out the same.

He'd given up on her. Given an ultimatum . . . and she lost either way.

This hadn't been worth the risk, then. And it didn't matter if she'd been wrong about him, that 1 percent, because now she would plead so that he wouldn't leave, and he'd say he loved her because she'd beg him to. And she'd keep asking him, because it'd be hollow when he said it, and she'd want the words to fill up the emptiness of it all. And she'd cling, trying to hold on to him, knowing her need was the reason he'd stayed, knowing her neediness would eventually push him away.

She tried to hold it in. But she could already feel it shattering open within her, projecting outward like sharp, broken glass, and there wasn't anything left inside that wasn't torn.

"Oh, Christ Jesus," Ethan said, his face white as he leapt toward her, his weight sending her staggering back until his body pressed hers up tight against the wall, his hand covering her mouth. "Don't let it out. I'm sorry. So damn sorry. I felt I was losing, and I tried to cheat—but I shouldn't have, not with this. Not with your heart. So just don't let it out, and I'll figure you. I swear to God I'll figure you."

He dropped his face into the curve of her shoulder, his breath a hot shudder against her neck. Charlie stared at the play of moonlight on the water outside. Slowly, she stopped shaking, and the pieces of her that had broken fell into place again, their edges smoothing.

She'd be all right. Even if he left, she'd get by.

And his body caged hers, but she was strong enough to push him away. His hand sealed her mouth, but a bite or a kiss to his palm would move it.

So she waited. And when Ethan raised his head, she hoped.

"I wouldn't have flown off," he said, and his palm slid from her mouth. "If going meant never coming back, I wouldn't have left. I'd have stood out on that deck until time made a statue of me, and I'd ponder all the reasons why a woman could need something so much, but not ask for it."

His gaze searched her face, but she couldn't speak. Just waited for the constriction on her throat to loosen.

"But no matter how long I stood there pondering, I don't imagine I'd get anywhere, because I'd focus on what you're needing, when maybe I should be wondering why it is you ain't *asking*. So I figure it must be one of those things that don't mean nothing if you got to ask for it."

Charlie trembled, and his thumbs wiped the corners of her eyes. He brushed a kiss across her lips before lifting his head.

"And I don't reckon I've ever told you how much I love you, Miss Charlie."

Her throat finally loosened, but a relieved sob broke from her instead of a response. She could only wind her arms around his neck and kiss him, *I love you* and *thank you* on her lips and tongue, trusting he'd recognize their taste.

And she recognized Ethan's as he projected it, bright and clean and strong—so incredibly strong. He drew back, and grinned before sweeping her up into his arms. "I also reckon this calls for the bed."

She'd have laughed, but his mouth was already on hers as he raced up the stairs, and he didn't stop kissing her for breath or speech, but asked with the thrust of his tongue and his body what she wanted. She wanted the pleasure of his blood for them both, and he trembled above her when she took it.

It was a long time before she eased away from him and lay back against the pillows. Ethan rolled on top of her and smiled crookedly, his hands tangling in her hair.

"You ain't slow, Charlie. You must've known what I felt for you. I thought for certain you did, or I'd have figured you the first night."

"I did know." She drew a shaking breath, and he skimmed a kiss over her forehead. "I just didn't know if *you* did."

He reared back at that. "I ain't slow either."

"I know. But you said your dad taught you a lesson about loving a woman too much. I didn't know if you'd ever let yourself—and if you couldn't help it, if you'd admit to yourself that you did."

His brows lowered, as if he were trying to figure her out again. "So as I wouldn't be hurt?"

She pressed her lips together and nodded.

"That would have been the wrong lesson to learn," he said, his voice rough. "You love a woman that much, so that life ain't worth living without her, then you do everything you can to see *she* isn't hurt. And once she's safe, you do everything you can to make sure you don't lose her. And if you don't give her everything she needs and she goes, you do everything you can to make it right again, because when she's hurting or needing something you can feel it, and it's like a poison tearing you apart, killing you slow. So you give her everything she needs or can't get for herself, and providing for her becomes a need as powerful as your love for her."

"Oh. Why didn't you tell me this, lay it out straight for me?" She felt her face beginning to crumple with another sob, but she punched his shoulder instead.

He grinned. "You're beating on me for it? I recall that you held on to your declaration an awful long time, Miss Charlie."

"I was afraid."

"Well, so am I." His grin faded. "There's another side to all of that, Charlie. Because when you love a woman that much, you need her just to keep moving every day. You've got to live—but without her, nothing much matters anymore, and the couple of hours you see her, and knowing that you're keeping her city safe are about the only reasons to keep going."

"Or the moment he sits at your bar," Charlie said quietly. "And when you see him, it's actually easy to smile."

His gaze moved over her features for a long moment, his throat working. "Yes," he finally said. "It ain't living as much as getting by, and I know it wasn't like this before I met you. Now there's something missing when you aren't with me, but I didn't want you to think you was a salve."

She wouldn't have. "Generally, those are bad for you, and you've already told me I make you a better man." Smiling, she wrapped her legs around his waist. "And 'getting by' is what you're doing when you have the salve. That's why you're trying to get rid of it, so that living feels right again."

He stared down at her, then finally shook his head, chuckling low. "You see, Charlie? I haven't been able to figure you at all, not since day one."

"I still think it's easy, but at least you won't get bored." She bit her lip, then said, "I won't use Sammael's blood anymore, but I'll have Jane keep sending it to me, just for those times when you can't show up those couple of hours a night. And what I don't use, we can store for any other vampire who might need it."

"You can do that, Charlie, if you like—but I reckon those times won't be all that often." When she looked at him, her gaze questioning, he told her of the offer Lilith had made.

Considering the reason he'd been assigned to Seattle was the looming threat of the nephilim, perhaps she shouldn't be quite as glad that he'd be there—but it was difficult not to be. And he seemed pleased by it, as well, which only made it better.

"So you'll be sheriff of this here town," she drawled when he finished, and although the rasp in her voice ruined it, his smile was broad and his laugh low.

And when it faded, his eyes were glowing, his gaze intense upon hers. "I'll lay it out straight now, Charlie: You need me as much as I need you, and that'll never change, and I ain't ever ridding myself of you. And if you ever rid yourself of me, I'll just follow you around, groaning real loud."

She grinned, her legs tightening around him. "I know a guy who did that once."

"Is that a fact?" His gaze fell to her teeth, and he shuddered lightly, all over, as if someone had whispered a wicked promise in his ear.

"Yes," she said, and turned her cheek against the pillow so that his mouth could begin exploring her jaw, the line of her

shoulder. "Just followed this lady around, drifting alo[ng] hind her, and taking her clothes off whenever he could."

"Well now, that sounds like a man of dubious characte[r.]"

"He was a good guy. Heroic, even. But he also ha[d a] speech impediment, and never said anything directly, whi[ch] was why he'd resorted to groaning."

"And I reckon the lady in this story doesn't make any kin[d] of sense."

Only because it was impossible to think when Ethan di[d] that thing with his tongue on her sense his tongue on her neck. "She makes perfect sense to me. And she hardly ever understood him, but she really, really wanted to. And he had no idea why he wanted her so bad, but she realized it must be because he kept climbing over the wall between their balconies, and sneaking into her apartment while she slept. And after he saw her naked, he just couldn't stop following her, because he loves pink things, and plump things, and titties—"

"I sure as hell do." He lifted his head, grinning; then he used his mouth to show her how much.

Her fingernails dug into his biceps. "Yeah. And . . . yeah. And she kept thinking about sucking on him—"

"With those sexy crooked fangs."

"Fuck you. They aren't crooked; they just aren't straight. And she wasn't thinking of sucking his neck, exactly . . . And it was his fault, because he kept talking about how he didn't wear underwear."

"I'm blushing awful hard now, Charlie."

"Is that what they called it back then? Blushing?"

"It just ain't manly to blush anywhere else. Women, now— they can blush all over. But this is where it's prettiest. So soft and wet."

"And his hands," she gasped. "And he had big hands—oh, God, don't stop doing that—and a voice that made her drunk just listening to it; drunk but not stupid, and never coming down from the high. And just looking at him made her heart stop, because he was so freaking sexy and funny and strong and *amazing* that—"

He nipped her inner thigh. "You hush, Miss Charlie."

She sang for him, instead.